PRAISE FOR

GEMINI CELL

"The best novel [Cole's] written so far . . . A military fantasy that combines intense personal anguish with elements of actual horror."
—Tor.com

"Myke Cole's novels are like crack: they're highly addictive, and this one is no exception."
—BuzzFeed

"Intense and explosive—Cole tells a hell of a story."
—Mark Lawrence, international bestselling author of
The Liar's Key

"The story is a powerful one . . . it takes some oft-maligned tropes of military adventure fiction and shows us how those things are supposed to be done."
—Howard Tayler, award-winning creator of
the webcomic *Schlock Mercenary*

"Think Vince Flynn plus a whole lot of magic mixed in and baked in hellfire, and you've got the gist of how awesome Myke Cole's new series is shaping up to be."
—Michael Patrick Hicks, author of *Convergence*

"Cole's books are an intriguing mix of fantasy and military fiction . . . [*Gemini Cell*] is outstanding."
—SFcrowsnest

"With each book, Myke Cole levels up . . . . . . *ell* is no exception. This is Cole's best . . . . moving, page-turning story that . . . .
. . . . . . Faction

"Myke Cole is a fant . . . . book he writes."
. . . . . Reviews

"This is some really go . . . . . . military/urban fantasy. Cole's style is fast-paced, immensely enjoyable, and delivers on both action and character in equal measure."
—SFRevu

continued . . .

PRAISE FOR THE SHADOW OPS NOVELS

"It's not *just* military . . . It's just a great book."
—Patrick Rothfuss, #1 *New York Times* bestselling author of
The Slow Regard of Silent Things

"Hands down, the best military fantasy I've ever read."
—Ann Aguirre, *New York Times* bestselling author of *Breakout*

"Fast-paced and thrilling from start to finish . . . military fantasy like you've never seen it before."
—Peter V. Brett, international bestselling author of
The Skull Throne

"Excellent, action-packed novels that combine elements of contemporary magic and superhero fiction with the type of atmosphere genre readers usually only get in military SF."
—Tor.com

"Arguably one of the definitive military fantasy novels."
—The Founding Fields

"[Cole] proves that an action blockbuster can have heart and emotional depth, while never skimping on the fireworks and explosions."
—Fantasy-Faction

"Myke Cole is an absolute gift to urban fantasy and military fantasy subgenres."
—Fantasy Book Critic

Ace Books by Myke Cole

SHADOW OPS: CONTROL POINT
SHADOW OPS: FORTRESS FRONTIER
SHADOW OPS: BREACH ZONE
GEMINI CELL
JAVELIN RAIN

JAVELIN RAIN

MYKE COLE

ACE BOOKS, NEW YORK

ACE

An imprint of Penguin Random House LLC
375 Hudson Street, New York, New York 10014

JAVELIN RAIN

An Ace Book / published by arrangement with the author

ISBN: 978-0-425-26965-7

PUBLISHING HISTORY
Ace mass-market edition / April 2016

PRINTED IN THE UNITED STATES OF AMERICA

10 9 8 7 6 5 4 3 2 1

Cover illustration by Larry Rostant.
Cover design by Diana Kolsky.
Interior text design by Laura K. Corless.

Penguin
Random
House

For Peat and Pete,
my brother and my brother

ACKNOWLEDGMENTS

Writing novel acknowledgments is always a fraught exercise. So many people other than the author are involved in making a successful book that it is inevitable you'll miss someone. Any omissions are my own, and I hope those slighted will accept my apology.

I want to single out for praise my tireless teams at Ace/Roc and Headline, and my agents at JABberwocky and Zeno. Thanks also to my audio publishers at Recorded Books and W. F. Howes, and extra-special thanks to GraphicAudio, whose gorgeous full-scale radio dramas have brought my books to life in a way I never imagined possible. Thanks also to Larry Rostant, who similarly evokes my world through imagery. I see my world because of you, and I am incredibly grateful.

Thanks are due to my beta readers, and in particular to Mallory O'Meara, who weathered the storms of my moods as she applied the same critical lens with which she brings incredible films to life. This book would not be worth reading if not for her.

Thanks also to my two tribes: the nerds and the military/police, both separate and intersecting, simultaneously teaching me to fight and giving me something to fight for.

And Peat, once more lighting the way and covering my six. Not a day goes by that I don't remember how very much I owe you.

The term "Javelin" denotes the seizure, theft, or loss of a national security asset with strategic impact. The term is followed by an explanatory code word indicating the severity of the incident and the nature of the response. Code word "Dry" indicates executive authorization of a diplomatic or clandestine response, with no action required from major commands. Code word "Drizzle" indicates a combined response involving assets from the State Department, the Office of the Director of National Intelligence, and the Joint Chiefs of Staff.

Code word "Rain" indicates a crisis of existential proportions representing a direct and pressing threat to the continued security of the nation. Javelin Rain incidents authorize any and all means necessary to bring the matter to a resolution as quickly and completely as possible.

—CHAIRMAN JOINT CHIEFS OF STAFF MANUAL 3250.03B
JOINT REPORTING STRUCTURE EVENT
AND INCIDENT REPORTING

The fear of death follows from the fear of life.

—MARK TWAIN

AUTHOR'S NOTE

A glossary of military acronyms and slang can be found in the back of this book.

CHAPTER 1
THE PLAN IS SOUTH

James Schweitzer's bare foot came down on a splintered root that punctured his sole, digging an inch-deep furrow in the gray flesh. His senses registered the cut, assessed the damage, dismissed it.

He felt no pain. The furrow in his flesh didn't bleed.

Schweitzer knew he should be horrified by what he had become. What little clothing remained on him was shredded, filthy, and stinking. The body beneath was a landscape of puckered purple-white scars, dotted with darker gray rents, wounds that would never heal, revealing the yellowed articulation of the bone beneath. His face was a dark horror, a parody of his features stretched over a skull that was mostly metal.

His eyes were gone. In their place burned twin silver orbs, thimbles full of metal-colored fire.

He was a Hollywood zombie. No, movie zombies shambled. Schweitzer picked his way through the forest as nimble as a cat, his body instinctively low, hands up and bone claws extended, ready for the fight that might find him at any moment.

His wife came behind him, their son slung across her chest. Schweitzer had tried to carry him, but Patrick wouldn't have it. Sarah Schweitzer knew her husband despite what death had made of him, years of love bound up in the magic that linked their souls, but Patrick was just a boy. Maybe, one day, he would develop the arcane sympathy that connected Schweitzer and his wife, but he hadn't yet, and he squalled and fought whenever Schweitzer came near.

Keep them alive. The words were a mantra, repeating in his mind. Over and over again, *Keep them alive.* His magically augmented hearing picked up the steady beating of Sarah's and Patrick's hearts, the rhythm keeping him from panic, reminding him that he hadn't lost them. Or had he? He listened to Sarah's panting breaths as she struggled to keep up. She was alive.

He wasn't. His embrace was cold, his skin hard from the glycerol they'd used to keep his veins inflated and resistant to wear. Even if they shook off the Gemini Cell, found a way to escape them forever, he couldn't stand at her side at art shows, laugh with her at parties, take her out to dinner. No matter how much he loved her, he couldn't be a husband to her anymore.

He glanced back over his shoulder, and his spiritual stomach seized as he realized how far behind him she was. Sarah was young and fit, but the monsters pursuing them were immortal, needing neither rest nor food. She stumbled, wheezed. Schweitzer forced himself to slow, to wait for her. The need to run was almost overwhelming; the dead muscles in his legs twitched with the desire to move on.

For the hundredth time since they'd fled together, he considered telling her to leave him, to take Patrick and find some place to lie low, to start over. He dismissed the idea as soon as it arose. He was the Gemini Cell's primary target, but they would never suffer someone knowing as much as Sarah did. As for Patrick, they'd either kill him or take him as their own, and Schweitzer wasn't going to let either of those things happen. The Gemini Cell had all the resources of a special operations regiment and intelligence service combined, but that paled in comparison to their Gold Operators, feral monsters, all as immortal and superpowered as Schweitzer himself.

No, Sarah and Patrick were safest with him. Only Schweitzer was strong enough to protect them. Grief for all he had lost ripped through him yet again, and yet again he quashed it. Grief was an emotion for the living. As was anger, or regret, or joy. He couldn't afford those luxuries now. He could take one thing from his former life: his oath as a Navy SEAL. *So others might live.*

He'd died trying to protect Sarah and Patrick. He'd been fortunate enough to get a second crack at it, and by God, he'd take it.

So others might live.

He turned his focus to the woods around him, leaping over a fallen log, landing on a stone barely larger than his foot and balancing there. The magic that animated his corpse gave him heightened senses. He could see for miles in different spectrums. He could sniff out a rose petal buried in a garbage heap. Now, he dialed his hearing out, straining to catch the sounds of dirt-bike engines or helicopter rotors, anything that might indicate that the Cell's agents were closing in.

Nothing. His boosted senses brought him only the sounds of beetles foraging in the dead leaves beneath them, the wind rushing in the canopy over their heads. The only smells were leaf mold and wildflowers and fresh water a long way off. No trace of humanity.

They were deep in nearly two million acres of forest spanning three states. Years of running counterinsurgency ops in the rugged mountains of Afghanistan had taught Schweitzer firsthand how hard it was to locate a single man on the run, even one with a family. All the drone cameras and ground teams backed by largest defense budget in the world couldn't make the haystack any smaller, the needles any bigger. He nodded and pressed on.

"Jim!" Sarah sounded winded and a lot farther behind him than he'd realized. He stopped, whirled.

She was bent at the waist, hands on her hips, breathing in labored gasps. Her pink hair was clotted with leaves and mud, her T-shirt ripped and filthy. Patrick flailed in his makeshift sling, all cried out but still struggling.

"Wait . . ." she panted. "Jesus . . . fucking . . . Christ . . . just wait . . . one . . . minute."

He had pushed her too hard, too fast. He had forgotten mortal limitations. It was a reminder of the chasm that separated them, and it tore his heart anew. "Sorry."

"Patrick and I aren't like you." She straightened, spat a long streamer of mucus-flecked saliva, and suppressed a coughing fit. "We can't keep going like this."

Her skin was pale and waxy, her eyes fever bright. He was hurting her, as his frequent absences had in life, all the missed art shows, her long nights at home alone caring for Patrick while he was away on ops. And now she was condemned to run like an animal, hounded by the undead, all because of him.

"I'm sorry," he said again, hoping that his tone conveyed just how much. "I'll slow down."

But he didn't want to slow down. The Gemini Cell wouldn't rest until it had them. He turned to go.

Sarah didn't move. "Where are we going?"

Schweitzer realized that he didn't know. Since they'd won the battle at Drew's farm and fled into the forest, his only thought had been an animal litany of *get away get away get away*. He cursed himself. That was feral thinking, better suited to jinn like Ninip, the monster who'd shared his own corpse. At last, he'd figured out how to exorcise the jinn and take full control of his body, but he wondered if Ninip hadn't corrupted him, warped him with its predator lust.

"Away," Schweitzer said. "We have to put miles between us and our last known position. They'll be launching from that old man's house." Drew and Martha, kindly old retirees who had taken Sarah in, and paid the ultimate price for it. More deaths laid at Schweitzer's door.

"Away?" Sarah asked. "That's the plan? We have to do better than that."

She was right, of course, but the feral side of him, the jinn side, as he was coming to think of it, snarled. She was slowing them down. "We can't stop," he said.

"Your goal here is to protect Patrick and I, and you're not going to succeed at that if we both drop dead of exhaustion. We need to rest."

"Sarah, I . . ."

"No, Jim. We are in this together. If you want to help me, that's fine. I accept your help, but I won't accept a leash. We need to come up with a plan."

One advantage to death was that Schweitzer had no trouble keeping his emotion off his face. He swallowed his anger and frustration, doubly intense because he knew she was right.

"Fine," he said, keeping his voice neutral. "The plan is that we keep moving as fast as we can, but slow enough that you and Patrick can keep up."

"That's not a plan."

"Sarah, they're coming."

"How are they coming? On foot? By helicopter? On horseback? How many of them? More monsters or people this time?"

He didn't answer, because the truth was that he didn't know. Death had given him superhuman physical capabilities, but it hadn't sharpened his mind. She was smarter than he was. Always had been. It was one of the many reasons he loved her.

Sarah sighed. "Didn't you say they were the government?"

Schweitzer nodded.

"The government controls the entire country, Jim," she went on. "That means that while we're getting away from them in one direction, we're heading toward them in another. This is *their* country. If they're as powerful as you say they are, they'll be able to tap police in any town we come to. There isn't anywhere to run and we can't stay in the woods forever."

"Then we get out of the country. We slip across the border into Mexico, or make our way to Florida and stow away on a ship bound for Cuba or Haiti."

"How?"

"I ran operations against drug cartels and human smuggling networks for years. I still know some of the players. I know how they operate. Let's get down there and then I can figure out a way to get us across the border."

"We need more specifics, Jim. How are we going to get across the border? I know you're trying to protect us, but we need a real plan."

"At least my plan comes with a direction. The plan is south. If you've got a better one, I'm all ears. For now, all we can do is keep moving. This forest is enormous, and that'll buy us some time at least."

"We can't keep moving unless we have somewhere to move."

"All right, then where do we move, Sarah? What place is safe for us now?"

"No place, Jim. That's my whole point. We can't hide from this threat forever."

Schweitzer swallowed his frustration, the need to keep going like an itch in his soul. "Then what do you propose we do?"

Sarah swallowed. Schweitzer could tell she was choking back tears. "What do you do with a threat you can't escape?"

The itch vanished. Schweitzer narrowed his eyes. "You stop it."

"You stop it," Sarah repeated. "We have to go on offense."

"Sarah, I spent months in that facility. I saw the guns, the people, the Gold Operators. We can't go up against that."

"You're right," Sarah said. "*We* can't."

Schweitzer's dead stomach clenched. "What the hell are you talking about?"

Sarah was silent for a long time. When she finally spoke,

the defeat in her voice made him cringe. "Jim, you're dead. Patrick and I are alive."

"What's that supposed to mean?" Schweitzer snarled, knowing exactly what she meant, knowing that she was right. He could feel the grief down the magical link between them, the desperation, but it didn't change the sinking feeling in his own soul. *She wants me to go.*

"You know what it means," she said. "It means that Patrick and I hunker down somewhere, and you find a way to make all this stop. You found me even though hell itself stood between us. You'll find me again."

"You saw what those things can do. You expect me to go up against an army of them by myself?"

"I saw you take on four of them and win." Three. Sarah had destroyed one, but Schweitzer didn't correct her.

"There are more than four! And that doesn't even count the living enemy."

"I don't know what else to do, Jim. I don't know how else we can stop this. Please . . . I . . . I love you, but you're dead, Jim. Patrick is alive. Protecting him has to be our first priority."

Patrick began to squall, pulling at his mother's shirt. Schweitzer searched his own mind desperately for a retort, for a way to make her stay with him, but the grief and anger clouded everything. "You're safest with me."

"You can't honestly believe that. The Cell wants *you*, Jim. If I go on TV, people can roll their eyes at a widow gone mad with grief, but nobody who sees you can deny what you are. Wherever you are, they will come. It's the government. They don't give up. They don't run out of money. You have to stop this threat."

"I won't leave you."

"Damn it, Jim," she shouted, tears glistening in her eyes. "You think this is easy for me? What about Patrick? Are you going to drop him off at school? Are you going to help him with his math homework? Do you expect him to spend the rest of his life running?"

The grief funneling down the link between them

triggered his own. His dead body still possessed the phantom limbs of life: he felt the shade of a tightening throat, the pricking of phantom tears at the corners of his eyes. His voice came out as a strangled cry. "Sarah, please. I fought so hard to get back to you. I can't lose you again."

She put her head in one hand, hugged Patrick tightly with the other, and wept.

"You're dead, Jim. We can't make love, we can't be together. You can't raise Patrick. We'll only slow you down. We're already slowing you down."

"I can keep you both safe."

"Jim, please. Please don't make this harder. If you push me, I'll just stay, and that's no life for either of us. Just . . . just . . . go and find a way to make them stop. Patrick and I are only human. We can't fight them. You can."

"I love you."

"I love you too. When this is over, you'll find me again, and we can . . . figure something out."

With that shred of a promise, thin as tissue, Schweitzer's SEAL side took control. *She's right. If you want to keep her, keep Patrick safe, you have to find a way to shut the Cell down.* "Chang."

"What?" Sarah asked.

"We can trust Steve Chang. He has the training. He has steel. He can keep you safe while I finish this. I wouldn't ask him to turn his coat, and I don't know that he ever would, but he loves you and Patrick as much as I do. He'll protect you."

"Jim," Sarah sobbed anew. The feelings along the link between them were tangled now, a riot of terror and love and grief and rage.

"What? What's wrong?"

"Steve's dead."

Schweitzer's mouth hadn't had saliva since the day he died, but he felt it had gone dry just the same. More phantom limbs, shades of the life he'd once had. "No."

Sarah was too overcome with weeping to answer. She only nodded.

"Did you see a body?"

"I don't need to."

"Then how do you know?"

"I *know*, Jim. The same way I knew that you were alive. I could feel it."

"Are you sure?" Schweitzer could hear the anger in his voice, the desperation, couldn't stop either. "Sarah, are you *sure*?"

She wept again, nodded. "Completely."

Schweitzer was too crushed by his own loss to focus on the tangle of emotions coming down the link from her. Steve Chang, his best friend, his teammate, gone. He struggled for a long moment before he found his voice again.

"How did he die?"

"I don't know. I just know that he did." Sarah's emotions became pinched, frightened. "He came around a lot at first, when we thought you were dead, but then he just disappeared. Chief Ahmad said he'd been deployed."

"And then you just felt it? He was gone?" Fear came flooding along the link from her. Schweitzer smelled the slightest hint of adrenaline in her bloodstream.

She nodded. "He's gone, Jim. That's all I can tell you." *No, that's bullshit. There's more. Something between her and Steve.*

"Sarah, there's something wrong here. What aren't you telling me?"

She only shook her head and wept. "I just . . . I just know he's gone, Jim. Please, just leave it at that."

And now Schweitzer's grief came on him like a wave, so strong that his legs shook. He grit his spiritual teeth and pushed it down, swallowed it. The questions rioted, the urge to interrogate her so strong that he suppressed a growl. There was something wrong with the way she was feeling, something more complex than the simple grief of someone mourning a passed friend.

Enough. Steve would have wanted him to be strong. He'd shown Sarah and Patrick enough of his underbelly for one day. When she was ready to tell him what she was thinking, she would. "He was our best option."

"I know," Sarah said, mastering her tears, drawing strength from Jim, as she had when he was alive.

"There are no good options here, Sarah. We can't go to a family member, no matter how far removed. Family's the first thing a targeter diagrams out. Close friends will be next."

He would have trusted his brother, Peter, to protect Patrick. Peter the golden boy, the model SEAL Schweitzer had aspired to be. *Proud of you, bro.* But Peter was dead, his body shredded in the wreckage of the downed helo in Afghanistan. He'd died when Schweitzer was still alive, before he'd known that death wasn't the end. He supposed Peter twisted in the soul storm now, or maybe there was somewhere else beyond it. It didn't matter. There was no way to know, and knowing wouldn't help him now anyway.

Sarah swallowed, nodded. "I'll think of something, but we're not going another step until we rest. That's not negotiable. You want to go on, you go ahead. Patrick and I are getting a few hours sleep."

"Sarah, I don't know that we have a few hours."

"Well, we damn well have to. We can't keep going. I can't see straight, Jim." She sat down where she was, not bothering to inspect the ground beneath her. She flopped over on her back, cradling Patrick against her chest. Her voice was already sluggish as fatigue wrenched her down into drowsiness. "And we could use something to eat."

"Sarah, let me carry you. I can tote you and Patrick without breaking a sweat."

She shook her head faintly. "We need to sleep, and Patrick is going to freak if you come near him. Can you get us some food?" And then she was snoring softly, her breath lightly wheezing, thick in a way that troubled him.

"Sarah," he said. She didn't respond. He knelt at her side, reached out to touch her, thought better of it. Patrick's face was turned away from him, his cheek nestled against his mother's chest. Schweitzer could tell from his breathing that he had collapsed into sleep the moment he had stopped bouncing in the sling.

Sarah was right, they needed sleep, and they needed food. Schweitzer sat back, pushed his hearing out to its very limit. A hawk circled miles out, crying out warning to any who would seek to approach its hunting grounds. An aircraft droned miles overhead, likely a passenger airliner, moving steadily away from them. There were still no sounds of pursuit. He dialed his hearing in closer, pausing at intervals to assure himself that all he heard were the sounds of the natural world around him. When he finally heard the snuffling of a deer drinking at a stream less than a mile away, he made his decision.

"I'll give you a few hours," he whispered to his wife. He bent to kiss Patrick's head, pulled back. Better not to risk waking him. "I love you," he whispered, then stood, turned, and took off running.

The wind was out of the south, blowing a steady two knots, bringing the sharp odor of the deer's hide to him, and more importantly, carrying his own scent away. He shifted his balance up into his midsection, slowing just enough to make his footfalls light. He brushed over the leaves, barely making a sound, the forest falling away to either side as the stream grew louder. At last, he saw an elbow of the water shining silver in the failing light, broken into glowing filaments by sharp rocks and jagged twigs. He heard the deer now, nosing in the water. It was breathing in deep pants, far apart. Gulping. It was thirsty then, winded from the climb to the stream.

Schweitzer advanced at a crouch, letting his senses dial in on the deer's breathing, concerned that the focus on the animal took so much of his concentration that it left him vulnerable to attack from another direction. He examined the branches above him, looking for a way to get off the ground and make a safer approach.

No time. Every second you're away from Sarah and Patrick puts them in danger. Get it done.

Schweitzer gave free rein to his jinn side, letting his

magical reflexes take over. His crouch turned into a loping crawl, wickedly fast, shoulders pumping as he knuckled over the uneven terrain, bone spines beginning to protrude from his head and back. This was the form Ninip had favored, an appearance in better keeping with its nature. When he'd shared the body with Ninip, taking this form had clouded Schweitzer's mind, submerging it in a sea of predatory lust. But now the jinn was gone, and the form was just one of many tools at Schweitzer's disposal, like his training. He put on speed, heedless of noise now, crashing through the underbrush. He heard the deer stop drinking, the creaking of its neck as it raised its head, muscles tensing as it prepared to spring away.

Schweitzer exploded from a patch of stunted trees, slamming into the animal before its eyes had so much as a chance to widen, locking his limbs around its thick body and sending it tumbling. The deer was strong, thrashing against him, the back of its skull hammering his face. It might as well have been a kitten compared to Schweitzer's magical strength. He locked his hands around the creature's chest, squeezing his arms together until its ribs snapped and blood fountained out its mouth and nose.

The coppery smell recalled the red joy he had known in Ninip's thrall. He had been able to forget himself, forget those who depended on him, forget the tasks left undone. There had been nothing but the feel of his body, his enemy, and the shrill joy of the kill.

But that had been before he knew his wife and son were alive.

He drove inward with his elbows, working the broken ribs until they pierced the heart and lungs, and the animal shuddered and lay still. He waited silently, listening. The forest had gone quiet around him. Still no sound of pursuers.

He rose, hefting the heavy deer easily over one shoulder, and sprinted back to where his wife and child lay. As he neared his back trail he could hear the faint patter of their heartbeats, the slow bellows of their breathing, each gust a moment apart. They were alive and still asleep.

He arrived at their side and slid the deer to the ground. He coaxed one of the bone spikes from his fingertips, skinning and gutting the animal, lost in the work until he heard the leaves rustle and turned to see his wife looking at him.

"Thanks, babe," she said. Patrick stirred weakly against her shoulder.

"Don't wake him," Schweitzer said. "He needs all the sleep he can get."

She nodded as he held out a long strip of thick, red meat. "Backstraps," Schweitzer said. "Best part."

"We can't eat it raw, Jim," she said.

He looked down at the steaming strip of wet flesh. "Right," he said, feeling farther from her than ever. "I forgot, sorry."

"I don't have a lighter. I don't suppose you have heat vision or something?"

"Something," Schweitzer said, scanning the ground until he'd located what he needed. He took a slab of bark and placed a stick against it, set his palms to either side. "Watch this."

He rubbed his hands back and forth. His magical strength and speed soon had the stick twirling to a blur, smoke rising from the friction against the bark. Within moments, it was burning brightly, and he picked it up, carrying it to a pile of leaves.

"Baby," Sarah said, sitting up, eyes widening at the burning tinder against the meat of his hand. "Doesn't that hurt?"

Schweitzer shook his head as the fire took, then set to clearing a ring around it. Sarah watched in silence as he built it, and the crackling flame sent embers sparking into the sky.

Schweitzer looked up at the thick canopy of trees, branches interlocking to form a green carpet that barely admitted sunlight. Even a powerful drone with an infrared camera wasn't going to be able to spot such a small fire through that. He hoped.

As he wrestled for a way to ask her what was going on, Sarah sighed. "Okay, champ. I can take it from here. Can you give us a little privacy while I get this cooked?"

Schweitzer's heart twisted. "Why?"

"Honey, I need Patrick to eat. He's not going to do that if he's . . . Please, Jim. Don't make this harder than it has to be. Patrick's had one hell of a shock. I just need him to have smooth sailing until we can figure this out."

The anger took him by surprise. *She doesn't trust me.* "Damn it, I'm going to have to leave you anyway." Schweitzer snarled. "Let me have another second with him. He's my son."

Sarah gave him a hard look. "Then you'll want him to eat without shitting his pants. Jim, I am doing my level best to accept the new reality of . . . what you are. You can't expect that of a child. Work with me here."

"You *want* me to leave." Her words made sense; his logical mind, the cold professional that was the Navy SEAL, accepted the calculus without batting an eyelash. But a deeper part of him didn't care. That part knew she was still hiding something from him. He could feel it in the sour edge of the emotions travelling down the link between them.

Sarah's expression softened at the hurt in his voice, and he cursed himself for letting it sound there loudly enough for her to recognize it for what it was. He couldn't control what she felt through the link between them, but he didn't have to make it harder on her by confirming it. Peter would have been disappointed. That wasn't the SEAL's way. "No, Jim. I don't. I just want to take care of our son."

Schweitzer could see that the exchange was hurting her too, that she was trying. *When she wants you to know whatever she knows about Steve, she'll tell you.* He could see himself through her eyes, a shambling horror, a walking corpse tied to her chest by the supernatural link their love had forged. There was no guile in the flow through that link now, only love, fear and exasperation. He knew he should say something, bow his head and tell he loved her, tell her that he understood.

But in the end, all he did was turn without a word, stalking off into the underbrush, letting his eyes roam the emerging heat signatures as they stood more starkly in the cooling air. Patrolling the perimeter gave the jinn part of Schweitzer his head, let the animal instinct to fight and defend take control. The sorrow and grief faded to a background buzz. Jinn Schweitzer didn't need to worry that his wife thought him a monster, that his son would likely grow up never knowing his father, fearing him as a thing that went bump in the night. Jinn Schweitzer was busy preparing to meet the enemy.

CHAPTER II
HUNTING THE DEAD

Cold air billowed out of the open refrigerator doors, bathing Doctor Eldredge in chilly white clouds.

Eldredge wrinkled his nose at the chemical-vanilla smell of the coolant and pulled the gurney out into the bare white room. The walls were dotted with metal nozzles. Half of them flickered with tiny blue pilot lights, the other half crackled with chemical frost. At the touch of a button, the contents of the room could be burned or frozen solid in seconds.

Jawid Rahimi stood, hands clasped. His eyes were shadowed, dark curls unruly under his round, brimless cap. He looked sad, preoccupied. The same whipped puppy-dog look that made Eldredge want to both comfort and shake him. It had been this way ever since Schweitzer had escaped.

Jawid insisted on continuing to wear his traditional dress, a long and impractical shirt and ballooning trousers. He still prayed five times a day, a damned inconvenience when they were on an op and schedules were tight. Eldredge didn't have much patience for religion, but the psychiatrist assigned to Jawid had recommended he be allowed it, that any attempt to forbid it would only make him dig in deeper.

Eldredge put on a smile in spite of his frustration, hoping it put Jawid at ease. He might want to shake him, to fire him, but Eldredge couldn't afford to lose Jawid. The man's magic was the basis of the entire program.

And Eldredge knew that being fired from Jawid's particular job was fatal. With what Jawid knew, with what he could do, there was no way the Director would ever just let him walk away.

Eldredge gestured at the corpse on the gurney, an Asian man, his body a network of scars. Tattoos were scrawled across his pale skin: a nautical star on his left pectoral, his blood type and serial number up his side just above the gaping hole where one of the Gold Operators had thrust its hand inside. A tattoo on his bicep showed his most important affiliation: an eagle perched on a trident crossing an anchor. In one set of sharp talons, it clutched the business end of a flintlock pistol.

"You recognize him?" Eldredge asked.

He realized it was a silly question the moment he'd spoken. Of course Jawid recognized him. He'd tracked him, had helped run the op that took him down. His name was Steve Chang. His brother SEAL and best friend, James Schweitzer, was somewhere in the middle of the George Washington National Forest, a needle in a haystack nearly two million acres large.

Jawid nodded. "You want me to put a jinn in him?"

Eldredge sighed. "It's been a few days since his death. Do you think his soul is still there to work with?"

Jawid placed a hand on the corpse's forehead and closed his eyes. "He's still in there." Jawid opened his eyes, but they focused on the middle distance.

"Jawid," Eldredge said.

The Sorcerer jumped, eyes snapping to him. "Sorry."

"What's wrong?"

"Nothing . . ." Jawid looked down, face pained.

Eldredge swallowed his anger, took a moment to calm himself. The psychiatrist had warned him that the Sorcerer wouldn't respond to confrontation. He needed to be coddled. "Jawid"—Eldredge forced a gentle tone, his knuckles white around the gurney handle—"I need you to focus here. It's all going to be all right."

"Schweitzer escaped because of me," Jawid whispered.

"That's not . . . entirely true." Except that it was. Schweitzer had plumbed Jawid's past, discovering that his own wife and son still lived. It had been a watershed moment for Schweitzer, the instant he discovered that he was a tool, and not a partner, of the Gemini Cell. Jawid had stared at the video monitors as Schweitzer wreaked carnage on the facility, carving a bloody path to freedom. Men and women, the closest Jawid had ever come to friends, lay in tatters in the corridors. His greatest failure splashed in red across the walls. And now Eldredge had to make him feel better about it. *Damn it, I am not trained for this. I don't know how to be a therapist.* "You want to make this right? You have to help us catch him."

"What if we can't catch him?"

"He's got his wife and toddler with him. They're not immortal. They have no magic. He's not going to abandon them. Trust me, we'll catch him."

Eldredge winced as he realized that he was trying to reassure himself. It wasn't just Jawid's failure. Schweitzer had escaped on Eldredge's watch too.

Jawid looked down at Chang again, his face wistful, eyes looking off into the middle distance again. God, dealing with his moods was exhausting.

"We need to get it right this time," Eldredge said. "I need you to fight hard to preserve Chang's soul. I don't want the jinn pushing him out."

Jawid looked up. "I never want the jinn to push the soul out. I always fight to keep it. It's just . . ."

"I know it's hard, Jawid."

"You don't know. You've never worked magic."

Like a whining teenager. Eldredge bit back his retort. "I

suppose you're right," he breathed, "but Chang was Schweitzer's best friend; we need to interrogate him. He might know some of Schweitzer's connections. Family members or friends we may have missed. A clue to where he's headed."

"The jinn are not interrogators. They are . . ."

"I *know* what they are." Eldredge's impatience got the better of him. "I know this is challenging and that's why I'm asking you to *try*. You need to push on this one. I need you focused; I need you to put the effort in."

"We have drones and reconnaissance teams. They can find him."

"Maybe they can and maybe they can't. That forest is enormous. We need every advantage we can get. If there's something that Chang knows that can help us, we can't afford to pass it up."

"I'm sorry, Doctor. I just . . . I have been sad for home lately."

Jawid's loyalty must be transferred to this institution, the psychiatrist's report read. *So long as it remains embedded in his tribal roots, he will never be truly reliable.* "This is your home," Eldredge said, putting a hand on his shoulder. "Schweitzer escaped because he was special. He escaped because there was . . . something in his spirit that let him beat the jinn. Chang was the closest man in the world to Schweitzer, and I can't shake the hope that that means they are *alike* somehow. Maybe alike enough that Chang could be a Silver Operator, too. That may be what we need to find Schweitzer, to catch him."

"If Chang is the master of his own corpse, he will never hunt his best friend for you. Even if I could do it, it won't work."

"Try anyway."

Jawid paused, stalling. "You can't blame Schweitzer for leaving. He only wanted to be with his family."

The truth was that Eldredge didn't blame Schweitzer. The Cell had lied to him about Patrick and Sarah, had kept him a virtual prisoner. But he wasn't going to indulge

Jawid. The Sorcerer didn't need a friend to agree with him. He needed a boss to get him on task.

"Schweitzer is dead," Eldredge said. "He can't be with anyone. At least we offer him a way to help keep the world safe so the rest of the living can be with their families. You need to remember that."

Jawid straightened, nodded. "Okay. I will try." He placed his hand on Chang's face again, looked awkwardly at Eldredge. "Do you think . . . you could leave me to do this alone? It is strange to be watched."

"I watch you every time you do a Summoning," Eldredge said. "Does it matter whether it's through a camera or in person?"

"No, I suppose not." Jawid turned his head away from Eldredge and closed his eyes. Eldredge watched as his breathing slowed, deepened. At last, his body gave a tiny shudder, and Eldredge knew that he was working his magic. The muscles in Jawid's jaw moved; his eyelids twitched. Eldredge would have thought him in the midst of a dream if he hadn't been standing. Jawid murmured words, so soft that Eldredge couldn't make them out, the mumbling of a sleep-talker.

Except that Eldredge knew Jawid wasn't talking in his sleep, that the words of his mouth mimicked those coming from his consciousness, communicating with the souls that drifted in some world that Eldredge couldn't see. At last, Jawid grunted and whispered. "I have him."

Eldredge couldn't keep the excitement out of his voice. "Can you save Chang? Can you keep him in there?"

Jawid and the corpse opened their eyes at the same time.

Jawid's were dark and distant, red-rimmed from lack of sleep.

Chang's were gone. In their place burned two flames, deep gold shot through with tiny threads of silver. Jawid looked at the silver and sighed. *"Allahu akhbar,"* he said over and over again. "Thank you, Allah."

And though he didn't believe in God, Eldredge echoed him. "Thank you, Allah." The silver threads meant that

Chang was holding on, that the jinn had not driven him out into the void and taken the corpse for itself.

"Who is it?" Eldredge always asked this. The question was partly motivated by a search for patterns, something that could help him understand the nature of the spirits Jawid drew across the line and bound into the bodies of the dead. But more than that, it was simple curiosity. The jinn were always ancient, and Eldredge thrilled at the idea that somewhere in the depths of the corpse before him was the soul of someone who had died millennia ago.

"He calls himself Partolan," Jawid said. "His hair was red, his skin tattooed in blue."

"Anything else?"

Jawid shrugged. "He is a lord of some kind. They always are."

"Can you talk to Chang directly?"

"No. He is there, but he is not as strong as Schweitzer was." The silver threads in the eyes were thin. Schweitzer's had burned solid silver from the start.

"Maybe he will gain ground," Eldredge said.

"Maybe." Jawid didn't sound convinced. He sounded exhausted. "Can you leave me alone with him, Doctor? It will . . . help me to focus."

Eldredge paused. He didn't want to take his eyes off Jawid, not for a moment. The man was unpredictable, in need of supervision. But a good supervisor knew when to back off and let things evolve. Standing here staring at Jawid accomplished nothing.

"All right."

"I will try harder," Jawid said. "I will."

"I know you will," Eldredge said, turning to go. But the truth was that the Director was losing patience, and Eldredge wasn't sure at all.

He felt sick panic boiling in his belly as he returned to his office to punch up the video feed that would allow him to watch Jawid's progress from one of the thousands of hidden cameras throughout the facility. Jawid was right that they had every technical advantage in the hunt for

Schweitzer. Feeds from half a dozen drones, Ranger teams on the ground, and spotters in the air. Local law enforcement prowling the edges of the forest. But Eldredge had run hundreds of ops in areas this large and remote. Single men, even burdened by their families, were hard to find, and that was when they weren't immortal supermen who could hear a pin drop a mile off.

He shook his head, dismissed the thought. A free Schweitzer could out the program, could confront the public with the truth that magic was real, that death wasn't the end, that the government didn't really know how it worked or how to control it. That couldn't be allowed to happen. Schweitzer had escaped on Eldredge's watch; the buck stopped with him.

There's more here, Eldredge knew. The risk Schweitzer presented to the program wasn't the only reason he wanted him back, but he couldn't think about that right now. To do so would be to lose focus as surely as Jawid had.

Eldredge needed his head in the game. He pulled up his laptop and called the Director's office, steeling himself to make his report. He'd promised progress and thus far had failed to deliver.

In the Gemini Cell, that kind of failure wouldn't go unpunished for long.

CHAPTER III
CALIFORNIA SUNSHINE

Dadou Alva walked through the California sunshine, smiling. Californians were always smiling. Frowning would mark her as an outsider, drawing as much attention as openly wearing the compact pistol she had tucked into the small of her back. She carried the gun for contingencies but knew to save the last bullet for herself. Her boss had made it clear: discovery was tantamount to death.

She had spent most of her life underground and she basked in the sun's strange warmth, the feel of the air on her skin. She was used to taking pleasure in the small luxuries: breathing clearly, a full belly, a clean body, and a warm bed. The people around her had no such appreciation. Americans never ceased to amaze her. They bickered and complained about the silliest things: reception for their mobile phones, whining that they brought them the wealth of the world's knowledge in five seconds instead of three. They were the richest, most comfortable people in the world, and they still managed to be miserable. Nothing was ever enough for them.

Dadou shook her head and laughed. American luxury

had lifted her up out of the broken asphalt and septic mud of Port-au-Prince and given her things she had only dreamed of all her life. Actually, that wasn't entirely true. American luxury provided the wealth that created the Scorpio Cell, the vast and sprawling secret infrastructure that supported her, but it was her magic that made them want her in the first place.

She followed the directions in the text message, turning down the narrow alley where it cut behind the pizza parlor. As she glanced in the open door to the kitchen, she surveyed the cooks. They were completely convincing to the average observer, slack-jawed, broad-shouldered men in white aprons stained with marinara sauce, working with the bored and distracted look of veterans of underpaid, menial jobs.

Dadou recognized one of them. His hair had grown out from the buzz cut he'd worn as he stood to attention outside a door of her office, his military uniform so clean that it looked as if dust dare not touch him.

The alley ended at a low cinder-block building, white paint flaking from the surface of a metal roll gate. A rusted sign hung over it, nearly covered in graffiti and stickers: CORONADO IRONWORKS. Clusters of weeds crowded the broken path leading to a single metal door. She glanced over her shoulder, careful to make a show as if she were inspecting her back pocket, as her countersurveillance instructors had taught her. She caught a glimpse of the men in the pizzeria kitchen, looking alertly out the open door. They were "covering her six," as the American soldiers liked to say, a comfort to her as she faced the door and tried the handle.

It didn't move, but she felt it warm as the pulse reader the Cell's agents had connected to the handle scanned the signature in her blood. There was a click and the door swung open.

The interior matched the outside. A single fluorescent-tube light cast shadows over the pitted cinder-block walls. Trash clotted the corners along with the discarded needles and condoms where druggies and prostitutes had plied their trade. The whole place stank of desperation and stale piss. She smiled. It reminded her of home.

A thick length of rope had been looped over the flaking iron remains of a long-unused sprinkler system, hanging down to a thicker knot. A man hung by his wrists from it, skin gray-white. He had thinning hair plastered across the clammy surface of his forehead. His head hung, body limp.

A man stood to either side of him. They were dressed self-consciously to imitate homeless people, complete with stereotypical watch caps, threadbare overcoats, and fingerless gloves. Dadou could tell that the filth on their clothing had been recently applied, knew that the gloves were fingerless so as not to impede the smooth action of their trigger fingers. One of them turned alert, killer's eyes on her. "You're late," he said.

"Komik," Dadou snorted. "A wizard is never late. She arrives precisely when she means to."

It was a quote from one of the endless films they showed in the Scorpio Cell's rec room, and both men smiled at the response, but she could feel them tense. They didn't like to be reminded of her magic; it frightened them. That was good. Dadou found that men were more likely to do what she asked them when they were frightened or aroused. Much of the time, one was linked to the other.

"He can still talk?" she asked.

"So far," one of the men answered.

Dadou leaned forward and seized a hunk of the man's hair. "Wake up, Rodriguez."

His head rolled back, his hair wet in her hands, eyes staying stubbornly shut. *"Reveye, sak tè.* Wakey, wakey," she said. Nothing. "It will go easier for you if you talk to me." Nothing.

She turned to one of the thugs. "You said he could still talk."

The man cursed and jammed a thumb behind Rodriguez's jaw, working it back and forth until the prisoner screamed, eyes opening and glaring at Dadou with a hatred that made her take a step back.

But only a single step. She took another forward and seized his hair again. "Your brother picks up the money you send him at Salto del Ángel. When is he coming next?"

Rodriguez stared. His mouth worked silently.

"Clearly, he appreciates it, *non*?" Dadou asked. "I'm sure he'll break in here any second to rescue you."

"Fuck you. I'm not telling you shit."

So clichéd. Like a bad movie on Tele Jeunesse. She gripped his hair tighter. "Why are you being an idiot, Rodriguez? What do you think you are accomplishing?" She pulled down on his head, his wrists straining against the knotted ropes. "You feel that? That's real. This isn't a movie. You're not an action hero. No one is coming to save you. This ends in one of two ways: you talk and you live, or you refuse and then we hurt you and you suffer and you talk anyway and afterwards, you die. You're not a hero, Rodriguez, and your brother is a murdering bastard."

Rodriguez found his feet at that, jerking toward her before being pulled back by the rope, shouting a stream of Spanish that she couldn't understand beyond knowing it was unkind.

She reached into her vest and took out a picture, waved it in his face. "You see this helicopter? Nice and crispy, isn't it? Did you know there were kids on it? Let me hold it closer so you can see." She tapped the edges of the photograph with her thumb, pointing out the black lumps that had once been hostages.

"Your brother took them," Dadou said, "and he burned up our helicopter rather than let us rescue them. That's where your money goes. To terrorists who kill babies. This is what your brother uses his magic for, to burn up rescue helicopters. You're no hero, and your brother isn't either."

"Fuck you," he spat blood, narrowly missing her face. "You fucking bitch!"

"*Raz,*" Dadou drawled. "Last chance to do this nicely."

Rodriguez swallowed. "If you're going to torture me, just get it over with. It won't work, anyway."

Dadou smiled. "I would never torture you, *moun komik*. People say anything when you hurt them badly enough. You would scream and mix lies with truth and listen for what you thought I wanted and tell me that just as fast as you could. Anything, just to make the hurting stop. By the time we untangled the lies from the truth, we would have lost even more time. I want to find your brother quickly, before he can use his magic to do more damage."

"That's why you want him, for his *brujería*. Not for hurting no fucking kids. So, you'd better torture me, because it's the only way you'll get me to even lie to you."

Dadou sat cross-legged on the dirty floor before him, relaxed her shoulders. The truth was that this was the answer she'd known he would give, that she'd wanted him to give. It gave her the excuse to do what she'd been planning to do anyway. "I don't need lies, Rodriguez. I need truth. And I also have the *brujería*. Which is why I don't need to torture you.

"I told you that you'd talk, and you will."

Dadou gathered the tide of her magic around her, closed the eyes of her physical body, and pushed her spirit outward. She reached out into the void, racing through the blackness. There was a time when the inky dark had felt thick as molasses to her, but she had been a *Sèvitè* since she was four years old, and the journey was second nature to her now. She reached the soul storm in moments, the light broadening across her vision, filling her ears with screaming.

The tangled mass of souls whirled about her, the distinct undertow lapping at her like the waters in the bay where she'd swum as a child. She kept her distance, sifting easily through the voices, discarding the half-mad shrieks of apology, dire promises of vengeance that would forever remain unfulfilled.

Dadou drifted on the edges of what she called the *gwo fantômes*, the cyclone where the dead churned. She listened patiently, pushing enough of her consciousness into the twisting hell to let those within know she was present. The strongest would make themselves known. Sooner or later, they always did.

Dadou became conscious of a quiet ferocity from deep within the storm. It emanated from a spirit just as hungry and violent as all the others, but not wasting its energy on words. Instead, it clawed its way steadily to the edge, relentlessly following the tide of Dadou's magic, until it was close enough for her to single it out.

Dadou reached out and touched the presence, letting it mingle with her magic. The experience was always heady when she first touched a soul. It was a sudden immersion in the sense of a person, a storm of emotion and experience coming on in a rush. Like all of the *mistè*, this one was freezing cold, ravenously hungry, desperate to reach the beating hearts and flowing blood it knew were just beyond its reach. It wanted to know some shred of warmth, even if only for a moment.

Dadou's spiritual eyes pictured the *mistè* as a young girl, barely older than twelve, a red plume flying from a bronze helmet covering her pin-straight black hair.

I am Hua Mulan, the spirit declared in a little girl's voice. *I am the flower of Wei, the lord commander of the three armies. Kneel before me.*

The language was unfamiliar, but it didn't matter. Souls communicated at a level beyond speech, and Dadou had no more need to translate the creole of her home when she replied. *I am honored to meet you, Mulan. I am here to give you what you most desire, in exchange for a favor.*

You do not bargain with the blood of Emperors, the *mistè* said.

Dadou only smiled patiently. *Call it a gift, then, bestowed upon a faithful subject as reward for an act of devotion.*

What devotion do you offer me?

I will return you to the world of men. Living men. Men that breathe and bleed. Blood that can be yours, so much that you can bathe in it.

Mulan grinned in the blackness. *Go on.*

Dadou could feel the *mistè*'s eagerness. It attempted to hide its anticipation, failed. It practically shivered with excitement. Dadou smiled inwardly. *Take my hand.*

The *mistè* let Dadou coil her magic around it, flashing another image of a little girl in armor, bronze halberd over one shoulder. Doubtless it expected Dadou to recognize her and be cowed.

Dadou only drifted back, pulling the *mistè* with her, down the magical link that brought her back to her physical body, the endless depths of the void slipping past her in an instant. Mulan struggled as they came closer, Dadou's magic intensified, and the *mistè* felt itself beginning to be roped into the form Dadou intended, compressed into the flow of the *vodou* that pulsed in her veins. But by then, it was too late and Mulan was within her, filling Dadou with such an intense sense of power that she doubled over. She opened her physical eyes back inside the filthy cinder-block walls and looked at Rodriguez.

"I warned you," she said through gritted teeth. "I gave you a chance to do this another way."

She focused her magic and Bound the *mistè* into his body.

The two thugs backed away as she moaned in relief, lips curling in disgust at the sexual sound. In truth, it was closer to pissing after holding it in for hours, the doubled tide of magic pouring out and into Rodriguez.

Dadou could feel Mulan driving hungrily at him, desperate for his warmth and blood and life. Dadou tried to follow Mulan in, to see the souls mixing, to understand what was happening now.

There was the brief moment where the *mistè* and Rodriguez's soul were joined, and Dadou came to truly know both of them. Mulan had been a child general, taking the place of her ill father in the army of some ancient emperor, rising through the ranks to become his concubine. Rodriguez was a two-bit thug who had grown up in the Colombian ghetto, cutting his teeth first on shell games and pickpocketing before graduating to second-story work.

He'd never amounted to much, even as a criminal, but his brother had.

With the dead, this next part was easy. The Binding was simple, and Dadou had only to concentrate on the silence within, pushing her magic out and letting the jinn do the rest.

But Rodriguez was alive.

Dadou could feel his heart pounding, a steady rhythm of hammerblows that shook both Mulan and her. The heat of his blood might as well have been a searing furnace after the endless cold of the void. Where the souls of the dead were silent, the living shouted their connection to the world. Dadou could hear the soul's link to everything in Rodriguez's body. His cells dividing. His nerves reporting the pain in his wrists. The sick panic in his gut as he felt Mulan tearing into him.

Dadou weathered it all, feeling her physical teeth clench as she focused her magic on Binding Mulan into Rodriguez's body. Rodriguez's soul recoiled at the invasion. Dadou could feel his body contracting, muscles going rock hard, veins dilating. Her physical ears could hear his strangled howl, could smell the stink as his bowels let go.

Yet still the heartbeat hammered. This was the closest she'd yet come to success. The living soul would tear the body to pieces resisting the incursion of the *mistè*. Mulan would have to be held back just enough to let the Binding finish before it was turned loose.

The *mistè* howled, scrabbling toward Rodriguez's soul, enraged and enraptured by the nearness of life. *No,* Dadou said to her, *not yet.*

Mulan strained against the chains of Dadou's magic.

Rodriguez screamed, his soul spasmed, and Dadou heard the sound of bones grinding, muscle tearing away from tendon.

Dadou coiled her magic back, pulled with everything she had. *Just wait for a moment,* she shouted to Mulan. *Just a moment and you'll have what you want.*

She might as well have pulled against a mountain.

Mulan's only answer was a strangled shout of its own. The *mistè* redoubled its efforts, pulling toward Rodriguez. Dadou was overwhelmed by images of Mulan's swinging fists, bronze squares flashing. At last, the wild beating of Rodriguez's heart began to overwhelm her, and Dadou felt her magic slip as Mulan strained forward. The *mistè* shouted, pulled and broke free, Rodriguez's vitality and Mulan's fury kicking Dadou back and into her own physical body, the link broken. She felt a moment's disorientation as her physical eyes opened. Reality always shocked her when she returned to it, the universe suddenly a warm, hard thing of sharp edges and foul smells.

Rodriguez breathed his last. Swathes of purple mottled his pale chest where the vessels beneath the skin had burst. One of his pectorals had detached, slid into his armpit. His eyes stared sightlessly, the sclera completely red. Blood bubbled out of his mouth with his death rattle.

Dadou cursed, stood. The thugs backed away. Dadou knew what they had seen, Dadou sitting, teeth gritted, frowning in concentration as Rodriguez's body slowly clenched, purpled, and died.

So close. Just another moment and I would have had it. It was the same problem every time. She couldn't perform the Binding quickly enough, locking the jinn in place before the victim's body tore itself apart from the shock of the incursion.

The thugs stared at her, horrified. The luxury that Americans enjoyed went hand in hand with a mad insistence on the sanctity of human life. It was not so back home. You learned quickly that people die easily, saw firsthand that life rolled on regardless.

"I got what I needed. *Mèsi.* Clean up here. Bring the body back to base," Dadou said.

She tried to keep her voice casual, but even she could hear the resignation. Another failure. The Director would not be pleased. She turned to go.

"You're supposed to wait another hour before you leave," the thug said.

"The Director will want to hear about this immediately."

"I have my orders," the thug said.

"And I have mine," Dadou answered. "I also have the *vodou* if you'd care to try and stop me." She nodded at the Rodriguez's cooling remains. *"Sa se pa vre?"*

The man's jaw set and Dadou grunted in satisfaction. It was as close to fear as these hard-operator types ever came. She turned on her heel and left, her back itching as she waited for one of them to try and stop her.

But they let her go, and the copper stink of blood followed her for a block or so before the breeze from the Santa Monica Bay whisked it away.

Back in her cell underground, the bright azure of the California sky locked away by miles of earth, her laptop chimed.

Dadou was just emerging from the shower, and she wrapped the towel around the wet mass of her dreadlocks, glorying in the water still dripping off her muscular body. She didn't bother to cover her nudity. Only one person ever called on her laptop, and she could never tell if he was bothering to look at the camera or not. At forty, Dadou knew she looked better than many half her age. Most girls spent their days preening and waiting for a man to lift them out of want. Dadou spent hers training. The difference was as obvious as it was stark.

She went to the computer, tapped in her password to unlock it.

"Good afternoon, Miss Dadou." The voice coming through her laptop was a mechanical rasp, as if the speaker had a mouth full of buzzing hornets. Dadou knew that there was better software out there, programs that could hide the speaker's voice without adding this creepy element, but she also knew that the Director preferred horror-show theatrics. She supposed it was no different from how she cowed the men she worked with, and she respected it.

"Good afternoon, *Direktè*," she said. "How's the view from the top?"

"Anxious," he replied, "I have received some concerned reports from my element leader at the temporary wetworks we established for your latest foray."

Dadou laughed through the thick rage she felt sour her stomach. Frightened men were worse than old women, always filing reports and making complaints. "You know how these 'pipe hitters' are, *Direktè*. They run screaming at the first sign of the *vodou*. Everything is fine."

"I hear Rodriguez did not talk, and that your efforts to Bind a spirit with him ended his life."

"*Se sa, Direktè*. Both true."

"Perhaps you do not appreciate the need for progress in this particular operation."

"I came close this time, *Direktè*."

"How close?"

"Very close. If I'd had another moment, we would have had it, a *mistè* in a living body."

"You've been close before, Miss Dadou. It only counts for horseshoes and hand grenades."

"I'll get it. I'll get it soon."

"I'll be delighted when you do. In the meantime, Rodriguez is dead, and we are no closer to capturing his brother. That man's magic is too valuable to let go unchecked. We need to bring him in or bring him down."

"I know."

The silence on the other end of the line was as close as the Director ever came to an outward expression of anger. "Miss Dadou, I am at the helm of a considerably well-resourced organization. Surely there is some insight you can provide me as to where the problem lies so I can find a way to help you?"

"There's nothing, sir."

"Then, what is the problem? You said this would work."

"It *can* work. I know it can. The problem is the Binding. It has to be done quickly, before the . . . shock of the

Binding destroys the host body. It is so much easier with the dead; I don't know how to explain it."

"Yet you must try."

"It's the speed of the Binding. That's the problem."

"Is there anything we can do to make that happen faster?"

"Not unless you've got another Sorcerer to help me."

Again the pause, and this time Dadou couldn't tell what emotion lay behind it. At last, he spoke again. "Another Sorcerer."

She squinted at the laptop, as if she could look through the blank screen to see his expression. "Not just any Sorcerer. Another *Sèvitè*. One who speaks with the dead."

Silence again; this time it dragged on.

"Sir? Are you still there?"

"I'm thinking," the Director answered.

Dadou's gut clenched. "Dare I ask what you are thinking about?"

"I'm thinking about another problem I have, on the East Coast. You might be able to help me with it. In turn, I might be able to help you. Forget Rodriguez, turn everything over to the watch captain, and pack a bag.

"I want you in Virginia by tomorrow."

CHAPTER IV
BRIEFING

Doctor Eldredge sat at the cherrywood desk and stared into the video teleconference monitor. The light beside the camera was green, indicating that his image was being relayed to the person on the other end, but the move wasn't reciprocated. Eldredge had been working for the Director for most of his adult life now, and he still had yet to see the man. He didn't know his name or even what his voice sounded like. The deep rasping that came over the phone or video teleconference line had to be the work of a voice modifier.

Of course, the Director didn't know Eldredge's name, either. Eldredge had worn his moniker so long that he thought of it as his own. There were days he couldn't remember his real name, a trio of foreign-sounding words that described a stranger he had known a lifetime ago.

"Doctor," came the Director's voice over the line. Eldredge had heard it at least a hundred times in his career, and it never failed to give him shivers. Eldredge could almost feel the man's satisfaction as the video conveyed the revulsion on Eldredge's face. "It's good to see you."

"It's good to *see* you too, sir," Eldredge answered, cocking an eyebrow.

The Director chuckled, distinguished from coughing only by cadence. "The security of this operation is my chief responsibility. Given the recent breach, I think my concern is justified. Wouldn't you agree?"

Eldredge felt his face color. The Director was referring to Schweitzer's escape. Schweitzer had been Eldredge's greatest achievement and his worst failure. He was the only Operator the program had ever produced whose own soul had triumphed over the jinn bound into his corpse. On Eldredge's watch, he had become the first Operator capable of ethics, of restraint, of anything other than the predator's instinct to kill. And on Eldredge's watch, he had escaped. He took the Director's meaning. Compartmentalization was a key part of keeping every aspect of the program secret. That meant that you didn't get to know what your own boss looked like. "Of course, sir."

"I knew you'd agree. What's the SITREP?"

The Director's insistence on military acronyms was the one clue Eldredge had to his identity. Civilians learned and used acronyms too, but only a former military man mingled them with everyday speech until it became a kind of creole.

"Jawid has succeeded, sir. Chang is paired with a jinn. From Jawid's description, he sounds like some ancient Celt or Norseman." Before Schweitzer had taken control of his own corpse, he had been paired with the soul of an ancient Akkadian god-king. All the jinn were older than dust, powerful, and hopelessly evil.

"And Chang?"

"Jawid says he's in thrall to the jinn," Eldredge said. "He's hoping we can learn something that will help us to locate Schweitzer."

"Outstanding. How soon until we send the teams?"

"I'm certain Schweitzer and his family are in the George Washington National Forest, sir, but we've got nothing more than that. I already have Blue One, Two, and Six over the target. So far, they've got nothing."

"I thought those were your best direct-action teams."

"They are my best *regular* teams, sir. Schweitzer has all the capabilities of a Gold Operator and the presence of mind to leverage years of training with the SEALs. That forest is over one point eight million acres."

"So, engage the Gold teams. You can add Chang to one of them. There would be a certain poetic justice to that, don't you think?"

Eldredge's stomach clenched. The Director was all too quick to employ the Gold Operators, but the living dead monsters were ruled by their lust for blood. Any time they were put in the field, there was a risk of a massacre. Eldredge forced a shaking breath before he was calm enough to answer. "Respectfully, sir, the Gold teams are unpredictable. Every time we use them in public, we run the risk of collateral damage with the potential to compromise this program. I'd rather engage them only when we're sure of the target."

"Get out there with the Blue elements and use your magic knife."

Eldredge's hand moved to his white coat, feeling the hard outline of the KA-BAR utility knife Jawid had ensorcelled for him. The blade was old and pitted from the sea salt that had scoured it during the Normandy landing when it had bounced along Eldredge's father's hip as the young marine had waded ashore.

Eldredge remembered handing it to Jawid when the Sorcerer had first been brought in, still covered in Band-Aids from healing cuts and taking a handful of antibiotics to drive out the parasites that had colonized his gut during years of hard living in the Afghan mountains. *Use this,* Eldredge had said as Jawid's hand closed around the handle. *Show me what you can do.*

The knife didn't look any different. It was hard to believe that the slim metal blade contained anything as mighty as a jinn, but Jawid had been ensorcelling talismans almost as long as he had been ensorcelling corpses, and Eldredge had seen the proof with his own eyes. *This jinn*

was mad in life, Jawid said when he handed the blade back.
*Death has not made him sane. He will not abide another
soul near him.* Eldredge had kept the blade concealed in his
waistband ever since. When one of the Golds had gone feral
and leapt for him, he'd managed to rip the blade from its
sheath and plunge it into the monster's calf. The thing had
gone limp as the jinn inside was banished back into the
void.

And something else.

Why was it glowing? Eldredge had asked.

*I do not know. Perhaps the jinn inside is angry enough
to touch the metal.*

Eldredge patted the knife, remembering a line from one
of his favorite books. *My sword Sting. It glows when
enemies are near.*

Not orcs but jinn. The closer they came, the brighter it
glowed.

"That knife's effective range is less than two hundred
yards, sir," Eldredge said. "Until we have a better fix, I'd
just be underfoot. Besides, I'm needed here to look after
Jawid."

"How is he doing?" the Director asked. He sounded bored.

"He's . . . shaken by Schweitzer's escape, sir. Doctor
Empath is having a tough time getting the whole story out,
but I've been having his food dosed with sodium amytal,
and it's making him open up a bit more. It seems Schweitzer
pillaged his memories, learned his wife and son were still
alive, which was what predicated his escape. Jawid is . . .
fragile. He lacked the strength of character to stand against
Schweitzer. The experience left him shaken."

"Empath tells me Jawid is pining for a family."

"That's true, sir. He was apparently betrothed before we
rescued him from the Taliban. He has remarked that he
desires children."

"Will this be an obstacle?"

"I'm not certain, sir. It's definitely a major distraction,
even a preoccupation for him. He lacks the . . . patriotic

motivations that drive the rest of us. This isn't his country. He's lonely, to be frank."

"Perhaps we can assign him a mate. A roll in the hay might put it to bed. No doubt one of the analysts would be willing to dive on that grenade for the sake of the mission."

"Respectfully, sir, I don't think it's sexual. I mean, that's part of it, but I think what he really wants is to feather a nest. He wants to make a home. You know the tribes in Waziristan, sir. Family is the only thing they hold more sacred than their faith." Eldredge thought of his own nights furtively masturbating on his cot, an efficient exercise designed to take the edge off a raw need that he would have surgically removed if he could. A part of him mourned the loss of the life he could have had, the woman he might have married, the children he might have raised. *That ship has sailed. You only have time for one life, and you chose this one.*

"That's not possible," the Director's voice was flat. "Magic has put him beyond that. Jawid must accept that he's not in the world as others are."

"I agree, sir, but that is precisely what he won't accept." Eldredge thought of Jawid's fearful eyes, the sad turn of his mouth. He had been a boy captured and abused by religious madmen when the army had found him. The Sorcerer had never had a chance to chart the course of his own life. *I wish there was some way to help you, but magic is like cancer. You don't ask for it, and it changes everything.* Eldredge was silently grateful that he'd been spared magical ability. His life wasn't that much different from Jawid's, but it was self-determined, and that made all the difference.

The Director was silent for a long time. "Is he reliable?" he finally asked.

"Honestly, sir? I can't say. There's something going on with what Schweitzer did to him that he's not telling us. Doctor Empath is sure of it. I spend a lot of time getting him over crying jags. He may need a vacation. Maybe we can send him somewhere, under guard, without freedom of movement, but some R and R, at least."

"There's no time for that, especially now."

"I know, sir, but if we lose our best asset, we're going to have bigger problems."

"Which is why I'm engaging a backup plan. Jawid isn't this program's best asset. I'm pulling Scorpio Cell's Sorcerer and bringing her here."

Eldredge managed to keep the surprise out of his voice. "Understood, sir, and you know I'm grateful for the help. But won't that necessitate closing down Scorpio's operations? That's going to give China a big leg up."

"We'll have to worry about that later. Schweitzer is a loose nuke, which is how it's been presented to the President. He's declared this a Javelin Rain–class incident. All options are on the table."

Eldredge swallowed. He knew the Director was being literal. The Javelin series of code words was generally used to describe nuclear incidents. The President had been lied to. He'd been told they'd lost a nuclear warhead, and not a magically reanimated, superpowered corpse. The power that lay in that level of secrecy terrified him.

"Understood, sir. Are you going to tap the reserve?"

"You told me you don't have a lot of confidence in that Sorcerer's skill. Has your position changed?"

"No, sir. It's just that you said that all options were on the table . . ."

"All effective options. We're not desperate yet. Scorpio's Sorcerer is very, very good."

"Yes, sir. I'm excited to meet her."

"She'll be here tomorrow. Pair her up with Jawid and get them to work. I want Schweitzer found yesterday. Every second he's at large jeopardizes not only the safety of this program, but of the entire nation."

"Understood, sir."

The Director's voice took on an edge. "I've been very lenient with you, Eldredge. I put you in charge of this program and gave you a free hand because I was confident in your ability to get the job done. Don't make me a liar. You blow up whatever you have to. You kill whomever you have to. You steal and lie and break every damn law in the world if that's what it takes to bring Schweitzer down.

"Destroyed. Not captured, Eldredge. You make sure there's no piece of Schweitzer left bigger than a softball. It's safe to assume that his wife and child are fully aware of our operations here?"

It was a rhetorical question. Eldredge's throat went dry as he nodded.

"Unfortunate," the Director's modified voice rasped. "Make sure you deal with them, too."

CHAPTER V
TOUCHING DOWN

Hours passed. Twice, Schweitzer resisted the urge to stalk back to his wife and ask her what was going on. He put thoughts of Steve Chang out of his mind. He avoided pushing back into the emotional link between himself and Sarah. Sarah could feel it on her end too, and he knew what it would tell him anyway. He could hear Patrick murmuring to her, the sizzle of cooking meat, the slow smacking of their chewing. He began to tune his hearing to make out their conversation, then decided he didn't want to, and dialed further down to focus on their beating hearts. The twin pulses reminded him of what was important: they were alive. He had done what he said he would he would do, would continue to do it.

At last, he turned and slithered on his belly, keeping to the shadows of a low copse of trees that got him close enough to the tiny orange-red flower that was their dying cooking fire. The smell of venison was strong enough to bring predators, but those same noses detected the strange, chemical odor of the glycerol and pungent cocktail of humectants and cell conditioners that kept his dead flesh supple. Schweitzer could hear the padding of tiny feet, the soft rustle of wings far overhead, but the animals always steered clear the moment they drew close enough to smell him.

Sarah had kept the fire low and stamped it out the moment she no longer needed it, not drawing any more attention to their position than necessary. At last, Schweitzer's patience wore out. "Babe," he said. "We have to go."

Patrick stiffened, and Sarah bundled their son against her chest, hiding his face in her armpit and stroking his hair. She sighed. "I know."

"Can you manage now? Can he?"

She nodded. "We'll have to."

"I'm sorry. I'll be more careful with you. I'll try to remember that you're . . ."

"Human." She looked up, eyes wet. "And you're not anymore."

"I don't know what I am, baby. I know I still love you and Patrick. I know I'd do anything for you, and that I'll keep you safe no matter what. I know that I would never have stopped looking for you, not for a minute. They tricked me, Sarah." He knew she was right, knew he'd have to leave, but he needed to know that she understood before he did.

She cradled Patrick closer to her, reached out one hand.

Schweitzer crawled from the shadows a little way, reaching toward her. His son squirmed, but Sarah pressed Patrick's face more tightly against her, shushing him. Schweitzer crept quietly toward them, straining until their hands met, fingers clasped. He could feel the warmth of her hand, the steady rhythm of her pulse below the skin. She looked away, and he could see her working to suppress a shudder. She raised his hand to her mouth, kissed it.

"Oh God, Jim," she said. Her tears pattered on his knuckles. "I miss you."

"I'm still here."

"You smell like formaldehyde. You feel like cold rubber."

"Doesn't change anything."

"I know, baby; it's just going to be . . ."

The sound of the birds overhead solidified, thickened. Schweitzer heard a sudden snap as a vast pair of wings unfurled, catching the air and slowing the bird's descent. But the sound was too loud, too sudden, pregnant with the vibrating ring of metal.

Not birds.

Schweitzer seized Sarah's hand and yanked on her arm. She cried out as her shoulder wrenched in its socket, but Schweitzer managed enough leverage to throw her away from him. He rolled into a crouch, but not before he saw a long line of rounds stitch the ground beneath where his wife's arm had just been.

He craned his neck, caught the faint outlines of angels settling into the canopy, metal-framed wings falling from their backs as they descended. *Gliders. They knew I'd pick up on helo rotors from too far away.* They must have jumped from high altitude and deployed their wings only at the last possible moment to get them as close as they could without alerting him. Gliders meant they had no way to run. They were in the fight to win or die.

Them or him. Them or his family.

Schweitzer launched himself to his feet, claws and horns extending fully, jaw unhinging. "Run," he hissed to Sarah. "I'll find you."

"And get caught out alone? Not a chance." She thrust Patrick against her chest and bent to lift a rock.

The men began to descend from the canopy, slowly floating toward the ground. Schweitzer narrowed his eyes. He could see no ropes, no means of support. They were kitted out as operators: tactical vests, helmets, modified carbines nestled in the crooks of their arms, sighting in at Schweitzer. The first round cracked, and Schweitzer felt an impact in his cheek as the bullet holed it and whisked out the other side. Schweitzer knew that the shooter was targeting a three-inch triangle over his face. Schweitzer had trained to put his rounds in the same spot for his entire career as a SEAL. It was the fastest way to put a living target down.

But Schweitzer was no living target.

He leapt, rocketing across the intervening distance, claws piercing one the enemy's throat before he had time to pull the trigger. His head lolled silently and he went limp, sliding off Schweitzer's claws, sinking slowly to the ground.

The other men finished their descent, boots touching gently on the forest floor as if they had been set there by an invisible hand. Schweitzer could feel the column of hot air rising up off the ground. He could feel a flow in the midst of the air, a shimmering energy that permeated his veins, resonating with the substance that kept his dead body moving. Magic. This was how the men had floated down from the high trees.

"Jim!" a thick Afrikaner accent, one he recognized. A man blazed in the sky, floating eight feet above the ground, wreathed in crackling lightning.

The split-second distraction was all the floating man needed. He flicked his wrist and the wind rose, vaulting one of the operators over Schweitzer's head toward where Sarah crouched behind him.

Schweitzer leapt straight up, catching the operator's ankle. The operator's leg snapped as Schweitzer swung him over his head. Schweitzer reached out with his other hand, grabbed the man's weapon, and broke it free from the sling with a single twist of his arm, sending his enemy sailing back toward the floating man, crying out in pain as he went. The floating man laughed and rose two feet, and the operator whipped under him and crashed into a tree, fell limp to the ground.

"The fuck are you doing here?" Schweitzer grunted. He remembered the floating man now. Raees Gruenen, a South African mercenary who had been contracted to help Schweitzer's team with an op in Botswana a lifetime ago. The Gruenen he knew had never floated. Schweitzer pulled the carbine up into his shoulder. A light on the weapon's upper receiver flashed red and he felt the trigger seize. They'd been developing this tech right when he'd been killed. The weapon wouldn't fire without the operator's wristband close by.

"Guess I'm just talented," Gruenen said. "Had some wild dreams and woke up in the air. Brave new world, eh?" He opened a hand and lightning sprang from his palm, plowing into the ground and blowing Schweitzer off his feet. He tumbled through the air, shoulder slamming into his son, popping Patrick free of Sarah's grip. The three of them rolled over and over through the smoldering leaves.

"Sarah?!" Schweitzer scrambled to his feet just in time to feel one of the operators' boots brush his head as he leapt over him, borne on the updraft of Gruenen's magic. Schweitzer flailed out a hand, brushing the man's calf. The enemy landed behind Schweitzer and stepped on Patrick's arm, making for the greater threat that was Sarah.

She roared and rose to meet him. The operator raised his weapon and squeezed off a round before she crashed into him, snarling, wrapping her limbs around him like a spider embracing prey.

Gruenen frowned. "Aim needs work, though." He extended his hand again, and Schweitzer threw the useless carbine at him. It spun into the next burst of lightning, the metal sparking and the magazine exploding in a crackle of gunshots. Gruenen rolled in midair, dove low to escape the sudden detonation of rounds.

Schweitzer turned back to his family. Patrick sprawled on his face, bawling. He was red-faced and terrified, but the immediate threat wasn't to him. Sarah held the operator too tightly to throw a punch, and the enemy raised his hand, hooking two fingers over her sternum, yanking down on the cluster of nerves and vulnerable windpipe behind it.

The pain must have been excruciating, but Sarah was already screaming, leaning forward, fastening her teeth on the man's face. He shrieked as his nose and upper lip shifted, blood squirting over Sarah, misting the ground beneath their feet.

Schweitzer thrust his claws into the man's lower back. The enemy's upper body stiffened, his legs went suddenly limp, and Sarah let him go. He turned toward Schweitzer, his face a twisted red horror, nose and upper lip sloughing away below the semicircular tears left by Sarah's teeth.

Schweitzer let him fall, grabbing his carbine, yanking his wrist up along with it.

Sarah spit out meat, blood trickling out of the corner of her mouth, and turned to Gruenen. "Stay away from my son."

Gruenen got to one knee. "You crazy fucking bitch," he said, raising a hand. Schweitzer could feel the current of Gruenen's magic coalescing, focusing. The sky above them darkened, and Schweitzer could smell ozone, feel the static charge gathering in the air.

"That's my wife you're talking to, asshole," Schweitzer said, sighting the carbine one-handed, raising the dying operator's wrist to the bottom of the handle. The light on the receiver went green, and Schweitzer fired.

In life, Schweitzer would never have had the control to aim a carbine one-handed. In death, he was as steady as a rock. A small, dark hole appeared in Gruenen's forehead. His eyes widened, then crossed. Twin trails of black blood leaked out of his nose, and he pitched forward on his face, his current suddenly gone, the forest going deathly silent.

Schweitzer paused, listening. The animal sounds had vanished. Only those insects too small to get away from the fight quickly could be heard, burrowed as deep as they could go into the fallen leaves. Patrick's sniffling reminded Schweitzer that his boy was alive. Whether or not he was hurt was another matter.

He turned to go to him, stopped himself. The boy didn't need to be scared any more than he already was. "Sarah, Patrick might be hurt. Can you . . ."

She crouched, her face and shirt painted with the operator's blood, eyes still fixed on Gruenen's corpse. "Was he flying, Jim?"

"Yes, baby. He was."

"What the fuck?"

"It's magic. Same stuff that is keeping me upright and walking. There are other kinds. I fought a man who could mold his own flesh. They called it Physiomancy."

"How are we supposed to run from these people? How can we fight them?"

Schweitzer could hear the edge of panic in her voice, forced his own to stay calm. "Baby. Sarah. Look at me?"

She didn't move, but her dark eyes flicked in their sockets, sliding to meet his own. His wife's eyes were slits, focused, locked into fight mode long after the threat had passed. This was hurting her, the kind of hurt that would last.

"Sarah," Schweitzer said. "You're right. We can't beat them with technology, and we can't beat them with magic. So, we have to beat them with heart. We control the one thing we can control."

"What's that?"

"We don't quit. We stay in the fight until they kill us. We don't break and we don't give up. Can you do that?" He put steel in his voice, willing the words across the intervening distance, praying they stiffened her spine.

Sarah only stared at him, eyes still narrowed, as if she wasn't entirely certain whether or not he was a threat. He focused inward, retracted his horns, spines, and claws, heard the slight slurping sound as the tips slid below the skin.

"Sarah. Can you do that?" he asked again.

She nodded.

"Say it."

"Say what?" she asked.

"Say you won't quit."

"I won't quit." Robotic repetition. She didn't mean it, not like he needed her to. But it was a start.

He nodded. "Okay. Patrick will freak if I pick him up. Will you please see to him?"

She turned, took a step. Her leg didn't support her weight and she fell to her knees. Schweitzer reached her in a single stride, followed the scent of fresh blood to her hip. "Fucker shot me," she mumbled.

Schweitzer extended a claw and sliced into her waistband. The dirty fabric broke apart, peeling back from pale skin, slick with sweat and dusted with dirt and bits of leaves. The operator's round had clipped the meat over her hip, parting the skin neatly. Blood sheeted down below, soaking her thigh. Schweitzer could see the soft glint of exposed bone, going jagged where the bullet had tumbled, breaking off a small fragment.

Her head lolled against his shoulder, and Patrick howled for his mother. Schweitzer looked up at his son, saw the boy facedown in a soft tangle of vines. Clusters of arrowhead-shaped leaves covered Patrick's face. He seemed whole enough, but Schweitzer knew that plant, knew that even now the oil covering it was working its way into his son's skin. Patrick would be an itching, screaming mess by nightfall.

And they couldn't afford screaming. Because the Gemini Cell wouldn't have just sent Gruenen and a single fire team. They were a recon force, spotters deployed to locate Schweitzer and his family. And that meant the main thrust of the search couldn't be far behind.

They didn't have much time.

Schweitzer took one more look at Sarah's wound and raced to Gruenen's corpse. "Baby?" He called to her as he rolled the body over onto its back, began checking the pouches in the tactical vest. "Baby? Remember what you said. Don't give up, Sarah. Don't quit."

But Sarah didn't answer, her pale face settling in the crook of her arm, her mouth opening, her eyes shut against the gathering gloom.

CHAPTER VI
MAMA DADOU

Jawid straightened, the stiffness in his back reminding him of his devotion. It was one of a series of small sacrifices that made his daily prayers cathartic. He raised his hands, softly whispering, *Allahu Akbar. Allah listens and responds to the one who praises Him.*

Dear Allah, be with me. Help me to find Schweitzer. Protect me from Eldredge. Turn his anger from me. I will be patient. Bring me forth from here and send me home, where I can have a wife and children of my own, that I may spend the last of my days praising You and living as You intended.

He bent to roll his prayer rug, stowing it in the corner of his cell, the one flash of color in the otherwise bare expanse of white and stainless steel. It had seemed the height of luxury when he had first arrived, after years of sleeping out in the open on rock, root, and frozen mud. The hot showers, electricity, and endless food seemed the stuff of paradise. Now, just a few years later, Jawid saw it for what it was: the thing the *Talebs* had warned against, a prison of comfort that was designed to keep him locked away from Allah's plan for mankind. He had no wife, no children, struggled against an enemy not his own, for ends that were valued only by the infidels. The sinking feeling that his life had gone wrong had solidified into a curdled horror, equaled only by the certainty that the Gemini Cell would kill him the moment they suspected he had real plans to leave.

The Qur'an counseled that there was no greater blessing than patience. He would watch; he would wait. He would find a way.

Until then, he had work to do.

He keyed in the code that slid open the door, no less a cell for the fact that he could leave it. He stepped out into the plain white corridor outside the ops center. They blindfolded him for the trips aboveground, so he had no idea how deep the complex went, but he imagined he could feel the great weight of the earth above him, the sun huge and bright over the false office complex that guarded the entrance.

He entered the elevator, waited through the silent descent, the flickering of digital numbers the only indicator that he'd moved at all. There were no signs in the facility. An interloper would be unable to find anything, but Jawid knew the way from memory. He made two sharp rights and found himself in a corridor that narrowed until only a single man could walk along it. Three-foot-thick seams appeared at regular intervals as he proceeded, home to massive metal barriers that could instantly seal it off.

Jawid struggled against claustrophobia, making his way toward the door at the far end. It was much thicker than the one to his room, the transparent palladium panel giving a distorted fishbowl view of the plain white interior.

Chang's corpse stood motionless in the middle of the room, back to the door. A Gold Operator had killed Chang with its claws, extending them up until they pierced his heart, leaving long rents in his side that extended halfway around his back. They were stitched shut now, crude purple-gray scars over raised welts an inch high. Chang's back was tattooed with angel wings, cresting his shoulder blades above a blotched scrawl that read ONLY GOD CAN JUDGE ME.

Jawid could feel the eddying current of magic pouring off the corpse, knew that for all his stillness, Partolan was hard at work within the dead vessel, warring with Chang's soul. Jawid pitied Chang. His own life was a twisting purgatory, an enslavement to the agenda of unbelievers. But even that was far, far better than an eternity of unlife chained to the side of a jinn leapt from the breast of the *Shaytan* himself. The jinn were infinitely cunning, infinitely strong, infinitely evil. How Schweitzer had managed to best one was beyond him. He tried not to think about it. Because, if Schweitzer's soul was so honored by Allah, then what did that say about Jawid and what he had done? What he was still doing?

Chang-Partolan stood completely still. Jawid summoned his current, sent it rippling through the door, feeling it mingle with the eddying tide that whirled around the standing corpse. Jawid focused his magic, opened a channel, and spoke to the jinn and Chang at once. *Good morning, I have come to . . .*

A surge of animal lust came pouring up the channel he had opened between them. Jawid felt his knees go weak. He stumbled a step back down the corridor, terror competing with his instinct to sever the link and roll his magic back. He regained control of his body just before the tipping point, saving himself from a nasty tumble to the hard, concrete floor. The red wave that had assaulted his senses had been pure, uncontaminated by the smallest trace of humanity. He hadn't felt Chang at all.

His vision came back into focus, his hearing registering a rhythmic pounding in time with the vibrating of the cell door. Tiny cracks were appearing in the surface of the palladium panel, white spider webs of breaks in the transparent metal extending with each successive blow.

Jawid could see Chang's corpse hammering itself against the barrier, desperately scrabbling to get at him.

Bone claws emerged from the shredded stumps of its hands, fingers hanging rent and useless like the sepal leaves of some bladed flower.

The thing's eyes burned pure gold.

Jawid did fall now, panic stealing what little strength remained, sitting down hard on his bony backside, the pain of the impact not even registering in his shock.

Partolan had pushed Chang back out into the void. There would be no insight into Schweitzer. There would be no repeat of Schweitzer's strange success, no new Operator with silver in his eyes who was something more than an animal. Jawid had failed again.

And in the Gemini Cell, the price of failure was high.

Partolan threw Chang's disfigured corpse against the door. The thick metal shuddered, squealed, and held. For now.

But that didn't mean it would hold forever. Jawid walked backward on his hands until he could get his feet under him, then jumped up, thumbing his commlink. "I'm in access corridor three. My subject has gone gold. I need a lockdown."

He was already turning, running back the way he had come. He fought against the instinct to keep his eyes on the threat. It didn't make a difference; facing Partolan or running from him, he was just as dead.

Eldredge's voice sounded in his ear. "Calm the hell down; stay where you are. We're right around the corner. We'll be right there."

Jawid knew that Eldredge wanted him to stay where he was, but the panic gripped him, and he felt that his heart would stop unless he moved his legs. The cell door shuddered behind him, and he could hear a faint whining, the mewling of a predator overwhelmed with desire by the nearness of its quarry.

He ran, the motion of his body burning off a tiny fraction of the terror, both of what lay behind him and what lay ahead.

He reached the end of the corridor, his sandaled feet

slapping against the concrete, and slid out into the junction as he turned the corner toward the elevator.

He rebounded off of something soft but firm, staggered backward, his nose suddenly filled with the pleasant odor of clean sweat, soap, and a woody, dry smell that reminded him of roots stretching below the earth.

Eldredge's hands were thrust into the pockets of his long white coat, his shock of hair spraying in every direction at once. Jawid had never once seen the man with his hair combed.

The pleasant smell came from the woman standing beside him. She was at least four inches taller than Jawid, made more towering by the pile of dreadlocked hair atop her head, bound in leather thongs twined with beads and tiny shells. Her body was lean as a whip and so strong, Jawid could see the striations of her muscles sliding beneath her dark skin. She wore a tactical vest and cargo pants bloused into combat boots. A pistol nestled in a paddle holster tucked against one lean thigh. Her eyes were dark and crinkled with amusement, her full lips ghosting a smile.

Jawid's eyes swept across her powerful shoulders, graceful collarbones, lean neck. The analysts in the Gemini Cell never bared themselves so. The sight of her naked shoulders mesmerized him. Her eyes were hard, pitiless, but no less entrancing for all that.

"Whoa, there!" She laughed, putting out a hand. "Who's this?"

"This," Eldredge sighed, "is our Sorcerer, Jawid Rahimi, who cannot seem to follow simple instructions, I'm sad to say."

Jawid started. The magical current from Partolan had died off, only to be replaced with a new one, every bit as powerful, but darker, deeper, the edges of it mixing and probing at his own.

It came from the woman.

"Easy, now," the woman said. "What's got you running

like a chicken?" Her accent was deep and drawling. Jawid could not place it.

"Jawid," Eldredge said, "this is Dadou Alva."

Jawid's jaw dropped; he shut it forcibly, eliciting another laugh from Dadou before he could form words. "She is . . . like me." The thought transfixed him as he studied the feel of her magical tide, the monster battering down the door behind him all but forgotten. Jawid knew there were other Sorcerers in the world, but always they were enemies, targets of the program he had helped to build. He had never known of another working for the American government.

Eldredge nodded as if this were obvious, as common as the grass. "We pulled her from Scorpio Cell to assist you here."

"Achante," Dadou said, extending a hand.

The thought of touching a woman who was not a relative both terrified and thrilled him, and Jawid felt the lust surging in his hips and belly, stiffening him beneath his robes. Dadou waited, her smile fading.

God forgive me, Jawid thought, then reached out and took her hand. Her skin was dry and calloused, and her grip strong enough to make him wince.

"Looks like our timing couldn't be better," Eldredge said. "Can you tell me what the hell is going on?"

Jawid tore his gaze away from Dadou, breathed deeply. "Chang is gone. The jinn has the body."

Eldredge cursed and Dadou's smile vanished. "You're certain?" Eldredge asked.

Jawid nodded. "I saw his eyes."

"Show me," she said.

Jawid froze. "I . . . I don't know if the door will hold . . ."

Eldredge cursed again. "Then we don't have time to stand here discussing it, do we? Go!"

The command jarred Jawid into motion, and his sandals slapped the concrete back the way he came, the soft padding of Dadou and Eldredge's feet coming behind him. The door still trembled in its frame, Chang's dead face pressed against the cracking pane of palladium, Partolan dancing behind the gold flames of his eyes.

Eldredge stared for a moment before cursing a third time. "Seal access corridor to prime subject," he said into his commlink. "Barrier one. Prime for freeze."

"Barrier one, section one is primed" came the response, buzzing in Dr. Eldredge's commlink loud enough to be heard.

"Do it." Eldredge said.

Liquid nitrogen burst from the nozzles in the walls as the thick steel partition slid out of its home in the ceiling, dropping to close off the cell and its rapidly failing door. Partolan let out a savage howl, echoing down the tight space before the barrier slid home, the seal so tight that it cut off all sound behind it. The flow of magic around the jinn dampened from the interference, but Jawid could still feel it whispering through the thickness of the metal.

He turned to Eldredge. The old man's eyes were hard as flint.

Jawid struggled, blinked, looked at the floor. But the terror had him now, and he knew he could not stop the tears from coming. He had failed. His elation at discovering that there were other Sorcerers like him working for the government was eclipsed by the realization that she was there to replace him.

Schweitzer had escaped on his watch, and now, at long last, Eldredge had lost confidence. Jawid couldn't get the job done, so Eldredge had brought in someone who could.

This was the Gemini Cell. Jawid wouldn't be fired. They wouldn't simply let him go.

"Please." Jawid was disgusted by his own voice. His legs trembled and he sank to his knees. "I'm sorry. I did what I could. I thought Partolan understood he had to keep him. I'm sorry. I will find a way to fix this. Please don't . . . don't . . ."

Dadou frowned down at him, disgust flashing across her face in time with Eldredge's deepening scowl.

"Get up," Eldredge said. "Stop being so dramatic."

"Please." Jawid reached for Eldredge's legs. "I beg you . . ."

Eldredge jerked away. "That's enough!"

Eldredge's hand disappeared inside his coat. *He's got a gun; he's going to shoot me.*

Jawid briefly considered fighting, dismissed it. He was no warrior, as the *Talebs* had told him so many times. He had made a mockery of so many things. He would make a mockery of this as well. Instead, he closed his eyes and turned his mind to Allah, to reflect on Him in his final moments. It would hurt, but not for long, then paradise would be his.

Allah, the merciful and compassionate. You know I am a coward and a weakling, but I hope You will judge me gently.

A stirring of the air above his head, a hand descending. Jawid tensed for the blow, for the bullet to tear through him.

Instead, there was the dry smell of roots below the earth. A hand settled on the back of his neck, warm, callused. It massaged the knotted muscles there, spreading warmth through his shoulders.

"It's okay," Dadou said. "It's okay. Everything is going be all right, dahling." Her voice was like warm milk.

"I'm sorry," Jawid said.

"I know, dahling," Dadou said. "But it's going to be okay. Mama Dadou is here to help."

Jawid still couldn't bring himself to open his eyes, though the softness of Dadou's voice made the fear begin to subside. "You're going to replace me. You're the new Sorcerer."

"Pas enkie twa, mon chouchou," Dadou said, the lilting of her voice approaching a song. *"Men anpil, chay pa lou."*

And Jawid did open his eyes now, her face filling his vision. Her skin was wrinkled about the eyes, her mouth lined, and deep creases walking from the corners of her mouth to the edge of her nose. She had seen hard use, this woman. She had known trials. He could not take his eyes from her.

"I don't understand," he whispered.

She smiled, and the world went warm around him. "It means don't be ridiculous, dahling," she drawled. "Together, you and I are going to do great things."

CHAPTER VII
PATCHING UP

"Stay with me," Schweitzer said. He paused long enough to hear Sarah's response, a slurred murmur that couldn't be called a word.

Gruenen stared sightlessly up at the sky, the look of surprise frozen on his face. The bullet hole in his forehead was dime-sized, but the back of his head was completely missing, the shattered eggshell remains testifying to the bullet's force. Schweitzer dug through the pouches in Gruenen's tactical vest. He didn't have to look; his hands knew each item as soon as they touched them, could almost guess where they'd be located. There was the pistol in its chest holster, three loaded magazines tucked just below. There was the knife snapped in behind it, just outside the body armor's intercept plate. He made a mental note to check the handle later. His own had been hollow and packed with supplies. Down over Gruenen's gut he found water-cleaning tablets, a headlamp. Not what he needed. Not now, anyway. *Come on, come on, damn it.*

Patrick had gotten to his hands and knees, crawled to his mother's side.

"Don't touch her!" Schweitzer yelled.

Patrick shrieked, but he obeyed.

The sound tore at Schweitzer, but he couldn't afford to have Sarah getting poison ivy on top of her wound. He only knew what little casualty care was necessary to stabilize a patient until medevac could dust them off. But there was no helo coming here. It was on him. Being yelled at was the least of what his son had suffered over the past few days.

He abandoned the vest, moving to the drop pouch strapped to Gruenen's thigh. He dug past a smartphone and a small wad of papers before his fingers closed on what he sought. "Sarah! You're going to be okay!"

It was a bulging ziplock refrigerator bag. He'd carried one just like it for his entire career; every SEAL did. He cursed himself for not remembering where he'd kept it, losing precious seconds in the search. Schweitzer popped it open, turned it over as he raced back to Sarah's side.

Tourniquet, alcohol pads, roll after roll of sterile gauze.

And the dark-green vacuum-sealed packet that he would know by touch alone. HEMOSTATIC AGENT was stenciled across the front. CAUTION: WILL CAUSE EXTREME BURNS.

Schweitzer rolled Sarah onto her side and ripped the remainder of her bloody jeans away from the wound, trying to ignore the exposed striations of muscle, the steadily flowing blood. He tore open one of the alcohol pads, wiping his hands as clean as he could before putting on the thin rubber gloves. He then turned to the wound, rinsing it with the alcohol, trying to scrub away as much of the dirt, sweat, and burned residue as possible. There was no sign of the round, and he was sure the bullet had torn straight through. That was good. He wasn't equipped for surgery out here.

Sarah groaned. "Ow. Fucking ow," she said weakly.

"This is just foreplay," Schweitzer said. "Hard part comes next."

She looked up at him, eyes focused. "Bring it."

He smiled as much as the skin stretched over the metal armature of his jaw would allow. "That's my girl. Here we go."

He fished the black plastic bite stick out of the trauma kit and pressed it to her lips. She accepted it between her teeth and met Schweitzer's eyes, held them.

Schweitzer felt Patrick's hand against his hip, glanced down to see his son, one hand on him, the other on his mother's boot. Schweitzer felt a surge of emotion at the sight of his boy voluntarily touching him, fought it down. *Keep the bubble. Focus.*

"Lock it up, lock it on," he said to Sarah, then tore open the package of the agent and dumped it into the wound.

The yellow powder began to sizzle the instant it came into contact with Sarah's blood, turning a deep red-orange as it sank in, sending up thin puffs of ochre smoke that stank of chemicals and cooked meat. Schweitzer thrust his fingers into the mass, pressing the powder deeper in, pinching the edges of Sarah's flapped flesh closer together. He wasn't careful about where he put his hands, and he could feel the heat of the agent burning through the gloves, scalding the fingertips beneath. That was fine. He wasn't going to need to be fingerprinted anytime soon.

"Going to fuck up my manicure," Schweitzer said, as Sarah's hand snaked out and gripped the back of his neck, pulling him down until their foreheads touched.

Her face had gone the color of rotten fish, her eyes burning. Her forehead was sweating so intensely that it ran down her temples. Her teeth ground against the bite stick audibly.

But she did not scream.

"You are a machine, you know that?" Schweitzer asked her as the first wave of agony subsided and Sarah relaxed a fraction, gulping air.

"I don't know why you hate me so much," she said, spitting out the bite stick. "I bore you a child, for Chrissake."

"Guy can't come back from the dead and be hunted by the government in peace," Schweitzer said, rocking back to examine his handiwork. "It's always nag, nag, nag."

The wound sizzled, but there was no visible blood flow, and the edges seemed elastic enough to withstand some movement. It would dry over time, and that meant it would crack. There was also no way to tell if she wasn't bleeding internally. Sarah's life could be pouring out below the surface of her skin, and neither of them would know until she collapsed. She needed medical attention, and she needed it soon.

He would worry about that later. First, he had to see to the boy.

"Don't move," he said, turned to Patrick.

"No! No!" his son said. "Mommy! Want mommy!"

"Shh, now," Schweitzer said, pulling the boy closer as gently as he could. "Mommy's going to be okay. I have to fix you now."

Patrick whined and called softly for his mother, but he submitted as Schweitzer tore open more alcohol pads, wiping down his face and hands, anywhere the exposed skin had touched the poison ivy.

At last Schweitzer released him, sitting back, letting his augmented vision dial down into the infrared spectrum. Red blotches covered Patrick's face, arms, and hands, the heat blazing out to Schweitzer's magically powered eyes as the skin below the surface became inflamed by the plant's oil.

He'd missed the window. Patrick was going to be in a bad way very soon.

Sarah was sitting up, gently touching the edge of the wound, hissing.

"Knock it off," Schweitzer called to her. "You'll infect it."

"It's going to get infected either way," she said. "We need something to keep it clean."

Schweitzer pointed to the corpses of the operators. "They'll each have trauma kits. Should be enough alcohol and sterile pads to handle that for a while. Anyway, we've got another problem. Patrick rolled in poison ivy."

Sarah winced. "Maybe he's immune. Not everybody gets it."

"He's got it," Schweitzer said, "and bad. He's going to be a mess very soon."

"Is there anything in the trauma . . ."

Schweitzer shook his head before she'd finished speaking. "I must have packed a hundred of those things in my life. It's for handling gunshot wounds, not stuff like this. We need calamine, hydrocortisone, and some cold packs."

"Maybe he can ride it out."

"Do you think he'll ride it out?"

Sarah cursed. "No. He'll scream his head off. What's the worst-case scenario?"

"For poison ivy in a kid? Anaphylactic shock. We can't have that, Sarah. We've got to fix this."

"We need a drugstore."

Schweitzer nodded. "There's one in every small town. I'll break in at night and get us what we need. Might be I can steal some antibiotics for you, too."

Sarah rolled onto her knees, and he raced to her side. "Baby, you have to . . ."

"Stop," she said. "Get your head on straight. You want to risk breaking into an alarmed store in the middle of the night like some petty thief? You think that's going to make us safer?"

She slowly got to her feet, wincing. Schweitzer winced with her, reaching out to support her elbow, backing off at a look from her. "I'm fine," she said. "I can stand.

"Jim, that team was coming for *you*. We have to split up. You have to go after them, and you have to do it now."

Schweitzer swallowed the grief and rage, let it pass down into his spiritual gut to churn there. The SEAL was in charge again; he was focused. "Okay. Just let me get you to a town and make sure that you have what you need. Then we'll come up with a plan."

"Jim . . . Please don't think this is easy for me. I just . . ."

He raised a hand. "Sarah, I'm with you on this. I just want to make sure there isn't another team inbound that might catch you out in the open. Once I'm certain we've got some breathing room, I'll leave. I swear I will."

The grief churned in him, rose up through his spine so

that he felt it in the back of his throat. He knew it was riding the link to Sarah, that she could feel it too.

"I love you, Jim" was all she said.

"I know you do," he said. "It doesn't change anything. Let's get this done."

She looked down at herself. "I'm a mess. I look like I've been through a battle."

Schweitzer cocked an eyebrow. "You have been through a battle."

She quirked a smile, the tiny motion a gut-punch reminder of how it felt to have things normal between them. "Can you find me a river? I'll wash up." She pointed to Gruenen's corpse. "Those are plain khaki cargo pants. No camouflage pattern. They're clean enough."

"Those are tactical pants. They're made for operators."

"You're telling me hikers never buy and wear that stuff?"

Schweitzer paused. She was right.

She looked down at her shirt and pullover. They were dirty, but not beyond salvage. "We can wash these. If anyone asks, I can say we were camping."

"This is risky."

Patrick ran to her, and she stripped off her pullover, bundling him in the cloth before picking him up, keeping the inflamed skin well covered. "What's more likely to raise the alarm: a hiker wandering into town out of the woods and buying some common first aid supplies, or a break-in in the dead of night?"

She had always been smarter than him. The elite reputation of the SEALs was a legend that even the SEALs themselves bought into after a while. There were precious few people who could pop that bubble, remind Schweitzer of his own limitations. Sarah was one.

And in the face of her logic, he found himself telling the truth. "If I lost you, I don't know what I'd do."

She smiled sadly at that, touched his hand. "You're not going to lose me, Jim. Not if you leave the thinking to me, anyway. Now help me get these assholes stripped, and then let's get me cleaned up."

Schweitzer was glad to get to the business of salvaging everything they could from the corpses. They took two of the carbines and their matching wristbands, Schweitzer equipping himself with every spare piece of medical equipment and ammunition he could fit on his body, carrying the load of three men. He put on gear more out of habit than need, and was surprised at the comfort of the tactical vest and thigh-strapped go-bag's familiar weight. Sarah rigged herself out as best she could, slinging the carbine like a pro, or at least a gifted amateur. Schweitzer silently thanked himself for the hundredth time for all the time he had spent forcing her to go to the range.

They left the corpses for the coyotes. As they picked their way through the woods back to the river where Schweitzer had killed the deer, he could hear the beetles already starting.

"Feels wrong." Schweitzer jerked his head in the direction of the bodies.

Sarah gestured to the black, clotted furrow in her hip. "So does this."

At the river bend, Sarah stripped and waded fearlessly into the freezing water, Patrick propped on her hip. Schweitzer didn't even bother chastising her about catching his son's poison ivy, and instead crouched, alert for threats, watching the water sluice down Sarah's body.

It glittered on her pale skin, standing up in gooseflesh, making the colored surface of her tattooed arms ripple. Her hair slicked back behind her ears, sending the water running down the graceful curve of her spine. She set Patrick down on the bank and bent to scrub at her shirt and pullover, caught Schweitzer looking.

"What?"

"You're beautiful," he rasped, suddenly aware of the distance between them. Sarah, still a young woman. Still beautiful and fertile, her body ready to carry the second child they'd started talking about before he'd been killed. He looked down between his knees, unable to meet her eyes, closing his own to avoid seeing the useless gray piece of meat that had once been his penis, nestled between the mass of hideous scar tissue and clumsy surgical stitching that was the body around it.

"I'm sorry," he mumbled before he had a chance to stop himself.

Sarah didn't answer, finishing in silence and lifting Patrick back onto her hip after she'd dressed. Her wet clothing wound up draped over Schweitzer's broad back as they travelled on, spread out and drying. The silence stayed with them for a long time. Schweitzer desperately wanted to bridge it, but there was simply nothing to say.

"So," Sarah said eventually, "drugstore."

"I'll find a road." He paused, dialing his hearing out as far as he could, grateful for something else to think about. At first there was nothing but the trickle of the water, the soft scrabbling of squirrel claws as they raced through the trees. And finally, somewhere in the distance, so faint he could barely make it out, the low droning of a motorcycle engine, a Big Twin like the one he'd stolen to make his way back to Sarah. That meant roads, civilization.

"That way." He pointed.

His wife nodded and they pushed on, Patrick beginning to fidget, pawing at his face, sniffling as his skin turned red under the constant attention.

CHAPTER VIII
WHAT IT'S LIKE

The door chime roused Jawid from his prayers.

He sat in the same position he used for his formal prayers, his left leg folded in so tightly that his thigh touched the ground. The cramped posture sent pins and needles through his hips, but he savored the sensation as a reminder of his devotion to God.

He stumbled to his feet, so surprised he forgot to answer, staring until whoever was outside lost patience and the door opened.

Dadou stood in the doorway, her eyes crinkled into a smile. She'd traded the tactical gear for a pair of slim-fitting jeans and a tank top that bared the slopes of her breasts and the strong muscles of her arms and shoulders. Jawid could count on one hand the number of times he'd seen a woman so revealed, and each time, he'd spent at least a week begging God's forgiveness for his sin. But standing here before Dadou, he found his mind far from repentance.

"Bon apre-midi, chouchou," she said. *"Ki jan ou ye?"*

"I was praying," Jawid said, feigning irritation he did not feel.

The smile left Dadou's eyes. "Yes. Eldredge told me you were a godly type. They don't listen, you know."

"God always listens." Jawid forced himself to relax. "Whenever I am not working, I am here, praying."

Dadou entered without asking, surveyed the bare surroundings. "And just think of everything you could be doing with that time, *non*? If you weren't spending it talking to something that isn't there."

"You think you're smart, but God will judge you."

"He has already judged me," Dadou laughed. "God and I have been at odds for a long time now. As you can see"—she gestured to her own hard body, her clean clothes—"Mama Dadou isn't doing so bad."

She sat down beside him on the bed, her shoulder brushing his. Jawid felt the heat of her through the thin fabric of his robes.

"When I first learned that magic was real," Jawid said, "I was not surprised. It was but one more example of the many ways in which God shows He can do anything."

"Or *Shaytan*," Dadou answered.

Jawid started at her use of the Arabic word for the devil. "How do you know that word?"

"Poor does not mean stupid, my friend," Dadou smiled. "I've always been amazed at how godly men like you always assume the good things in the world are God's doing, when you have no evidence that it isn't the devil behind them."

A sick ball formed in Jawid's stomach. The truth was that consorting with jinn was specifically forbidden in Islam, but Jawid wasn't sure that the things from the soul storm were truly the jinn described in the Qur'an. But there was no one to discuss it with. If there were other Muslims here, Eldredge had not introduced them to Jawid. The so-called chaplain wore a cross on his collar and spoke always of Jesus, and the doctor who Jawid was forced to constantly speak to only smiled silently when he spoke of his faith. There was no imam to advise him, no qaadi to judge him.

Jawid breathed deeply, letting his pride and anger go out on his breath, trying to expel the lust that rose in him at Dadou's nearness. "Sometimes, I think this is my punishment, that I am trapped here for my sins."

Dadou nudged him with her shoulder. "Back in Haiti, they raised us to be afraid of being women, to hide when we bled, to never want a man. They called those things sins, and I spent a lot of time hating myself for them. But you reach a point where you go over the edge, *non*? Might as well enjoy yourself. Plenty of time to repent while you're burning in hell."

"I am not going to hell," Jawid answered, but he wasn't so sure.

"No," Dadou breathed. "I don't think you are."

"Magic is proof of God, but in the end you all continue to worship your science. You just assume there is an explanation, that if you just look hard enough, you will find it."

Heat came into Dadou's voice. "'You all'? I use magic, same as you."

"Yet you refuse to believe in God."

"I never said that I don't believe, *chouchou*," Dadou said. "I believe with every bit as much passion as you. God exists, and He's a bastard, a mean little boy who pulls the legs off spiders."

Jawid knew he should grab her by her arm and throw her out. She was only a woman, after all. But he looked at the hard muscle of her arms and realized that throwing her out would not be so easy. And the truth was that he wanted the warmth of her shoulder touching his much more than he wanted her out of his cell.

Dadou placed her hand on his knee, just high enough to send shivering sparks up his leg. "Let's not fight. I came here to help you."

He couldn't answer, unable to control his breathing, to tear his eyes from her hand.

"You're not the only one who's alone," she said. "I have never met another person who can do what I do. Actually, that's not true. There was one, but I killed him."

The words broke the spell woven by her hand on his knee. Back home, no one could reach adulthood without seeing killing in abundance. Most of the men he had known were killers, but never the women. "You've killed?"

Dadou's face went serious. "With my own hands, *chouchou.*"

The dread certainty that she was telling the truth overwhelmed him.

Jawid blinked. It was strange, but the fear her words inspired only made him want her more.

"So, tell me what it's like for you?" Dadou asked, as if they had just been talking of the weather.

"I have never killed." Jawid said. *That's not true. You've never killed with your own hands, but to say you haven't killed at all is a lie.* Another sin piled on the growing mountain.

Dadou laughed. "Not that, *moun komik*! I meant what is it like for you to use the *vodou*?"

"You mean the magic."

She nodded. "I see a storm. All the people who ever lived and died are tangled in it."

"I see the same thing," Jawid answered. "They are screaming. It is awful."

"It is hell," Dadou said, tears forming in the corners of her eyes. "Do you have any idea how long I have been waiting to hear someone else say that they saw it too? That I am not crazy?"

"Of course you're not crazy. Do you think the American government would deal with you if you were?"

"The American government has a long history of doing very stupid things."

"In this, they are not stupid."

"I know that, but it is not the same thing as hearing it from someone else."

Jawid's heart swelled at the thought that he was helping her, that he was finally talking to someone who understood what magic did. "I see bodies, but also through bodies. It is chaos. It is impossible to see where one ends and the next begins."

Dadou was nodding, tears tracking down her face. "That's exactly right."

"It is terrible," Jawid said, "and I fear that some day it is where I will wind up."

"And yet you still believe in God."

"I do, and I pray He will save me from it. He is the only one who can."

Dadou shook her head, cuffing the tears away with the back of her wrist. "Then I will pray the same. *M'espere bondye rete avèk ou e gade ou.*"

"This is what helps me think that maybe what we do isn't evil. Maybe this is God's plan, to have us reach out and pluck the souls of the worthy from hell, give them a second chance."

"Eldredge tells me you call them 'jinn.'"

Jawid nodded.

"I call them *mistè*, and I do not think for a second that they are worthy."

Jawid looked at his lap She was right, of course. The jinn were unspeakably evil.

Save one. Save Schweitzer.

Dadou's voice was flat. "Have you met a single one of them that was not a monster?"

"No," Jawid lied.

"Make no mistake," Dadou said. "What we do is not benediction for the deserving. We summon devils, and we put them to use."

"Yes." Jawid nodded. "But without it, what would I be? A slave to stronger men. This has given me my life."

Dadou nodded. "It is the same for me. I would be groveling in the gutter in Port-au-Prince if not for the Americans. I owe for that, and so do you."

"But . . . how much? When is the debt paid? And what comes after?"

Dadou tilted her head, looked into his eyes. "If you could have any after you wanted, what would you choose?"

Jawid started to answer, looked down at his lap. Who was she? A stranger. "It is . . . easy to talk to you."

Dadou laughed, touched his shoulder. "Of course it is, *chouchou*. We are the same, you and I. You know what our magic controls?"

"Devils."

"Communication. It is a way of talking. Have you ever tried it with a living person?"

Jawid shook his head. "It's impossible. Life is . . . too loud."

Dadou smiled. "*Se sa*, but see you said 'loud'? It's a sound to you. Summoning is really communication. And that is why you like talking with me. Because, deep down, our magic is already doing that."

Jawid smiled. "That's . . . crazy."

"Is it any crazier than a man sitting in the sky and telling you to get on your knees five times a day?"

Again, Jawid knew he should be angry, but it was so good to talk to someone. Not a doctor, not a superior, not even an American. Someone like him. The silence stretched and he realized he was staring at her.

She didn't seem to mind. "So, if you could have any after, what would it be?"

"A wife. A family. Isn't that what people do?"

Dadou's face went hard for a moment, her eyes narrowed, the muscles on her neck tightening just a fraction. He sat up. "I'm sorry; I've made you angry."

But as she turned back to him, her smile returned, only sad now, her eyes wide and mournful. "No, *chouchou*. Don't be silly."

Relief warmed his belly. Of course he was mistaken. "You looked unhappy."

"I was only thinking that I had never let myself hope for such a thing. Our lives have been like the storm where the dead live. We are twirling this way and that. One day, we live in the mud and then we have the *vodou*, and suddenly we are killers in another country. Who thinks of family then?"

I do, Jawid thought, but he could not speak, because he felt like his stomach had shrunk into a tiny ball at the thought that this woman, this beautiful woman, might feel the same way. Was this magic too? Perhaps they really were communicating without words, like Dadou said.

She sighed. "But this is misty-eyed talk. We are neither of us ready for an after. We must focus on the now."

Her words were a bucket of cold water down his back. The warmth in his belly vanished, replaced with the knot that reminded him of his failure with Chang, his failure with Schweitzer.

He knew it made him seem weak, but he couldn't stop himself from asking. "So, you are not here to replace me?"

"Of course not," she said, "but . . . I would be lying if I said the *Doktè* was happy with how things have gone."

Jawid looked up at her. "What did he say to you?"

She put her hand back on his knee, smiled, and some of the warmth returned. "Don't worry about it, dahling. I can handle Eldredge. He just needs something to put you back in his good graces. Some success."

"How?" Jawid asked.

Dadou moved her hand up his leg now, just a fraction of an inch, but enough to cause his head to spin.

Her grin widened, her teeth gleaming under the fluorescent lights. "Let me show you."

Dadou sat up, rubbed the sore spot below her shoulder blades that had cramped as she hunched over the computer. In Port-au-Prince, people were nothing, scrabbling in wreckage like insects. There were a few, a very few, who had the money to be actual people, to have their lives count in any real way, to be loved, remembered. For most, living was much the same as dying, an involuntary function as random as the weather.

In America, it seemed that everyone mattered. Almost everyone, anyway. There were mountains of paper, computers full to bursting with legacy. Every doctor visit, every school grade, every idle thought on the Internet. She wondered how big the Gemini Cell's file on her was. She had been an actual person for only a few years now, but she didn't doubt that was more than enough time for the American government to put her in their endless databases, to note their speculations on her sanity, health, potential.

They'd certainly dredged enough up on Jawid Rahimi.

Here was a digital photo, recovered from a Taliban laptop by a Special Forces team. Jawid was dressed in fabric so gauzy it billowed, perched on the knee of a hard-faced, bearded warrior. The man's skin was tanned like old leather, his eyes sharp in a way that spoke of a lifetime at war. One hand was curled around the barrel of an assault rifle. The other rested lightly on Jawid's hip, long fingers disappearing over the curve of his thigh.

Jawid was younger, his light scruff of a beard shaved away. He was made up like a woman, thick lines of black around his eyes, cheeks and lips rouged. His own eyes looked haunted. Distant. Dadou had seen that look many times before. Her sister's eyes had looked the same way. Dadou's might have too, if she hadn't killed the man who'd hurt her.

Dadou turned back to the case files and the notes of the psychologist assigned to profile Jawid, under the duplicitous title of HEALTH RISK ASSESSMENT. She had read them so many times that she knew them by heart, but let her eyes read over the words regardless.

Subject's village was attacked by combined elements of the Taliban and Haqqani network, though subject believes the attack was not religious in nature but rather related to intertribal rivalry over access to grazing lands. Subject's grandfather, who he revered, was killed. Disposition of the rest of his family is unknown, but ground branch was unable to locate and they are assumed dead. Subject was taken as "boy" by band leader and subject to routine and repetitive sexual assault before rescue.

As a result of this experience, subject suffers from Post Traumatic Stress Disorder 309.81, with the following second-order effects: Generalized Anxiety Disorder 300.02, and Major Depressive Disorder, Recurrent (severe, no psychotic features)—296.33. Symptoms include intensely low self-confidence and preoccupation with religious observance. Subject has lionized his family and childhood, and seeks to recreate that experience, preoccupied with marriage, children, and a return to his tribal roots.

Fear-Up, Pride-in-Belonging, and Hammer-of-Justice approaches yielded negative results. Subject responds dramatically to female influence, and has basis for a substantial Madonna-Whore Complex that will likely prevent him from forming meaningful romantic relationships without persistent therapy.

Recommend increased SSRI as a bulwark against both depression and libido and mirtazapine to reduce anxiety and increase appetite (subject is eight pounds underweight). Appealing to subject's religiosity remains counterproductive, as subject's religious beliefs are strongly weighted against magic use and likely to focus subject even more firmly on his goals of marriage and family.

It is possible that appealing to subject's pathology may yield more positive results. A female honey trap operator may make inroads, but it is unlikely that subject will respond to someone who is not a religious Muslim, and Waziristani tribal courtship rituals are notoriously slow. This could be circumvented by a talented operator with a powerfully connecting common trait.

Dadou smiled. *My magic. That's the common trait.* They had underestimated his weakness to sighs and touches. Jawid was as horny as a schoolboy and would likely have responded to any pretty girl who seemed willing. But she had to admit the magic helped. She thought of the look in his eyes as he described the soul storm. *Do you have any idea how long I have been waiting to hear someone else say that they saw it too?* She had told him, *That I am not crazy?* That had been no lie.

He was like a little boy who had been given something

too big for him. He was innocent and adrift, and it tugged at her heart. The world needed more boys. By the time they became men, more often than not, they were like the one who had hurt her sister, like the killers who'd flanked Rodriguez in that warehouse back in California.

Stupid. You are here to do a job, and you will do it.

She turned back to his file, read it again. So much concern, so much attention.

How many people back home wandered every day in a PTSD-induced fog? How many had minds broken by rape, torture, the horror of watching their own children die because they could not feed them? Nobody kept files on them. There were no smart doctors making careful notes, staying up late worrying how to fix them. They were not actual people, not people who mattered. If not for her magic, Dadou wouldn't matter either.

The door chime sounded, startling Dadou up from her chair. It would be Jawid again, tugging at his scraggle of black beard and staring at her chest. He was so nakedly obvious in his hungers, showing the world how best to manipulate him. She almost felt bad as she went to the door, letting a smile play across her face despite her irritation at being interrupted.

Almost.

But the smile died as she saw Eldredge standing in the corridor, glowering from under his bushy white eyebrows. Where Jawid was the very picture of naiveté, Eldredge was stone. "We need to talk," he said.

Dadou sighed and stood aside, gesturing into the cell. "Have a seat." She motioned toward the chair at her desk. Had it been Jawid, she would have motioned toward the bed.

Eldredge ignored her. "We need progress."

"Progress in what, *Doktè*?"

"Don't play with me. I just had a rather . . . uncomfortable conversation with the Director. He's of the mind that you need to push Jawid harder."

"This won't come from pushing, *Doktè*."

"I don't understand why you can't involve me in this operation. I have worked with Jawid longer than anyone else in this program. I know him. I can help."

Dadou laughed, cupped her breasts. "I'm afraid you lack certain assets necessary for this work."

Eldredge swallowed his anger, breathed for a moment. When he spoke, his voice was even. "Doctor Empath has told me about his levers. I understand that you are leaning on . . . particular ones. What I don't understand is how this is going to help find Schweitzer. We lost Chang. We don't have anyone else to hand that we could possibly mine for information, even if they were able to resist the jinn . . ."

Dadou put up a hand. "Do you ever wonder how Schweitzer found his wife?"

Eldredge froze, mouth open. At last, he closed it. "Of course. I wonder that every day. The prevailing theory is that he has some kind of link to her."

"*Se sa, Doktè.* You must understand that what we do, at its heart, isn't summoning. It is . . . a kind of talking. We know so little about the *vodou*. Perhaps there is some way that Schweitzer can talk to his wife. His soul to hers. Very romantic, *non*?"

"Are you sure this link exists?"

Dadou spread her hands. "This is the *vodou, Doktè*. I am not sure of anything. Except for this: I must be left alone to work with Jawid if I am to have any chance of finding your missing Operator. Jawid and I have a better chance if we work together, and we can only work together if you leave us to it."

"Have you made any progress at all?"

"Tremendous progress, *Doktè*. Jawid and I have gone into the void together; we are learning from one another. But these things take time."

She could hear the edge of excitement in Eldredge's voice. "If you're right, the implications are staggering. The ability to . . . find an Operator? But you're talking about Sarah, and she's alive. So, it would be the ability to find a *person*."

Dadou patted the air with her palms. "I don't want to over-promise. We are a long way from that. I am merely telling you what we are chasing. In the meantime, you must work on finding Schweitzer the old-fashioned way."

"We are gearing up the follow on to Gruenen's team. There are three towns nearby. We think Schweitzer will head for one of them. He will need supplies for his wife and child."

"If you can get us close enough for the Golds to feel his magic, we won't need to worry about links. It will be a fox hunt."

"I would rather not use the Golds if we can avoid it." Eldredge swallowed. "How much more time do you need?"

Dadou shrugged. "Jawid's heart is not in this. He is . . . distracted. Unhappy. To do this right, he needs to focus. I am doing what I can, *Doktè*."

"The Director is emphatic that this move quickly."

"Tell me something, *Doktè*; when was the last time you had a woman?"

Eldredge blanched, then turned red. "I am not going to discuss that with . . ."

Dadou laughed. "I thought so. I am not surprised. You have been locked down here for so long, *non*? If you were not so rusty, you would remember that these kinds of things can't be rushed. That would be the fastest way to make him feel like it was . . . false, *ou konprann*? I have to let it roll until it boils."

"And how the hell will you know when he's . . . boiling?"

Dadou tapped her temple. "I will know."

"The Director doesn't think we can run this program with a single Sorcerer. We need Jawid's head in the game."

"*Pas enkie twa*. His head is in the game."

"Doctor Empath isn't so sure."

Doctor Empath doesn't have him staring at her tits all day. "I've got this."

"If there are any resources you need . . ."

"Just time and a little patience," Dadou said, then, glancing meaningfully at the door, "and some privacy."

Eldredge frowned. He opened his mouth to speak, closed it, left still shaking his head. Dadou let him hear her hiss of a chuckle as she slid the door shut.

She took a deep breath, let it go before returning to her computer. Jawid was easy. She had seen the way he looked at her, the way his breathing changed whenever she touched him. If his file was any indicator, he'd never even touched a woman who wasn't a relative. She already had him. Getting him to agree to help her Bind *mistè* into a living subject would be much harder.

She thought of the lie she'd just told Eldredge. It was clumsy, to be sure, but the Director had been clear. Her orders came directly from him, and Eldredge was to be kept in the dark until the project was ready to be revealed.

Eldredge might look like a wise man with his white hair and his white coat, but in the end, he was a man. Dadou had met many, and most were, at their root, like Jawid. You started with sighs and glimpses of skin, then moved to guile and finished up with threats. Sooner or later, they did what you wanted.

Still, she would tell the Director of their conversation. *Leave him to me,* the man's modulated voice had rasped. *He will be of no help to you in this.*

I understand, Dadou had said. *But will he be an obstacle?*

If he becomes one, you will let me know, the Director had said. *And I will deal with it personally.*

She punched up her laptop and called the Director's line.

His rasping voice answered. "You're calling about Eldredge."

Dadou smiled. She didn't doubt that the Director had her monitored. They'd taught her to sweep a room for recording devices when they'd brought her on, but she also didn't doubt that any device they used would be designed with her training in mind. "However did you know?"

"Because I spoke to him a little while ago, and I know him to be a man of action. You must understand, Miss Dadou, that he lacks certain pieces of information that are critical to his estimation of your progress."

"I gave him the story we agreed on. About the links. About how Jim Schweitzer found his wife."

"The best lies are mostly truth, Miss Dadou."

"Mostly."

"Anyway, when I deem Eldredge ready to handle it, I'll have him read on. I have some doubts about his ability to fully appreciate the criticality of what we're doing here."

"It's your show, *Direktè*. I only work here."

"But Eldredge wasn't wrong about our need for progress. How is Jawid coming along?"

Dadou was silent for a moment. "I am almost there; he just needs a little push."

The Director didn't bother to keep the frustration out of his voice. "You sound . . . reluctant."

"Your psychologist's assessment is correct, *Direktè*. He wants a woman. That's the lever."

"If that is the lever, Miss Dadou, then you are to pull it, and with all expediency."

Anger boiled in the back of her throat. She thought of her sister, of the long parade of men who had tried to tell her that she belonged to them. "I . . ."

"Listen to me carefully, Miss Dadou. I want to make sure I'm perfectly clear"—the Director's spoke slowly, enunciating each word—"that while you are a critical asset to this program, you are not so critical that I will tolerate shirking. I brought you here to do a job, and I need you to *do* it."

Fear doused her anger. She knew the kind of power the Director wielded. She knew what he could do, what he would do. "Sir," she said. "It will be very tricky. The process of Binding a jinn into the living is . . . ugly . . . bloody. It may . . . frighten someone so delicate. I will have to bring him in at precisely the right moment. It's like pitching a source, *ou konnen*? You don't ask the question unless you already know the answer."

"Then make sure you know the answer. He wants a wife; he wants a family. Promise to marry him and have his babies."

The anger boiled in the back of her head, mixing with the terror in her gut. "I'm not sure that . . ."

"Let me tell you something about my leadership style, Miss Dadou. I don't get involved in the operational details of any of the programs I run. Instead, I recruit the most talented people I can find, and trust them to do whatever is necessary to get the job done. I trust them to do their jobs, Miss Dadou. I don't micromanage them. I am an executive. I *execute*."

He bit off the last word, raising his voice just enough to underscore the point. He waited for Dadou to reply, and when she didn't, spoke into the silence. "Do we have an understanding, Miss Dadou?"

It wasn't until she tried to answer that she discovered her mouth was dry. "We do."

"Excellent," the Director said. "I look forward to great progress in your next report."

Then he cut the connection. Dadou stared at her laptop for a long time. Jawid was just a man. It was nothing that she hadn't done before.

She looked in the mirror and ignored the void in her gut, swallowing the pinpricks of tears forming in the corners of her eyes.

Allergies. Everything in America was strange and new. She'd get used to it.

CHAPTER IX
HONESTLY, OFFICER

It was the kind of Shenandoah town where Schweitzer had kept promising to take Sarah: old clapboard barns converted to antique shops and used bookstores, little cafés hung with the work of local artists, the semipermanent stalls of a farmers market. As the years rolled by and they never visited, she didn't nag him about it. *I always thought there'd be time*.

The corpse of her husband looked over at her. The face of the man she loved was only faintly visible on the gray-purple skin stretched over its mostly metal skull. Jim's beautiful gray eyes were gone. The silver balls that replaced them were chilling, their flickering dance a constant reminder of the strangeness of the new world she'd woken up to in the Sentara Princess Anne Hospital. This was not the man who had fathered her child. This was not the man who had made her feel so safe, not because he could protect her, but because he could help her to protect herself.

But the magic that linked them would not be denied. She could feel it dragging at her chest, a physical thing, a ship's line tying them together. The love in that channel was thick and solid, as if everything they'd shared when Jim had been alive had been distilled into it, something she could smell and taste and touch, but outside of her. A museum piece. It reminded her that she loved him but was not in love with him. It was obligation and legacy and the raw knowledge that only he could protect her son from the monsters that were just like him in every way, save the color of the flames that burned in the eye sockets of their skulls.

That same link had nearly betrayed her as she had betrayed her husband. *No, it was not betrayal.* When she'd slept with Steve Chang, she'd thought Jim was dead, would never have done it otherwise. *You shouldn't have done it, anyway.* She loved Steve, but not in that way, and their love-making had been more a desperate flailing for something other than panic and agony, grasping for anything that felt good, even for a moment.

There was nothing to be gained by telling Jim. He had lost enough. The link between them had tipped him off. He knew something was wrong, but he also knew her well enough not to press her, and the urgency of their situation didn't exactly lend itself to a deep conversation at the moment. Even in this, her hiding something from him, they were working together.

Because the truth was that the core of their marriage had been more than passion. It had been the yoke they'd worn together, harnessed and straining for common goals. She looked at Jim now, not as her lover and the father of her son but as the person she would be working with to get the mission accomplished. *Oh God, Jim. I miss you.*

Jim stared back at her, his dead face expressionless, devoid of the slow movement that breathing provided. She could feel his own emotions pushing down the link to her: love, but also desperation, and a rising impatience with her all-too-human limitations.

She ruffled Patrick's hair. "You'll have to find a way to keep him quiet."

"I'll figure it out."

"Don't hurt him." She wished she could take the words back as soon as she spoke.

Jim looked away, and Sarah felt the pulse of anger, humiliation, and pain along the link. "He's my son. What the hell do you think I'm going to do?"

She knew she should apologize, try to salve the hurt. But the truth was that Jim was dead now, and she worried that with each passing day he grew less and less in touch with the demands of the living. She grunted and turned back to the gorgeous scene unfolding below them.

"I'm not seeing a drugstore," he said.

"There's a drugstore. See that?" She pointed to a road winding its way up a hill that had been cleared of anything taller than a blade of grass. The sign beside it was large enough to be read at this distance. BRYCE RESORT, BASYE, VA.

"Looks like a ski resort," he said.

"It is. Big enough for a hotel. No way they're not going to have a way for guests to buy aspirin."

"Doesn't mean they'll have what we need for Patrick." The boy stared sullenly down the hill, rubbing absently at the growing red welts on his arms.

"Itches," Patrick whined.

"I know it does, sweetheart," Jim said, "but you can't scratch it. No matter what."

Patrick ignored his father, looked up at Sarah instead, his eyes questioning. "Do as Daddy says," Sarah said.

Patrick was sullen, but he stopped rubbing his arms. She spoke quickly, before Jim could say anything, before she had to reckon with the pain filtering down the link between them.

"Ski resorts run year-round," Sarah said. "Big ones do, anyway. There'll be a zip line and mountain bike trails and a conference center. They'll have what we need."

Jim grunted. "Not too late to do this my way."

Sarah's answer was to stand, dusting off her pants. "He's going to start screaming bloody murder the minute I walk away."

"I'll head back into the woods far enough that nobody will hear him. He'll cry himself to sleep eventually."

She bent, gave Patrick a long hug. "I can't even begin to think how this all is hurting him," she said.

"Best not to," Jim answered.

They looked at one another then, and Sarah felt a tremor pass along the link connecting them. She suppressed a shudder at the sudden intrusive memory of Steve moving on top of her and inside her, watching him couple with her as if she hovered outside her own body, looking down at his pumping hips, her trembling shoulders. Could Jim tell? Did he know? She had thought she was certain he didn't, but the magic had power beyond anything she understood. It enabled her to know things that she shouldn't. She had been able to tell where Jim was and how far away. She knew that Steve was dead, had been certain of it the same way she'd been certain that Jim was alive.

She looked at the grinning skull of his face, the embalmed skin stretched across it. *Not alive. Not anymore.*

She kissed the top of Patrick's head and tried to ignore his cries as Jim bundled him into his dead arms and turned for the woods. *Commit to the fight,* Jim had taught her. *Go all in and stay in until one of you is down. Half measures are how you lose.*

She walked down the hill, her clothes mostly clean, her stride mostly even, reciting her story, falling into character. Nobody would ask, but if they did, she was camping in the forest and had hiked in to grab some medical supplies. The ground sloped sharply, the sun warming her neck and shoulders. Birds shouted out competing claims to territory and roots crunched under her boot soles. For a moment, she could almost believe she was alone, walking in the sunshine toward some Shenandoah Valley art town, instead of on the run for her life from an army of the undead.

She took refuge in that thought, turned away from her anxiety over Patrick, the museum piece of her love for Jim heavy in her chest, and spared a glance for her surroundings. A low barn had been converted to an antiques showroom to her right. An ice cream parlor, closed for the winter, topped a trio of a barber, sandwich shop, and small motor repair store. Further along, the art galleries and coffee shops crowded the narrowing road as it wound its way toward the ski resort. There were few people on the main road between the ski resort and the town proper. A young couple with a baby in a sling smiled at her, another set of parents smiled sheepishly as they tailed screaming children. None gave her more than a second glance.

She passed the repair shop and angled toward the broken gravel road that began the long climb to the resort's top. She felt the aching in her hips and knees, the fatigue brought on by nights out in the open on hard ground. Too little sleep and far, far too much walking, Patrick's dead weight always on her shoulder. This entrance was designed for families coming from a long way off, driving cars that could carry them the miles up the hill to the main entrance. The view would be spectacular, but the climb would be punishing.

Sarah sighed, set her teeth, and headed off.

As she passed the corner, her eye caught a flash of white and red. A drugstore stood at the end of the row, sign bleached from long years in the sun. The glass door was propped open with an old brick. Rows of detergent bottles were on display in the dirty window.

A brown car was parked in front, a five-pointed gold star emblazoned on the side. SHERIFF was written beneath it in angled letters, then SHENANDOAH COUNTY. The light bar on the roof glinted at her.

Sarah felt the sour panic boiling in her stomach. It was useless to fight it, Jim had taught her. Far better to acknowledge its presence and factor that into your decision-making. Grappling with fear honestly was the only way to mitigate its power over you. She kept walking, not looking at the cruiser again. For a normal person, it would just be part of the scenery, and Sarah was normal. Nothing to see here, folks. Move along.

The car wasn't idling. The windows were rolled up and the doors locked. It could be parked for a minute; it could be parked overnight. The sheriff might be inside the store or on vacation in Florida. *Make a decision. You either go up that hill and see if there's another store or you go inside this one. You do not wander around in circles, drawing attention to yourself while your son's poison ivy gets worse.*

Her hip. She felt the throbbing ache of the divot in her flesh, the steady heat that she prayed was the aftereffect of the clotting powder and not an infection. She looked at the winding road up to the ski resort again. Steep, long, the broken gravel would spin a tire, slip with each footstep.

She muttered a silent apology to the training Jim had given her and let pain and fatigue make the decision. She turned to the store's open door even as she told herself that it was time and not exhaustion driving her to this choice, knowing it was a lie.

The inside of the store was organized and warm. Posters advertising everything from whitening toothpaste to chest rubs were yellowed with age, but the shelves were neat and well stocked. The silver edges of an old-style black metal cash register glinted under fluorescent lights. Behind it, an older man stood chatting, his enormous belly spilling over the brown braided leather belt that held up his khaki trousers.

A sheriff's deputy leaned in toward him, hard lines of her jaw creased in a smile. Her uniform was brown and gold to match the car outside, her hair wound into a long braid coiled into a bun that popped out just below the edge of her ball cap. The deep lines in her skin spoke of a life out in hard weather. Her hand, sporting a gold wedding ring, was tapping against the butt of her pistol. Her head swiveled as soon as Sarah walked in, smile never fading, eyes out of the conversation, fixed firmly on her.

Sarah suppressed the sudden urge to turn and leave. *No. That's what someone with something to hide would do. You're here shopping.*

Sarah smiled and looked up at the white poster-board signs hanging from clear fishing line over each aisle. *Calamine.* She headed to the aisle marked SKIN CARE. She bent, heart hammering, making a great show of scanning the rows of white and yellow bottles, the panic rising until they were all a plastic blur, labels unreadable. She felt a sharp pain as the cauterized skin over her wound stretched taut, and worked to keep a grimace off her face.

"Help you find something, ma'am?" The man behind the counter's voice drifted over to her.

"Got any calamine lotion?" she asked, hearing the edge of fear in her voice, praying the deputy didn't notice.

"You're in the right aisle," the man answered. "Should be two shelves from the bottom. Look for the pink."

"Pink, right," Sarah said, focusing. *Don't lose the bubble,* Jim's voice echoed in her head. Where was he now? Could his magical senses tell him where she was? She felt for the link but was interrupted by footsteps coming toward her. "It's okay," she said, looking up to the man, "I can find . . ."

The deputy stood there, eyes crawling over Sarah, looking for indicators. "Let me show you," she said. "I practically live here." Her voice was high, with a slight southern twang. Clusters of freckles dotted her cheeks and nose.

Sarah swallowed. She only noticed these kinds of details when she was truly panicked. She swallowed; it was an indicator, but she needed it to get her voice back. "I've got it," she said, tapping a pink bottle that she hoped was calamine.

The deputy's eyes flicked to it, and Sarah could tell she'd missed her guess. "What else are you looking for, ma'am? Might be I can help you."

"Sure," Sarah said, standing and working the kinks out of her spine, wincing at the pain in her hip. The deputy didn't appear to miss that one, either. *Engage her. That's what a normal person would do.* "Need aspirin, hydrogen peroxide, and antibiotic ointment. An extra tent stake would be awesome if you sell that stuff."

The deputy relaxed a bit at that. "You camping out here?"

Sarah nodded, following the woman into the next aisle.

"Been a disaster so far. Tent blew over, my son cut himself 'trying to help.'"

The deputy nodded, handing her a bottle of aspirin and moving farther along the aisle. "Boys do that," she said. "Got two of my own. Spend half my time putting Band-Aids on 'em. You need a doc? The ski lodge has an EMT on call."

"Nah, he's fine. Just scraped up. My husband's with him."

The deputy nodded as Sarah collected the rest of her things and headed to the counter. "How long you in town?"

"I'm not in town," Sarah smiled. "Just discovered that we hadn't packed enough. We don't do this a lot."

"Where you from?" The man behind the counter's voice was light, and his eyes easy and open compared to the deputy's.

Good lies are as close to the truth as possible. If there was an APB out, then the information Sarah was providing would be giving the deputy what she needed to make a positive ID, but that was a risk she was simply going to have to take. "Tidewater," she answered. "Outside Norfolk. My man's in the Navy. You?"

The man laughed and even the deputy seemed to relax. "Been here my whole life." He handed her the purchases and her change. "Now, you be sure to thank your husband for his service from us."

"I will," Sarah said, picturing Jim's dead face.

"Bye, now," said the deputy, as Sarah turned and left. She could feel their eyes on her back, following her out. She forced down the urge to hurry, keeping her stride even and casual. She strained her eyes, hoping against hope that the conversation would start up again, that she would hear the light strains of their chatter, showing they had turned from her and back to the life before she'd wandered into town.

But instead, she heard the crunching of shoes on the gravel behind her.

"Ma'am?" The deputy's voice.

Sarah froze, thrust her hands into her pockets to stop them trembling, forced herself to turn, smile. "What's up?"

Please tell me that I forgot my receipt . . .

The deputy had hooked her thumbs into her gun belt, took a few steps closer, looking at her feet. She stopped outside striking range, crossed her hands in front of her buckle, looked up. "Ma'am, I've been in law enforcement all my life. I've got something of a sixth sense when it comes to trouble. There's trouble here. Is there anything you want to tell me?"

Sarah rolled her eyes and tried to keep from bolting. "Trust me, if there was something I needed police help with, I'd be asking."

"You running away from something, ma'am?"

Sarah fought the urge to swallow again, put a little edge into her voice. "I'm a thirty-three-year-old mother. I am a successful artist. I am married to an amazing man. What the hell would I be running away from?"

The deputy looked sheepish. "That's what I'm trying to figure out."

"Well, there's nothing to figure. I'm going back to my camp. We'll sharpen a stick or something for the stake."

"Ma'am, you look a little banged up. This amazing man of yours, he hitting you?"

And now Sarah did swallow, tamping down on the sick certainty that this woman wasn't going to let her go.

"They just keep doing it unless you stop them," the deputy said. "I see it all the time. Happened to me once. No shame in admitting it."

"No, no," Sarah said. "Jim would never do that. We're just lousy campers, is all."

There was a long silence, during which Sarah was suddenly very conscious of how empty the street felt, deserted save for her and the deputy, eyes narrowed and tracking Sarah's hands. *Commit to the fight,* Jim's voice in her head. *Even long odds are still odds. Make a plan.*

Sarah didn't want to hurt this woman who was, in all likelihood, trying to protect her. But she had driven a knife through the throat of a man who would have kept her from her son, had bitten the face off another. She would not hesitate if that's what it took to get her back to Patrick.

At last, the deputy sighed. "All right, ma'am. I'll let you be on your way. If you change your mind, I eat my lunch in my car right here most days. Just come on down and we'll talk it over. No need for a report or anything. Just us girls."

Relief flooded Sarah with such intensity her knees went weak, but she put a smile on her face. "That won't be necessary, but thanks anyway. It's good to know that people like you are out here, keeping us safe."

The deputy smiled but said nothing, eyes kindly suspicious.

Jim had taught her this technique, how police and military interrogators had been trained to use the silent stare. Most people abhorred silence, and would fill it with anything, clues, even confession, if it went on long enough.

But Sarah was not most people. She turned on her heel and took a long and confident stride back toward the woods. It was the sort of purposeful step she imagined an innocent woman would take, the fast pace of a camper anxious to get back to her living husband and child, who were just out for a pleasure trip and not being hunted by the government. She felt the deputy's eyes on her back, but each step lifted her confidence. *Keep going. Long strides. You've got somewhere to be. Move quickly, but don't run.*

Sarah felt a stinging in her hip, then a sudden warm wetness.

Too fast. Too long. Too confident.

The wound had reopened.

Before she could stop herself, Sarah had clapped her hand to her hip. Her jeans were already soaked, the red stain easily seeping through the thick fabric to glisten wetly in the sun. Even a casual observer couldn't miss it.

She was already turning as she heard the deputy's shocked voice. "Ma'am? My God, ma'am, are you okay?"

The deputy's eyes were wide. She was already advancing on Sarah, eyes fixed on the spreading bloodstain on her hip.

"I'm fine," Sarah mumbled, backpedaling.

"Like hell you are! You sit down right now; we're going to get you help." The deputy thumbed the radio clipped to her shoulder. "Don, I'm going to need your help over here, Fairway and Ridge. Ten fifty-four, uncontrolled bleeding. Over." Sarah's stomach turned over. She knew this type of cop. There was no way she would let her go now. They would take Sarah to a hospital. That meant identity checks. It meant radio chatter. It meant the Cell would find out.

Make a decision. She had no doubt the deputy could draw and fire before she could close the distance between them.

The radio crackled a reply, but it was lost in the blood roaring to Sarah's ears. Her vision was graying at the edges, coming into crystal clarity as she focused on where the deputy was vulnerable, how she would disable her before she had a chance to draw her weapon.

No. Even if you could, you're not going to hurt her. She's done nothing wrong. She's trying to help.

Sarah backpedaled faster, her hip throbbing. "I said I'm fine! Leave me alone."

"Ma'am, you are badly hurt. You are not going anywhere until an EMT tells me that you're not going to bleed out. I am trained in first aid. Just let me stop the bleeding until we can get an ambulance here."

Tires crunching on gravel, another police cruiser pulling up alongside.

Now or never.

Sarah broke for the line of storefronts, her boots spraying dirt and making her feel as if she was wading through molasses. She heard the dull clunk as the deputy dropped the radio and it banged against the body armor beneath her shirt. "Oh, shit. Ma'am! Stop right now! Go, Don, go!"

Tires peeling as the driver of the other cruiser threw it in gear and picked up speed. Sarah ran with every ounce of will she possessed, feeling the seared wound in her hip tear wider, fresh blood soaking her waistband. The storefronts drew closer with dreamlike slowness. *Damn it, Jim. You were right. You should have just come in the dead of night and stolen this stuff.*

She heard the sudden roar of an engine, the sound of

crunching gravel, and the other cruiser leapt around the building corner, fishtailing to a stop between her and the door. The driver jumped out and took cover behind the engine block, pistol trained on Sarah's face. "Police officer!" He shouted through a thick accent. "Stop right there! Let me see your hands!"

He had a black flattop cut close enough for a Marine to envy. He was a caricature of a southern county cop: huge paunch and jowls, red pug nose, aviator glasses. His ball cap had flown off in his hurry to draw down on her.

Sarah slowed, stopped. She wouldn't do Patrick any good with a hole in her head. She looked left and right, saw only the female deputy slowly coming closer, eyes locked on her gun sights, staring down the barrel at Sarah.

There's no running now, she thought. *Only dying.*

Another thought came close on its heels. *Maybe that's best. If they take you, they can use you to get Patrick, to get Jim.*

Her husband was a superpowered immortal. He might be able to rescue her, and she knew he wouldn't stop trying until he succeeded. And that was the problem. Because there were other superpowered immortals, and as soon as they had confirmation of where she was, they would be coming.

She swallowed. *I'm sorry, baby.* She felt the tremor of the communication pass along the link, could feel Jim tightening at the other end. He would be coming. Even now, he would be coming for her.

"On your knees," the male deputy said. "One knee at a time, nice and slow. Right knee first."

Sarah hesitated. "Ma'am, do it right now!" the female deputy shouted.

Patrick. She wasn't sure Jim could care for him. But then again, she wasn't doing such a great job either.

She heard gravel scuffling as the female circled around to triangulate her, keep both guns on her without the risk of shooting one another.

"Knees!" the man shouted. "Do it now!"

"We're trying to help you!" the woman called.

Sarah willed herself to run, but her legs refused to obey her. *Oh God, baby. I'm sorry.*

"Fuck you," she said.

"Damn it." She heard the female stalking toward her, the loud *shick* as she snapped open her metal baton. "This is going to hurt you, ma'am. Watch it, Don."

"I've got her," the male said, angling his head to get a better sight on his weapon. "I've go—"

And then his head was gone, and the bright red of his arterial blood was spraying into the sky, mixing with the powdered glass of his cruiser's shattered windshield.

Something had landed on the cruiser's roof, its weight bowing the car inward, the windows exploding in sprays of shining dust. It crouched, slowly rising, gray-white body slashed across with the deputy's blood, as if it had been hit by an errant paint roller dipped in crimson.

It was one of the monsters she'd fought back on Drew's farm. It looked so much like Jim. It wore the same leering skull, the same Frankenstein stitching, the same haunting imprint of the living thing it had once been. Bone spikes projected from its elbows, hooked upward from its shoulders. Purple-black mottles showed where it had been grafted together, woven and stitched from the fabric of other corpses. It raised its head on a stub of a neck held to its torso by an armature of metal cables straining beneath thin scraps of dead flesh.

Its eyes were twin flames.

Bright gold.

Gunshots. The female deputy was screaming now, her cop's sangfroid a memory. In its place was the sound of a little girl, hiccuping sobs as she poured on panicked fire, in no danger of hitting anything.

Sarah leapt back from the monster on the cruiser, looked over toward the deputy.

"Run!" Sarah shouted to her.

Gray shapes loped along the blasted gravel path to the ski resort, at least ten. She could hear the distant growls, the sound of breaking glass. There were more of them in the town. She whirled, trying to pick a safe direction. The way she'd come looked clear.

"Run," Sarah breathed, shoved off the ground, started running.

"Wait!" the deputy screamed.

Sarah didn't wait. Because she knew what these monsters were. Because just three of them had nearly been more than a match for her and Jim together. And now there were more than double that number, racing through the streets of Basye, crashing through the storefront windows, savaging the occupants. Sarah stumbled through a slick red pulp that had once been a person. She swallowed bile and ran as fast as she could, knowing it was useless. There was no way she could outrun these monsters, no way anyone could.

"Wait!" the deputy shouted again, whether to her or to the Gold Operators, Sarah couldn't tell. Her world narrowed to the six inches in front of her face, the burning agony in her hip as she ran as fast as she could.

"Waaaaaaiiiiiit!!!" The deputy dragged out the scream a third time, trilling on until it ended in a wet ripping that reached Sarah even across the wide distance she had opened up in her panicked run.

She could hear the pounding gallop of feet on the road behind her. If an animal had been pursuing her, she'd have heard the panting exertion of its breath as it put on speed. But the Gold Operators didn't breathe, and they came on silently, revealed only by the light touch of their clawed hands and feet on the ground. She could feel her back prickling at their nearness, heard the change in their gait as they went from four limbs to two, reaching toward her.

She threw herself to her right, crashing through a window. For a sickening moment, she felt the surface vibrate and hold, thought she would bounce off and into the arms of her pursuers, but then the glass gave way and she fell in, sprawling across the concrete floor.

The glass made a jagged carpet below her, and she left

skin on it as she rolled to her hands and knees, lurched back into a run.

She was in a potter's studio, rows of tables, each with a wheel, fanning out before a central desk below a grease board. Cupboards lined the walls, bulging with bricks of clay.

Two women crouched behind the desk. They were both blonde and fortyish, hair in buns meant to keep it clear of clay. One was shouting frantically into a phone.

"Fucking run!" Sarah shouted to them. She tore between tables, eyes roving frantically for a back door.

The woman stared at her and she ran past. "Nobody is coming to help! Move!" she called back over her shoulder.

They shouted something at her that she ignored, concentrating everything she had on running. She glimpsed them starting to run after her, knew they were too slow, too late.

Sarah tried to shut out the sounds, to focus instead on finding a back exit, to not hear the tinkling of the glass as the Gold Operators came through behind her, the slapping of their bare feet on the concrete floor.

The studio ended in a wall of metal shelves stacked with boxes; if there was a door hidden behind them, Sarah didn't have the time to search for it. She swallowed the sick panic that boiled in her stomach and turned to the side window. She tried to avoid looking at the central desk, but it was impossible.

The two women had bought her precious seconds. Three Gold Operators were crouched behind the central desk, up to their elbows in red. The screaming had stopped, replaced by growling and liquid gurgles. Blood had begun to spread out on the floor, as if a bucket had been upended. *I didn't know there was that much in a human body.*

Something thick and wet flew out of the feast, struck her in the shoulder as she slammed into the window and crashed through. The metal frame groaned on its hinges and slammed open, spilling Sarah out into the side street.

She rolled to her knees, oriented herself, and raced toward the ridge where she'd crouched with Jim.

She kept her eyes straight ahead, focused on her pumping legs, on ensuring the muscles were stretched to the limit, that she was putting on as much speed as possible. She knew that if one of the Gold Operators decided to pursue her, it could close the distance and overtake her in a matter of seconds.

But all around her, she could hear the ripping flesh, the shattering glass, could see the low gray shapes in her peripheral vision. There was enough living prey to keep the monsters busy. She didn't know how much time the unfortunate population of Basye had bought her, but she was determined to make the most of it. She poured her desperation, her fear into the channel that linked her to Jim. Jim could hear a twig breaking from a mile away; there was no way he could miss the screaming as Basye came apart around her. *Come on, baby. Get your ass over here.*

The thought was followed by a stab of guilt. He couldn't leave Patrick in the woods, and bringing the boy would mean bringing him into danger. But *damn*, now that she saw a chance to live, she realized how badly she wanted to.

She ran on, the solid road giving way to broken chunks of asphalt and then to the flat expanse of gently rising grass. Her hip screamed at her; she could feel the edges of the wound ripping wider with each long stride. The plastic bag full of the supplies she'd bought to clean it was lost in the wreckage somewhere behind her. *All that for nothing.*

It seemed as if she ran through molasses. A soft fog was forming in the corners of her eyes, stubbornly staying in her vision after she blinked. She raised a wrist, rubbed hard at her eyes, let it drop. The fog remained. It might be infection or blood loss, but she was starting to come apart. Her vision became a stutter-flash of staccato images, like an old film reel running too slow.

One moment, she was running on open grass, and then the grass was suddenly interspersed with packed gravel,

and Sarah vaulted something boxy and black. She heard a
low hiss, smelled the dull scent of gas. She glanced down
long enough to see that she was running through a small
grill park, the white canisters of propane scattered among
the half-cooked hot dogs and hamburgers, grills knocked
on their sides as the Golds had lit among the families here.
A woman lay on her side, cut in half, face pressed against
the black bars of a hot grill. Sarah was grateful the corpse's
head was turned away from her, so she couldn't see what
the metal was doing to its face, but she could hear the sizzle
and pop of the melting skin, could smell the cooked-meat
stink mixing with the stench of the leaking gas. Her gorge
rose and she focused on picking her way through the field
of scattered propane canisters. The gravel thinned and
Sarah gulped air, feeling her lungs inflate with hope with
each passing stride. The Gold Operators may have come for
her, but Jim had said they were driven by bloodlust, happy
to slaughter whoever was closest. By the time they realized
their original quarry had escaped, she would be in the
woods and with the one person in the world who could
protect her. *And what then? You're bleeding out and you
know it.*

Something heavy and hard hit the backs of her knees,
sending her flying.

Sarah didn't even have time to land before she was
snatched out of the air by her ankle and swung around. She
felt the tendon cry out, the bone creaking against the strain.
*If my ankle breaks, I can't run, and if I can't run, I can't get
back to my son.*

And then the ground rushed up to meet her and she was
tumbling across it, the sharp grass tearing at her face, a
propane tank smacking into her gut, knocking the breath
out of her, her vision going black. She skidded across the
ground, flopped and rolled for a few feet, and finally slid to
a stop on her back. She groaned, struggled to suck in air.
Get up get up get up get up.

She could hear a slow tamping in the grass, something
stalking toward her.

Sarah scrambled with both hands, hoping to come across a rock, a stick, anything she could use as a weapon. But she didn't look away. When it made its move, she would be ready.

The Gold Operator looked like it had once been an Asian woman, slight and lean. Its body was remarkably well preserved, with only a long gash across its throat that had been lasered shut, the long burn scar puckering between holes where stitching had failed. There was even the stubble of hair clinging in patches to the skull. The mouth was drawn in a wide smile; the only spines were two short bone spikes protruding from the gray remains of small, high breasts. She couldn't have been more than twenty when she died.

But its eyes were the same hungry gold flames as the rest. It advanced like a stalking cat, shoulders hunched, clawed fingers spread, enjoying Sarah's distress. It whispered something in a voice like broken glass, a low, harsh string of language that sounded like Russian. The burning eyes flicked to Sarah's belly and she noticed that her shirt had hiked up during the tumble.

And then Sarah's fear overpowered her, and she scrambled back on her hands, because she knew what the Gold Operator was thinking, could imagine those teeth and claws slicing into the taut skin of her stomach, digging out the soft organs behind. "No," Sarah said in spite of herself. "Nonononono."

The Gold bent at the waist, smile widening further, until the face threatened to rip open, cheeks stretching so thin, Sarah thought she could see daylight through them. Thin, articulating tusks slipped out of the corners, curling around below the mouth, sharp points clicking together.

Sarah scrambled back, trying to get her feet under her, succeeding only in tangling her ankles together and folding her legs painfully beneath her thighs.

Her knuckles barked painfully on something hard and cool behind her. The propane canister that had knocked the wind out of her rolled away. She reached for its edge, felt her fingers close around the thick metal ring of the valve guard handle.

The Gold Operator shrieked and lunged.

Sarah shrieked back, throwing herself to the side and using her momentum to wrench her arm forward. The heavy tank swung so hard, she thought her arm would tear out of its socket. For a moment, she feared she'd missed and the tank would pass through empty air, turning her around so the Gold could savage her back instead of her front.

But then she was rewarded with a heavy thud that sent a satisfying tremor up her arm as the tank crashed into the Gold Operator's head, sending it stumbling back. She heard a soft crack as one of the thing's tusks snapped off.

It crouched, howling, bone spikes sliding out of its fingertips.

The tank settled back into her grasp, bottom thudding into the ground beneath her. She pushed herself up to her feet. For a moment, the world went gray and Sarah swayed. *No no no stay up stay up stay up.* She blinked, shook her head furiously, nearly sobbed in relief as her vision came clear and she found she was still up. She had a handle on it now; she was standing. She was fighting.

She heard a familiar hissing, close by now, followed by the faint rotten-egg stink of the gas. The valve had been jarred by the blow, the pressurized contents starting to leak out.

Sarah smiled, lifted the tank.

She couldn't outrun a Gold. This would either work, or it wouldn't.

Either way, she was fighting, and in spite of the life slowly leaking out of her hip, in spite of all she had lost over the past months, it felt amazing.

She screamed defiance and hurled the tank at it.

Sarah didn't wait to see what Gold's reaction. She was already turning, already diving for the ground, throwing her arms up to shield her face, watching through slitted eyes.

The Operator grinned, raised its bone claws, and slashed the tank out of the air.

Sarah heard the metallic clang as the razor-sharp bones struck the tank, saw the sparks as they ripped it open. Only then did she allow herself to close her eyes.

She didn't hear the explosion. She was only conscious of sudden heat roaring over her, of a high ringing in her ears, of the feel of something sharp and hard cutting through her side, her cheek, her arm, her shoulder.

She lay for a moment, breathing. *Maybe I've lost too much blood; maybe the explosion got me too. Maybe the Operator survived and will cut into me any second . . .*

But a second passed, then two.

Sarah opened her eyes.

There was precious little left of the thing. Scraps of gray meat twitching in a black pit of ash dotted with smoldering grass. Sarah turned her attention to herself. The pain in her hip was worse than ever; the fog was still gathered in the periphery of her vision. She was weak as a kitten, but she wasn't going to die just yet. She sat up, passing her hands over her body, assessing the damage. If another Gold came, it wasn't as if she were in any condition to outrun it now, anyway.

She blinked; another dead thing stood there. Rage flooded her. She was so close. She was almost home free. She snarled, preparing herself to fight. She wouldn't make it easy.

And then she saw its eyes. Burning silver.

Jim.

"Fucking . . . took you . . . long enough . . ." Sarah breathed, unfolding her legs and staggering unsteadily to her feet.

Jim was looking over her shoulder into the town. "Are you okay?"

"Do I fucking look okay?"

"Fair enough. You're standing, so that's something."

"I can walk. Come on." She turned back toward the town.

He stopped her with a hand on her shoulder. "Sarah, this is bad; we have to go."

"I can't." Her lips were numb, her hands shaking. She tried to take a step, found she couldn't. "I lost my bag. I have to go back and get my bag."

She saw it now, even as her vision grayed and the ground pitched unsteadily beneath her. She had come to town to get supplies. If she just left the bag behind, then it was all for nothing, and she couldn't have that. She had to go back.

Jim cocked his head to the side. "Your bag? Oh God, baby. Your hip."

He reached for the sopping wound, and Sarah saw he was going to stop her. She had to get her bag. But she was so tired. She slapped his hand away. "Don't touch me."

"Baby." The rictus face grimaced. "We have to go; we have to get you some help. You're going to bleed out if we don't treat that."

"The bag!" Sarah shouted. "It has Patrick's calamine!"

Jim cast a worried glance over his shoulder. She heard the howl of the Golds getting closer. "We're going now." He reached out, scooped her up like she was a toy, threw her over his shoulder. His grip suffocated her. The press of his cold, dead skin was more than she could bear. She gagged on the faint smell of glycerol.

"Get off me!" she screamed. "I can walk!" Though she wasn't sure that was true.

"Not this time," Jim whispered as he set off running so fast that the grass turned into a green blur beneath his feet. "This time, I'm carrying you."

CHAPTER X
COLLATERAL DAMAGE

Eldredge sat in the swivel chair, facing the monitors. The huge screens dominated the ready-room wall, expensive liquid crystal displays framed in businesslike stainless steel.

Every one of them showed sickening carnage.

Here was a trio of Gold Operators overturning a shuttle bus, dragging one of the passengers out through the driver-side window. There was a Gold Operator stalking out of a burning building, the crisped corpse of what Eldredge assumed had once been a person impaled on a single bone horn projecting from its forehead. As he watched, the propane tank on a parked RV exploded, the flames racing up the side of the vehicle to engulf the building beside it.

They moved like a flock of geese, the tip of their vaguely triangular formation led by the Gold Jawid had made of Chang's corpse. They forged deeper and deeper into the town, drawn by the promise of those they hadn't yet unburdened of their lives. There were too many still cowering in cellars and closets. It would be the devil's work convincing the Golds to give up the hunt and get on Schweitzer's trail.

Eldredge flicked his gaze to two screens set down and to the right of the rest. One was dark, reflecting his mop of white hair back at him. The other showed a pale green and orange palette of a map, flashing teardrops corresponding to each camera shot overhead, feeds from the drone cameras independently tracking the scene from ten thousand feet above. Right now, they were all clustered around a dot nestled in the broad green patch that took up most of West Virginia. BASYE, it read, or it had read before the feeds had engaged and the densely packed orange teardrops had blotted out the words.

"This is not good, sir," Eldredge whispered.

"No, it's not, but it's a price I'm willing to pay," the Director's voice replied from the speaker below the dark screen. "The Gold teams are engaged because Schweitzer is nearby. It's just a matter of time until we find him."

"Sir, did Dadou . . . say anything to you?" Eldredge's stomach tightened.

"You know she did. I brought Dadou here to find Schweitzer, and she's close to doing just that."

"Sir, I think her theory of an emotional link shows promise. It matches up with my thoughts about how Schweitzer located his wife and son so quickly. We need to give that angle a chance to work."

"Of course, but in the meantime, Gruenen's team has given us a location."

"An *approximate* location, sir. Not specific enough to risk using a Gold team, let alone . . . Jesus, it looks like you used all of them. Schweitzer is west of there, and he's widening his lead every minute."

"I am done being played for a fool by a single Operator and his living wife and child. We should have caught them all long ago. Approximate is good enough. They have the scent now; they'll find him."

"Sir, they are not finding him. They are pillaging."

"Pillaging? How dramatic."

"Sir, are you not seeing what I'm seeing here?" Eldredge swept his hand across the abattoir that had once been a

Virginia resort town. "Basye has over twelve hundred residents. Add in tourists and you're talking at least fifteen hundred."

"I understand this must shock you, but this is a Javelin Rain incident, Eldredge. We're authorized for whatever measures are necessary to bring things to a speedy resolution."

Eldredge bit down on his anger. The Gemini Cell had always killed. It was part of the job, what Eldredge had accepted when he'd come on board. But never in these numbers, and never at once. "We're talking about an entire town. Of Americans."

"Have you been laboring under the delusion that we don't target Americans, Doctor?"

"This isn't an American in another country. This is on American soil." But even as Eldredge spoke, he saw the holes in his own logic. They had targeted dozens of Americans on home soil over the years. *It's the scale. It's the scale that bothers you. It's the carelessness.*

That thought was followed by another, even more chilling. *It's not the scale. Working with Schweitzer has broken something loose. The joint has come unglued for you.*

"Schweitzer's last op was off the coast of Hampton Roads," the Director went on. "Are you forgetting Operation Stable Hammer? That took out a city block in the most densely populated city in the country. We have to take lives so that we can save lives, Eldredge. This isn't your first day on the job. You know this."

Eldredge sucked in his breath, tried to gather his thoughts. He looked down at his lap, but the grisly scene unfolding on the screens still danced in his peripheral vision. He knew that even though he couldn't see the Director, the man was surely watching him. The thought kindled anger and resolve.

"We can't control them, sir," Eldredge said. "They're animals. They go for whatever heartbeat is closest. Schweitzer's heart isn't beating. We have to do something."

"That's right," the Director said. "*You* do have to do

something. Which is why you have Dadou Alva putting her head together with Jawid. It's your job to extract results from those two, Eldredge, and it's my job to extract results from you. The sooner we get Schweitzer, the sooner we can pull the Golds out. You seem so hell-bent on an exact location before the Gold teams are employed, so I'd like to hear your plan on getting one."

"Dadou is working on it, sir."

"How is she working on it? How exactly does this link theory of hers work?"

"I'm not clear on that, sir. Right now I'm pretty much proceeding on a basis of 'trust me, I know what I'm doing.'"

"I am not entirely comfortable with that basis."

"It's magic, sir. I'm open to ideas if you've got any."

Silence.

"Well, you can chat with her about the collaterals after all this is over," the Director finally said. "Talk to Dadou, have her and Jawid rein the Gold teams in, get them headed in the right direction."

"What do you plan to tell the press, sir? There's no way a massacre of this size is going to stay out of the public eye."

"Gas explosion. Happens all the time in these country towns."

Eldredge couldn't resist casting a glance up at the monitors, shuddered at the sight of the broken asphalt strewn with the corpses hewn beyond recognition. "That doesn't look like a gas explosion, sir."

"Not yet." Eldredge could hear the Director's smile. "Go talk to Dadou. Find Schweitzer. I am tired of how long this is taking."

Eldredge caught himself running, forced himself to slow down.

He remembered standing outside Schweitzer's cell just a few days ago. The undead SEAL had been talking about a comic book, his telepathic projections translated through Jawid. *There was a scene where a prisoner passed a letter to another,* Schweitzer had said. *"It is the very last inch of us,"* she said of integrity, *"but within that inch, we are free."*

Schweitzer's last inch had been needless notions of his former life: nodding, sitting, scratching his head. Eldredge's last inch was not running to do to the Director's bidding. He breathed deeply, slowing himself to a walk and biting down on the voice in his head that told him delay was tantamount to suicide.

Jawid and Dadou were in the prep room, seated on one of the metal gurneys, eyes closed, thighs gently touching. Eldredge knew that for Jawid, touching a woman was a very big deal, and he doubted the Sorcerer was focused on the task at hand. It also meant that Dadou was making inroads on his affections, as ordered. *Progress.*

The refrigerated units were closed, with the corpses inside. A monitor above them showed the carnage unfolding in Basye. Whatever Jawid and Dadou were doing, it wasn't focused on this world.

Eldredge thought of clearing his throat, stopped himself. They might be close to finding Schweitzer's exact location. He couldn't risk interrupting that. He leaned against a wall instead, thrust his hands into the pockets of his white lab coat. The coat was completely unnecessary, but the look helped calm the analysts and military members in the facility. It was better to project the image of a doddering scientist and not the brains behind a military program dedicated to developing weapons from beyond the grave.

He waited, feeling ridiculous, and finally sighed, cleared his throat loudly.

Dadou's eyes stayed closed, but the corner of her mouth quirked. "We are working the *vodou*, *Doktè*, but that doesn't mean we can't hear you."

Eldredge smiled, feeling his cheeks redden. "I'm sorry."

Neither Dadou nor Jawid moved. The bare, still room made Eldredge's skin crawl. He was at least used to seeing corpses arrayed on the gurneys. The two Sorcerers sitting silently was unnerving. "No need to apologize, *Doktè*. How can we help you?"

"The Golds are rampaging through Basye, heading in every direction except the one Schweitzer ran in. I need them reined in. I need them going after him."

Jawid tensed at this, but Dadou's smile only widened. "The Golds are not easy to convince, *Doktè*."

Eldredge bit down on his frustration, struggled to keep his voice even. "Convincing them is your job. This was the whole point of putting you two together."

Dadou smiled, as if at some private joke. "We're very, very close to being able to do just that," she said.

"You are out of time," Eldredge said. "The Golds are massacring that town. There's a pretty bad body count and it's only going to be higher by the time it's over."

Dadou shrugged. "It is an addiction. Like rum or sleeping pills."

"What is?" Eldredge asked.

"Slaughter," Dadou said. "Do you like your beating heart? The warm blood in your veins?"

Eldredge frowned. "You're wasting time."

"Do you?" Dadou's smile didn't waver.

"I've never really thought about it, to be honest. I guess I take it for granted."

"All those who do not touch the *vodou* do, because we never have to live a single day without it. Our bodies are always warmed by blood. Our hearts always beat. When these things stop, so does our perception of them.

"But the jinn, as you call them, live thousands of years knowing the absence of both. And when they are returned, they want it more than anything. They want to bathe in blood, if only so they might enjoy the smallest reminder of life for even a moment. With time, it becomes compulsive. Like all compulsions, it eventually becomes all-encompassing."

"Not for Schweitzer."

For the first time, Dadou's smile faded. "No, not for him. He is different."

"What makes him different?"

Dadou's voice was cold. "I have never touched him. But once we have him, I intend to."

"Well, I need you to get on that. I can't have the Gold teams ripping a hole in every human inhabitation they come across. I need you to influence them."

Dadou's smile returned. "Your so-called jinn may be addicted to shedding blood, but that doesn't mean they don't have their own wills. I can't control them."

"Schweitzer could."

"Schweitzer is rare. Maybe even unique. And the only jinn he ever controlled was the one in his own corpse."

"Damn it, stop playing games. Can you get the Golds moving on him or can't you?"

Dadou opened her eyes, glanced over at Jawid. Her smile faded. "Yes," she said, confidence slowly dawning on her face. "Yes, I think we are ready now."

Eldredge swallowed, found the courage to say the next words. "Good. I'll leave you to it. I need you on this right away, and I'll need your report the moment you're done."

"All right, *Doktè*. We'll get started immediately."

Eldredge paused, swallowed. "One more thing. You're right about Schweitzer being unique. That's why I need him brought in alive."

Now Jawid opened his eyes. "Schweitzer is not alive," Dadou said.

"You know what I mean. I want his corpse returned intact and with his soul still in it."

Jawid's eyes shone with gratitude. Dadou was inscrutable. "Those were not my orders when I was pulled from Scorpio Cell."

"New orders. We need him." Eldredge pictured the Director as a tall man in a black suit, pistol in his hand.

"Why do we need him?" Dadou asked.

"Because we have to understand him," Jawid answered.

Eldredge nodded. "If this program is ever going to be effective, we have to find a way to control the Gold Operators. Even trained dogs are more reliable." But Eldredge knew that wasn't the whole truth. *Schweitzer is a good man. Floating in that chaos for eternity is less than he deserves.*

Dadou's face was stone, but her eyes smiled again. "And I assume you have no objections to his wife and child being put down, also per my original orders?"

Jawid turned to her, eyes widening. She put a hand on his knee, squeezed, and the Sorcerer stayed silent.

"No, they should be brought in alive as well." Eldredge tried to keep his voice calm.

"That will be a . . . challenging task. Some might say impossible," Dadou said.

"Can you do it?"

"We can try, sir," Jawid answered for her.

"Try hard."

"Why do you care?" Dadou asked.

Because if I have a way to keep Schweitzer united with his family, even as prisoners, I will do it. Because if I can do that, then maybe I'm not completely evil. "I'm working on a theory that living family members can be used as a means of control. Hostages are a crude method but often an effective one. You said yourself that love, if it's intense enough, is itself a magical bond."

Dadou didn't look convinced at all. "I'm not certain you fully appreciate how it works, *Doktè*."

"Oblige me."

"You're the boss." She shrugged. "The Director may not be happy with this turn."

"I'll deal with the Director. This is my call."

Dadou nodded, and Eldredge turned and left. Eldredge knew he would have to explain his actions, but he doubted that even the Director would order Schweitzer or his family destroyed once they were in custody. Not if Eldredge could come up with a convincing-enough argument for keeping them. What he had was thin, but he would work on it. The Schweitzer family was dead either way; he had nothing to lose by trying.

Save his life.

CHAPTER XI
TOGETHER

Dadou and Jawid sat in front of the video monitor watching the pack of Golds race through Basye's burning wreckage. Chang's golden-eyed corpse ran in the lead, forming the tip of a long, narrow delta of gray flesh. Dadou had seen it before when Golds were deployed in groups. The pack followed the fastest and strongest one. She supposed it was because they thought it would lead them to the most abundant slaughter.

Or maybe it was something else. She didn't know. She had never seen this many Golds in one place before.

"Well," Dadou said as Eldredge left. "It seems we have a task before us."

"An impossible one." Jawid looked at his lap, eyes sad.

"Nothing is impossible." Dadou leaned toward him. "We only need to try."

He looked up, lip trembling, eyes wide. The melodrama made her sick with anger and she drove her fists into her lap so he could not see them clenching.

She kept her voice gentle. "Remember when I told you that magic is a conversation?"

"Yes," he answered. She watched his eyes darting to the curve of her chest, back up to her face. His file said he came from a religious hinterland where they never saw a women unveiled. She had dressed accordingly, a tank top to bare her arms and shoulders, long trousers bloused into combat boots.

"We need to reach out to the *mistè*. To talk to them." *Keep raising the idea of conversation, of connection.*

It was clearly working. Jawid's eyes were dewy with a mix of desire and admiration. "There is no talking to them. They are beasts."

Dadou smiled, shrugged her shoulders, watching his eyes follow as her breasts rose and fell. "Beasts can still be clever when it gets them prey or a mate. They can be devious. Do you think the *mistè* answer our summons because they must? We *can* force them, but it is so much harder. Better to convince them it is what they want."

"Yes." Jawid nodded. His face fell.

"Does that upset you?" she asked.

"I promise them . . . I promise them blood if they will help me."

"So?"

"It is the blood of men they want. I am promising them murder."

"Everyone does a thing because they want a reward. A dog will guard your house for a bone and a pat on the head. A soldier will fight for money or if you wave the right-colored flag in front of him. Is it any different to offer a *mistè* the thing it prizes the most? You are only doing what you must, *chouchou*."

"They are hungry for blood."

"The *mistè* are hungry for *life*. They have been dead so long that they have forgotten that living is about more than warm blood and a beating heart. With time and practice, we will teach them again."

"How?" Jawid look doubtful and hopeful in equal measure.

"It is a conversation, as I said. You convinced them to follow you into the world of the living, to let themselves be

Bound into a corpse. You can convince them to go after Schweitzer. This Partolan, the one you put in Chang, it is out front. It is the one we will talk to."

Jawid shook his head, a hint of flush behind his beard. *He doesn't want to fail in front me.* A good sign. "It has what it wants. It is in the living world; it has the chance to kill. Why should it do anything I say?"

"Because you won't be alone. Because we will go and speak to it *together*."

"We can do that?" His eyes lit. "Working magic beside one another isn't the same as working it together, truly sharing it."

She shrugged, tried to look bored. "We can try." She forced the bored look to shift into shy uncertainty. "That is, if you want to?"

Jawid smiled. "Of course I do. "

She took his hand, brought it to her, careful to let the back rest on her thigh. She heard his breathing quicken, could feel his pulse racing in his hand. Too easy, really. He was like a little boy.

"I . . . I . . ." He wouldn't admit that he didn't know what to do next. It was always this way with the deeply religious. They would rather run screaming off a cliff than confess ignorance of anything. If she didn't offer help, she would sit there, listening to his stammering forever.

"It's all right," she said. "Just do what you usually do. Seek the void, and I will seek you."

She closed her eyes, Drew her magic about her, and sent it spiraling out into the fabric between the two worlds. The truth was that she'd never done this before either, was as nervous as he was. She didn't know if it would work, didn't know what she'd do if it didn't.

But she hadn't clawed her way out of the gutters of Port-au-Prince by shrinking from risks. Her eyes closed and the cold dark of the void settled around her, and for a moment, her stomach clenched in panic at the thought that she had lost him, that he was far away, seeing the soul storm from a different angle, and that he wouldn't be able to hear her.

Then she felt his current, stronger here, more intense. It was his emotion distilled, nervousness and wonder and delight and overpowering lust. The void was as empty as ever, only the faint line of the soul storm breaking the black monotony. *Are you with me, Jawid?*

His presence beside her pulsed, invisible but as evident as if he'd been a glowing star. *I am. Allahu akhbar, I am!*

She suppressed her annoyance and laughed, trying to send him a pulse of delight. *I knew it would work. I knew it. I knew we could do it together.*

Allahu akhbar.

Are you seeing what I see? she asked. She knew perfectly well he was, but the shared experience would help him feel a bond.

The storm, he answered, *in the distance.*

Se sa. Can you find your jinn? The one you put in Chang?

Of course I can. I have done this many times. She felt his wounded pride, his need to impress, more lust.

She felt his magic concentrate, pull them forward together. She had always viewed her own connections cutting through the void as a blue lane, and she was shocked to see that Jawid's looked much the same, a ribbon of azure pushing through the uniformity and ending somewhere in the distance. She edged her presence toward the line, reaching out with her magic to dip into it.

She felt the presence at the other end instantly intensely enough to make her reel. Rage, lust like Jawid's, only darker and more urgent, and above all, a tautness, like a piano string tuned nearly to breaking, every straining atom tuned to the frequency of carnage. She pulled herself back from Jawid's connection, gasping. *That is the jinn?*

That is the one I put in Chang. It is called Partolan. It is . . .

Strong, she finished for him. *But you are stronger.*

You've felt it. How can you say that—

Stop it. You are a Sorcerer. You survived months with the warriors who defeated both the Russians and the

Americans. You have run ops for the greatest military in the world. Whatever you need to move this Partolan, you have it.

Jawid hesitated. She could feel him trying to summon the courage to reach out to Partolan, failing.

She pushed her presence out toward him, pulsed an image of her hand taking his. *Go on; I am with you.*

He sighed, pushed off into the channel, and Dadou went with him.

Instantly, the rage and hunger slammed into her. This Partolan was powerful, both in strength and appetite. Jawid's terror was palpable. Dadou felt it instantly, could tell that Partolan felt it too.

I am the one who called you. I am the one who gave you life again, Jawid said to it. *You must do as I command.*

Dadou nearly rolled her spiritual eyes. The *mistè* were always proud, always haughty. It was exactly the wrong thing to say. She could feel Partolan's contempt come reverberating back up the link between them.

It sent an image of itself in life, a squat, naked man, so hairy that Dadou almost thought him an ape. His hair and beard were fiery red, thick and matted. Blue paint covered his skin, spiral patterns that interwove with crude pictures of men and animals. In one hand he held a primitive, copper-headed spear. The other was hidden behind a rudimentary shield, rawhide stretched over a wooden frame. *I am Partolan, father of nations. I kneel to no one.*

Dadou had promised herself that she would let Jawid handle this, knew it would help him build confidence, but he was already putting them on the wrong footing. She had to step in. *Do not kneel,* she sent to Partolan, *only follow.*

She could feel Jawid stiffen at her intervention, but he composed himself and answered. *There is one who escaped. One like you. He flees to the west. You must go after him.*

Dadou cursed inwardly at Jawid's use of the word "must."

Partolan only laughed. *Why? There is sport enough*

here. Why should I chase the dead when I am hip-deep in the living?

We need him, Jawid said.

You need him, Partolan answered. *I need nothing save a spear in my hand and ground enough for my chariot to run.*

If she let Jawid keep talking, Partolan would never obey them. Ancient lords respected only strength. It would do no good to hold back bargaining chips.

You will have all the spears and all the ground you require, she said, *but you will only have them if you help us.*

And if I do not?

Dadou sent an image of an American bomber flying low over the ruins of Basye, black metal cylinders plummeting earthward, a lake of fire that turned every Gold for miles into gently drifting clouds of ash.

Partolan was quiet; the lust and rage were reeled back as it considered. This worried Dadou more than the rage. Thinking monsters were the worst kind.

So, then I will return to the void and wait for the next Summoner to call me forth.

You will not go back to the void if the body I put you in is destroyed, Jawid lied. His deception was plain in his heightened anxiety, the emotion flowing back down the link to Partolan, who only laughed.

I think you are a stupid thrall, Partolan sent back. *I will speak with the woman.*

You will return to the void, Dadou answered, ignoring the humiliation emanating from Jawid, *but it may be that you will not be called again.*

I will be, Partolan answered. *The strongest always are.*

He had drifted in the soul storm long enough to know, and it didn't matter either way. Schweitzer was getting away. They needed him to move now. She had only one card to play, and now she had to play it. Dadou sighed. *Then I will give you something more, something greater.*

What more could I possibly want? I am in the sunlit world. I am swimming in blood. I have rid this shell of the coward who believed he was a great warrior because he

*was given machines that let him strike blind men in the
dark from a field away.*

A dead shell, Dadou answered.

She could feel Jawid's emotions shift, humiliation giving
way to confusion.

You can offer me a living one? Partolan asked.

No, she ca— Jawid began.

*I can—*Dadou cut him off—*but only if you go west and
after the one we seek.*

I think you are lying, Partolan said.

I am not lying, Dadou answered. *You can stay here and
stop the hearts of others, or you can go west and have one
beating for your very own.*

And if you are lying?

*Then I am lying, and after you have taken your quarry,
we will send you out to kill more, because as you have said,
you are the strongest, and the strongest are always put
where the fighting is thickest.*

Partolan was silent, considering. Jawid's emotions went
sour. Shock and fear mingling with anger. Dadou ignored
it. She would deal with him in a moment.

Well? she sent back to Partolan. *We don't have much
time.*

Very well, Partolan replied, though she could feel his
excitement down the link Jawid had opened. *Where does
this hunt take me?*

For now, only go west, Dadou replied. *We will guide you
as you near him.*

Make sure the . . . others . . . make sure they follow you,
Jawid added.

Partolan laughed again. *They always follow me, as the
carrion crows follow an army. Because they know that is
where the feast will be greatest.*

And then Jawid cut the link, the blue lane winking out,
his presence pulling back from her. Dadou said nothing,
only shunted her magic back and pulled herself back into
her physical body, opening her eyes back in the room, the
video monitor showing the delta of Golds turning, veering

away from the ruins and streaming out of the town to the west.

"What . . ." Jawid began, "what was that? You lied to it. You can't put it in a living body."

Dadou shrugged. "*Se sa, chouchou.* That's right."

"It will be angry that you lied. It will never do anything for us again."

Dadou laughed. Jawid's eyes were wide, his Adam's apple bobbing as he swallowed. "No, dahling. Partolan will be in a living body and grateful to us for putting him there. It will be the beginning of a great partnership, just like yours and mine."

"But you can't . . ."

"You're right, *chouchou*, *I* can't. But *we* can."

Jawid sat in stunned silence, eyes as wide as dinner plates. Dadou suppressed a laugh, reached out, and took his hand again. "I know this is a shock to you. I know about your work on the Virgo Cell. I know how it turned out."

He stammered, head shaking gently, and Dadou suddenly wished they were back in the void together so she could feel his emotions, know if she'd pushed too far, too fast.

"They were abominations. They were murders. It is one thing to put a jinn in the body of the dead, but putting one in the living—"

"—is the greatest work two people can accomplish together. Look at what we just did! Partolan is a savage animal. We *turned* it, Jawid. You and I. We went into the beyond together and we bent the monster there to our will. There is nothing, *nothing* we can't do if we do it together. Can't you feel that?"

Jawid snatched his hand back, shook his head. "Not this. I will not do this."

The anger was a ball in her throat and she choked as she swallowed it down. He *would* do it, and all of this posturing and pious angst were just wasting her time. Her hands twitched. She wanted to choke the life out of him, to shake him until his neck snapped.

Instead, she took his hand again, and he let her guide it back to her thigh, rest it there. "Very well, *chouchou*," she said. "It doesn't matter. We have done what we set out to do; we have turned Partolan to our will."

Jawid glanced up at the monitor and Dadou saw the flicker of pride in his eyes, the twitch at the corner of his mouth. "It was mostly you. You should call Doctor Eldredge and tell him," he said.

She squeezed his hand and he squeezed it back. "We'll call him together."

He glanced sidelong at her, then at the floor, suddenly shy. But Dadou could tell the hook was in, and it was only a matter of reeling now.

He would help her, and soon.

Doctor Eldredge punched the cipher code into his office door and entered the closet-sized space, slumping in the rolling chair at his desk. The cheap wooden surface was cluttered only with papers and office supplies, the edges of his laptop monitor. There were no pictures of family, no Christmas cards stood on end. No knickknacks. *Is that why you want Schweitzer back? Because you felt a connection with him? Because he was something other than the work?*

The thought made Eldredge feel pathetic. It didn't matter anyway; whatever his motives, he had to get Schweitzer back, he had to find a way to corral the spiraling appetite of the Golds.

He reached into his waistband, pulling out the KA-BAR fighting utility knife. The weight of the weapon in his palm steadied him. He hadn't noticed his heart had been racing until he began to feel it slow. With this, he could defend himself. It wasn't much, but he wasn't completely helpless against the superhuman might of the Golds.

It also meant that, if he could just get close enough, he could find Schweitzer himself. Slim hope, but slim was better than none at all.

The chime sounded at his laptop. He winced as he

pushed the button to connect, he wasn't ready to talk to the Director just yet.

But it was the ops boss on the other end. "White, this is ops."

"Go ahead, ops," Eldredge said.

"Sir, we just got word from the eyes-on over Basye."

Eldredge sighed relief; even if the news was bad, at least ops didn't scare him. "What's up?"

"The Golds are surging en masse to the west. Observers report them in pursuit of one Operator, one woman, and one little boy. That's confirmed. We've got him."

Eldredge felt his stomach turn over. They didn't need links anymore. Dadou's fox hunt had begun.

CHAPTER XII
PURE GOLD

Schweitzer felt his wife go unconscious. He rolled her off his shoulder and into his cradling arms. Her head lolled, drool trailing from the corner of her mouth, but the pale sclera of her eyes rolled back and the pupils inside the deep brown irises fixed on him.

"It's okay, baby." He tried to keep the worry from his voice. "We got out of there. We're safe."

It was a lie. His augmented hearing could make out the frantic padding of the Gold Operators as they hurried after him, fixed on the scent of Sarah's blood. He could feel the constricted flow as her veins dilated, her circulatory system responding to the loss of blood. Precious little was making its way to her brain He glanced down at her hip. The wound was completely open now, the flesh beneath burning hot.

"Baby?" he asked again.

She blinked, made no response. Her eyes glowed with fever. He reached down the link that connected them, felt only confusion, exhaustion.

Patrick had wandered out from the shelter of the rock where Schweitzer had left him. He'd known the boy would, had counted on him not being able to get far. He knew that racing up on his son would terrify him, but there was no time.

Patrick was sobbing, walking downhill through a low thicket of berry bushes, slapping at the thorns. His face was a red mottle of poison ivy rash, the heat beneath the skin so intense that it glowed to Schweitzer's augmented eyes. The boy turned and screamed at the skull-faced gray monster bearing down on him. Schweitzer shifted Sarah back to his shoulder and scooped Patrick up, folding the boy into his mother's arms, switching Sarah back to his own. Sarah clutched Patrick tightly to her, repeating the same words Schweitzer had said to her just a moment ago. "Oh, baby, it's okay. It's okay," she breathed. "Mama's got you."

Schweitzer tightened the muscles in his arms and chest, but his family flopped like rag dolls as he vaulted a downed log. Sarah and Patrick hunched closer as the tree branches tore at them.

A whooshing sound to his right told him one of the Golds had leapt into the canopy, was pushing off a tree trunk in an effort to get ahead of them.

Schweitzer came down, skidding on his heels as he tried to stay upright. The Gold Operator hit the ground in front of him, landing on its shoulder, rolling down the grade. It extended a hand, trying to stop its momentum and get onto its feet. In life, the thing must have been at least seven feet tall, with shoulders like a linebacker. Bone spikes jutted from the point of each. One of them dug into the ground as the thing began to rise, sending it into a tumble again. It stuck out a hand to change the direction, forcing it into Schweitzer's path.

To slow was to lose Sarah and Patrick, to lose everything.

Schweitzer didn't break stride. He counted his steps, made sure that his right foot was swinging forward with everything he had.

He felt some of the small bones in the top of his foot snap as his instep slammed into the Gold Operator's ribs. But some of the crunching bones were not his own, and the monster launched into the air, flipping head over feet until it struck a trunk hard enough to crack it, Gold Operator and tree going over in a splintering crash.

Schweitzer took long strides to keep himself upright, each one hammering Sarah as his arms shook. She screamed, and Patrick screamed with her, wrapping his arms around her neck.

Schweitzer heard a snarl as another Operator galloped along behind them, reaching out to snatch at his heel, missing by inches. Rotor blades were sounding in the distance.

"Put me down," Sarah gasped.

"Are you fucking crazy?" Schweitzer asked. "They'll kill you."

"*You're* going to kill me if we keep going."

She was right. They had to get that wound closed.

A rock hammered into Schweitzer's shoulder, knocking him off-balance. He pitched into a roll, taking the impact on his head and neck, locking his core muscles to use his own bulk as a shield for Sarah and Patrick. He felt one of his cervical vertebrae snap.

He flung himself off of his wife and child, springing clear. The crack in his spine would have paralyzed a normal man, but for him it was just a footnote. The structural integrity of his back held, and that was all he needed for now. There was no time to turn to Sarah or Patrick. The thing that had thrown that rock was coming on fast, ignoring him to angle for the beating hearts of his wife and son.

His augmented hearing picked up racing wind and he knew the Gold Operator had leapt immediately after it had thrown the rock, was descending on him from above. It hit him just as he looked up, sending him rolling. Something hard and metal slapped against his thigh, spinning fast enough to burn his skin. For the living, the first thing adrenaline robbed you of was your fine motor skills. SEALs trained to compensate, emphasizing big and easy movements. They didn't waste time punching. The striking surface of a fist was tiny.

Though Schweitzer no longer had adrenaline in his

body, the training held, and he clubbed the Gold Operator's neck with his forearm, striking solid metal hard enough to crack his ulna and to throw his enemy off.

Schweitzer rolled to his feet, clenching and unclenching his fist. The break was hairline thin; he could still use his arm. He turned to his enemy rising to its feet.

He could glimpse flashes of the slate-gray skin, the now familiar clumsy surgical stitching common to its kind, the flashes of burning gold he knew were its eyes. But most of it was covered by thick metal plate that looked bolted to the thing's skeleton, screw heads and lug nuts crowned with rust. Its left arm had been removed below the elbow, replaced with a metal armature clenched around a circular saw spinning madly, buzzing like an angry hornet.

That's for me. This thing was custom-built to cut me to pieces.

But whatever the machinery, the Operator lusted for beating hearts and warm blood. Schweitzer was cold and dead.

Sarah swayed on her feet, limping away, Patrick dragged along by one wrist, face chalk white.

The Gold turned from Schweitzer, the spinning blade missing Sarah by inches as Schweitzer tackled it to the ground. It bucked, snapped at him. Schweitzer held on, using his weight to pin it in place, wrist locked on the metal forearm, pushing the blade into the dirt. The buzzing muffled; dirt and rocks sprayed into the air.

He could hear the thudding of feet on earth, the speed of the intervals too rapid for living men. Other Golds, inbound. At least a klick out but closing fast.

Schweitzer lifted his weight long enough to get both hands around the metal shaft that had replaced the Operator's arm. The metal bolted to the thing's body gave it the weight advantage, and it used it, pulling against him, trying to rip the spinning blade out of his hand. Schweitzer kneed it in the face, kneecap rebounding off the metal plate bolted to the skull.

He pulled with everything he had, bracing one foot

against a root. There was no way to bring his training to bear now; this was a contest of raw strength against strength, and the monster beneath him had the advantage of an extra hundred pounds of metal.

Schweitzer felt the saw slide an inch, another. He was losing his grip on it. The Gold Operator hissed.

Patrick cried out, then Sarah.

It was unforgivable to break concentration now. Schweitzer knew he should keep his head in the fight, but he was powerless before the sound of his wife and son's voices raised in fear.

He looked up.

Gold Operators were cresting the rise behind them, gray shapes flashing between the tree trunks, coming closer. One was in the lead, not galloping on all fours but jogging steadily, gray-white fists clenched and pumping before its bare chest.

Steve Chang.

Death hadn't changed Schweitzer's closest friend much. Bone claws emerged from the shredded remains of his hands. There was what had once been an ugly wound in Chang's side, three matching jagged holes in the opposite shoulder, all stitched shut with more care than Schweitzer was used to seeing in these monsters. Chang's head was down, the skull shaved. Schweitzer could see the top half of the eagle, flintlock, and trident Chang had tattooed on his arm the day after he'd pinned on. Schweitzer had sat in the chair next to him, waving the twenty-dollar bill he'd bet that Chang would wince before the two-hour job was over.

Schweitzer couldn't remember the last time he'd been that happy to lose twenty dollars. Because it meant Chang could hack it. Because it meant they could stick together.

He knew the thing stalking toward him wasn't Chang, but he had come to know that face so well that he recognized it even though Chang's head was lowered.

Oh God, brother. They got you. They fucking got you.

Was this what Sarah was hiding from him? That they had made Steve into a Gold? Steve was dead. His best friend, his brother. The closest person to him on the team. Sarah had told Schweitzer of the persistent, nagging belief that he was still alive. Had she told Steve? Had Steve gone looking for him? Had the Cell found out and . . . done this to him?

The thoughts drowned in sick sadness. Steve Chang, dead. He remembered watching the banner on the bottom of the TV screen as the news relayed Peter's death even before the Navy could send a chaplain to tell the family in person. U.S. NAVY HELICOPTER CRASHES IN AFGHANISTAN—17 DEAD. Peter, gone. And now Steve. A brother by birth and a brother by shared trials, both family.

The grief nearly overwhelmed him. Hope mingled with it, mad and fluttering. Because if Chang was an Operator, that meant that Schweitzer might still be able to reach him. Chang was a SEAL, as strong a man as any Schweitzer had ever known. Maybe he hadn't gone Gold? Maybe he was coming to save them.

Then why does it look like he's leading the charge? Why aren't the other Golds attacking him? He knew it made no sense, but his dead heart still surged at the sight of his best friend. He wanted to abandon everything, run for him, pull him into a hug.

No. That's not Steve. You are looking at a corpse.

But while Schweitzer had lost focus, the Gold Operator beneath him hadn't. With a jerk of its metal limb, it ripped the spinning saw free and lunged.

For Sarah.

Schweitzer dropped his weight on the thing's arm, giving Sarah a moment to twist away, dragging her son with her, the saw swinging wide and digging into the tree trunk beside them. Schweitzer rolled off it, felt the Gold struggle to jump to its feet. Schweitzer grabbed its ankle, twisted his back and pulled. The Gold Operator spun off the ground, saw breaking free of the wood, the flat of the blade rebounding off Schweitzer's head, notching the top of his ear. The Gold Operator flew, spinning in a slow circle until it smacked into Chang and sent them both tumbling back into the pack of monsters ranging through the trees.

The shock over seeing Chang would have to keep. "Hold on to Patrick!" Schweitzer shouted, then scooped Sarah over one shoulder and leapt for the trees. The branches gave, but not before he was able to leap for the next one, Sarah folding herself over his back and shuddering as the sharp branches dug at her, Patrick wailing like a siren.

Schweitzer's vision became a staccato of still images. Branches, tangled leaves, blue sky. He pulled them along as fast as he could, arms and legs pumping, wood splintering with each leap. The forest floor sped by beneath them, and Schweitzer lost all sense of where he was heading, focused only on the sound of his pursuers smashing through the wood behind him. Part of him railed against the lack of a plan, but SEALs also knew when it was time to throw planning to the wind, when it was time to fight like an animal. When it was time to run.

More images. Pulses of gray and pale blue. Skin taut over tight muscle. Flashes of flickering gold.

Splintering from overhead.

More of them, in the trees.

Schweitzer thudded into a landing on a thick bough strong enough to hold, overbalanced, let his momentum carry him forward to the ground.

The jarring landing forced a cry from his wife. "Jim, stop."

There was no time to stop. He kept running, trying to lock her in place with his arm, unable to stop her bouncing regardless. He could feel Patrick crushed against his neck, the tightness in her arms as she held him there. "Jim, I can't keep hold of him."

He raised a hand to Patrick, trying to pull the boy from Sarah so he could secure him under his arm. Patrick screamed and kicked, began to slip free.

Schweitzer slowed to keep him from falling, and the first Gold Operator was upon them.

Sarah spasmed in his arms, dropping Patrick and pushing off Schweitzer's chest, breaking free as the Gold's gray tongue whipped over Schweitzer's shoulder, missing his wife by inches and wrapping around his neck instead. The Gold Operator lacked discipline and training. It squeezed, cutting off his windpipe, a futile tactic against a being that didn't need to breathe.

Schweitzer reached back, pointing his fingers and punching into its mouth, feeling a long tooth scrape along his hand until the crux of his forefinger and thumb snapped it off. He grabbed the tongue at its root, yanked forward.

The thing came over his shoulder, biting down on his hand as he'd known it would. Schweitzer hooked his fingers through the golden flames, found the edges of the skull, pulled forward and down. The Gold turned in the air, slammed down on its back, ribs cracking. The sound of the pursuit drawing closer fueled a desperate strength. Schweitzer knew that the second best thing to cold professionalism was hot rage. Lukewarm was the zone where you lost the fight.

He channeled his despair into a stomp that collapsed the Gold's chest, crushing the sternum and revealing the gray edges of a heart pierced by its shattered ribs. He lifted the thing by its neck and hauled it over his head, slamming it on the ground again and again, stomping and wrenching.

Crack. Crack. Crack. Bones crunching like gunshots. The thing writhed in his grip, but it was helpless to fight, first against his brutal strength and then its own steadily reducing armature, as its own bones broke into fragments. He threw the thing away, writhing as it rolled but powerless to rise. He thought briefly of the gun he'd taken from the operator on Gruenen's team, but the weapon was gone, the sling having snapped during his flight through the trees. It didn't matter. A gun would do no good against this enemy.

Sarah was on her knees. Her skin was chalk white, her hip a sheet of red. Her beautiful pink hair was streaked with blood, leaves, and the grime of the forest floor. *I'm losing her.*

Crashing, branches breaking. The Golds getting closer. Chang was somewhere at the front of the pack. Schweitzer turned back to Sarah, reaching for her. "Get ahold of Patrick," he said.

She reached down with surprising strength, swatted his hand away. "We can't. They're too many and too fast."

She got shaking to her feet, pushed Patrick roughly into his arms. The boy cried, reached for her, but Sarah's eyes were pitiless.

Schweitzer's spiritual stomach turned over. He didn't bother keeping the panic out of his voice this time. "Sarah, we don't have time. What the fu—"

"You're right"—her voice was calm—"we don't have time. I'm leading them away. Get Patrick out of here."

She took a shaking step away from him, got her legs under her, started to move more quickly.

Schweitzer knew how much blood she'd lost, could feel her lowered body temperature, could hear her weakened heartbeat. He was amazed at how much strength she showed, but even Sarah at her fastest couldn't compare to his superhuman speed. He reached her in a single step, snaked an arm around her waist. "Baby, I am not dealing with this martyr shit right now! They are going to . . ."

She screamed, tore at his arm, flinging it off her. "Save my son, damn it!" He could feel the rage and desperation down the link they shared.

Something gray flashed in their peripheral vision. Schweitzer reacted instinctively, grabbing Patrick's wrist tightly with one hand and punching out with the other, snatching the incoming Gold's arm and swinging it around into a tree trunk with enough force to send the thing into the wood a half an inch. He followed with a knee hard enough to shatter its pelvis. It collapsed under its own weight, slumping to the ground, reaching out to stop its fall.

Patrick yanked at Schweitzer, trying to twist away, but the boy may as well have struggled against a metal vise. Schweitzer turned his attention to the immediate threat, reaching over the Gold's head and yanking down on a thick bough, driving the splintering branch into the monster's shoulder, pushing the wood through its chest and down into its ravaged hips, until at last he felt the softer surface of the earth beneath, and the monster was staked in place. He kicked it in the ribs savagely, once, twice, until his toes passed into the hollow beyond.

"Sarah!" He ran to her, hearing the rest of the Golds crash closer.

"Jim, for the last time, take Patrick and run! I'll get them to follow me!"

"Sarah, no!"

"Didn't you see Steve? He's with them."

"That's not Steve, Sarah. That's . . ."

"Maybe he's like you, Jim. Maybe there's some of him left in there."

"You've lost too much blood; you're not thinking straight. Sarah, Steve is dead. That is something else wearing his corpse."

Her eyes were fever bright; Schweitzer could see the dark circles under them fading to pale white from blood loss. "He loves me!"

Schweitzer tucked Patrick against his side, reached for her waist. "Fuck this. I am not wasting another sec—"

Sarah grabbed his wrist, gritted her teeth, and concentrated so hard that she screamed. The link that bound them throbbed, the dull pulse of emotions went from a thematic buzz to a sudden spike as Sarah desperately pushed her feelings for Steve Chang down the channel.

Schweitzer froze, stunned.

It was the most intense burst of emotion from her yet, so strong that it evoked the link he'd been able to forge with Jawid, to plunder his memories, to learn that his wife and son were still alive. The link began to throb with memories, images.

The tangled burst surged out of Sarah: love, so strong it crackled, but not for him. Loss and need, despair so keen that it was a hole inside her, a yawning gulf opening below her, vast and black and endless, a living soul storm. The desire to feel warm and safe, desperate and heady, dull and addictive. Love, not romantic, not lustful, tangled now, lost in the fear of the void of loneliness. Tripping up her judgment, chewing away at caution, until the only thing she wanted was to not feel awful, just for a moment.

Sweat, moaning, flesh on flesh.

This. This is what she had been hiding from him. Steve had come around after Schweitzer had been killed. Steve had done what a brother was supposed to do. He had taken care of Schweitzer's family.

Steve. We were supposed to be brothers; how could you?

A part of him knew he wasn't being fair. Both Sarah and Steve had every reason to believe that Schweitzer was dead. His best friend and his widow were trying to move on, build something new. If Schweitzer had been dead, he would have wanted her to find someone else, someone who could make her and Patrick happy.

But he wasn't dead, not really. Not in the way that would dull the pain of the revelation that his wife had slept with his best friend.

"I'm sorry, baby," Sarah whispered so softly that only his augmented hearing allowed him to make out the words.

James Schweitzer couldn't move. For all his magical might, he stood rooted to the spot, hurt burning in his silver eyes.

Sarah turned and ran.

She moved with incredible strength and speed for someone so badly wounded, a desperate tapping of her reserve to lead the chase away from her son. She ran with everything she had, arms and legs pumping, straight toward the pack of monsters that were finally emerging from the wood. She ran and Schweitzer stood, his spiritual nerves still paralyzed with the shock of realization.

The Golds reacted as Sarah predicted. They veered after her, ignoring Schweitzer's cold corpse and Patrick's smaller, fainter pulse. Steve Chang led them, though whether he was led by the nearness of blood, of a beating heart, or his love for Sarah, Schweitzer couldn't tell. The corpse of Schweitzer's best friend put on speed, dogging Sarah's heels, close enough to put a hand on her shoulder. And now Schweitzer found himself praying that Sarah was right, that it really was Steve Chang in there, that he was battling the jinn for supremacy of his own body, as Schweitzer had.

Because even as his paralysis broke, he realized there was no way he could reach her in time. Not now, not with Patrick in tow, not with so many enemies so close together.

He tried anyway. He crouched to leap toward her, tucking Patrick into his belly, locking him firmly in place with one arm. One of the Golds flagged behind the pack, a tall thing with impossibly long limbs, scrabbling along the ground like a spider. Bone spines sprouted from its back in looping lines that matched the curve of its ribs, covered with leaves and clods of dirt. It darted toward Sarah, saw the other Gold Operators would have made short work of her before it arrived, and turned for closer prey.

It leapt, catching the tops of Schweitzer's feet before he could clear it, sending him rolling.

Patrick tumbled from his grip, got to his feet, and raced away from the fight into the woods behind them. Schweitzer rolled, came up on one knee.

Chang had caught Sarah, had turned her around. His hand was on the back of her neck, his head bent to look into her eyes. One of the other Gold Operators tried to surge around him, and Chang backhanded it into the brush. His other hand, the one on Sarah, looked gentle. Sarah raised her own to grip his wrist. They looked like lovers, leaning in for a kiss.

Maybe she was right. Maybe Chang was as Schweitzer had been with Ninip. Maybe there was enough of him left in his own body to hold his humanity. Schweitzer's heart rejoiced, because it meant that Sarah might live.

Chang lifted his head.

His eyes were shining, shimmering gold. Untarnished, pure.

"Sarah!" Schweitzer shouted. "That's not Steve!"

But the jinn wearing his best friend's dead skin had already started to squeeze.

No. Oh God. Sarah, no.

Schweitzer screamed. A wordless, high cry. A ringing grief so keen, it cut the air. Schweitzer hadn't known he had such sounds in him. The SEAL was gone, leaving only the grieving husband, reeling in shock. The love of his life. The mother of his child. The woman he'd fought so hard to get back to.

Blood shot out of Sarah's nose. Her hand on Chang's wrist pulled frantically, the backs of the knuckles purple. Her chalk-pale skin turned the same gray as the dead things pursuing her. She opened her mouth to scream, but only blood came out, thick and dark. Schweitzer heard the cracking of bones.

Oh God, Sarah. He tensed to spring again, heard Patrick scream, the scuttling of the bug-like Gold racing over the cold ground after him.

Clear fluid sprayed out with the blood, Sarah's eyes glazed, and Schweitzer knew his wife was gone. The link between them buzzed, faltered, cut off. Rage and grief competed in his dead gut, his legs straining to push him after the body of his wife, to wreak useless revenge, to kill things that were already dead.

The SEAL bulled the impulse aside. *Sarah is dead. Patrick is alive. Grieve later.*

Sarah's voice, panicked, feral. *Save my son, damn it!*

The Gold reached Patrick, grabbing ahold of his ankle. Patrick shouted, fell, twisting free of the Gold's grip, sprawling on his face.

Schweitzer spun, flung himself after the insectile Gold. He grabbed the spines, hauled himself up onto the creature's back. The monster swatted at Schweitzer. Schweitzer snatched one flailing wrist, held it easily, then the other.

Schweitzer slammed the Gold's wrists down, impaling both arms on its own spines. The thing flailed, rocking its shoulders, stuck fast. Schweitzer's mind chanted a ceaseless litany as he worked: *SarahGoneSarahGoneSarahGone.*

Patrick was up and running, heading blessedly deeper into the woods. Schweitzer made sure he had a fix on his son, then reached back, seizing one of the Gold Operator's flailing ankles. He bent it back, pulling on the leg until the knee snapped, spiking it on the spines as well. He grunted, placing one knee on the monster's head, driving it deeper into the dirt. "Hold still, you fucker."

When he was done, the Gold was bundled in a neat package, shuddering as it tried to untangle itself, broken limbs sagging under their own weight, impaled on its own spines.

Patrick had disappeared into the woods, but Schweitzer could hear his son's footfalls and sobs. Schweitzer glanced over his shoulder to see if any of the Golds would follow.

He looked away before he could focus on the details, pick the lines out of the quivering red gray mass behind him. The shredded mess that had been Sarah.

Grief and horror warred within him until his training locked them down. For now, he only needed to know one thing. He had a few minutes to find his son and widen the lead on the pursuit. They wouldn't be coming after him for a little while at least.

They were busy.

CHAPTER XIII
PROGRAM REVIEW

Senator Donald Hodges looked like he had stepped out of a library portrait. The effect was so pronounced that Eldredge half expected a gold-leaf frame to appear around the man's head. His jaw was chiseled, just beginning to run to distinguished jowls. His hair was a shellacked dollop of cream. His face was creased in a semipermanent expression of warmth.

The creases didn't reach his eyes. They were steel gray, never settling in one place for long. Now they were narrowed, watching the digital map on the monitors. Faint green lines sketched out the elevation of hills and the path of streams, dotted with dark blotches that were stands of trees. Layered over it were seven blinking gold triangles, floating as the Operators they designated moved. Four were still, covered with red X's.

"We can effect repairs on them, sir," Eldredge said. "In some cases, Schweitzer broke the bones so completely that they'll need complete alloy armatures. Even then, they still may not be fully mission-capable, but we won't know until we fix them and put them back through trials."

There should, of course, have been a silver triangle marking Schweitzer's position, but there wasn't.

They'd lost him. All that damage, that bloody massacre, and they'd still lost him.

"Doctor Eldredge"—Hodges's voice had a slight New England aristocratic lilt—"the exact amount of the line item that funds this program is classified in channels known only to myself and the President."

"Yes, sir."

The Senator brushed some imagined dust from his lapel. "But I want you to believe me when I tell you that it's an awful lot of money. I'd even go so far as to call it a staggering amount of money."

"I believe you, sir." *Now stop wasting my fucking time and get to the point.*

"You should," Hodges said, not getting to the point at all. He gestured to the expensive liquid crystal screens, the ergonomic office chairs, the stainless steel and graphite furniture frames. "We've spared no expense with your program."

It wasn't his program, but Eldredge figured it was best to let the overstatement pass. "We're very grateful, sir."

Hodges looked down at him. "Well, gratitude is always a good thing. It's nice to know one's contributions are appreciated."

They're the taxpayers' contributions, you self-important ass, Eldredge thought.

"But do you know what I like even more than gratitude?" Senator Hodges went on, stabbing an angry finger at the screen. "Results.

"So, perhaps you can explain to me why this . . . shall we just say more-than-adequately-funded program, is now responsible for the wholesale slaughter of a popular Shenandoah resort town, laying waste to several miles of countryside, all for the ultimate loss of a single man and his little boy?"

"We got the wife, sir." The words made Eldredge's stomach twist.

"Do you think"—Hodges's mild voice slowed—"that I give a damn about the wife? Do you think we called Javelin Rain on some hippie artist from the ass end of Norfolk? Schweitzer. Where is Schweitzer?"

Eldredge took a deep breath, repeated the same answer he'd been giving for over an hour. "We don't know, sir."

"This is the biggest deployment of Gold Operators we've ever endeavored, supported by as many conventional operators as we can beg, borrow, or steal. He's a walking corpse burdened by a screaming child. He's in the continental United States in a specific national park. How the hell is it that your Golds can't find him?"

"They're . . . they're animals, sir."

"What the hell is that supposed to mean?"

Eldredge knew that he needed to pick his next words carefully, that the Director would be furious if Hodges lost faith in the program based on something Eldredge said. "They are driven by their appetites," Eldredge said. "Like dogs. They have some free will, but in the end, they go after what they want."

"And what is that?"

"Blood, sir. They're addicted to the stuff."

Hodges pursed his lips. "And Schweitzer doesn't have any blood."

Eldredge sighed, stood. "Glycerol, sir. Keeps everything lubricated so he can move without seizing up. But if you're a Gold, that doesn't tickle your pickle, as my dad used to say."

"The boy . . ."

"Is small. Fainter heartbeat, less of the stuff they're after."

"And you're sure of this?"

Eldredge thrust his hands into the pockets of his white lab coat. "No, sir. This is magic. Jawid's not even sure of it and he's the one using it every day. When we still had Schweitzer, he told me that the jinn were both addicted to blood as the stuff of life and angry at those who still lived for living. He said it was some kind of twisted mix of dependence and vengeance. But I don't think even he was sure, and he's not around to ask."

"Well, that's the crux of the matter. How the hell do you propose to get him back?"

"More of the same, sir. We round up the Golds and have Jawid and Dadou parlay with them. We can trot out incentives to nudge them left or right."

"Incentives?"

"Livestock, sir. Or convicts."

"Convicts?" Hodges's lip curled. "You mean people?"

Death row inmates, but people all the same. The Director had only recently floated the idea. It didn't sit well with Eldredge, but he couldn't let that show. "It's just to get their attention. We dust them off before the Golds catch up with them."

"Can you guarantee that?"

Eldredge was quiet for a moment. "No."

"I see."

Hodges folded his arms across his chest. "Okay, so you do your human sacrifices and your Sorcerers send the remaining Golds out after him."

"No, sir. The Sorcerers round them up, and we lock them back down. We don't drop them in again until we're sure that we're right on top of the target. What happened at Basye has convinced me that we just don't have the control we need. I am not risking collateral like that again."

"Collateral happens in war," Hodges said.

"Respectfully, sir, this isn't a war. It's an experiment gone haywire. I have not yet looked in a mirror and faced what just happened out there. I'm putting it off until after I get Schweitzer back, because I don't want to lose focus. But sooner or later, I'm going to have to, and it's going to sting."

"You're not getting him back," Hodges said. "You're destroying him."

"Sir, that is the wrong call. Schweitzer is unique. Throwing him away would be like turning your back on a gun because you prefer swords. The Golds are wild dogs. Schweitzer is a person. He is a rational, ethical, thinking person, and when you combine that with what magic has made of him, there is no limit to what he can do."

Hodges's eyes narrowed. "Is he your friend?"

"No, sir. He hates me too much for that. Even before he got away, he harbored resentment at not being in control of himself and his own fate. He never trusted me. But the truth is that he is a good man, probably better than either of us, and we did him wrong."

"We gave him a second chance."

"We lied to him about his family. We kept him prisoner here. Do you know what tipped the scales for him? The point when he finally pushed the jinn out and dominated his own body?"

"Enlighten me."

"When he began asserting himself. When he began defying orders and saving people. When he acted less like Ninip and more like Jim Schweitzer. He's good, sir, and that's what makes him different. That's what makes him strong. I want this program to be good, so we're not going to destroy him. We're going to get him back and find out what makes him tick."

"You yourself have told me multiple times that Schweitzer is more powerful than any Gold Operator."

"Not more powerful, sir, as powerful. He combines this with a highly intelligent, rational mind that has the ability to discipline itself. He's also able to access his training and experience in a way that the Golds can't. He's not blinded by bloodlust. He can think."

Hodges waved the words impatiently away. "Whatever, Doctor. You know what I mean. Schweitzer is more . . . dangerous than the Golds? He's a tougher adversary?"

"Yes, sir. That's accurate."

"Doctor, every second Schweitzer eludes us, we run the risk of him deciding that he'd rather go in front of a TV camera than fight. He could grant interviews to bloggers, or decide to walk into the middle of Times Square. That would be a very bad day."

"Yes, sir. It would."

"I am this close, Doctor, *this* close to just ordering that entire forest razed. Bomb it until no two stones are left atop one another."

"If your goal is to avoid press, sir, that might not be the best move."

The politician's mask fell away. "Don't talk to me about what the best move is, Eldredge. You lost Schweitzer and now you've failed to recapture him. Even men more charitable than I might call your judgment into question at this stage of the game."

Eldredge had no answer to that.

"We are not capturing anyone," Hodges went on. "We are going to pinpoint a location, we are going to cordon it off, and we are going to have a Spectre cover it with enough fire to shred every chipmunk, ant, and inchworm down there. Then we will bomb what's left. We'll chain the story to Basye, say it was another rupture farther down the same gas line."

"You might want to make sure there are actually gas lines running through there first." *Good lord. How does a man this stupid get elected?*

"Don't get cute with me. I need you to locate Schweitzer so that we can get this done."

"Sir, please. That's the wrong call."

"There is only one thing you need to know about this call, Eldredge," Hodges said, "and that is that it isn't yours to make. I am done negotiating with you. I want to speak to the Director."

"Sir, he can be . . ."

"SOCOM is making a power play and the Secretary of the Army is delivering a passionate argument for why his branch is the only one in the service capable of acting as the executive agent for what they're calling the 'Arcane Domain.' That means your precious program here would be dissolved. That means all your resources would be moved to MacDill. Maybe they'd let you stay on. Maybe not. You want to avoid that happening? Let me talk to your Director."

"The Director prefers me to handle these interactions, sir. He doesn't talk to anyone." *That's not true, though, is it? He talks to Jawid and Dadou now.*

"That's fine," Hodges said. "I'll just call my staffer and let her know that I'll be voting to give SOCOM control."

Eldredge sighed, nodded. "Give me a minute, sir."

He walked down the hall to his office and took a moment to cool himself down. His desk was buried under stacks of paper, chaotic and sprawling: personnel files, budget spreadsheets, lists of equipment, and project schedules. The morning operations and intelligence briefing was still on his computer screen, half prepared for presentation to the Director the next morning. That briefing was the Director's main window on to the day-to-day operations of the Cell, the litany of tasks that, after all these years, it seemed only he knew how to do. Eldredge had lost count of how many times he'd prepared the document. The thought made him tired.

He double-clicked the shortcut labeled simply COMMS and waited. A moment later, the Director's voice whispered to him through the speaker under the monitor. "Ah, Doctor. I'm glad you called. Did we work out the coolant contracts?"

"Almost, sir. Entertech is negotiating the purchase, but we're having a tough time coming up with a justification for the bulk order. Entertech is well backstopped. They'll look legitimate to anyone investigating, but it's still not a good idea to make anyone suspicious."

"Surely there's some front technology we can claim to be using. Say it's for a nuclear plant."

"That's not liquid nitrogen, sir. That's helium, or molten salt, or just lots of water."

The Director made a strangled cough that Eldredge decided was meant to be a sigh. "You'll figure it out, Eldredge. You always do."

"That's not why I called, sir."

"One more thing: I do want the reserve Sorcerer brought to this facility. I know he's not the best we have, but I want him on deck in case this situation with Schweitzer grows

more complex. Might be we can find a way to put him
to use."

"Understood, sir, I'll take care of it. That's still not why
I called."

"Why, then?"

"It's Senator Hodges, sir. He's here."

"I'm aware." The man's voice was distracted, tired. "I
trust you are handling him."

"He's not happy that we lost Schweitzer. He wants to
talk to you."

A pause, then: "Find a way to put him off."

A chill worked its way from Eldredge's balls up his
spine to freeze the base of his skull. *Has he gone insane?*
"Sir, did you hear me? It's Senator Hodges."

"I know perfectly well who he is, Eldredge."

"Then you know that he's the man who funds this
program."

"I do. I'm not available right now. I need you to handle
this."

"Sir. He can defund our line item. He can shut everything
down. He's threatening to put us under the army, make us
report to SOCOM at MacDill. In Tampa, sir. They'll make
us tear everything down before we move."

"No, they won't."

"With all due respect, sir, how the hell can you know
that?"

"Trust me. Things are about to change. We're going to
find Schweitzer."

It was a moment before Eldredge could speak. Scenarios
raced through his mind. The Director was on drugs. The
Director was insane. The Director was under duress. He
forced himself to breathe evenly, spoke as if to a child. "But
we just lost him. Finding him means more teams out, more
helos up. More gas and more bullets and more bribes to the
press and police. More drones in the air and sources on the
ground. All of that costs money, and Senator Hodges can
make the money stop."

"What we're doing is more important than money."

"Sir, I . . ."

"I said handle him, Eldredge. Don't make me tell you again."

The connection cut and Eldredge stood, balling his fists. The Director was insane if he thought he could snub Senator Hodges. *Maybe he knows something he's not telling you?* That had to be it. Why else would he risk losing funding?

Eldredge was shocked to feel a sick swell of relief in his gut, mingling with the anger and frustration. An end to the program would mean he would be free of this place and this man, whose will he had served for years despite never having seen his face.

It wouldn't bring redemption, but it would bring change, time above ground, the voices of people whose names he could know, whose faces he could see somewhere other than at the office.

That wasn't redemption, but it was something.

He didn't realize how long he'd been sitting there until a knock sounded at his door. A soldier stuck his head in, face sheepish. "Sorry, sir. The Senator said he'd been kept waiting long enough."

Eldredge spun in his chair. "All right, I'm com—"

Hodges pushed past the soldier, stuck his immaculate coiffure into the room. "Your response isn't exactly endearing me to the program, Eldredge."

"I'm sorry, sir. It's just that . . ."

"I already told you that I was done talking with you. My business is with the Director; now, am I on his calendar or not?"

Eldredge exhaled, looked down. "I'm sorry, sir. He's unavailable."

"I see."

"Sir, I can assure you that . . ."

"Spare me, Doctor. I appreciate your efforts, but I think I know everything I need to. My staff will be in touch."

"Sir!" Eldredge stood and followed him out into the hall. Hodges didn't turn, didn't so much as acknowledge his presence, and Eldredge was not so stupid as to try and stop him, to do anything more than watching his receding back as he entered the elevator that would take him to the helo hangar, where his bird back to Washington was spun up and waiting.

CHAPTER XIV
ON TO THE LIVING

Dadou slid closer. The touch of her thigh against Jawid's own horrified and thrilled him in equal measure. He had grown used to voices inside his head. The magic brought them, the sorcerous link that conveyed both emotion and language between him and the souls of the dead. But there were other voices too, his grandfather Izat for one, who had been the ulema, the religious leader for the small cluster of huts that clung tenaciously to the slowly shifting rock face where Jawid had grown up. They had held on for generations until the *Talebs* had fired their mortars into them. Thousands of years undone in an instant. Izat had lost his life then, but Jawid still heard his voice now.

And come not near unto fornication. Lo! it is an abomination and an evil way. Jawid could hear the old man's voice as if it were he and not Dadou who sat beside him, leg brushing his own.

That village had seemed the whole world to him all those years ago. Jawid knew better now. All those huts, the goat paths and the mosque, the wells and even the trampled field where the men played *buzkashi* could all fit in one

corner of the squad bay where the Gemini Cell kept its
helicopters. Jawid didn't know how many levels the
underground complex had, but he knew he could have fit
ten of his villages in just one of them.

The world was so big, and there was so much that his
grandfather hadn't even imagined. *Do not let the infidels
blind you. Follow the way of those on whom Allah has
bestowed His grace, not of those who earned His anger,
nor of those who went astray.* Jawid supposed Izat spun in
the soul storm now, his admonitions mixing with the
regrets and misdeeds of millions of others across time. All
the prayers and all the studying and all the righteous living
made no difference. Jawid had clung to the belief that only
bad men went there, the sort of monsters that he called back
into the corpses of the newly slain. Ninip, Partolan, an
ancient archer who called herself Hippolita. A part of him,
deep in his heart, knew this was wrong, but he had believed
it with a stubborn faith that allowed him to do his work.

Until Schweitzer.

And if Schweitzer had gone to the soul storm, then *all*
people must go to the soul storm, the Muslims and the
unbelievers, the righteous and the wicked. Every last one.

Jawid inhaled Dadou's smell: soap and roots, clean and
earthy. She was not a Muslim. He did not have his parents'
permission. But the world was vast and complicated beyond
anything the wisest men he had known had ever imagined.
Surely, God would not judge him harshly for loving her.

"Look at those curls." Dadou hooked a long finger in a
lock of Jawid's thick black hair, gave it a tug, laughed as it
sprang back. "Boink." She pulled again, released. "Boink."

Jawid's head felt as if it were stuffed with cotton. He was
stiff beneath his robes, worried she might see, wanted her
to see. "It's too long" was all he could manage. He sounded
like he was gasping. Because he was.

She laughed again. "You're so cute."

"I like that you laugh." He almost never saw women
back home, and when he did, they were shrouded in burqa.
They could have been laughing uproariously or weeping fit

to fill a valley and he would never have known. The women here had men's names and never even smiled.

"That's what you like? When a woman laughs?" Dadou sounded surprised.

"There isn't a lot of laughing here."

"Plenty of cryin' to be done in our line of work, dahling," Dadou said. "You make hay while the sun shines."

"Do you like our line of work?" Jawid asked.

Dadou shrugged. "You want to talk about work now? I thought we were talking about you."

Jawid's cell seemed close and dark, his bed impossibly small. But it was private enough, and Eldredge had been giving him more of a free hand lately.

"I don't understand this." He turned to her. "You are a . . ." He couldn't bring himself to compliment her beauty; he didn't understand how men did it. He knew he should recite poetry, compare her to a flower or a jewel, but his head was spinning with the nearness of her and he couldn't find the words. "You are . . . different. I don't understand why you are touching me . . . talking to me. Because you like my hair?"

Dadou laughed a long time. Jawid didn't like this laughter. It felt harder. It bled the softness, the quiet intimacy out of the air. He felt his cheeks flush, tried to smile along with the joke. Failed.

"Oh, *mon petit chouchou*," Dadou said. "Don't be angry. I'm not laughing at you. No, it's not just the hair. Though it is pretty."

"What, then?" Jawid had always believed that he would first see his wife on their wedding day. The look he'd stolen at Anoosheh had almost cost him his life. She would also be seeing him for the first time; whether he was beautiful or not would not be at issue. If he was, he wanted to know; he was hungry to know, to hear her say it.

Dadou paused, sighed. Her eyes were huge, the pupils blending with the dark irises, so big that the sclera drowned in them, tiny slivers of white in an ocean of black. "Have you ever met another person with the *vodou*, Jawid?"

The loneliness in her voice evoked it in his own heart. "No," Jawid answered, his voice thick.

"*Se sa*. I don't know how I knew there must be others out there who were like me, but I knew. Maybe it is because of the *mistè*, how we link to them and they to us. It is a . . . community, *non*? But I never met anyone. You can feel it when it is real. The *vodou* has a touch."

"Like standing in a river, only it flows through instead of around you."

"*Se sa*," Dadou said again, "only the river comes from you, and you can feel it coming from others. But I never did. I always searched for it, but I never found it. After a while, I started to wonder if I would be alone forever."

Jawid only nodded. How could this be wrong? She *knew* him.

"And then the Americans came and took me," Dadou went on. "Do you remember when you first came here? Everyone is so rich! Then I finally did meet others with the *vodou*, but it was only to kill them. Once, I ran an op on a *Sèvitè* who used a homeless shelter as a cover. Most of her charity cases were dead."

"She was like us? A Summoner?"

"*Non.*" Dadou shook her head. "This was different. She did not call the *mistè* as we do. She did not venture into the beyond. She simply made the dead stand up and walk. They only moved by her will, not their own."

"A Necromancer, Doctor Eldredge calls them."

"*Nécromancien*. That's what we call them back home. Even then I was alone. I couldn't even find someone like me to fight."

"You killed her?"

"I sent my *sòlda yo an lò*, my 'Gold Operators,' to deal with her. Against them, her creatures had no chance. Even among the dead, it is better to be clever than stupid."

She paused, turned her head to look at him, and he could feel the current flowing from her, a liquid note of kinship. Here was someone to whom he need make no explanation.

She would just understand. How could Allah oppose this? How could this be sin?

"All my life, I have never known someone who could understand," Dadou went on. "I have never thought I could have a family of my own. Not a brother or sister, certainly not a husband. I didn't even know I could have a friend. Back home, everything was family. Now there is nothing. So, yes. I like your curls, and I like your eyes. I like how you are a grown man, but you shake and stutter like a little boy. But most of all, I like that you *know* what it is to live like this. I think this is part of why the program has put us together. They are not stupid. They know what we want, and they think by giving it to us they can keep us loyal."

Jawid felt as if he were floating. He could feel bubbles in his blood, so heady and intoxicating that he could no longer distinguish between the magical current and the giddiness brought on by Dadou so close beside him. "And what do you think?" he husked.

"I think," Dadou answered, "that in this one case, I am happy to be their puppet."

She leaned in. Jawid knew he was supposed to do something. He had seen enough infidel television and movies, but the truth was that no one had taught him, and it was one thing to know how people did a thing, and another to have practice.

But Dadou didn't mind. She giggled, whispered at his stiffness. "*Se byen, chouchou.* Let me drive."

Jawid was glad, because he wasn't sure that he could move under his own power now, anyway; the bubbles in his blood had made him weak, and the floating sensation was now competing with terror. What if he was clumsy? What if it made her change her mind? Made her laugh at him? And there was Izat and Allah Himself, shaking their heads in disappointment. *An infidel,* they said, *and you unmarried.*

Dadou's lips met his, and they were soft, the smell of her blotting out his senses. He could feel her dreadlocks brush his nose, his chin, his chest. He tried to return her kisses, but pursing his lips didn't seem to be what she wanted. She kept pulling away, then darting back in, following some rhythm that he couldn't understand. He raised a hand tentatively to the small of her back. He desperately wanted to touch her legs and her breasts, to plunge his hands into her hair, but his arms would not obey him. He was so terrified to do it wrong. He could not bring himself to think of Dadou as a wanton, but she knew so much more than him. At last she reached down, grasped his wrist, brought his hand to her breast. She was so soft, so beautiful. Shocks ran up his arm, as if he had touched a live wire. He left his hand there as she dropped hers, not knowing what to do, afraid to ask.

Dadou paused. "This is your first time?"

It was a simple question, but Jawid could not bring himself to answer.

She lifted her hand to his again, squeezed. "Like this," she said, her breath coming ragged. "Not so hard."

Jawid felt his hand move under her own, the whole world vanishing save for the softness of her beneath his touch. "I'm sorry," he said before he'd known that he'd spoken.

Dadou laughed, kissed him again. "Don't you worry, dahling. Mama Dadou will teach you everything you need to know, and the first thing you need to know is never to say you're sorry." But he couldn't help himself. Jawid apologized again and again as they fumbled through the act, wincing internally each time.

Izat's voice was clear in his mind. *When you enter upon your wife, you have first to perform two rak'ats and then hold your wife's head and say, "O Allah! Bless my wife for me, bless me for my wife, give her bounty out of me, and give me bounty out of her!" Then you can do what you want.* But Dadou was not his wife, and the moment they shared seemed to be made of spun glass, as though any interruption might shatter it.

"I'm sorry," he said again, cursing himself even as he said it. This time, it wasn't even for her. It was for Allah and

Izat and Anoosheh. He was weak, and he was lonely, and he knew that he would be judged anyway.

Dadou stayed on top of him, his hand still crushed to her breast. His back had begun to ache, and he realized he was clenching his body so tightly that the muscles were hard as rock. He tried to relax, tried to stop his mouth from moving, but he failed and he failed, and in the end, he said "I'm sorry" again.

Dadou stopped him with a kiss, easing her hand down into his trousers, grabbing his flaccid penis, squeezing it, pumping it. "It's all right, dahling," she breathed over and over, "it's all right." Only now Jawid felt his face flush in humiliation. When he touched himself, when he thought of her, of nearly any woman, he had always been rock hard, but now the one time that it mattered, his manhood was as soft as the cushion of Dadou's breast. *Will she think I am unmanned? Am I unmanned? Will it never get hard again?*

But Dadou squeezed tirelessly, leaning down every so often to kiss him. He was getting a little better at that, parting his lips just enough to admit the tip of her tongue, bringing them gently together each time she pulled away. After what seemed like forever, his penis felt rubbed raw, but it was a little harder, at least.

Dadou stood, slid her trousers down to her knees. The curve of her was all hard muscle, only the faintest hint of the edge of her hip rippling over the bone beneath. A wicked scar, thick and badly healed, ran from the side of her buttock down her thigh before winding its way behind her knee and out of sight. The evidence of rushed, rough stitching made him think of the Golds, and then his penis was soft again, but by then Dadou had mounted him.

She spat in her hand, a harsh sound, massaged it into her cleft. She guided his limpness into her, but it was so dry that she winced, and spat again, and again, rubbing and rubbing until there was enough wetness to get him inside by dint of sheer pushing.

And then the thought that he was doing it, actually making love to a woman who was not his wife, overwhelmed him. He had thought it would be the physical feeling, but it was something else. The knowledge that he defied Allah and his parents and the millennia of tradition that he had felt as heavy as the mountainside he'd grown up on, it was so incredibly, deliciously *wrong*. The thought set a fire in his loins, and before he knew it he was harder than he'd ever been.

Dadou grunted. She rocked back and forth, moving her hips like a saw. She closed her eyes tightly, concentration on her face. The workmanlike look diminished his own arousal, but the motion and the thought could not be denied, and within seconds, the pressure in him had built to a flood, and he slapped his palms on the bed, gripping the sheets tightly.

He cried out, feeling like the whole world, all his magic and all his soul and everything in him was letting go inside her. She was looking at him now, her movements slowed, satisfaction in her eyes. "That's good, *chouchou*," she said. *"Li bon."*

And then it was over, and he lay flat on the bed, all his muscles unclenching. A voice was chanting, "I'm sorry, I'm sorry, I'm sorry," over and over and over, and it took him a moment to realize that it was him. He closed his eyes, was amazed at how suddenly tired he was. All he wanted to do now was sleep.

"You don't have to be sorry," Dadou said. "You've done nothing wrong." But he kept saying it, couldn't stop.

Will she get with child? he wondered, amazed at how the thought both delighted and terrified him. Surely Allah would judge him less harshly if a son came from all this?

And suddenly his heart was full, swelling fit to burst out of his chest. He sat bolt upright, wrapping his arms around her, burying his face in her chest, breathing in her smell. He felt himself going soft inside her, fluid leaking out around him. It slid down his abdomen, soaking the sheets. He knew that seed staining his clothing made him impure in the sight of Allah, was fastidious about cleaning when need and weakness compelled him to touch himself. But now he didn't care. He loved this woman; they had joined. She would be his wife. He didn't care that she was an infidel; he didn't care that they had joined outside marriage. He didn't care about anything except for her.

Tears streamed down his cheeks and he pulled her close. Dadou's back went stiff. He could feel her pulling gently away. Perhaps she was frightened, but he would set her at ease. They could not have done what they had just done and not have love come of it. It was too wonderful, too magnificent. He gripped her more tightly.

"Gah," she gasped. "Easy, *mon cheri*. You are going to break my ribs."

"I'm sorry," he gasped, releasing her to cuff away a tear, kissing the tops of her breasts. "*Allahu akhbar*. That was wonderful."

"I'm glad," she said, touching his hair awkwardly. Of course. She was frightened. Loving someone was a frightening thing.

"I was betrothed," Jawid said, "but now it is you. I love you, my Dadou."

He felt her ribcage hitch against his face, her belly spasming. She was crying too; it was too much for her to hear him say it. He strained his ears to hear her say the same things to him.

A dry coughing, staccato barks from the back of her throat.

Laughter.

Dadou disentangled Jawid's arms, putting a hand gently but firmly on his throat, pushing him back down to the bed and sliding off him. The thin mixture of her saliva and his seed ran down her thigh, ignored. She grinned at him, but the smile didn't reach her eyes.

"Love?" she asked. "You are too kind to me, Jawid."

Jawid tried to look stern. He was a man. It was not for her to deny how she felt. He opened his mouth to refute her, but the words felt childish even as they formed in his head, so instead what he said was, "After what we have done . . . we must be married."

Dadou stared at him. "Married."

"It is what is right," he said, aware of how petulant he sounded, at a loss as to how to sound any other way.

"Married." She swallowed. She was trying to contain something. She was struggling, too. It was so sudden, but it didn't matter. They didn't have the luxury of families to match them, of a common faith. Jawid had felt her magical tide flowing around and through him; he knew he would never feel that again with anyone else. "What is right," she said, "depends on where you stand."

Jawid's stomach felt as if it was packed with ice. The swelling in his heart reversed itself, became a violent contraction. "You don't know what is right. People cannot do what we have done and then just . . . just . . . go on. This is God's will."

"God's. Will." She bit off each word, and the look in her eyes made Jawid suddenly afraid. He remembered their first private conversation together.

You've killed?

With my own hands, chouchou.

Who knew what she could do? What she would do? *Don't be ridiculous. She is still only a woman, and now she is yours. She only needs time to understand.*

Dadou drew a deep breath, closing her eyes. When she opened them again, the anger was gone. "I am . . . not sure I am ready. This is . . . sudden."

He stood, took her hand. It felt hot, the muscles in her fingers stiff. She twitched, as if she meant to pull away from him, stopped herself. "This is not a thing one waits for," he said. "We are *joined*; don't you see? What if a child comes of this? Will we raise it like an animal? We must marry."

At the word "child," Dadou's eyes snapped back to him, the simmering anger more intense than before. "I will consider this," she said. "I just need time."

"Time for what? What can I do to sway you, my love?" His heart was suddenly full again, and he choked on his tears, throwing his arms around her neck. She was as hard as iron, unmoving. He didn't care; he loved her. "Ask me whatever you need to be sure. I will do anything."

She reached up and broke his grip as easily as if he were a child, pushed him back until his legs hit the bed and he sat down hard. The anger in her eyes had been replaced by a coldness that frightened him more. "Anything."

"Anything," he nodded, love and terror mixing in his gut.

"I need your help with . . . some work."

Sick relief washed through him, making Jawid's knees weak. Part of him was disgusted at himself for wanting this conversation to be over, for being frightened to push her on the matter. He was the man, and what they had done made Dadou his tilth, his fertile field. *Go to your tilth as you will,* the Qur'an said. She was his now. She would come to see it; he would make her.

But not now. Maybe not just yet.

"What work?" he asked, disgusted at the quaver in his own voice, hoping against hope that she wouldn't hear it.

If she noticed, she gave no sign. "The most important aspect of our work," she said. "This is big, bigger than anything we've done before."

He felt his eyes narrow. A part of him mourned the loss of the conversation about love and marriage, the other part of him was roused by curiosity. "What do you mean?"

"I'll show you," Dadou said, taking his hand and pulling him up, leading him to the door.

"No," Jawid said. "We have . . . joined. We need to wash. We are unclean."

"We can do it later," she said. "I know what you smell like."

"It's not the smell," he said, "it is ritual impurity; the Qur'an says that . . ."

Dadou stopped short, her shoulder suddenly immovable, so that he bounced off her and staggered back a step. "I do not read your Qur'an. Do not mistake me for a Muslim. Back home, many people mistook me for a Catholic. These assumptions are . . . not helpful."

"We must," Jawid said, dropping her hand and heading to the bathroom. "Come."

He saw the struggle behind Dadou's eyes, the two Dadous, one murderously angry and the other warmly smiling, doing war with one another. At long last, the smiling Dadou won and she sighed. "All right."

She suffered through his prayers and even consented to wash herself. She let him lead her to the bed and draw her down next to him. "I love you," he said, and she didn't answer, but she put one hand on his head and traced circles in his chest hair with the other. He floated on the tide of joy and contentment, feeling the sparks through his whole body at her touch, his eyelids slowly growing heavy. He snuggled his face into her chest and shut his eyes. Not to sleep, just to inhale her smell and feel her softness against him.

But he knew he had slept for hours when he finally opened them again. The softness of Dadou's breast had been replaced by the firm cushion of his pillow. She was standing, looking at him, as if she had been waiting for him to wake the whole time.

Jawid opened his mouth and the danger returned to Dadou's eyes. "You said you would do anything," she said. "Did you mean it?"

And then she was pulling him along again, and even though she frightened him, he was grateful, because the touch of her hand meant she still loved him, meant that he hadn't dreamed what had passed between them.

She led him into the stairwell and took him down several winding flights, down a bare corridor lined with doors. The facility was big, but Jawid had been here a long time, and while he had been down each corridor at least once, they all looked the same. White, sterile-looking cinder-block walls, stainless steel doors with keypad locks above each handle. At last, they came to a door with a red sign engraved with white lettering: RESTRICTED AREA WARNING: IN ACCORDANCE WITH THE PROVISIONS OF THE DIRECTIVE

ISSUED BY THE SECRETARY OF DEFENSE ON 10 DECEMBER 2005.

Dadou turned to Jawid, put a hand on his shoulder. The touch felt intimate at first but soon tightened painfully. "This task comes to us straight from the program director. It is not from Doctor Eldredge. He does not know about it and you must not tell him."

Jawid's mind filled with questions. She had talked to the Director? When? How? Jawid had heard Eldredge mention him, but never anything beyond that. Why couldn't they tell Doctor Eldredge? Eldredge was his jailor, but he had been kinder to him than anyone. But the dangerous look was in Dadou's eyes again, so all he did was nod, swallowing.

Dadou gestured back to the sign: UNAUTHORIZED ENTRY IS PROHIBITED. ALL PERSONS HEREIN ARE LIABLE TO SEARCH. PHOTOGRAPHY OF THE FACILITIES IS PROHIBITED WITHOUT SPECIFIC AUTHORIZATION FROM THE COMMANDER. *DEADLY FORCE IS AUTHORIZED.*

Jawid felt the muscles in his back cramp, a chill rippling beneath them as a bead of sweat worked its way from the back of his neck to the top of his buttocks. Dadou keyed in the code, the lock beeping and clicking open. She turned the knob and dragged him inside.

The room was simple enough, an old freeze-burn cell of the sort they used with Operators. The scorch marks on the wall had been painted over sloppily, the smell of the drying paint still lingering in the air.

A single recessed fluorescent light shone down on them from the ceiling, the plastic cover partially melted and streaked with cleaning fluid where some enterprising soul had tried to scrub off the soot before finally giving up.

Below it was a padded chair like the one the post dentist had Jawid lie in when he worked on his teeth. It had straps over the legs and arms, wide and strong-looking, with shining metal buckles.

A man struggled against them. He mumbled around a ball gag, powerful muscles bulging as he pushed against the straps fruitlessly. One eye was blackened, a lump rising just below his forehead. Jawid had seen enough gunshot wounds to recognize the hole in his shoulder. It was dressed, gauze soaked with still-moist red going brown around the edges. Whoever this man was, they were trying to keep him alive.

Dread blossomed in Jawid's stomach. He knew what the work was now and why Dadou had brought him here.

"Our new work is the same as our old," Dadou said. "Only the vessel is different. It should be easy."

Jawid stared, nausea rising up his throat. He looked at this woman that mere moments ago he had thought he would marry, and shuddered.

A man. Not a corpse. A living man.

They were going to put a jinn in him.

CHAPTER XV
ALL THE DEAD
CAN DO IS PROTECT

Schweitzer ran.

Patrick bounced in his arms, no longer screaming. The boy had tripped over the line of terror and sadness into a pale-faced silence, meekly accepting the rough ride of Schweitzer's panicked gait.

Schweitzer was just as numb. *You turned and ran while monsters killed your wife.* From what little he'd seen, there hadn't been anything left bigger than a softball.

Oh God. Sarah. He pushed the vision of the red ruin of her body aside, only to find it replaced with memories of their life together. Applauding from the audience as she'd stood to accept the Best New Artist award from the Tidewater Chamber of Commerce. They'd made love in his car that night, so blind with passion that one of them had kicked the window out.

He remembered kneeling on the deep pile of the kitchen throw rug, his head in Sarah's lap as he shook and cried, the phone swinging by its cord, sentenced to hang after delivering the news that cancer and grief over Peter's death had finally taken his mother's life. His brother and his mother, just months apart. *I can't be strong right now,* he'd sobbed.

She'd run her fingers through his hair, letting her hand drop to the back of his neck. *You don't have to be, babe,* she'd said. *I can carry us until you're ready again.*

It was one of the rare times Schweitzer ever fully gave himself over to another human being. It had taken him the rest of the night to get it together, and he had never felt so safe. She had his six. She wouldn't let him fall.

Had he told her how grateful he was? He couldn't remember.

You're a coward.

No. You ran because she told you to. He'd run because she'd told him to save their son.

He slowed, dialed out his hearing, listening. He could hear the helo rotors still in the distance, vainly circling above the canopy where the fight had gone down with the Golds, no doubt searching for him. He'd opened up a good-enough lead on them while they were busy with Sarah.

She'd bought him the time he needed. He had to make good on that.

He looked down at Patrick, pale as death save for the puffy red blotches on his face and arms, his blond hair so streaked with dirt and gore that it looked black. The boy was terrified of him. He would only respond to his mother. He needed her.

Schweitzer needed her too.

Sarah's body had been destroyed, which meant her soul would be in the void even now. His link to her had helped him find her in life, would it in death?

Just a quick second, he told himself, *just to see.* He had let her die. He had watched her die. He needed to tell her he was sorry. *You should have saved her. You should have found a way.*

Sarah was the strength he'd drawn on to do the dangerous work of a SEAL, and the lifeline he'd followed out of the Gemini Cell's facility and back into the sunlit world. Their love was a thing so strong that it was a magic in and of itself, a bond that linked them through death and time and distance.

A part of him, the cold professional who carefully weighed risk and outcome, stayed focused on the mission, knew there was no good reason for this. Schweitzer couldn't bring her back to life, had no way to comfort or even communicate with her in the chaos of twisting souls.

But that part of him was crushed under the heel of the other part, the husband and best friend, the man who had known and loved Sarah from the moment he'd met her. That part of him had to see her in the beyond, just to know, just to . . . *just to say goodbye. You didn't thank her enough. You didn't tell her what she meant to you. Not clearly enough. Not nearly often enough.*

Schweitzer had felt the pull of the link between them even when he'd thought her dead, and he still felt it now. It pointed into the darkness of the void, the place where Sarah now tumbled, sucked into the spinning chaos of the soul storm.

Schweitzer turned his focus inside himself, felt the darkness at the edges of his physical form, pushed out into it. The cold of the void wrapped itself around him. He felt the edges of his own body slip past and recede.

Schweitzer felt the undertow of the soul storm, slowly reeling him in, hungry and grasping. He pushed against it, holding his position, keeping a watchful inner eye on his own body in the distance. He concentrated, reaching out for Sarah's presence, trying to feel the link that joined them.

There it was, so faint he could almost miss it. Sarah's distilled soul, always coming to him in the same way: the touch of her rosewater perfume, a phantom scent he could follow to its source. He inhaled deeply, filling spiritual lungs with the fragrance. It grew stronger as he went, clearer, until he could almost see the edges of the stream, the smell leading arrow-straight into the storm.

This close, the screaming was deafening. Schweitzer's spiritual ears pulsed with the chorus of shouts beginning to move past mere hearing, speaking directly into his mind. A litany of battle cries, regrets, and last testaments. Schweitzer felt them chipping at the edges of his consciousness, trying to suck his identity into the tangle, desperate to turn it over and over until he didn't know who he was anymore.

Sarah was somewhere in there.

Schweitzer pushed deeper, hauling himself up the trail of his wife's perfume, calling her name. He was forging too far, too deep. The undertow had seized him, was pulling him deeper and deeper into the throng.

A part of him didn't care. He was desperate to reach Sarah, no matter what the cost. He snarled, pushed on. But the other part of him, Schweitzer the SEAL, forced him to slow, to push back. *You're no good to Sarah, to anyone, if you get lost in this morass. Withdraw for now. Come up with a plan. Come back when you're ready.*

The thought of Sarah screaming and tumbling in the maelstrom almost made Schweitzer continue, but then his own voice put the hammer down. *No good to Sarah. No good to yourself. No good to Patrick.*

Patrick.

Save my son, damn it!

Schweitzer turned back, following his own sense of self back into the limits of his body, feeling the void shrug off and reality snap into place with a ringing that sounded in his ears.

Not ringing, crying.

Patrick was sprawled on his face, nose bleeding.

He'd dropped him. He'd been so focused on exploring the void that his body must have relaxed. He'd dropped Patrick on his face.

"Oh, my god. Oh, Patrick. I'm sorry," Schweitzer knelt and scooped up his son, dusting the dirt off his face, checking the scratches. "You okay, little man? Daddy's sorry. Daddy's so sorry."

He'd had years to build a bond with Sarah, something that could sustain their relationship in times of trouble. He'd had far less time to build it with Patrick. Their relationship was truncated, stopped cold the moment the men who'd murdered Schweitzer had entered his home. His uncle Peter was dead. His uncle Steve was dead. Now his mother was dead. All the warm hearts and kind faces who were ready to teach Patrick how to be an adult, all snatched away before the boy was old enough to appreciate how much he needed them.

Patrick sniffled, but the crying stopped. *He's getting used to me. He's starting to realize that just because I look like a monster doesn't mean I am one.*

"Want Mommy," Patrick said, cuffed at the poison ivy rash on his face.

Schweitzer folded him to his chest. "Me too," he said, feeling tears that would never come, the rigidity of his tear ducts, dried and hardened. The grief threatened to swamp him. His chance to be a father to Patrick had been stopped before it really started. They had no relationship beyond Schweitzer's duty to keep him safe and alive. "I want Mommy, too."

He looked back down at his son, filthy, scratched, and with a serious case of poison ivy. He'd lost Sarah. He wasn't going to lose Patrick, too.

And the boy would never be safe at his father's side. Not now.

"Okay, pal," he said, scanning their surroundings, dialing his hearing out for the sound of a neighboring road, a town, even a group of hikers.

"Let's get you fixed up and then find some place safe for you."

Though where that place was, Schweitzer didn't know.

In the end, Schweitzer broke into a convenience store.

He waited for Patrick to fall asleep, then tucked the boy over his shoulder and moved silently down into the parking lot, where he made Patrick a bed of cardboard and plastic bags. "Just for a sec," he whispered, more to himself than his sleeping son, and stood.

Patrick huddled, ragged and filthy, in the nest he'd built.

His Tiny Tim, his beggar boy. *Oh God, Patrick. I've failed you.* And now he was walking away, leaving his child alone in the dark like an after-school special.

"I don't know what else to do," Schweitzer whispered aloud as he jogged over to the drugstore loading dock, tried the handle of the rusted blue door. The SEAL in him had replaced Ninip as his partner in internal dialogue. *Parenting is for the living. All the dead can do is protect.*

The door wasn't alarmed. The tight-knit relations of a small town were enough to deter most of the crime. It was hard enough to steal from a stranger, and in these little hamlets, everybody knew everybody. For those who could overcome the instinct to do right by one's fellow man, a stout lock did the job.

But Schweitzer didn't know anyone here, and his magical strength twisted the lock off its mounting like it was soft clay.

Inside, darkness shrouded the stainless steel racks of greeting cards, laundry detergent, and shampoo in orderly rows. He remembered corpses in the same orderly rows when he'd stormed a freighter off the Virginia coast. He'd had a beating heart then, had breathed sweet air. *Stop it. Focus.*

He grabbed a child's backpack from a section of the store marked by a giant cardboard ladybug with the words BACK TO SCHOOL blazoned across her back. He filled it with rubbing alcohol, calamine lotion, hydrogen peroxide, sterilizing pads, gauze, medical tape, and two boxed first aid kits. To this he added a Coleman stove and plenty of fuel, cans of spam and beans, and bottles of water. He grabbed a child's elf costume. The tights and shirt were brown and green, at least, and they were clean. At last, he leapt the counter into the pharmacy, snatching up a double handful of orange plastic bottles of antibiotics.

He paused, listening. Hushed whispers in a house some distance away. Someone had heard some noise, was debating going to check it out, being talked down by a worried wife. Schweitzer heard the relief in their voice as they acquiesced. No one was coming.

He rummaged back through the bag, paused as the moonlight caught his hand. It was shredded, more bone than flesh now, the ragged gray striations of the muscle visible where the skin had been peeled back, or burned off, or simply rubbed away. He could only imagine what it must look like to Patrick, to anyone. Dirt packed the holes, bunched around the tendons.

Schweitzer cursed and roved the aisles until he found a roll of duct tape. He spent fifteen minutes taping over the various gaps and rents, pausing every so often to listen for breathing, footsteps, any indicator that someone was drawing closer. No one was. He could still hear Patrick's breathing, slow and steady and even. The boy was where he left him, sleeping.

Schweitzer surveyed his handiwork. Striped with duct tape, he looked . . . less horrible, but no more human. It would have to be enough. He shouldered the bag and headed back out the door.

He crouched beside Patrick, gently lifted the boy up and over his shoulder again. His son didn't struggle, didn't moan, gave no indicator he'd noticed at all. He was dead weight on Schweitzer's shoulder, his slow breaths the only indicator that he was alive. The events of the past few days had taken that much out of him, or it was simply safer in dreams than in the waking world.

Schweitzer made sure they were a good distance into the woods, and that the only sounds near him were animals, before he bent to his task. He cleared the ground as best he could and lay Patrick down, then set to work cleaning himself with bottled water and alcohol before doing the same to the boy's face. Patrick didn't scream when he came awake, merely stared at his father sullenly as he submitted to being washed, cleaned, and then liberally smeared with the calamine. Schweitzer cleaned his cuts and bandaged them as best he could. It wasn't until he was mostly done that he realized he had been humming softly out of instinct, an old nonsense lullaby that he'd used to sing to his son at bathtime.

Patrick looked up at his father, staring exhausted into his skull face, his burning silver eyes. "Daddy," he said.

"Yes," Schweitzer choked the words out. "I'm your daddy."

"Are you a monster?" Patrick's eyes were wide.

Schweitzer almost said no, stopped himself. Patrick had seen so much. It would do no good to lie to him now.

"Yes," Schweitzer said, "but there are different kinds of monsters, sweetheart. Some are good monsters, and some are bad monsters. Daddy is one of the good ones."

"Good monster," Patrick said.

"Yes."

"Mommy. Want Mommy."

"I know, sweetheart," Schweitzer answered. What else could he say?

The imagery from the link between them flared in his mind; he fought the memory down, but not before it gave him a painful glimpse of what had transpired. Sarah had been with Steve. She had fucked him. She had loved him. She had belonged to him.

She thought you were dead. What the hell did you expect?

There were so many questions he wanted to ask her, both wanting and not wanting to know the answers. *Were you sure I was dead? Did you try to see my body first? Was Patrick close enough to hear? Was it good? Did you come? Did you think of me?* But above it all were two questions pulsing in alternating tandem, one blinking on as the other blinked off: *Why? How could you? Why? How could you?*

His mind was quick to provide him with a flood of cuckold's fantasies: Chang's sweating back, Sarah's nails drawing red lines across it. Schweitzer still remembered the soft moans she made, the dirty words she used, the way she said "please" when she was close to orgasm. He remembered them now in vivid detail, always with Chang in the foreground. His wife, his best friend, a cliché out of a bad movie.

The vision was replaced by the blurry distance, Sarah as a red mound, pieces of her detaching, the gray shapes of the Golds fighting over them. Schweitzer inventoried each lump. That might have been her arm, or her elbow, or her foot. He hadn't focused enough to tell; he'd known he wouldn't be able to bear it.

The temptation to go after her, to quest into the void, was so strong he almost succumbed, but he forced himself to look back at his son. *Sarah is dead. Patrick is alive. Take care of your son.*

"Come on, big man," he said, taking his son's hand, "let's get you somewhere safe."

Patrick held his hand, toddled along beside his father. Frightened, shaken, but starting to realize that the thing beside him wasn't going to hurt him. Maybe the duct tape over the wounds helped, but Schweitzer doubted it. Schweitzer had to stoop low to walk beside his son, knew he should scoop him up so they could move at a faster clip. *Not just yet,* he thought. *Let the boy walk for a moment. A few minutes won't make a difference.* More likely that it would, but Schweitzer forced himself to match his son's fumbling gait anyway.

"Good monster," Patrick repeated.

Schweitzer nodded. It hurt to hear it, but that didn't make it any less true. "The best."

"Where we goin'?" Patrick asked.

"Well, where would you like to go?" Schweitzer asked. His own mind worked feverishly. Where could he take Patrick that was safe? The Gemini Cell was a classified program embedded deep in the intelligence community; that meant it likely had its hooks in all over the country, the ability to tap local law enforcement or the FBI. They clearly had mercenaries at their beck and call, if Gruenen was any indicator. Where could he go where they couldn't find him?

Patrick tripped over a root, clung tightly to his father's finger to stay upright. Schweitzer began to swing him up into his arms, relented when Patrick squalled, "Nooooooo," continued to let the boy toddle at the maddening, slow pace.

Sarah was right. They want you. They aren't after Patrick. They'll take him if they can get him, but that's a lot more likely if he stays with you.

No. He's dead if you leave him. You're the only one who can protect him.

Protect him to what end? What did he think would happen? He was a walking corpse, animated by magic. He was a horror to look at, an immortal being purpose-built for war. Did he think he could go back to life as a father? Drop Patrick at the school bus each day? Go to his high school football games? Teach him to ride a bike? All of that was lost to him. His focus had been too tactical. It was time to pull the camera back, time to ask the big question. Sarah was dead.

Why go on?

To protect Patrick. That was the obvious, the only, answer. *What do you want for him? What could be salvaged from this mess? He's still young. He can heal. He will have a hard time with what he's seen, but he can get past it.*

You can't have a normal life. He can.

But not while the Gemini Cell existed. Eldredge had seemed kindly, Jawid naïve, but Schweitzer's tour through the Sorcerer's memories had shown him what he needed to know. They would do anything, absolutely anything to further their "program." While they lived, Patrick would never be safe.

While they lived.

In all his time with the Cell, Schweitzer had never seen another person who could do what Jawid could. Maybe killing him would stop things cold. Maybe by holding him hostage, Schweitzer could extract a promise of Patrick's safety. Maybe by surrendering himself, he could get them to forget the boy. All of those plans were paper-thin, all of them more likely to end up with both him and his son physically destroyed and sent to the soul storm, but Sarah was right that they were better than the current option: run senselessly, endlessly.

And all had one thing in common: they were dangerous. Infiltration missions requiring a lone operator with powers like his. He couldn't do it with Patrick under his arm. He had to find somewhere safe for the boy.

A hundred strategies rose in his mind and were instantly discarded. He could drop Patrick at an orphanage. He could find a kind and good adoptive family desperate for a child. All were ridiculous. All would put Patrick and whoever took him in at terrible risk. Families weren't experts in OPSEC; they wouldn't know how to keep his son's origin a secret. The Gemini Cell would find them.

His mother and brother were dead. Sarah's sister was a flake with a mild drug habit and a string of questionable boyfriends. Her father was gone, her mother in the early stages of Alzheimer's. He needed someone frosty, someone trained.

He needed SEALs.

His heart sped up as he thought of Chang. The man had been completely dedicated to Schweitzer, his family as an extension of himself. He would have risked anything, gone any distance, to keep Patrick safe. *Maybe that's why he fucked your wife. Because he loved her.*

Stop it. This won't help.

Chief Ahmad was a company woman. Her first and sole loyalty was to the nation. She would never sell out a teammate, but her by-the-book attitude meant that if the government came knocking, she'd salute and do what she was asked. He couldn't ask her to take that risk. Ditto for Lieutenant Biggs. Martin was a religious fanatic who believed an invisible man in the sky had told him to hate gay people. Who the hell knew what he would get up to? What things he would ask Patrick to get up to?

That left Perretto.

Schweitzer's heart quickened a little at the thought. As the lone Coast Guard assigned to the team, he was outside the decision-making circle. If any of Schweitzer's brother SEALs had been co-opted by the Gemini Cell, it likely wasn't him. Schweitzer knew he had two children of his own. Perretto had botched his takedown during their last mission together, nearly getting the whole team killed. He was still stinging over it, but that didn't change his heart. Schweitzer remembered his quick and irreverent sense of humor, the mischievous turn of his mouth. Was he the sort of man who would defy his own government? Who would take in a child with no questions asked? Schweitzer had no idea, but he did know the bond between operators was strong, and Perretto was the best chance he had.

Schweitzer knew that after his botched job, he wouldn't stay with the team in Little Creek; he'd be "reattached" to his original unit, the Pacific Tactical Law Enforcement Team in San Diego, California.

Nearly three thousand miles away.

Schweitzer nodded internally. The distance would do double duty. It was a place to run to; it was a direction to run in.

And he knew just how to get there.

CHAPTER XVI
DOESN'T ANYONE KNOCK ANYMORE?

The analyst did her level best to look nonchalant, but she was trained to crunch numbers, write software, and pull needles out of giant data haystacks. Working for a spy service didn't make her a spy. Eldredge could see all the classic tells, refusal to make eye contact, increased breathing, sweat sheening from the hollows of her neck where they showed through her thin green blouse.

"What do you mean, I can't see Jawid and Dadou?" Eldredge racked his brain for this analyst's name. Joseph? Daniel? "I am the lead scientist on this program."

"I'm sorry, sir," she said, trying to keep the quaver out of her voice and failing. He decided her name . . . her cover name, at least, was Matthew. "They're cloistered right now."

"What the hell does that mean?" It was times like this that the kindly Samuel Clemens look he'd worked so hard to cultivate backfired. On the one hand, it made others more likely to trust and open up to him; on the other, it made them less likely to obey him when he was trying to put the hammer down.

"It means they're unavailable, sir," the soldier behind her answered. "It means you need to check back later."

Eldredge scanned the man's blouse for his rank, noticed there was none displayed. That meant he was assigned directly to the Cell. It meant he wasn't going to blink, but that wouldn't stop Eldredge from trying. "I was here when they brought Jawid in. I have been with him every day since. I have never, not even once, been denied access to him."

The soldier shrugged. "Guess there's a first time for everything."

The analyst frowned at the floor, looking pained.

"This is going to be bad," Eldredge seethed, hating himself for not having more self-control, "for both of you."

He spun on his heel and stormed back to his office, feeling the soldier's smug grin burning against his back the entire way.

Eldredge slumped into his chair, crossing his arms over his chest, staring at the clutter on his desk. It soon became clear there was no answer there, so he pulled up the commlink and called the Director.

He heard the low buzz, saw the icon blink as the call went through.

Nothing.

What the fuck is going on? The Director had never failed to answer him before. Eldredge wracked his brain, going back the years since he'd come here. His secretary had at least answered. Eldredge had never had to wait more than fifteen minutes. He'd just assumed that the Director lived in his office, worked around the clock. *Like me.*

Eldredge broke the connection and pulled up the overhead layout tracking the Golds. The triangles flashed. They were fanning out west, moving in a pack. Schweitzer had moved off along a ravine, and Eldredge was betting that he'd followed it. The mop-up team showed as a blue square, hovering over the last place they'd seen Schweitzer. They were busy cleaning all traces of the Golds' presence.

They were dealing with what was left of Sarah Schweitzer's corpse.

Eldredge had only glanced at the image before turning away. The Golds had been in a frenzy. They had been thorough. There wasn't much left. Eldredge swallowed his revulsion. Sarah was a threat to the program; he knew that. He knew what the price would be if she were allowed to leak details to the public. He knew how they would react. The Gemini Cell would be shut down, and repulsive as they might be, the alternative was worse. But it didn't change the fact that Schweitzer was a good man and Sarah a good woman. *What would you have done? Asked them nicely to come in? You know as well as anyone that Sarah Schweitzer wasn't going to allow herself to be captured.*

More lives would have been lost if a human team had tried to engage Schweitzer. He'd watched the videos of Operations Jackrabbit and Nightshade over and over again. He knew what Schweitzer could do. Sarah had a good heart, but it was still just one heart weighed against the dozens or even hundreds that Schweitzer would stop beating if mortal humans tried to capture him. The Director had done what he had to.

So, why did it feel so wrong?

He looked back to the map, watched the blinking phalanx of Golds sweeping south and west, drawn by the promise of the heartbeat they had missed, Schweitzer's son, Patrick.

Sarah would have blown the whistle on the program. He'd read her file. He knew how she'd fought like a cornered bear to save her son when her husband had first been killed. *She wouldn't have let it go. She would have found a way to have revenge.*

But Patrick was a child. He was far too young to understand what he'd seen to be believed, even if he could communicate it.

Yet there were the Golds, running down his trail. Eldredge pulled the map out until the red rings representing the circling drones came into view. He toggled from camera to camera, trying to find one that had a clear shot through the dense forest canopy. He cycled through the feeds until he saw the flickers of gray shapes, then dialed in on the ground below.

And froze.

He called up the commlink and dialed another number.

"Ops," came a woman's voice.

"This is White," Eldredge said. "I'm punched into Eyes Seven, and I . . . I don't like what I'm seeing."

"Are you sure you have a clear view, sir?" the ops boss asked. "Might be you're not sure what you're seeing."

Eldredge fought the ball of rage threatening to make him shout. You never got anything done that way. "I have a clear view. It looks like the action element has found . . . something."

The ops boss sighed on the other end. "Yes, sir. That's a campsite. We're waiting for them to finish and then we'll send the mop-up team to their position."

"So, you knew what I was seeing." Now Eldredge couldn't keep the edge off his voice.

The ops boss sighed again. "Just trying to make sure we're talking about the same thing, sir."

"How many?"

"How many what, sir?"

"How many did they kill this time?"

"We won't be able to get a count until the mop-up team gets there, sir. The Golds aren't exactly great at math. From what I can see, it looks like somewhere around twelve."

Eldredge dialed in further, maximized the camera feed, squinted at his screen. "Jesus . . . Are those . . . are those uniforms?"

"Yes, sir." Ops sounded bored. "Looks like Boy Scouts."

It was a long time before Eldredge could speak. "We just massacred a scout troop."

"The Golds aren't responding to the incentives, sir. We were hoping you might be able to talk to the Ops Taskers." She meant Jawid and Dadou.

"Keep me posted," he said, and cut the connection.

"We will, sir," she lied just before the line went dead.

Eldredge stood, whirled, and stormed back to the lab

entrance. The analyst had gone, but the same soldier was there, hands crossed behind the small of his back, eyes fixed on Eldredge's approach.

As Eldredge came within striking distance, the soldier put his hand out. "Sir, please. Don't make me . . ."

But Eldredge could tell that his narrow shoulders and white hair had already put the soldier at his ease. He didn't believe that this old man with his bushy moustache and white lab coat was any threat at all, wasn't prepared for any real resistance.

Eldredge knew he wasn't strong enough to fight him, was flying by his gut now, the strange feeling of working without a plan both exhilarating and terrifying. He needed to talk to Dadou and Jawid for just a moment. He had to find a way to bring the Golds under control. He'd figure the rest out as he went.

The soldier's expression went from smug and unafraid to shocked as Eldredge brought his hand up, spread his first two fingers and poked him in the eyes.

The soldier sputtered, seizing his wrist, bending double.

Eldredge reached smoothly under his elbow and grabbed the door handle. It was one of the newer ones, with an embedded palm reader, which was probably why they'd posted the guard in the first place. Eldredge felt it warm as it read the signature of his pulse and unlocked.

The soldier grabbed his elbow, blinked tears. "What the hell do you think you're . . . ?"

Eldredge smoothly switched hands, using his free one to turn the knob and open the door. He shook the other arm free from the guard's grip. "What are you going to do? Beat up an old man?"

"If I have to," the soldier said, seizing Eldredge's arm and jerking it back, locking his elbow, and bending his wrist painfully. "You have lost your goddamn mind. Jesus, you little shit."

Eldredge struggled, unable to match the younger man's strength, knowing he was already beaten but refusing to give in. The soldier put more pressure on his arm, and

Eldredge bent at the waist, desperately trying to give his shoulder some relief from the feeling that it might pop out of its socket.

And then the soldier froze. Eldredge looked up from beneath his brows, and all thoughts of pain vanished.

Jawid and Dadou crouched over a chair, faces drooping in shock and guilt, like cheating lovers caught in the act by a husband who came home early. But Eldredge's mind only briefly acknowledged them, turning instead to the chair and the figure bound in it.

It was padded and fitted with buckled restraints, like some fetishist's dungeon prop, stuffed black faux leather with thick white stitches. Or, at least, he thought they were white. The entire assemblage dripped with blood, sheeting from the body of the man strapped into it. He looked like he'd bled from every orifice in his body. Thick crimson runnels streamed from his nose, his ears, his mouth, his genitals. Beads of the stuff had formed on his face and chest, as if he'd sweated it.

Eldredge looked at the purple blotches just beginning to form across the man's body. There were no visible lacerations, no bruising. This man hadn't been cut or beaten. He'd torn himself apart from the inside out.

"You shouldn't be here." Dadou sounded sheepish.

"What the fuck is this?" Eldredge asked, the words choked off as the soldier hauled on his arm, dragging him back.

"Let him go." Dadou sounded tired. "You've already failed to keep him out."

"Sorry, ma'am," the soldier said, sniffing and blinking, releasing Eldredge, who staggered forward a few steps before straightening.

"Get out and close the damn door," Dadou barked at the soldier. Eldredge had just enough time to glare at the soldier before he complied.

Jawid stammered, shot a terrified glance at Dadou. She gestured, a mere movement of her wrist, palm outward, and the Sorcerer instantly stilled, shoulders slumping. "I'll handle this," she said.

"That"—Eldredge stabbed a shaking finger toward the man in the chair—"does not look like a corpse."

Dadou placed two fingers against the dark line of the man in the chair's carotid, slowly going an unhealthy shade of purple. The tips came away wet and crimson. "He is dead."

"He is recently dead," Eldredge said. "That is fresh blood."

"Dead is dead," Dadou said. Jawid swallowed.

"You killed him. Who was he? What the hell is going on here?"

"What is going on here is not your concern, *Doktè*."

Dadou was leaner than the solider he'd just evaded, but her body was all muscle, and there was something in the set of her mouth and eyes that made him think that she'd be more than happy to mete out those consequences herself. The soldier was a man in a uniform doing his job. Dadou had the look of a person who had a different relationship with the value of human life. The thought made his heart rate speed up, but he didn't let it show. "I run this program, damn it. You do not tell me what is or is not my concern."

Dadou stepped closer. "You do *not* run this program, *Doktè*. You are an employee, the same as I. This program is run by the taxpayers of the United States. You are just a public servant."

"I am the public servant from whom you take orders. There is a chain of command."

"Yes, there is, and you are bound by it just as I am. My orders come from a higher authority, and if you have concerns, you are welcome to take them up with him."

Eldredge's blood went cold. "The Director ordered you to murder someone? Why?"

"We are in the killing business," Dadou said. "Or had you forgotten? The targets, the incentives, the collateral damage. Why is this one suddenly a problem?"

It was a good question. Eldredge only knew that it was. *Because you met Schweitzer,* he thought. *Because you got to know him. Because he made you realize that there is more going on behind those burning eyes.* He thought of the town of Basye, the offhanded casual manner in which the Director dismissed all those deaths.

That doesn't look like a gas explosion, sir.

Not yet.

He thought of the ragged remains of the scout troop, the ops boss's bored tone. *We won't be able to get a count until the mop-up team gets there, sir. The Golds aren't exactly great at math. From what I can see, it looks like somewhere around twelve.*

He thought of the ruined pile of flesh scraps, all that remained of Sarah Schweitzer.

"Wait here," he said. "Don't do another goddamn thing until you hear from me." He spun on his heel and stormed off, breezing through the door and past the soldier, who was chattering something into his radio. Dadou shouted something at his back, but Eldredge ignored it, the bit already between his teeth. A small part of him knew the truth, that he was leaning on momentum now, that if he stopped, the fear would take control, and he would lose the will to do what he was about to do.

This is what Schweitzer would do.

He stormed past his office and into the stairwell alongside the single elevator shaft at the end of the hallway. He took the steps two at a time, following the elevator shaft up one floor, two, then three. This was the subsurface level, the place he'd foolishly allowed Schweitzer to live on, never thinking he would try to make his break. *He played me. No, I don't think he was the type to play anyone. He wanted to be closer to the surface because it felt more like living. And that's what he wanted more than anything, to be alive.*

At last, he crested the top flight, threw open the door, and marched across the hall to the opposite doors. They were big and metal, the only ones without cipher locks in the whole facility. That was because the Director's vestibule lay beyond, manned by his secretaries twenty-four hours a day. They were drawn from a pool of block-faced and broad-shouldered professionals, humorless, each one dedicated to protecting the Director's privacy. Eldredge had only met them the few times the Director had been unable to take his calls, or when he'd had to drop off a thumb drive for the Director's eyes only, a file too big or too sensitive to send over the network.

The fear pricked at the back of his neck, and he felt his knees wobble. *If you keep going, you might well be killed. But if you stop now, you'll live, and hate yourself for every second that you do.*

He dropped his hand to the handle of the KA-BAR, tucked into its sheath in his waistband. The feel of the ridged leather handle steadied his nerves. He thought of his father, advancing under the withering fire of German guns. *This is just a conversation, and the Director is just a man. Grow a pair.*

He drew the KA-BAR out. It was an antique weapon, but a weapon nonetheless, and the sharp edge against his thumb would remind him of that.

He froze, blinked.

The blade was glowing.

A jinn was nearby. Eldredge stared at the blade, then looked around. Apart from the stairwell door and the doors to the Director's vestibule, there was nothing.

He paused, listening. The only sound was the static hiss of the climate control system blowing air through the vents overhead.

Was the knife . . . broken somehow? Had the magic gone sour? *No, magic isn't machinery. It doesn't wear out. It has never been wrong before. A jinn is near.*

He sheathed the knife, squared his shoulders, and with a final glance at the air vents, opened the double doors.

The secretary was already rising from behind the ebony desk, her reflection distorted by the stainless steel walls. "Doctor Eldredge, you didn't call. How can I help you?"

"Mark, good to see you." She could have been swapped with any of the other secretaries who manned the station and he would have been hard-pressed to spot the change. He hoped he'd gotten her cover name right.

"It's always a pleasure," she beamed, the polished presentation contrasting with the tension in her muscular arms. The welcoming smile didn't reach her eyes.

"Sorry for not calling in advance, but something's come up and I need to speak with the Director."

"Certainly, Doctor," Mark said, sitting down in front of her computer. "I can block you out for a video conference right away."

"Thanks"—Eldredge tried to keep his tone casual—"but I think this time, I need to talk to him in person."

Mark's smile went from forced to pained. She snorted a quick laugh. "Come on, now, Doctor. You know the Director doesn't see anyone."

"He sees you."

"Not very often. I'm afraid he values his privacy very highly, as I'm sure you understand. It's critical that we keep all aspects of this program, and identities in particular, as compartmentalized as possible."

Eldredge looked around for a chair, but there wasn't one. The office wasn't designed to accommodate those with a mind to wait around. Eldredge leaned on the corner of the desk, ignoring Mark's sour look. "Well, this is really important. I need to speak to him right away."

His eyes drifted over the ebony desk's reflective surface. It was bare save for a phone and a computer, one of the upright models where the monitor housed the whole works. Sticking out of its side was her ID card, inserted to allow her access to the network.

Eldredge glanced to the door to the Director's office, noted the black contact pad beside it. He couldn't be sure that Mark's card would unlock it, but he bet it would.

"Certainly." Mark clicked her mouse and brought up the Director's calendar. "Is this an emergency? I can . . ."

Now or never. Eldredge thought of the man in the chair, swollen and bleeding. He thought of his order to Dadou to bring Jim and Patrick in alive. He thought of the Director's drunken tone when he told Eldredge to handle Senator Hodges. He thought of the fires burning in Basye, the bodies in the streets. *Now. The Director has lost his mind. You have to talk to him now.*

Eldredge wasn't as fast as he once was, but he was more than fast enough to reach out and yank the card out of its reader, turn, and reach the Director's office door in three strides. He slammed the card against the contact pad.

Nothing.

Mark spun in her swivel chair, leapt to her feet. "God damn it . . ."

Eldredge cursed, tapped the card against the contact reader again and again. Could he have been wrong?

A sharp beep brought relief so strong that he nearly sagged against the door.

Mark's hand settled on his left wrist, clamped down painfully. "This is going to hurt you a lot more than it's going to hurt me."

Eldredge drove for the door handle with his left hand, but Mark's grip was like iron, and he knew he wasn't going anywhere. His right reached back for the KA-BAR, whipped it out of its sheath, the blade glowing so brightly it nearly blinded him. *Idiot. What do you intend to do with that? You're going to stab her?*

But Mark let him go, leaping back at the sight of the raised blade. "Fine. Let's do this the hard way," she said, pulling open one of the desk drawers, hand reaching inside.

Eldredge saw the black plastic of a pistol in her hand as he slid through the door and felt it click shut behind him.

The room beyond was freezing.

A second click sounded as the door lock engaged, sealing him in darkness so total that he thought he had gone blind. He raised the knife, holding it up like a torch. The light slowly adjusted his eyes, casting dancing turquoise shadows around the small space, energy smoking in the refrigerated cold.

Eldredge slowly became aware of a high, clacking sound, traced it to himself. His teeth were chattering, breath coming in plumed clouds from his nose and mouth.

The KA-BAR's light intensified, glowing so bright that he had to hold it at full arm's length away from his slitted eyes.

"I don't recall you having an appointment." In person, the Director's voice was a wheezing, high-pitched rasp. The sound of it stole the last of Eldredge's resolve, and fear and revulsion took the reins, forcing him back a step until his back pressed up against the door. He fumbled for the handle with his free hand, failed to find it.

The teal light finally found the corners of the room, showed the edges of a plain concrete floor. The ceiling stretched high above them, a pitch-black shaft leading who knew where, beyond the reaches of the brave light. The room was bare of furnishings. A wheeled computer stand stood in the center, a closed laptop resting on the single narrow shelf.

The Director stood behind it. His muscular frame was draped with an ill-fitting black suit, a tie askew at his throat. His hands hung at his sides, covered by thin leather gloves. A single piece of stretched white fabric covered his head and face, a reflective surface against which the light played. He looked like a store mannequin poorly dressed for display. Only the movement of his lips under the white cloth gave any indicator that he was the one speaking.

Behind him, three Gold Operators stood along the featureless far wall.

Their bodies were withered, ancient, the old muscle looking hard and narrow as braided plastic, the skin stretched across it brittle and peeling. They were crowned in beaten gold and tin, stepped geometric patterns of plants and faces, animals and people, all surmounted by the blazing corona of a stylized sun. Their necks and chests were hidden beneath massive pectorals of the same metals, studded with rough-cut gems that refracted the KA-BAR's light. Their waists were draped in dirty linen, gone to dusty rags at the fringes of what had once been gorgeous metallic brocade. Their withered feet were tied into rotten leather sandals, hints of bone showing through where the toes had worn away. Their arms were drawn up in X's across their chests, hands resting over their collarbones.

Their eyes burned, tiny pinpoints of flickering light, staring straight ahead. Without pupils, he could never tell when a Gold was looking at him or not.

"I assume there is a reason for this downright suicidal intrusion, Eldredge," the Director said.

"Sir, I . . ." He couldn't form words. Couldn't think. He could only stare at the Director's shrouded silhouette, at the gloriously arrayed living dead behind him. Why had he come here?

"Eldredge." The Director slowed his words. "You barged into my office. Now, if you want to barge back out again, you had better tell me why."

The threat jarred Eldredge's nerves, brought some of his focus back. He became conscious of the cold again, realized that terror wasn't the only reason he was shivering. "Sir, I've just come from Dadou and Jawid. They . . ."

"Dadou and Jawid are cloistered, Eldredge. They're not supposed to see anyone until they have completed their latest project for me. I had them under guard for that very reason."

"You didn't discuss it with me, sir."

The lips under the white mask twitched, sliding against the cloth as the Director formed words. No other part of him moved. "I am not in the habit of discussing things with you. And you should not be in the habit of having things discussed. We have a chain of command in this organization. We follow orders."

Eldredge fought the urge to fumble for the door handle again. "Sir, they had a freshly killed subject in there."

"I know what they had in there, Doctor. I am the one who ordered them to have it."

"Has there been a change to the program? We don't—"

"We don't until we do, and we do when I say it is time. We are reviving the old program. Virgo Cell."

"Virgo? Sir, that failed for a reason. A living subject can't house a jinn; we have stacks of results that—"

"I have reason to believe that Dadou has had a breakthrough in this arena. Working with Jawid, she is making progress."

"Sir, I just came from the room, and that subject is dead. The manner of his death is consistent with the Virgo Cell failures."

"*That* subject is dead, Doctor. Maybe the next one will be as well. We will keep trying until we get it right."

"How many? If we're continuing along the lines of the Virgo program, these are *service members* we are killing."

"As many as it takes. Service members sign up to die. That is part of the oath they take when they enlist."

"And our oath as leaders is to only spend those lives when we must."

"Agreed. And we must. These are not good men, Doctor. We are using the ones who would be breaking rocks in Leavenworth, or on death row. This way, they serve their country even on their way out."

"Sir, this is out of control. The Gold Element just massacred a scout troop in the George Washington National Forest. This is right on the heels of Basye. We are going to out the program. We were set up to defend American lives, not slaughter them."

"We are defending American lives. Eggs to omelets, Doctor. You of all people know the threat we face. We are making the hard choice necessary to keep this nation stable."

Anger competed with the fear and, for a split second, won the upper hand. "Senator Hodges is furious. We can't keep being this careless. I need Jawid and Dadou full-time on getting the Golds wrangled back under control. We need to find Schweitzer and bring him back intact. We need to figure out what makes him tick. That's the only way, the *only* way we're going to be able to save this program. That's the only way we're going to be able to do this right."

"There is no *we*, Doctor. There is *me* giving instructions, and there is *you* carrying them out. I am fully aware of the disposition of the Gold Element. I am fully aware of the current operational taskers set before our magical assets. I am fully aware of the challenges this program faces in the Senate. I am fully aware of you contravening my orders and directing Jawid and Dadou to bring Schweitzer and his son in alive and intact. I appreciate you underscoring your concerns, and now I invite you to close your mouth and sit on them. I and not you will decide the best way forward. If you do not feel you can continue, please submit your resignation to Mark outside *after* you have apologized for whatever means you used to gain entry here."

Eldredge's mouth went dry. "Resign?"

"I grow tired of you questioning the decisions of executives. The Gemini Cell is founded on decisive action in the face of a rapidly growing and existential threat to the nation. We do not have the luxury of ethical struggles here. I value your work, Doctor. You have been an essential building block, a piece of the foundation of all we've built here, but if you labor under the delusion that you are *indispensable*, that we cannot proceed with what is arguably the most critical work in this nation's history without the earnest trembling of your most endearing mustache, then you are sadly mistaken.

"Do you know why you are still alive, Doctor?"

"I . . ." Eldredge felt his knees go weak.

"You know every line item in every contract we hold. You know the idiosyncrasies of every soldier and analyst we employ. This program is a tangled weave of a million different threads, and you know just where they are whenever I want them pulled. I will be honest with you. It would take me years to train someone up to the point where they could handle your duties with the efficiency and competence you show, even if I could find someone who wouldn't run screaming at the first mention of magic.

"But I will also be honest with you in that I will find a way to soldier on without you if all this doesn't work out. If, like Jawid, you suddenly decide that your heretofore singular dedication to the advancement of this program is wavering, that other priorities are coming to the fore, I will lose my patience. Because, unlike Jawid, you are not a Sorcerer, and that means you can be replaced.

"Now, I have suffered your uninvited entry into my *sanctum sanctorum*. I have *explained* myself to you, something I have never done in the history of this program. I am willing to chalk this up to some feverish humor of your brain and let it go, provided that you walk out of here, forget this entire ugly incident, and get back to work, this time providing whatever assistance Miss Dadou Alva requires. Her project is to be your first priority. You are to do whatever she asks. That is the alternative to your . . . resignation, Doctor. That is the choice before you."

There was no resigning from the program, Eldredge knew. He'd known it from the moment he'd first signed his nondisclosure agreement. It would be difficult to out the program even with specific evidence, because no one would believe him, but he also knew that the Director, even Senator Hodges would never risk it. Eldredge could dream of retiring from the government someday, living a comfortable life in Arlington, Virginia, under the watchful eye of the FBI, but resigning? Pursuing work in the private sector? Being free to travel to a foreign country or talk to the press? No way.

To resign was to die. Which, he supposed, was the Director's point.

"Do you have anything else you would like to say?" the Director asked. The wet, rasping voice. The completely motionless body, save for the lips rising and falling behind the white mask. No skin exposed at all, not a sliver.

Eldredge's hand finally settled on the door handle. He didn't realize that it had been questing for it all this time, the fear giving it a mind of its own. His head worked side to side, a refutation of a number of questions, none of which had been asked. *No, I don't think I can defeat you. No, I don't want to work for you anymore. No, I don't understand what's going on here.*

No, I don't want to die.

Unasked questions. The Director responded to the asked one. "No? Excellent. Dismissed."

The handle turned and the door opened. The three Golds along the wall twitched in time, leaning toward him. Eldredge quickened his step, nearly falling over himself in his sudden hurry to escape. The Director spread his fingers, turning one of his hands out, palm toward the Golds. They stopped as if he'd flipped a switch.

"Close the door, Doctor. We wouldn't want to let all the cold air out."

Eldredge stood gaping, grateful that his bladder was empty. It was Mark who reached across him, slamming the door shut.

The vision of the Director was seared on his brain. The dark room, the biting cold, the shabby suit pulled clumsily over the vaguely human frame, the head shrouded in white fabric, like a lamp bulb stripped of its shade. Every inch of skin covered.

I didn't see him breathe, Eldredge thought. *I didn't see his chest move at all.*

Only the lips beneath the fabric. Only the hand to gesture the Golds to stop, and only after a few minutes.

The room must have been below freezing. No living man could have survived in there long, not in such thin clothing. The warm blood in his veins would have eventually filled with ice crystals, gone solid.

But the living-dead Operators had no such concern. Their veins were full of glycerol, their skin waxen. Their chief worry was to preserve dead flesh that could no longer heal, and for that, you needed cold that a living man couldn't abide for long.

Eldredge shivered, and not from cold this time. The jinn were intelligent but slaves to their appetites. He'd always thought of them as animals, a step above trained dogs or messenger pigeons. So long as the blood addiction ruled them, they could never be a threat to humanity.

Animals couldn't think, couldn't plan, couldn't make grand strategies.

But Schweitzer did, didn't he?

Eldredge's mouth went dry. His eyes focused on his desk. He was back in his office with no memory of how he'd gotten there. He'd been so focused on the positives of Schweitzer's breakthrough that he'd been blinded to the threat behind the idea. *You wanted an Operator that could think. But what happens when that Operator's agenda isn't in sync with your own?* That made Schweitzer a threat.

And what if the Operator's agenda isn't in sync with humanity's? That made it a loose nuke.

Eldredge remembered his conversation with Senator Hodges, when he described the thing that Schweitzer was now. He'd told him that Schweitzer wasn't more powerful than a Gold Operator, but *as powerful. He combines this with a highly intelligent, rational mind that has the ability to discipline itself. He's also able to access his training and experience in a way that the Golds can't. He's not blinded by bloodlust. He can think.*

Eldredge leaned forward in his chair. His chest felt tight; his breath coming in whooping gasps. Sweat broke out along his brow and ran down his temples, tracking behind his ears. He put his hand to his chest. His heart was hammering, but it was doing it regularly. Not a heart attack, then. A panic attack.

He tried to slow down his thinking, to focus. What was the right call here? He couldn't get back in the Director's office, and even if he could, there was nothing he could do. He couldn't kill a dead man. He could go to the press. No. They wouldn't believe him, and by the time anyone could verify his story, *if* they could verify his story, he'd be finished.

Senator Hodges. Again, no. He had no way to contact the Senator. His regular reports went through the Director's office. The man had only visited the facility twice in the past year, and then with no forewarning whatsoever. And even if he could get off campus to contact him, he had no guarantee the Senator would help. Maybe the Senator even knew? *No, he wanted to see the Director, and the Director refused.* And now Eldredge knew why, knew why the Director refused to see not only the Senator but *anyone* all these years. Only his secretaries. Were there others?

But not Hodges. He remembered the man's curled lip, his threats to shut down the program. It would be one hell of a risk to reach out to him. Just because it would be news to him didn't mean that he wouldn't support it, or be angry at Eldredge for going outside his chain. Politicians served their own interests first and foremost.

Doesn't matter. You can't stay. Your boss is walking dead. You've got to get out of here.

He forced himself to stand, felt his knees wobble. He thought briefly of contacting Jawid, dismissed it. If the Director hadn't killed him where he stood when he'd stormed into the room and put two and two together, it was because he wanted to keep Eldredge on, felt he could still extract use from him even with his identity revealed.

That means you have time. They're not going to kill you. You can figure this out. Are you sure you want out?

It was the only real life he'd ever known. He remembered brief flashes of his past. The University of Illinois at Urbana-Champaign, his brilliance as a fluid engineer leading to a career as a Navy scientist. That's where the Cell found him. It seemed so long ago that thinking on it was like watching a biographical film about a stranger. No, the Gemini Cell was his life.

But he thought of the ruins of Basye, of the overhead camera's view of Sarah's shredded remains. He thought of the Director snubbing Hodges, of his lack of concern with an end of funding for the Cell.

He thought of his father on D-Day, tried to recall the last photograph he'd seen of him standing in uniform, rifle slung over his shoulder. Eldredge imagined his strong jaw, his determined gaze. He pictured his father under the withering Nazi fire, churning the sands of Omaha Beach around him, advancing steadily regardless. He knew what his father would do in his situation. But Eldredge thought of the Director's chest, how utterly still it was, even as his mouth moved, telling Eldredge to close the door to keep the chill air from escaping. Eldredge thought of the crowned Golds surging toward him, stopping at a twitch from the Director's hand, and admitted that he wasn't his father, never had been.

He knew that now.

CHAPTER XVII
THE PLAN IS WEST

"You ready?" Schweitzer asked his son. The metal wheels were thrumming on the rails, still a quarter mile out at least but as loud as pounding hammers to his magically enhanced hearing. He lifted Patrick up, tucking him tightly against his belly. Patrick hooked his hands into the ragged remains of his father's web belt. Even now he wouldn't suffer being close to the silver flames burning in Schweitzer's eye sockets.

But he wasn't crying, and the angry red welts on his face and arms were starting to recede under the medication's touch. Patrick still had his limits, but he was letting Schweitzer handle him more, responding to the sound of his voice. He was, with time, getting used to him. A part of Schweitzer grieved the development. He didn't want his son to live in a world where monsters, even good monsters, were a fact of life. He didn't want Patrick to understand that the walking dead came in varieties, that you could tell the tenor of their hearts by the color of the fire in their eyes. He could feel Patrick's youth warping under the pressure of what he'd been through, a plant permanently twisted by poisonous air. He turned away from the thought. He could no more dwell on it than he could on the thought of Chang's sweating back, hips pumping away at Sarah beneath him.

Schweitzer set off at a run, keeping his center of gravity low, arms locked to hold Patrick in place, keep the boy from bouncing too much. Patrick's hands dug into Schweitzer's forearms as he picked up speed, sliding along the duct tape that held his wounds closed.

"We're going to see the train!" Schweitzer said to him. "Don't you want to see the train?" The benefit of complete breath control meant that there was no panting, a weird even temper to his voice that defied the speed at which they were covering ground. "See the tracks?"

He spun Patrick in his arms, turning him outward as the ground rose alongside them, sloping gently up through a scramble of softball-sized stones until the surface suddenly flattened and twin metal lines cut across it, arrowing straight ahead and out of sight. The scent of creosote was cloying, interspersed with the thick smell of rust. The tracks began to vibrate, a high, metallic pinging sound as the train drew closer.

Patrick squinted as the wind picked up his hair, but he pointed at the rails before Schweitzer spun him back around to shield his eyes.

He felt the ground shaking, heard the metal wheels rumbling louder and louder, until at last he turned and put on a burst of speed, Patrick's shriek drowned out by the noise of the train rocketing past them. Schweitzer watched the cars stutter-flash past, the locomotive well ahead, the freight containers flying by, corrugated sides painted in giant block letters. Schweitzer ignored them, looking instead for the sliding car doors, the huge padlocks that held them shut. A normal man might be able to run fast enough to grab hold of one of the speeding cars, but without a solid foothold, there was no way he'd be able to break the lock and open the door.

A normal man.

Schweitzer broke from the cover of the trees and pushed

up the rise. The rocks slid under his feet, and for a sickening moment, he thought he might pitch under the spinning metal wheels, but he found his balance a moment later, picked up speed until he matched the car briefly. There was no keeping Patrick stable now. The boy jolted and bounced and cried as Schweitzer leapt, reached out, and hooked his fingers into the top of the lock, yanking downward. He felt the bones in his fingers tremble, and he sprang before they could give, providing him enough reach to clasp his entire hand around the piece of metal, shearing it away.

And now he did stumble, his strides lengthening, feeling his balance pitching toward the train, the gravity of the spinning metal wheels pulling him, as if they were hungry, eager to chew up his dead body and his son's living one with equal gusto. He fumbled Patrick, staggered as he caught him, reaching out a hand to push off the train's side.

He missed the train's side, slipping under the car and into the undercarriage; the top of the spinning wheel blazed heat on his palm. He snatched the hand back, overbalanced, began to fall. Patrick slid in his grip, tumbled. Schweitzer growled, snatched him under his arm like a football, pushed off with his legs.

His shoulder collided with the train door, hard enough to dent the metal. His body rebounded, then fell back in toward the spinning wheels. He reached out, desperation welling in his throat as his hand slid down the flat surface.

And settled on the handle, still trailing the remains of the broken lock.

His weight swung the clasp open, and the door hauled back, dragged by his body. He tucked Patrick in tighter, bracing himself for the door to slam into its terminus, the rubber stopper, making the whole structure shake. His arm straightened, taking his weight, and he grunted, pivoting his mass and pulling himself around, throwing them both into the car.

The door slid forward, Schweitzer's momentum momentarily stronger than the wind, and slammed shut, closing them in darkness as Schweitzer skidded into a pallet stacked with plastic pipes hard enough to shake them against the holding straps.

The train thrummed away beneath them, wheels pounding in time with Patrick's sobs.

Schweitzer lay still for a moment. He'd shut his eyes out of instinct, and he kept them closed, letting his other senses paint the picture of the car's interior.

A fresh breeze blew at them from the car's front end. A connecting door between cars, open. He could hear Patrick's little heart hammering away, just beginning to slow as his mind processed that he was safe, that they had stopped moving.

A second heartbeat, rising as his son's fell. It was bigger, a man's heart. That man was crouched at the far end of the car, frozen by the sudden appearance of Schweitzer and Patrick. He wasn't trained for this. The scent of it was in his sweat, pores opening to exude adrenaline, the high stink of norepinephrine mixing with the sweet smell of a dramatic spike in blood sugar. A civilian, then. That was good.

Schweitzer tucked Patrick against the stack of plastic pipes and rolled into a crouch, opening his eyes to let the silver flames dance for whatever audience they'd found.

It was a young man. He had risen to his knees on a dirty foam bedroll. A cloth knapsack was held together by patches and duct tape. His blond hair was formed into dreadlocks that trembled around his face. His chapped lips worked in his dirty beard as he said, "Hang on, man; hang on, man," over and over. A hobo, a stowaway. He must have hidden himself somewhere as the train was loaded, before the locks went on.

"Shut up," Schweitzer rasped. The young man did.

He knew he should kill him. The man had seen him, seen Patrick. No good could come from letting him live to tell the tale willingly, or have it surface under questioning. The average cop, even a very good one, wouldn't believe him. But the Gemini Cell would.

Patrick stirred against Schweitzer's thigh. "Mommy," he sighed.

Schweitzer cursed and slid the door open a fraction. "Jump," he said to the hobo. "Take the bedroll; leave everything else." The bag might contain food, or medicine, or camping supplies.

The young man started to speak.

"If you are not out of this car in the next five seconds," Schweitzer cut him off, "you are meat."

The boy nodded, raced for the opening, hesitated at the prospect of drawing near Schweitzer.

Schweitzer grunted and snapped out a hand, lightning-fast, tapping the boy's back. He squealed and jumped.

Schweitzer didn't look to see where he landed. The fall might hurt him, but provided that he could still move, he would be able to find help if the Gold Operators didn't find him first. Schweitzer felt a twist in his gut like the one he'd felt when he'd slaughtered the guards keeping him in the underground Gemini Cell facility. But as with them, he shrugged it off. They had been keeping him from reuniting with his family. This boy's life and health were not going to take precedence over Patrick's. He didn't want to hurt anyone, but if he was going to be a monster, then he may as well be one to protect his own.

He knelt beside Patrick, checked him over for cuts or scrapes. The boy came to him, folding against his chest, crying into the ragged remnants of his tactical vest. Schweitzer held him apart just long enough to ensure he wasn't hurt, then brought him back in, conscious of his own chemical smell, of the chill, rubbery feel of his skin. His embrace couldn't convey warmth, which came from blood. He didn't have any of that, not anymore. At least the child's costume Patrick wore under his ragged clothes kept him warm.

"It's okay," he whispered.

"Hungry," Patrick said.

The word tore at Schweitzer, a reminder of how quickly his own humanity was slipping away. He didn't have to eat, so it was easy to forget that others needed food. He didn't have to sleep, so it was easy to forget that others needed rest. *You cannot protect him if you starve him to death.*

Schweitzer tucked Patrick against his side and went to rummage through the bag. The filthy leather buckle parted at a twitch of Schweitzer's fingers, spilling out the contents: a plastic bag that contained at least a pound of marijuana, a battered copy of a paperback novel, plastic bags stuffed with pills, and a dead smartphone wrapped in its charger. Deeper in the bag were things Schweitzer could actually use: a rusted pocketknife, a box of matches that looked like they'd been dropped in water but dried again. A ball of twine and a packet of wet wipes. A few unopened packages of chemlights.

Two old and dry-looking granola bars, mostly crumpled inside their bleached foil packaging. *How the hell did this kid eat?*

It wasn't like there was a café car. The freight train had been heading west when Schweitzer had hauled himself and his son on board, and he slid the door open just wide enough to reckon the sun's position before shutting it again. Angling more south now, but still mostly west. He was trained as a maritime counterterrorism operator. If there had been a class on domestic rail lines, he'd missed it.

Schweitzer pulled out a can of beef stew from the child's backpack he'd taken from the convenience store. He slid out a bone claw, punching easily through the thin metal and working around the can, peeling it back, then he handed it to Patrick. "Here you go, little man."

Patrick took the can tentatively, sat staring at it. He brought it to his face, frowned, his upper lip quivering.

Schweitzer's dead stomach turned over. *It's cold, you moron. You need to warm it up for him.* If it had been mere stupidity, it wouldn't have caused his soul to contract in horror. But it wasn't. Schweitzer had forgotten that little children couldn't heat their own meals. He had forgotten that they needed help from their parents. He had forgotten how to be a father.

And if he didn't remember, Patrick would die. *You're*

*like a monkey playing with a gold watch. Just because you
don't want to break it, doesn't mean you won't.* He would
save Patrick from the Gold Operators only to lose him to
his own new state of existence.

*Oh God. Sarah. I need you. I don't know how to do this.
Stop. This doesn't help. Focus.*

Schweitzer set up the camping stove and set the can on
it. Patrick stared at them doubtfully.

"Come on, little man," Schweitzer said. "It'll just take a
minute."

"No!" Patrick said.

"Fine," Schweitzer proffered him the can again. "You
can eat it cold." *Idiot. He needs a spoon, at least.*

"No!" Patrick said, thrusting his hand into his armpit.
"No! No! No! No!"

Schweitzer winced.

"I don't want that!" his son shouted. "Hungry!"

But all of Schweitzer's magical power couldn't conjure
up a sandwich or a glass of milk. Anything to eat would be
somewhere out in the countryside around them, rocketing
past at one hundred and fifty miles per hour. If they jumped
off, they wouldn't get getting back on. And the Gold Operators were somewhere behind them, sniffing out their trail.

"That's what there is," Schweitzer said. "Sorry."

He held Patrick as the boy raged and sobbed, peeked his
head out the door again to reckon the position of the sun
once more. Still west.

He had no idea if they were on the same latitude as San
Diego. He had no idea if the train kept on in this direction
as it went. Maybe it would turn north. Maybe it would
double back entirely. He had no idea how to find his former
teammate.

But San Diego was west, and that's the direction that, for
now, they were heading.

It was something.

CHAPTER XVIII
PUSHED TOO FAR

Dadou came to Eldredge's office a few hours later.

She stood in the doorway, arms folded, shoulder casually resting against the jamb. "I told you that you shouldn't have come in there."

Eldredge swallowed the ball of panic in his gut, resisted the temptation to reach for the KA-BAR. Dadou was at least twenty years younger than him and athletic. She'd take that knife away from him and stick it in his eye. "Are you here to kill me?"

Dadou laughed. "No, *Doktè*. I'm a Sorcerer. We have people who handle the wetwork; you know that. The *Direktè* wanted me to talk to you."

"You . . . you've seen him?"

She laughed. "No. That's an almost unique privilege you can lay claim to."

Should I tell her? Maybe she already knows. Would it make a difference to her? "He's . . ."

Dadou held up a hand. "The less I know about him, *Doktè*, the better. All you need know is that he has been good to me, and where I come from, that kind of thing buys loyalty. *Eske ou konprann?*"

"I'm not going to try to talk you out of anything. Do I still run this program?"

"No, *Doktè*, you don't. But there is still plenty of work to be done, and we can use your help in doing it."

"The Virgo project."

"That's right. You've seen it now."

"I saw the aftermath of a failure. A bleeding corpse tied to a chair. We've been down this road, Dadou. We know exactly where it leads. You can't Bind a jinn into a living man without killing him."

"You Americans are all so smart; you know that? The less you know about a thing, the more sure you are that you have nothing to learn."

"I know what I saw."

"Weren't you a scientist before you came here?"

Eldredge thought of his lab at the university, whirlpools and model pipelines. Lab experiments to determine how fluid moved and why. "I still am."

Dadou laughed. "Really? You live in a world with a real afterlife. You live in a world where magic is real. How can you call yourself a scientist now?"

"Magic isn't . . . it isn't magic. There's an explanation. Just because we don't know the science behind it doesn't mean we won't learn eventually. There just hasn't been time to test, to study. We've been too busy . . ."

"Killing," Dadou finished for him.

"I was going to say 'protecting the country.' I still believe in science, Dadou. Magic hasn't changed that."

"Perhaps, but your analytical skills are poor. You lack a skeptic's natural ability to instinctively question. Just because you saw one corpse doesn't mean that they all end like that. Some people are stronger than others. Some resist the jinn with greater . . . enthusiasm."

"Are you saying that you've succeeded?"

"Come with me, *Doktè*. I want to show you something."

He stood, followed her down the corridor and into one of the cold storage units. "I hope this one is still alive," she said. "If he isn't, then you'll have to take my word that he . . . Oh, good."

She stepped up to one of the sealed access doors, thick steel with a panel of transparent palladium in the center. She gestured. "Take a look."

Eldredge stepped closer, squinting through the clear metal, adjusting to the sudden sense of vertigo that came from the fishbowl effect it always had on the view beyond.

A man stood in the center of the plain white room. His soldier's uniform was stained with fresh blood. He stood with his back to Eldredge, arms hanging loose at his side. His neck was crooked at what look like a painful angle, head rigid on his shoulder.

"Another Gold," Eldredge said.

Dadou laughed. "Golds are gray, *Doktè*. Does he look dead to you?"

Eldredge squinted, then his eyes widened. The soldier's neck was the angry purple-red of a sunburned bruise. That meant blood. He glanced around the room, looking for the telltale misting of the Freon injectors that kept the room refrigerated. Nothing. Dadou had put the soldier in here to keep him contained, not to keep dead flesh cool.

"So?" Eldredge tried to keep his voice even. "He's newly dead."

"Is he?" Dadou reached across Eldredge's face and rapped on the transparent pane.

The soldier jerked, pivoted on one foot, faced the door.

Eldredge stifled a scream as he recognized the soldier who'd failed to stop him from getting to Jawid and Dadou. His uniform was unbuttoned at the front, the angry purple flush extending all the way down to where his stretched T-shirt cut it off. Badly corded muscle stood out around the ugly bend in his neck, blotched in darker purple where veins had clearly burst. Fresh blood tracked from his nose and the corner of his mouth.

"Private First Class Welch felt so terrible about letting

you invade our privacy," Dadou crooned, "that he asked if there was anything he could do to make up for it. It turned out there was."

Welch's face was screwed up in agony, lips drawn back in a fixed grimace, teeth gritted together so hard that Eldredge was surprised they didn't crack. Men in pain moved, their lips twitching and chins trembling, but Welch's face was frozen, as if he had begun to scream and suddenly stopped. His eyes were wide, and Eldredge felt his mouth go dry at the sight.

Pupil and iris were nearly a matched purple-black. The sclera was the bright red of burst capillaries.

But they were whole, human eyes. There were no flickering flames.

Eldredge could see Welch's chest rising and falling rapidly. Hyperventilating, a rabbit's super-rapid, super-shallow breaths. At the sight of them, Welch took a staggering step forward, arms coming up. Eldredge knew the man was still alive, but he looked more the zombie than any of the dead Operators.

Eldredge gave a strangled cry and backed away from the pane as Welch lurched against it, hammering his hands against the palladium, leaving sticky red handprints. He gibbered in a language Eldredge didn't understand, the angle of his neck straining his windpipe and forcing the words out in a bubbling, choked wheeze.

"Jesus," Eldredge breathed.

"As you can see, he's very much alive," Dadou said. "I have done better, and I have also done worse, as you have seen. But I am improving, and with the right . . . preparation, I know I'll be able to get it right reliably in the near future."

"How . . ." Eldredge fought against the rising sickness in his gut. He had seen horrors in his time with the Cell, but this exceeded all of them. "How soon?"

"At the rate I'm improving?" Dadou asked. "Very soon, Doktè. Very soon. I suppose we should thank you for convincing Welch to volunteer."

Eldredge shuddered. He had gotten the drop on the

soldier for a split second, and the man had paid for it with his life. "Is this supposed to be a threat?"

Dadou flashed a vulpine smile. "The Director asked me to underscore the consequences of . . . how did he put it? Violating strict rules of need-to-know."

Eldredge's head spun. "Will he live?"

Dadou shook her head. "You're not asking the right questions, *Doktè*. Whether he lives or dies doesn't matter. What matters is what this means for the future of our program. We are on the brink of . . . expanding our capabilities beyond anything we ever dreamed of. I will be able to have one of our jinn wearing a living man's skin. I do less damage to the host each time, and eventually the jinn will live behind their eyes. Dominating only the spirit, the space inside."

"That's . . . possession."

"*Se sa, Doktè*. That is what you call it. For us, it is, as the soldiers say, 'an overmatch capability.' Do you know what a possessed man says, *Doktè*?"

Eldredge looked at her.

"Whatever you tell him to." Dadou's smile grew wider.

"How the . . . How can you control the jinn?" Eldredge asked.

"By giving them what they want more than anything else in the world. With the Gold Operators, we have created your horror-movie zombie. With Welch, we are creating your horror-movie vampire. They are in warm bodies with beating hearts. The frenzy is dampened. They can *think*."

Eldredge looked back at Welch, his frozen face pressed up against the transparent metal pane, smearing the bloodstains across his nose. "He doesn't look like he's thinking."

Dadou shrugged. "He is *much* better than a Gold, and as I said, I am getting better at this. I promise you, with time, I will be able to make them perfect."

Eldredge took a step back, shaking his head. Dadou put a hand on his shoulder.

"When they are perfect, they will be able to go

undetected anywhere we choose to deploy them. Think about it, *Doktè*. No more devastation as there was at Basye. A single Operator who responds to commands. We won't need to keep on with the Gemini program in the futile hopes that we'll get another Schweitzer."

Eldredge still said nothing, his stomach doing somersaults.

"Think about it! With a Silver Operator, we are dependent on the subject being . . . as unique as Jim Schweitzer. With a Virgo Operator, we'll be able to repeat the process at will. It will be reliable, a known quantity. A game changer. Isn't this what you wanted?"

Eldredge nodded agreement. *No,* he thought. *This is absolutely not what I wanted at all.*

His conversation with the Director came racing back to his mind with such force that he almost sat down on the floor.

Sir, did you hear me? It's Senator Hodges.

I know perfectly well who he is, Eldredge.

Then you know that he's the man who funds this program.

I do. I'm not available right now.

It explained Basye. It explained the Director's almost-insane willingness to deploy the Golds without a second thought. Because if the Director could turn a living person into a jinn answering to him, then he wouldn't have to worry about answering to anyone.

"How fast can you do it?" Eldredge asked.

"How fast can I do what?"

"How fast can you master this . . . putting a jinn in a living host?"

Dadou shrugged, but she sounded troubled. "It takes as long as it takes, but we have time."

Eldredge cocked an eyebrow. "Do we?"

Dadou grinned. "You're talking about Senator Hodges, aren't you? His threats to shut the program down and put us all under the Army."

"You know about that?"

Dadou waved a hand. "Of course I do. The *Direktè* doesn't trust you anymore. That means that he has to trust me. And I am not worried. Hodges is like all politicians. He yells and screams, and in the end, he does nothing."

"I'm not so sure you're right."

"It doesn't matter what you're sure about."

"Then why keep me alive at all?"

Dadou squeezed Eldredge's shoulder firmly, her fingertips digging in just below his collarbone. "You transgressed, *Doktè*. You violated compartmentalization protocols. But the Director has told me that in spite of what you've done, you're needed on this program, and he is giving you a chance. I need to know that you're with us, Eldredge. I understand that this may frighten you, but you of all people understand the benefit here? The Golds are like . . . *yon eksplozyon* . . . an explosion, *non*? This will give us a laser. No more . . . collaterals; no more shotgun blasts. Eggs to omelets."

Eldredge nodded, desperately trying to work saliva into his mouth, to keep his knees steady. Welch had slid away from the panel, was wandering aimlessly inside the cold storage unit, blood dripping from his twisted nose. He wasn't hurling himself against the door, which was an improvement over the Golds, but not by much. Maybe Dadou could do what she promised; maybe she couldn't. It didn't matter to Eldredge either way.

Dadou's grip tightened further, and Eldredge winced. "Are you on board, *Doktè*? The Director is giving you this one chance. We need to know that you're with us."

Eldredge couldn't make himself give her the answer he wanted, so he stalled for time. "What about Jawid?"

Dadou's eyes narrowed, a simmering anger gathering behind them. He winced as her grip tightened further. "*Sa se pa yon repons, Doktè*. Jawid is Jawid. I am asking if *you* are with us."

Eldredge shook off her arm. "Yes."

Dadou advanced on him, hands twitching. "You're absolutely certain?"

Eldredge's belly was sour with fear. Dadou looked like she was itching to strike him. "Yes, of course."

The anger vanished as quickly as it had come, and Dadou smiled again. "That's good to hear. I knew we could rely on you."

Eldredge took a step back, trying desperately to keep the horror off his face. He briefly considered telling her that the Director giving her orders was a walking dead thing, a corpse like one of the Golds, or maybe even Schweitzer, but he looked at her false smile showing entirely too many teeth and thought better of it. She wouldn't care.

"I'll . . . I'll go back to my office," he said.

"You do that." She smiled wider. "The Director would like you to pack it up."

Sick fear churned in his guts, made his chest tighten. It was a moment before he could stammer a response. "Wha . . . what? Why?"

Dadou waited, enjoying his discomfort. "He'd like you to move up on to the first tier, in the annex adjacent to his office. He thinks that, as part of the executive team, it would be good to have you close by."

"Of course," Eldredge said. "I'll go get on that right now."

Dadou said something to his back as he walked away, but Eldredge didn't hear and didn't ask her to repeat herself. It was time to go, as fast as he could and as far as he could. He'd figure the rest out from the road.

The moment he was back in his office, his knees went weak, the tightness in his chest worsened. He put out a hand to steady himself against his desk. He didn't have time. Even now Dadou was reporting the outcome of the meeting. He doubted he had convinced her, and it didn't matter if he had. He couldn't do this. Dadou was insane. If she achieved the desired outcome, she would be placing this power in the hands of a dead thing that had shown callous disregard for human life time and again. What would the Director do then? Would he put a jinn inside Eldredge?

He thought of the Director receiving Dadou's report, communing with the three monsters behind him, the things bedecked in ancient regalia, like kings ready to mount matched thrones. He shuddered at the thought. Maybe they were advising him to snuff out Eldredge even as he stood here wrestling with his own anxiety. It didn't matter. He was not working for a monster.

Another spasm hit him, a wave of nauseating weakness that almost took him down. More panic. The tightness in his chest solidified, welled upward, leaked out the corners of his eyes.

Not panic. Grief.

The Gemini Cell was the closest thing he'd had to a home for as long as he could remember. At first, it was a cool job, then a calling, and over year after year, it simply was. He had accepted the threat that magic posed, his role in stopping it. The horizon stopped drawing nearer. Schweitzer had been the first nail in that coffin, the first tremor of the realization that what he was doing might not be good, that *he* might not be good.

And now . . . those thin lips, wriggling like worms behind the tight weave of the white fabric . . . Welch's canted neck, purple muscles bulging. Eldredge shuddered again.

Quit fucking around. If you're going, get on with it.

He was going. Eldredge thrust his hands deeper into his pockets, hunched his shoulders, and did his best to look preoccupied. *You always chew your moustache when you're really bothered.* He tucked the corner into his mouth and chewed on it, as if he were contemplating a problem that required great concentration, headed for the double doors that led to the main elevator bay.

"Sir." A male voice, commanding.

Eldredge kept walking. Boots tramped as the speaker ran to catch up. "Sir! Sir! Doctor Eldredge!"

There was no way to pretend he hadn't heard him now. *Act natural. You're in the middle of something; you'd be irritated.*

He turned, frowned, faced a soldier he didn't recognize.

"You're wanted in the Director's office. In person. Not over the commlink, sir."

Eldredge's bowels turned to water. He had to pause for a moment, clenching his bladder to keep it from letting go. *They want to discuss things further, and by "discuss," I mean they want to fucking kill you.*

"I was just ordered to move my office up there. I'm getting started on that right now."

"I understand, sir, but apparently, he wants to talk to you first."

The Director had never wanted to speak to him face-to-face in all the days he'd been in the Cell. *Dadou told him she wasn't convinced. It's over for you.*

"Director's elevator is this way, sir," the soldier said, gesturing behind him. "It's been enabled for your use."

"I was actually on my way to the latrine," Eldredge said. "Let me drain the vein, and then I'll head on over."

"He was real specific, sir. He wants you to come now."

Eldredge paused half a second too long for a man who had nothing to hide. *If you go back in that office, you are not coming out.* He pointed at his crotch, cocked his eyebrow. "Sorry, man. When you gotta go, you gotta go."

Then he turned on his heel and hurried toward the elevators. He could feel the soldier's eyes on his back, the thrumming of the blood in his ears drowning out the sound of him talking into his radio, no doubt calling Eldredge's reluctance upstairs. *Don't overthink it. Even angry spirits from beyond the grave understand that a guy has to go to the bathroom. They'll wait.*

At the last minute, he veered away into the stairwell again, not wanting to risk being trapped in a metal box that could be shut down externally. He was slowly conscious of his excuse becoming painfully real. His bladder felt suddenly full, the need to vacate it overwhelming. *No way; you do not have time to stop for a bathroom break.*

He took the stairs two at a time, his bladder jostling with each step, threatening to open up. If it opened, then it opened. He could die just as easily with piss running down his leg.

One floor, then two; the air in the stairwell was close and musty, trapped in the narrow space between the cinder-block walls and the metal staircase. The lights were low, dull fluorescents running on a separate, lower-powered generator to allow them to stay lit in an emergency. It had never bothered him before, but in his sudden panic, the space felt claustrophobic, the coiling shadows ready to congeal into a clutching threat. The tight space seemed to absorb sound, close as a womb, ready to birth him into the daylight if he could just climb fast enough. The only sound was his own breathing, labored and panting, the rubber soles of his shoes padding over the grip tape on the stairs.

And something else.

A dull scrape, something leathery whispering over the surface above, trying to keep quiet and very nearly succeeding.

Eldredge froze, and suddenly the light around him brightened, took on a faint teal cast.

It was coming from his waistband, the light so bright, it spilled the banks of his white coat, colored the air around him. He reached back, grasped the grooved metal of the hilt, drew it out.

The KA-BAR blazed, the jinn locked inside so agitated that it practically smoked, thick turquoise light filling the air. It chased the shadows from the corners, bounced off the white doors and their silver handles, the dimly lit EXIT sign one level up. The one he wanted. The way out.

The scrape again, and a whooshing sound. Something big and heavy falling toward him.

Eldredge stumbled back as something tall and lean fell onto the landing in front of him. It was an involuntary move, born of shock and fear, but it saved his life. The shadow swiped for him, bone claws ripping through his lab coat and the shirt beneath, digging bloody furrows in his chest. He felt them score his ribcage, but his heart, his precious lungs, were spared.

The light from the KA-BAR washed over the thing,

reflecting off lines of rough-cut gems, playing across ridges of hammered tin and copper where they pushed through the layers of ancient dust.

One of the three crowned Golds from the Director's office. It must have been sent to ensure that he made his appointment. The striations of its gray muscles slid under skin gone thin as old cellophane. Its face was totally gone, any vestiges of humanity utterly wiped away. The bald skull was stretched taut with the old skin, peeling back in places to reveal the gray-yellow bone. The gold eyes flickered, brighter and larger than any others Eldredge had ever seen.

It said something in a language long dead, Eldredge guessed. What few jinn he'd heard described had been uniformly ancient. Its mouth folded into a tube, the jaw flexing and curling, until it was a lamprey tube ringed with sharp teeth. Its cheeks rose in a gross facsimile of a smile, and it lunged.

Eldredge shouted and leapt back, feeling his shoulders arc out over empty air. He tucked his chin, resisted the urge to flail with his arms. His one weapon was the KA-BAR, and he kept it tight against him as his shoulders slammed against the sharp lip of the stair. His head followed, stars exploding across his vision as he slid backward, each step cracking into his spine in steady, staccato rhythm, until his shoulder collided with the landing and darkness enveloped him.

He felt something heavy hit his stomach, knock the wind from him. His vision swapped places with his breath, air headed out, sight coming in. He was folded up around one sharp, bony knee, the ankle bent between his own legs, copper bangles sparkling with square-cut emeralds. A hand locked around his throat, the sharp edges of metal rings digging into the folds of his skin, drawing blood. Eldredge grabbed the wrist, pulled hard, desperately trying to swallow air. The wrist was so thin that his thumb and forefinger met with inches to spare, but it was stronger than iron and just as cold.

In the periphery of his vision, the crowned head reared

back, the lamprey mouth flexed. Dust pattered against Eldredge's face.

He tried to stab it in the back with the KA-BAR, folding his arm down, bringing the monster into a tight embrace that drove its knee deeper into his gut. The monster put its weight on his throat, and he felt his windpipe collapse as it grabbed his bicep, pushing his arm down.

Eldredge coughed, the edges of his vision going as gray as the monster's skin. He pushed with all he had, but he may as well have pushed against a truck. The monster pushed on his bicep, and his arm went flying back down to the floor. Eldredge bent his elbow, let his forearm drop, stopping as the knife struck the monster's back. He tightened his grip, felt the blade's edge catch, bite.

The Gold screamed, a high-pitched sound like a bird of prey, and Eldredge felt the magic in the knife discharge. The monster shook as the jinn in the knife lunged for it, spiritually grappling it, pushing it out and back into the void from whence it came.

The teal light went sky-blue, then white, so bright that Eldredge had to shut his eyes.

And then it was over.

The Gold King's body slumped against him, light as a bundle of dry sticks. He felt the crown slough off its head. It bounced down the stairs, clattering like a dropped pan.

And then there was silence, broken only by the pinhole wheeze of Eldredge's breath whistling through the tiny hole left in his crushed trachea. He sat up, the Gold King rolling away, little more than a dusty mummy without the jinn to animate it. He dropped the KA-BAR in his lap and clawed at his neck, frantically trying to suck in air. *Stop. Think. Panic won't save you. You have to fix this.*

He stiffened his thumbs, jamming them at angles in below his Adam's apple, pressing harder until he felt the edges of the airway, struggled against the nausea that threatened to swamp him. *Don't panic. You can breathe. That wheezing sound means you can breathe.* He pushed, massaging in and out, until at last he felt the airway spring open with an agony that blotted out his vision for the third time in as many moments.

He slumped against the floor, his neck searing agony, his tongue feeling several sizes too large for his mouth. *Get up. You can breathe, so get up! You bought yourself some time, but you don't know how much. You have to get out of here.*

He staggered to his feet, his back singing out as his spine took the weight of his torso. *Slowly. Start with one foot.*

He took a shaking step forward. A gleam of light caught his attention, brought his vision into focus. He slipped his hand around the KA-BAR's ridged leather handle. The jinn inside was sated with the banishment of its enemy, and the blade glowed so softly, he could barely make it out. He shook his head and winced as he swallowed involuntarily, slid the weapon back into its sheath in his waistband, and made his way topside again.

His tongue hung out of the corner of his mouth, the root of it thick and foreign in his mouth. His throat felt as if he'd swallowed a hot coal. His back and shoulders screamed with every step. Pins and needles in his butt and thighs.

But the pain was blotted out by the looming doorway, leading out of the stairwell and into the lobby beyond. Eldredge bit his lip, steadied himself, and checked his clothing.

His shirt was ripped and bloody where the Gold King's claws had sliced through. He pulled his coat tight, ensured that it covered him to the neck. It would have to do. He tucked his tongue back into his mouth and clamped his jaw shut. The movement caused him to swallow reflexively, the hot agony making his eyes water. He waited until the pain subsided to a manageable level, then opened the door, stepping out into the corridor beyond.

If there was an alarm, he couldn't hear it. To his right, the hallway ended at a door he knew led into the "corporate" foyer. This was the isolated facility's only cover, a manned receptionist desk that sported the Entertech logo, the corporate sponsor who'd lent their company name to the project, despite not knowing what it was used for. *Paid a pretty penny to get them to take that on.*

Eldredge turned left, walking down the long hallway and badging his way through a door, which opened with a click and hiss of air. The elevator beyond required another swipe of his keycard. They hadn't disabled his accesses yet. *There was no need. Who would guess the Gold King would fail to do its job?*

The elevator opened on a short hallway that ended in another sealed door. There were no guards. There was no need for any. As far as Eldredge knew, the blast-proof doors would only open for the electronic IDs of Eldredge, Jawid, Dadou, and the Director himself. Each step down the hallway was two kinds of agony, the first physical, the second the dread certainty that at any moment, one of the other Gold Kings would settle a bony hand on his shoulder, claws sinking in, slowly turning him around . . .

Don't be stupid; it hasn't been a minute since you fought the other one. They can't know yet. Still, he hurried the rest of the way and badged himself through the door marked simply CONTROL.

In the dark silence beyond, with his back to the door, he finally allowed himself to breathe. The small room featured a broad control board covered in buttons and blinking lights. The wall above was a series of monitors. This was the reason he had come here. The screens showed the inside of the facility from dozens of angles. There were other control rooms like it, manned by soldiers, but this was the only one that gave the full view: the cold storage chambers, the laboratories, the testing chambers dotted with burn-freeze nozzles. All the spaces where the true work of the Gemini Cell was performed. Even the Director's foyer was shown, the secretary's face bathed in the static glow of her computer monitor.

Eldredge saw no running guards, heard no alarm bells. He had a little time, at least. *Make it count.*

He needed to get out of here, and fast. There was no hope of going on foot. The Cell's cover facility was an office park in northern Virginia. He would escape into a city crawling with police in the center of his nation's seat of government.

He looked longingly at the helo bay, the limbered helicopters crouching like huge insects. The duty pilots sat around a crate, playing cards. They knew him as the Cell's lead scientist and would follow his orders without question. If he went down there now, he had no doubt one of them would fire up one of the birds and fly him anywhere he wanted to go. *But what will happen when he radios flight control for clearance to take off? Or worse, what will happen when you're already in the air and he gets a call from base?*

No, the helos were out. He looked instead at the motor pool. The cars were specifically chosen to be discreet, a range of sedans and compacts common in suburbs across the country. No white vans, no black sedans with tinted windows. Eldredge could see license plates from thirty different states and knew each one of them was backstopped enough to stand up to scrutiny. Two guards stood near the shack beside the giant, rolling steel garage doors. Since there was a possibility of exposure to outside view, they wore jeans and pullovers, sunglasses propped on their ball caps. But Eldredge could see the thin bands wrapping the paddle holsters in the backs of their trousers, knew there were high-caliber pistols nestled inside. Two killers, dressed to look like a couple of manual laborers on a smoke break.

Same problem there with the helos. They would let him check out a car, but they would also call it in. It also wouldn't take them long to chase him down even if he could get out of the garage. He needed them occupied. He needed the entire facility occupied, at least long enough for him to get a head start.

He checked the monitor in the arms locker. Claymore mines were stacked beside coils of det-cord, bricks of pre-casting Composition B. There was enough firepower in there to blow half the building sky-high, but he'd need to go several floors down to reach it, and unlike this control center, that *was* guarded, and by people who would look askance at his presence there. Like everyone working for the Cell, Eldredge had received at least rudimentary explosives training, but that didn't mean guards wouldn't cock an eyebrow at him attempting to check any out.

Besides, explosives weren't the Cell's real weapon. Those were the undead, immortal Operators, like the ancient, withered king he'd just dispatched. They were more powerful than any explosive. His throat throbbed as he thought of the creature's hand on it, slowly choking the life out of him while its gold eyes blazed into his.

And suddenly, Eldredge knew. He couldn't fight his way out of here, but he didn't have to.

Someone else would do it for him.

He flicked his eyes between the cold storage chambers. The Golds stood like statues in the center of each one. With no blood nearby, all the heartbeats on the other side of doors and walls they couldn't break, they abandoned even the tiniest pretenses of the living: sitting or pacing, twitching or scratching. Eldredge had only seen one Operator continue going through these motions, a nod to a humanity he desperately clung to. Schweitzer.

He caught himself glancing between cells, trying to pick the best one. *Just do it. You don't have time.* He settled on Gold Eight, a thick-limbed Operator who had been short and stocky in life. It squatted on muscular thighs, sharp elbows perched on its knees, facing the back corner of the room, so still that it looked carved from stone.

Eldredge matched the number over the cell door to the button on the console, flipped the plastic cover up. He thought of the ruins of Basye, the tangled remains of the scout troop. The Gold King's knee in his gut, the window of his vision slowly narrowing, going gray as he struggled for air.

The Director had been willing to unleash the Golds on an innocent town, on a bunch of children, on anyone who got in his way. He had been willing to unleash one on him.

He would do it again, Eldredge knew, the very moment he learned that the one he'd sent had failed.

Let him learn what it was like to face one of them down.

Eldredge punched the button, watched through the flickering monitor as the cell door slid open. Gold Eight jerked upright immediately, head snapping toward the sound. It paused only to open its mouth in a silent howl, then crouched down on all fours, knuckle-walking out the door so quickly that it seemed to blink off the monitor.

Eldredge knew the run-books by heart for every emergency protocol affecting the facility. There was only one that called for every guard to leave their post. Only one that turned every eye inward. Its code word was *Sunspot*, and it meant that a Gold had slipped its bonds, was loose in the facility.

Eldredge grabbed the radio that connected to the building-wide address system. He depressed the thumb switch, hearing the alarm sound in response. "All personnel, all personnel," he said into the speaker, hearing his words echoing through the hallways, in every room. "All personnel seal acc-points in East Wing, level two. East Wing, level two, is Sunspot. I say again, Sunspot, East Wing, level two."

It was, of course, the wrong information. The Gold was currently speeding its way down the open access tunnel on the level below, but it would take them a while to sort that out.

Eldredge wasted no more time, ignoring the pain in his back and throat, rushing out the door and back to the elevator, his impatience so great, he actually danced from foot to foot as the car rose and opened on the upper floor. He turned and raced toward the motor pool. He badged through the entryway just in time to nearly collide with the two guards shouting into their radios as they came on. "Doctor Eldredge!" said one. "They called Sunspot; are we sur—"

Eldredge cut them off with a gesture. "It's not a drill. Ruptured cold line put a crack in the door. There're three in East Wing. There's a flamethrower team there, but they could use someone at the junction acc-point. The duty roster isn't in the control room. I don't know where the axe team is, but I need one of you to check the rack room."

"Which—"

"Figure it out en route! Go right now!"

The men exchanged a glance, and Eldredge felt his mouth go dry. It was thin, and he knew it. Hopefully, they didn't know it too.

But you didn't get assigned to guard the motor pool due to a surfeit of mental acuity. A moment later, the men were shouldering past Eldredge, guns drawn, the door clicking shut behind them.

Eldredge stood for a moment in the sudden relative quiet of the motor pool. The cars around him reflected the fluorescent tube lights stretching across the unadorned concrete ceiling. The alarm still sounded, faintly audible through the thickness of the door. A light swirled overhead, washing all in honey-colored waves.

He made his way over to the shack by the door, reached in through the window, and slapped the broad green button inside. With a groan followed by the rapid clicking of chains, the door began to rise. Eldredge blinked at the daylight flooding in.

The keys were kept in the ignition. Eldredge chose a small subcompact, the kind of car that an old man living alone might drive on his weekly trip to the grocery store. He almost signed the logbook checking the car out, as he had so many times before, before remembering his situation. He got behind the wheel and started the motor, his mind screaming at him to rev the engine and peel out of the lot.

He didn't. He drove slowly and deliberately, praying he wouldn't draw undue attention as the facility locked down, that by the time they had the situation contained, it would be too late to catch him. Again, thin.

He drove by rote and memory, letting his hands and feet guide the car out of the office parking lot, down the access road, and onto the entrance ramp for 66 West, out into the countryside, toward Basye and the forests where Schweitzer had last been seen. The route brought him closer to the deployed Gold team, but they had long since moved on from Basye, and he doubted the Director would have them double back if it meant taking the pressure off Schweitzer. If he was going to hide, the huge forest where they'd lost Schweitzer was his best chance.

The highway traffic was thick but moving, and Eldredge blinked in the sunshine, looking at the other drivers. None so much as glanced his way, just one more commuter in a throng. If he ignored the pain in his back, he could almost pretend that he was just another person. He had been outside many times before, overseeing ops, meeting with potential recruits, but this was the first time he'd ever truly left. In spite of the pain and terror, in spite of the pit in his stomach as he realized that he'd left without supplies, Eldredge found himself excited. The forest lay ahead of him, and all the cars in the motor pool were kept with a full tank. After he passed the first police cruiser and it didn't turn on its lights, Eldredge actually began to hope he would make it. As 66 snaked past Warrenton and the signs of civilization around him grew sparser, he was able to turn his mind to formulating a plan with more substance than simply putting the Cell facility behind him.

What now? Would he run to the cops? Tell them that he was being chased by soldiers on the orders of a walking corpse in a bad suit and a white hood? They would hold him until they got direction from on high, and on high was precisely where the Gemini Cell was situated.

There was no one to tell who would believe him. He had lived in that bunker for so many years. He had no family with whom he was close. His room and his belongings were all back there, just a few floors below the crowned thing that had just tried to kill him.

The Gemini Cell was designed to take people in and keep them.

The only ones it let out into the world were dead. That had worked until Schweitzer.

Schweitzer.

The man was still out there somewhere. Eldredge surprised himself by using the title, was more surprised to find it was true. Schweitzer might not be living, but he was still a man. More, he was the one man strong enough to oppose the Cell. He'd escaped, he'd eluded them, he'd shredded seven Operators, stopped the Cell's only living Aeromancer. He had been retreating ever since he'd run, but Eldredge didn't think it was because he was afraid. He was doing it to protect his family, and now just his son. Eldredge thought of the raw heap of meat that had once been Schweitzer's wife, and shuddered.

No, Schweitzer was protecting his family. It would be a long shot for him to oppose the Cell head on, but he was the only being in the world who had a shot at all.

Eldredge thought of the Director, the three kings behind him. Two now, thanks to Eldredge. He had seen them. He knew. They would never let him go.

Schweitzer might be a thin hope, but it was the only one he had.

CHAPTER XIX
THE THINGS WE DO FOR LOVE

Jawid turned away from the ruined piles of flesh that had been the flamethrower team. They'd managed to catch Gold Eight on fire before it had reached them, but even burning brightly, it had still been able to rip them limb from limb before the axe men had arrived to cut it down.

The soldiers had finished with their axes and now knelt among the remains, working with their knives. Sunspot protocol said there should be nothing left larger than four inches square. Even with a burned corpse, that took time.

There was nothing for Jawid to do, but they'd called him down anyway, also according to protocol.

After a minute, one of the soldiers looked up from his knife work and cocked an eyebrow. "So, are we good here? No nasty surprises coming?"

Jawid shook his head. "Of course not. The body is destroyed. Even if the jinn were still inside, it couldn't harm anyone."

The soldier went back to slicing through a tough knot of bone. "So, no chance of it all . . . coming back together and giving us a fight?"

"None."

"Well, then . . . you're making me nervous standing there."

Jawid turned away, not knowing where he was walking, only that the burned-flesh stink of Gold Eight was growing fainter with each step. When at last he realized where he was, he stood outside a door, hand hovering over the only break in the otherwise reflective stainless steel surface. A black plastic plate had been slipped into two brackets, engraved in white letters. 202—ALVA, DADOU. SCORPIO LNO.

Jawid realized with a shock that he was frightened, sickened. And so he had come here. Because he loved her. Still, his hand hung in the air.

Knock, you idiot! You love her. Tell her!

But his hand wavered and would not move. He forced himself to think of her softly parted lips, her hips rocking against him, the earthy smell of her throat. But he had to force himself to recall, for when he didn't, a different vision took the fore: Dadou's curled lip, the rage simmering behind her eyes, the taut muscles in her arms and shoulders. Long, graceful fingers flexing. She had killed before. She could kill again. Magic had given Jawid many things. Strength was not among them.

Have some courage. She is your tilth now. What would you prefer? To stay here and put jinn in living men? He shuddered as he thought of corpse after corpse, of the men writhing in what Dadou called her *chèz espesyal*, her special chair. Their eyes bulging out of their heads, their arms straining against the straps, their death rattles sounding as Dadou threw up her hands in exasperation. *Kèt! We are so close. The next one. It will work with the next one.*

Jawid didn't doubt she was right. They were close. He could feel the living soul being pushed aside, making room for the dead one they were attempting to Bind in with it.

But he could still smell the smoking remains of Gold Eight, mixing with the copper tang of the soldiers' spilled blood. How had it gotten out? Had the door mechanism broken? Had someone been careless? Would he be blamed? It didn't matter; Jawid felt his guts roil, his breathing coming faster. He could suddenly feel the closeness of the corridor around him, the weight of the earth overhead. Wherever the jinn were concerned, there was always blood, one way or another.

He had to talk to Dadou. He had to take her away from this place. They had joined. They were one in the eyes of Allah now. The escape of Gold Eight was a sign. Allah was telling him it was time to take her and go.

And soon as the thought occurred to him, Jawid knew it was right. *Allahu akhbar.* He had to talk to her now. Allah was with him. No matter how Dadou frightened him, he would tell her of his love.

You reached out to Schweitzer, and look what happened. Jawid could remember himself opening to Schweitzer, and Schweitzer's sudden lunge into his own memories. *This is why he escaped.*

And now he was doing the same with Dadou, making himself vulnerable to her. The thought chilled him, stayed his hand as he tried to knock again.

What is your other choice? To stay here forever? How else would a Gold have gotten out save by the will of Allah? He has sent you a sign. You wanted a family. She is your one chance.

His knuckles finally scraped against the metal. Once. Twice.

Jawid was about to turn away when he heard the soft click of the door opening.

Dadou's face in the crack of the doorway was the one he feared. Her eyes burned, narrowed slits sizing up targets. Her fingers curled around the doorjamb as if she were about to throttle it. Jawid froze as her eyes found him, simmered, unchanging, no recognition in them. He was just something close enough to hurt.

An instant later, the corners of her eyes turned up; her mouth followed. "*Chouchou.* You lonely?" She swung the door wide, stepped back so he could enter.

"The alarm . . ."

"I heard. It's been handled."

"How did it get out?"

She shrugged, the ease of the motion troubling him. "Occupational hazard."

"They called me down to . . ."

"I heard that too." She motioned him inside. "Come in."

He had been in her cell once before. It was the opposite of his own. Clothing was heaped in the corner, mostly tactical gear, the sort he'd seen the soldiers wear when they weren't in uniform. There was one long dress of brown and gold laid out next to a pair of leather sandals beaded with seashells. They both looked very old. He had never seen her wear either one. Her bed was unmade, pillows lying on the floor.

A shrine had been built in the corner opposite the clothing, a riot of objects surrounding a framed portrait of the Virgin Mary: a doll's head, a plastic Christmas tree, a string of beads and a bottle of rum, a plastic skull and a heart-shaped mirror. Just below the image of the Virgin was an unframed wallet photograph in black and white. It was curling at the edges, yellow cracks working their way through a smiling man holding two little girls.

Dadou noted his stare. "That is my *vodou*," she said. "It keeps my family close."

"You believe that?"

She smiled sadly. "Sometimes, it helps to try."

"But we know what happens to the dead. We know that doesn't make a difference."

"Do we now? You believe that a magic man in the sky gets angry when you make pictures of him." The anger returned to her eyes.

"I'm sorry." He cursed himself. She hated when he said that. *Tell her the truth.* Holy Qur'an said that Allah did not forgive the worship of idols.

But he saw the murder in her eyes and quailed. He had not come to fight with her on this. That was for another day. Once they were together and away from this place, he would ensure she built no more shrines to idols. He watched as she forced the anger down, covered it over with the smile.

"Anyway"—he tried to sound relaxed, but his voice came out terrified instead—"I didn't come here to fight."

Dadou sat on the bed, patted it. The action should have stirred him, filled his head with thoughts of love, but all he could think of was the risk he was taking, and his manhood wilted. Nobody left the Gemini Cell, certainly not a Sorcerer. *Do you believe in the power of Allah, or don't you?*

"I didn't come for love, either," he said.

Dadou leaned back on her arms, her breasts rising toward him, cocked her head to the side. *"Trè kirye,"* she said. "What did you come here for?"

"The truth is . . ." And now that the moment had arrived, he found he could not say it. "The truth is . . ." He stammered, his tongue suddenly too big for his mouth. *Just say it! Why is it so hard to speak the truth!*

Dadou's face went serious. "Stop," she said. *"Rete, chouchou.* Nothing good can come of what you will say next." She pushed herself to her feet, pointed her finger at him. "Time for you to go. We will talk more tomorrow."

But by then, he'd found some sliver of strength. It was little more than an ember, barely enough for him to call himself a coward, but it was enough to speak. "The truth is that I love you. We are joined. You and I are to be together. And if you will not see that on your own, I only ask that you give me the chance to show you. If you come away with me, we will make a beautiful thing together, as God intended when He joined us. I know we are different, but all people are from God, and God will smooth these differences until we go forward as one. We only need to give it a chance. I love you, Dadou. You must be my wife."

"We were doing so well," she said, her voice flat. "We were making such progress. We were working. You had managed to keep your stupid mouth shut for *days.* I thought we were . . . how did the *Doktè* say it? Out of the woods."

"Please," Jawid said. "I love you."

"Love." Jawid could hear the rage rising in her throat. "Love," she said again. "What the fuck do you know about love?"

"I know that when a man and woman do what we've done, that means they love one another. And I know what the Holy Qur'an says, that those who love one another must marry. Love is a thing that comes from God, Dadou." Jawid was angry now, and it felt good to be angry, because it made him feel safe, because maybe if his anger could match hers, she could not hurt him. His father had told him that when spiders joined, the female ate the male. That would not happen here.

Dadou blinked. Predator eyes. Like a coiling snake. Or a spider. "You think because you dip your wick a time or two that you are in love? You think your stupid god cares whether we stand at an altar and mumble some words?"

She stabbed an angry finger at her shrine. "*That* is not magic. *That* is not even god. I am a *Sèvitè*. I *know* what happens when you die. I have *seen* the soul storm with my own eyes. That is to help me remember my home, my family, where I came from. That is *not* because I believe an invisible man in the sky is looking at me and judging whether or not I build a pile of trinkets for him, and he certainly does not care who I fuck, or when, or why."

"Alva, this is wrong. Us being apart is wrong. What the Cell is doing is wrong. We are murdering people. We are making piles of bodies. And now a Gold has escaped. He killed some soldiers, not as many as when Schweitzer escaped, but still . . ." He shuddered.

"They are soldiers. They are paid to be killed."

"You didn't see . . ."

"I have seen plenty. More than you. It's the mission, Jawid."

"The mission? You sound like an American."

"I sound like someone who does their job."

"What is our job? Whatever the Director tells us. Why should we care what he wants or what he doesn't? America was never my home. I am from the mountains above Bibiyal and wherever the Baba Khel graze their herds. You are from Port-au-Prince. Americans helped us, maybe even saved us, but they didn't do it out of love. They didn't do it because they want us to be happy, or well, or right with God. They did it because they want what we can do. We are machines to them. We are . . . assets, they call it. I owe them nothing. And if I did owe them anything, it has been repaid. I want my own life now, and now that I have met you, I know what that life is supposed to be. It is to be us, together. I am going back to the Korengal."

"You are not going anywhere."

He ignored her. "You should see the Pech River, Alva. It is like a silver ribbon. You will come back with me, and we will make a home there."

"You are not listening to me."

"You are not listening to me! I am telling you that I love you!"

"You don't know what love is! You don't even know what a woman is!"

"Then you will teach me. You cannot be happy here. You cannot be happy killing people."

Dadou took a step toward him, and this time, Jawid didn't flinch back, closed with her. "I have never been happier," she growled.

"You are wrong. You don't want to leave because you feel you will not be safe. But you will be safe in the mountains with me. My family is there, and if you are my wife, they will protect you too. If we work together, we can escape. If we work together, we can survive. This is what the American army is always talking about, teamwork. We are a team. And together we can be gone and safe in my home."

"Now, you listen carefully." Dadou looked at him from below her brow, fists clenched. "There is *nowhere* you can run. There is *nowhere* you can go where they can't find you."

"You are wrong. It took them over ten years to find bin Laden. They never found Mullah Omar. And neither of those men had magic. Maybe they will find us, and together, we will be ready. We beat the Soviets, we beat the Americans before. *Ooba chi thur sur wawooshte, se yawa naiza, se sul naize.* I love you. That comes from God. He will see it through."

Dadou's anger peaked, and she shrieked, an incoherent animal noise.

"God?! God?!" She spat out the words. "Where was God when I crawled the streets of Port-au-Prince, down in the dog shit on my knees, sucking the cocks of old men for enough food to see the next dawn? Where was God when my brothers were killed for a rooster, when my sister was raped to 'teach her not to be so high and mighty'? Where was God when I lost my first baby? My second? When the army doctor told me I would never have any more?"

The fire of her anger burned his to ashes, and with it, his resolve. Suddenly, he was no longer angry. Suddenly, he was afraid. "You will have more," he said, but his voice sounded very soft, as if it came from a long way away. "We have magic. We can do anything."

"That is not how our magic works," Dadou answered. "It is not magic for making children. It is not magic for hiding. It is magic for speaking with the dead. That is all."

There was something in her voice now, something in her face, darker and more solid than what he'd seen before. His love had been a white-hot thing when he entered the room; now he could scarcely believe he had come at all, wished that Allah would reach down from heaven and turn back time, take him back to the hallway when he'd been hesitant to knock, make him trust his instincts. *No, you will have faith. You will trust in Allah.*

"I'm leaving," he said. "Come with me." He looked at her eyes and thought of female spiders eating their mates. He didn't want her to come with him anymore, only insisted now because it was Allah's will.

Dadou circled, stood between him and the door. "Don't be stupid. I am not coming with you, and you are not leaving."

"You are a woman. You cannot stop me from doing anything. I am done with this place and with this work."

Dadou said nothing. She crouched before the doorway, long fingers hooked. Her spider eyes looked eager.

"You are mine!" Jawid shouted. It was an angry sound, though fear was in possession of his body, as if it were a jinn driving his limbs. He reached out and grabbed her wrist, pulled her toward the door. She was a woman; he was stronger than her. That was the will of Allah.

Except that he knew he wasn't stronger than her, could see it in her ready stance, in the taut ripples of muscle. *Allah protect me.*

She dropped her arm, casually, gently, the look in her eyes never changing. He tried to yank his hand back, but she clamped his wrist to her side, as if she were made of solid iron. He pulled harder; she didn't move.

"Ah, *chouchou*," she whispered softly, not sounding angry at all. "This is going to hurt you a lot more than it is going to hurt me."

She whipped her head forward.

By the time Jawid felt the impact, he was three steps back, his vision a gray tunnel. Something wet and sticky was running into his eyes. The fear had given way to nausea, and he felt his stomach hitch as if it would try to push the panic out of his mouth. He ran, and suddenly there was pain in his nose, and he was reeling back from her closet. He had run into it. How had he gotten here?

Pain in the back of his head. She had grabbed his hair, was pulling his head back. *"Mwen regret sa,"* she said. "You think you fucking own me? You think you are the first man who has told me that I belonged to him?"

He grunted, the pain a fire in his scalp. It brought some of the anger he so desperately needed back. He pumped his arm, throwing his elbow back into something hard but yielding.

"Fuck," Dadou gasped, her grip on his hair loosening. He jerked his head forward and felt some of his hair rip out by the roots. Dadou whooped a breath, tightened her grasp on what remained, holding him fast. He threw the elbow again, but it found empty air this time.

Dadou was screaming, a litany of unintelligible Creole curses that finally descended into an animal growl. Jawid couldn't recognize her voice anymore; it scarcely sounded human.

His need to be free of her grip became desperate. He felt his lungs constrict, his heart hammering so fast and so hard, he thought it would leap from his chest. At that moment, he knew he would do anything to escape, suffer any indignity, anything if she would only stop hurting him. He had misread the sign. This wasn't Allah's will. Or, if it was, he lacked the bravery to see it through. "I'll leave!" he shouted. "I'm sorry! I'll leave!"

Dadou didn't hear him. "Think. You. Own. Me." She bit off each word. Her knee collided skillfully with his hamstring, perfectly placed to make the entire leg go numb. He leaned, desperately shifting his weight to his good leg, but Dadou held his head fast, and the pain proved too much for him; with a groan, he swung back to the weak leg, overbalanced, dropped to his knees.

"Stop!" he shouted, not even trying to elbow her now. There was no point in struggling against her. She was so much stronger than him, so much better at fighting.

"Now you want me to stop?" Dadou asked. "What happened to us belonging together? What happened to the will of your stupid fucking God?"

Her knee again, this time in the base of his spine. Jawid felt the vertebrae flex, strain, and finally give, a low *crunch* that sent pins and needles shooting down his legs at first, finally vanishing into numbness. The reality of it hit home. He was defenseless. She was pitiless. He was going to die. He tried to scramble to his knees, to find the strength to fight for his life, but his legs would not answer him and his arms and shoulders felt heavy, as if his veins ran with lead.

Dadou knelt over him, lowering him gently down, until his chest lay on the floor. He swatted at her weakly until she knelt on his hand, grinding the bones into the stiff carpet.

"Please," he whispered. "Please."

"You love me, eh?" she said. "I'll tell you a little story so you know the woman you wanted to marry.

"When I was little, we begged on the steps of a church. The nuns were good to us, but the mason who worked on the church wanted to wed my sister. He said some funny things. Things like what you said: 'I love you,' and 'God meant for us to be together.' And when she refused him, he raped her. Said it was a lesson, to teach her 'not to be so high and mighty.'

"My sister was a good girl. She never hurt anyone in her whole life. She was always smiling, always kind. Men see that in a woman and they think her weak. That's what you think of me, Jawid. That's what you mean when you say, 'I love you.'

"That mason was the first man I ever killed. I faced him in the church nave, in front of the altar of the God who said, 'Thou shalt not kill.' I didn't rush it, *chouchou*. I took my time.

"That is what happens to men who try to own me and mine, Jawid. You're a stupid animal, so I will let you live, but like all animals, you must be trained."

She reached down and grabbed his hand, bending his finger back until he felt the bones begin to creak. He screamed, thrashed, and the hand came away. Dadou cursed and flailed for it again, but Jawid punched out with a strength born of desperation, his thumb jamming into her eye.

Dadou shrieked, ripping his hand away and punching him hard enough to make his head bounce off the floor. "You fucking bastard!"

He tried to roll to his feet, but she grabbed his hair again, hammered his head down.

Izat was there, and Anoosheh, and his father and mother as well. The river sparkled behind them. The old man had his arms folded around a walking stick, his forehead creased with worry. "It will flood," he said. "You must take the goats to high ground."

"Where are the goats, Grandfather?" Jawid tried to ask, but he couldn't speak; his head hurt too much. The riverbank flashed red.

His mother's burqa shivered. Gold lights glinted behind the mesh veil. "The Americans are coming."

Jawid heard the roar of helicopters and tried to turn his head to see them, but the pain was too great.

He opened his eyes and suddenly, his family was gone. The river had melted into the iron-gray carpet on Dadou's floor, soaked through with red. Bits of wet gray slime floated in the fluid, along with yellow-white fragments.

His head whipped forward.

It was just Anoosheh now, washing in the river, as she had been on the day he had seen her. Her skin was the color of the dry ground, her hair as thick and curled as sheep's wool. She looked over her smooth shoulder, her graceful neck arching, caught his eye, smiled.

"There you are." Izat, at his shoulder. Jawid's bowels turned to water. The old man had caught him looking at her. He would be furious.

"I'm sorry, Grandfather," Jawid said, eyes filling with hot tears.

Izat put his hand on the back of Jawid's head, ruffled his hair. "I do not judge. That is for Allah only." He smiled. "He is merciful and compassionate."

Jawid felt relief so great that he sank to the dusty ground. "Thank you, Grandfather."

Izat kept his hand on the back of Jawid's head. "Don't thank me; thank Allah."

And then he whipped Jawid's head forward and threw him into darkness.

CHAPTER XX
WHY DID YOU GO?

Eldredge squatted next to the pickup parked in the discount store lot, grateful its owner had parked it nose into the light. The shadows pooled behind the tailgate, giving Eldredge plenty of cover as he unscrewed the license plate using the screwdriver in his car's toolkit, swapping the plates out with his own. The front was dicier, but the lot was deserted at this late hour, and he made short work of it. The Cell had given him basic training they'd intended to be used if he had to roll out on ops with fire teams. They'd never meant it to be used to make good his escape, but it had taught him enough to remember to swap the plates. It would throw off law enforcement, but not for long.

His body still ached, but not as much as before, and each time he woke up and saw the sun rising outside the window of his car, he felt lighter.

Because he was still alive. He'd evaded the Cell another day. *Why bother? What is the point of staying alive?* He was running nowhere; he had no idea where to find Schweitzer, the only weapon that stood a chance of bringing the Gemini Cell down. And then what?

But the truth was that he wanted to live. Even through the pain and the loneliness and the dislocation, he desperately wanted to live. Even in an old body, a damaged one. The strangers he passed on the road, families singing in SUVs, college students with their hatchbacks crammed with furniture, all occupied a different universe, one he could never set foot in. They didn't know that magic existed. They didn't know that the government had a hidden hand in it. They didn't know that hidden hand was attached to an arm no longer living, governed by a dead mind, cold and ancient, driven by an agenda they couldn't possibly understand.

It was isolating, but the isolation was followed by a fierce, animal need to protect them. These were the people he'd dedicated his life to keeping safe. These strangers. He'd sacrificed everything for them. He'd given up family and friends and future. Staying alive as long as he could wasn't so much more to ask.

In addition to the toolkit, the glove compartment had a tiny brown envelope with a hundred dollars in twenties, the petty cash included with each vehicle for road emergencies. Added to the forty in his own wallet, it was enough to buy a cheap T-shirt to replace his ripped and bloody one, keep the tank full, and eat at roadside diners for a few days, but the time was coming when he'd have to steal some more money to keep himself going.

When he'd last been tracking Schweitzer, he'd been heading west with his son in tow. That was an incredibly vague set of directions, but it was all that Eldredge had to go on. Years of working targets for the Cell had taught him some of the basics. *Focus on the target's immediate needs.* Schweitzer didn't need to eat or sleep. He didn't need clothing or shelter. There was no one for him to check in with. The entire world thought he was dead. Hell, Schweitzer *was* dead.

But Patrick wasn't.

The next morning, Eldredge bought a cheap scissor and disposable razor in a gas station. He shaved in the restroom and hacked his hair down. It looked wilder than ever, but it also looked different, and without his walrus mustache, he would be a little harder to recognize, at least.

Thirty minutes later, he pulled up outside the town's public library, little more than a couple of ramshackle trailers linked together and parked behind a church. Eldredge walked past its soaring white steeple and fresh-painted siding, and realized where the town fathers were putting their money. He'd been religious once, back in another life. He laughed to think of it now. Christians were always talking about the Rapture, a glorious day of the dead crawling out of their graves and walking the earth. They had the story of Jesus raising Lazarus, an example of shining hope, the benevolence of a kind and gracious God. For a time, Eldredge had even believed it. But that had been before he'd actually seen the dead walk, had learned firsthand that there was nothing kind or gracious about it.

Eldredge hauled the door open; it creaked on spring hinges and banged shut behind him. The library was as unimpressive inside as it was outside, just walls of beaten-looking pressboard shelves and stacked plastic milk crates jumbled with old and poorly used–looking books. Yellowing posters extolling the virtues of reading adorned the water-stained walls.

But Eldredge didn't mind, because he saw the two things he'd most hoped for. The first was that the library was empty save for the receptionist, a teenager who sat behind a battered and peeling desk, eyes glued to his phone.

The second was a computer sitting below a battered plastic laminated sign, which read PUBLIC INTERNET.

"Just going to use the computer for a bit," Eldredge said. "I'm afraid I forgot my library card."

The boy behind the desk waved at him, not looking up.

Eldredge sat down at the computer and woke it up, suppressing an almost violent need to run. He'd swapped out the plates, but it was still the same car. He'd cut off some hair, but he was still the same man. He was far from the Cell, but not far enough. They would find him, and every second he delayed made it more certain. *Focus; you can't run forever with no place to go. You have to do something.*

Doing something meant taking some risks. This would be his first. He knew the Gemini Cell could read his Internet browsing history, but he had to hope that either he wouldn't alert them, or if he did, that he would be gone before they found him here. He pulled up Google and searched for "Burglary and Virginia," narrowing his search results to those articles posted in the last week.

The results were staggering, and he wrestled with them for more than an hour, dialing in on drugstores. The thieves always took the same things: cash, drugs from the pharmacy. But Eldredge kept looking. It was the best lead he had.

Because when the mop-up team had found the bag Sarah Schweitzer had dropped, it had been full of supplies necessary to treat a bad case of poison ivy: antibiotic ointment, calamine lotion.

Jim Schweitzer's dead skin wasn't reactant to anything. He didn't have living nerve endings to report itching sensations. That stuff was for Patrick. Dead men also had no use for money, and Schweitzer was that rarest of creatures, the Boy Scout who always did the right thing. He wouldn't steal money beyond what he needed to take care of his son.

Even with Schweitzer's superhuman capabilities, he couldn't have gone far after escaping Basye. Not with a little boy cradled in his arms, crying and scratching at the swelling rash the plant's oil had set to burning beneath his skin. Eldredge narrowed his search. Robberies in and around Shenandoah County, focusing on the limits of what a man could do at a fast walk. Patrick would be nestled in his father's dead arms, but Eldredge knew Schweitzer's determination well enough to know that the man would never stop moving, no matter how much his son squalled.

Nothing. If there was a needle in the haystack, Eldredge couldn't see it. Judging by the pieces on blogs and local

Virginia papers, all anyone did out here was steal. The kid had stepped outside for his third smoke break when Eldredge finally came across a searchable crime blotter from a tiny police department in Timberville. It was basic and old-looking, but the information was up-to-date and, more importantly, he was able to search robberies and burglaries by type. The drop-down menu had a few options: ARMED, RESIDENTIAL, BUSINESS LARGE (>IO EMP), BUSINESS SMALL (<IO EMP).

Eldredge arched an eyebrow. "Here's hoping," he muttered to the empty room, and clicked through.

It was as he expected. "BUSINESS SMALL" burglaries were almost exclusively convenience stores and gas stations when this far out in the country. The blotter laid out inventories of the stolen property like all the other articles. Drugs and cash, always drugs and cash. Eldredge rubbed his eyes as the kid came back in, looking askance at the strange old man who'd been sitting at the public computer for over two hours.

"How's it going over there, sir? You need any help?" the kid asked.

"I'm fine," Eldredge answered, barely noticing he had spoken.

Because he'd just clicked on a link, and there it was.

A little town called Fulks Run, less than twenty miles southwest of Basye. A healthy man could have walked it in a full day. Schweitzer would have been able to make it by nightfall.

There were pharmaceuticals stolen, but they weren't the usual targets: sleep aids, painkillers, opiates, and narcotics. A few bottles of antibiotics were missing, and the rest of the aisles had been ransacked, leaving almost everything of value in place. The thief had packed a child's school pack with first aid and cooking supplies, what food was available.

Calamine lotion was listed among the missing items, along with a child's Halloween costume.

There were a thousand possible explanations. Maybe it was a prank. Maybe the antibiotics were part of a homemade drug recipe. Maybe the thief was a crackpot with a penchant for dressing up his dog. It didn't have to be Schweitzer.

But somehow, Eldredge knew that it was.

There were no major highways leading to Fulks Run, and the drive seemed painfully slow, despite the fifty-five-mile-per-hour limit on most of the bigger roads. Eldredge kept it strictly at the limit; despite his impatience, he absolutely could not afford to get pulled over now.

Fulks Run itself was little more than a wide space in the road, a collection of vinyl-sided houses that were just a step above trailers. It was rustic and beautiful in the way that drew rich, urbane government contractors from DC on romantic-getaway weekends with their wives and mistresses. The convenience store was alongside a diner just off the main drag, sheltered in the shade of the thick Virginia pines that made up the edge of the National Forest.

The investigation was long since concluded, any broken windows repaired. The blotter had said the break-in occurred at night, when no one was working. It wasn't like he could interview the clerk. Why was he even here? He walked past the windows once, twice, drew a few stares before adjourning to the diner. *You need to figure this out fast or you are going to get caught.*

Ah, hell. You're going to get caught anyway. The Director would be angry. It would not be painless. It would not be quick.

Eldredge ordered a coffee and avoided making eye contact with the waitress, who acted like an old man wearing dirty clothes was an everyday occurrence. He ran his fingers through the tangles in his hair, feeling the grease that had settled in over the past day. It would get harder and harder to blend in, unless he was trying to appear homeless.

Think. This was the last place he was. Where would he have gone?

Away from the Cell; that meant south or west, or both. He could be in Arizona. He could be in Florida. He could be anywhere. *No. He has no transportation. Wait. If you can steal a car, so can he.*

"Jesus." He couldn't stop the words from tumbling out of his mouth. He didn't even know if it was Schweitzer who'd robbed that store. He had nothing to go on. Any minute now, the local sheriff was going to come in and . . .

"Hey, can you turn the volume up on that?" Eldredge pointed to the flat-screen TV hanging behind the counter, the only thing remotely modern-looking in the place. It was turned to the news, showed a young man in his twenties with a dirty yellow beard and matching dreadlocks. He looked like a privileged runaway, or one of those children of CEOs who decides to spend a year homeless on the streets of a big city. His face and body showed the signs of weather and rough living, but the set of his mouth and the hurt entitlement in his eyes told Eldredge that this was someone born into money. The kid had been worked over badly. One eye was swollen shut, and thick black stitches showed where a long gash had been sewn shut in his forehead. One ear was cauliflowered.

The news banner marquee rolled past too fast for Eldredge, but he could make out the words: CLAIMS TO HAVE BEEN THROWN FROM TRAIN BY ZOMBIE.

". . . had a kid with him; I think he kidnapped him," the man was saying.

The TV cut to a sheriff in a dark green uniform, gray moustache quivering on red jowls. "Of course, we are taking Mister Colridge's story seriously, and will keep you updated as we have more information. However, given the outlandish nature of his claims, and the positive results of his drug test . . ."

"That kid is crazy," the waitress said, drowning out the sheriff's next words. "I used to know . . ."

"Shhh!" Eldredge jumped out of his chair, jamming a finger against his lips.

"No need to be a jerk," the waitress said, sauntering away with a wounded look.

The news had already cut to the next segment, a story about a car wreck on I-64. The young man's face was replaced with a burning segment of blacktop rolling through the verdant Shenandoah Valley.

But Eldredge was already digging through his pockets, fumbling for the money to pay the check.

Because he'd managed to hear the young man say one more thing in spite of the waitress's nattering, a burst of profanity the news station had only just managed to bleep out.

"His eyes, man. They were silver. They were on fucking fire."

CHAPTER XXI
LAST RESORT

The need for supplies forced Schweitzer off the train somewhere in Kentucky. The magic that augmented his senses didn't come with a built-in map, and he was sure of their location only by virtue of a state border sign that whipped past while he peeked out a crack in the door.

The poison ivy was healing well, but Patrick's steady sobbing had been replaced by something far more troubling, a stone-faced silence, inscrutable eyes that looked shockingly wise in such a young face. Life in the SEALs had been a steady parceling-out of hell; Schweitzer's life had been spent wading through the depths of human depravity, the sewers peopled by human traffickers, narco-terrorists, and those organized-crime operators strong enough to threaten the power of states. It had offered him a glimpse of not only what was done in those depths but how it impacted those it was done to. He looked at his son again and shivered. He'd seen those eyes before. He knew what they meant.

But even a steady diet of traumatic terror couldn't dampen Patrick's need to eat and sleep, and so Schweitzer jogged his way along, his boy nestled against his shoulder now, cheek placid and accepting of the cold, dead skin beneath it. Patrick would grow up in a world where it was possible to trust a corpse. As far as Schweitzer knew, he was the only one who could be trusted. Anything else remotely like him would kill Patrick as soon as look at him. He thought on that, on the hard conversation that he was going to have to have, how he was going to explain all this to Perretto, if Perretto would even speak to him, or would just draw and fire when he saw what Schweitzer had become? He would worry about it when he got closer; for now, the only plan he had was to keep moving, to keep his son fed and alive and as far from the Golds as possible.

Schweitzer kept returning to his augmented hearing, straining to hear a stealthy approach, a muffled hiss, anything that might indicate the approach of pursuit, but there was nothing. If the Gemini Cell had his trail, then they were not following it for some reason or had found a way to silence pursuit effectively enough to take him unawares. He doubted that, but he couldn't doubt the fact that Kentucky was disappearing under his feet, a steady drumbeat that took them west, moving through the woods just off the roads, ducking low whenever he heard a car approaching.

After two days, he had become a petty thief. The routine of smash-and-grab robberies of boutiques and small shops was too easy, given his powers. *You are an immortal superman*, he told himself, *and you use it to lift premade sandwiches and bottles of sports drink from gas stations*. It was for Patrick, he reminded himself; that had to make it okay.

He told himself this as he broke the lock off the freezer cabinet in a gift shop that was self-consciously rustic, lacquered rough wood garlanded with plastic ivy and flowers. Patrick was getting better about being alone, learning to sit tight and keep quiet, secure in the knowledge that this cold, dead thing that claimed to be his father would return eventually and would bring food with it when it did. He'd promised the boy ice cream, and he intended to deliver. The trick was to be quick enough that Patrick wouldn't lose patience and start wandering off. Schweitzer was confident that he would overhear anyone drawing near. He scanned the soggy cardboard dividers, the brightly colored packaging. What hadn't Patrick tried yet? Schweitzer remembered Peter passing him a tricolored rocket pop, blue eyes crinkling at the corners as Schweitzer's face lit in response to the sweet tang of it hitting his tongue. Would Patrick have a similar reaction? Had he ever tried a Creamsicle? Schweitzer felt another stab of grief as he realized that he didn't remember. He thought of Patrick's hard eyes, wondered why he was bothering. *You are dead. You are just trying to get him to a safe place. That doesn't require ice cream. There is no fathering left for you to do.*

But he remembered his early days of unlife, navigating his dead body around the refrigerated cell they'd kept him in. He hadn't had to sit, but he had. He hadn't had to nod or shake his head when he "spoke" through Jawid to Eldredge.

But he had. Those tiny gestures had saved his humanity, and his humanity had cast out Ninip and given him himself.

Sitting for him, ice cream for Patrick. It was something.

He snatched a chocolate-dipped Popsicle out of the freezer. Best to go with the classic when he wasn't sure what Patrick's tastes were. He straightened, closed the lid as gently as he could, slipped the broken padlock back through the hasp. The longer the morning shift took to notice the break-in, the more time before they called it in. He turned to head back to the corner of the store, where Patrick sat among a pile of plush toy owls. He wouldn't play with them, Schweitzer knew. He would stare off into the distance, face pale and eyes blank. *What did you expect? For him to chatter, babble, and play nice while you rob the place?*

Schweitzer paused, concentrating, dialed his hearing out, straining to pick out anything from the chorus of usual night sounds: insects chirruping, distant cars, and the stealthy padding of nocturnal mammals going about their routines.

Heavy breathing, the thumping of running feet.

Male, out of shape, hoofing it alone down the center of the main drag. Schweitzer sniffed the air. It was still too far out for him to smell the fear in the interloper's sweat, but he could hear it in the high edge of his labored breathing. The man was terrified. Wincing huffs. In pain, too.

Schweitzer dropped the ice cream and hefted the bag of canned food as he raced to the back of the store. Patrick was standing, one toy owl in each hand. He was making low noises in his throat, flying them in circles over his head, one chasing the other. His eyes still had too much thousand-yard stare in them, and he was not smiling, but the small gesture of genuine childhood made Schweitzer's dead heart clench. He wanted nothing more than to stand there and watch his son just be his age.

The thumping steps, the heavy breathing. Closer now.

There was no time. *He can't be a kid. Not for five minutes. Not ever.*

He raced to scoop up his son, saw the surprise on Patrick's face as he swooped in, shifting briefly to fear as he caught him around the waist and swung him up over his shoulder. Schweitzer knew he should say something, make it appear he was attempting to play, but all of his senses were focused on the sound of the breathing and the feet, the lone man running closer and closer. A tiny part of him registered the damage he was doing, that this was hurting Patrick, but the focus of the SEAL and the super senses of the magically augmented being bulled them aside. *Got to see what I'm dealing with here. Need high ground.*

There was a staircase behind the register, but it was close to the storefront window, in the direction of whoever was coming. Schweitzer pushed open the back door to the building, but he still couldn't prevent it from squealing on the hinges he'd broken getting in.

The footsteps slowed to a jog, then stopped. Whoever it was held their breath as they tried to listen. *Damn it.* It didn't change anything. He still needed the ground. Patrick might have been frightened by the speed with which

Schweitzer had appeared and scooped him up, but he was quiet for now, settling into the familiar rhythm of nestling into his father's shoulder.

Schweitzer turned and looked up. The building could barely be called two stories, more like a single floor and an attic, but it was higher off the ground than anything else around. It would have to do. Schweitzer jumped. The strength in his legs with so great that he barely had to crouch to get the momentum he needed. Patrick pressed close as the wind swept over them and the weathered brick wall rushed past. For a brief moment, it was only the two of them, washed by the light of the moon and the cold blast of the passing air. Under other circumstances, it would have been wonderful.

He vaulted the lip of the roof and put his son down on the torn tar paper. Behind Patrick, Schweitzer could see the open door leading down into the storefront. "Shh," he said, putting a finger to the gray smears that had been his lips, before making his way to the opposite edge.

A man stood in the street, head sawing left and right, dirty white hair wild on his head. Schweitzer recognized him, not just his face and body, but the tenor of his winded breathing, his bouncing gait. *It can't be. Why the hell would they send him alone?*

It didn't matter. It would be good to kill him. Schweitzer conjured Sarah's mangled corpse in his mind and prepared himself to spring.

The man reached into his waistband, pulled out a long-bladed knife. Teal light spilled off the blade, so bright that it washed the street before him, chasing shadows into the gutter. He turned away from Schweitzer, and the light dimmed, he turned back toward him, and the light grew brighter. He took a step toward the building, lifted his eyes to the lip of the roof. "Jim!" he shouted.

There was no doubting the voice. It was Eldredge.

"I know you're there!" Eldredge called. "Please! I just want to talk! I need your help!"

Scrabbling in the darkness behind him. Patrick was

stirring, crawling on his hands and knees over to his father. Schweitzer put out a hand and he stopped, crouched, listening.

"Jim!" Eldredge took a step closer, and now Schweitzer could feel the magic washing off the blade, the current eddying toward him, faint but powerful, the light brightening as it drew nearer.

Schweitzer stood, head and shoulders rising above the roof's lip. His SEAL mind told him he presented a good target for a sniper, backlit against the moon. It was bad tactics, but there was something in Eldredge's voice, his ragged appearance, that let him take the chance. He heard no one else, and a sniper's round would do nothing more than punch a hole in him.

"You've got to be out of your fucking mind, Eldredge."

"Jim. Oh, thank God."

"You've got about thirty seconds before I rip your fucking head off." He was conscious of Patrick listening at his side. The boy had seen so much, curses and threats were nothing now.

"I know about Sarah, Jim. I'm sorry."

"Are you, now? I am too. Killing you might make me feel a little better about it."

"I'm dead anyway. I went against the Cell, Jim. I'm on the run. Sarah was the last straw."

Schweitzer could hear the lie in his voice, the change in pulse and breathing, the rush of blood as his heart pumped faster. Sarah might be part of the reason he'd left, but not the whole.

"Is that why you're here? You want me to do it before they do?"

"No. I want to live. I want you to help me to live."

"And why the hell would I do that?"

Eldredge's eyes were wide, his cheeks tight, forehead lined. Schweitzer saw no guile in him. He was terrified. He was desperate. "We both know the Cell will never stop hunting you. It's either you or them."

"I'm dead, Eldredge, in case you hadn't noticed. Now my wife is too. Let them come. I'll make a good fight of it."

"You have Patrick, Jim. He's with you."

"Patrick's dead." Schweitzer tried to put his hand on his son's shoulder, but Patrick had moved back from him. Schweitzer turned his head to look for his son as he spoke to Eldredge. "Funny thing, but life on the run from a SOF unit that fields killer zombies isn't conducive to the health of small children."

"You're lying," Eldredge said. "Patrick's alive, but he won't be much longer if you don't stop the Cell. You're the only one who can do it, Jim. Whatever you may think of me, I didn't have a hand in killing Sarah. Our interests are aligned here."

"What the fuck do you expect me to do? Go running back to Virginia with my son in my arms?" The deep shadow on the roof forced Schweitzer to dial into the infrared spectrum to find his son. Patrick was standing now, walking toward the open door downstairs.

"I will stay with him," Eldredge said. "I will keep him safe."

"Don't move," Schweitzer whispered to his son, then leapt. The movement and the emotion that drove it were so sudden that he didn't realize he intended to kill Eldredge until he was already in the air. Shades of Ninip, Schweitzer's jinn self, made manifest.

He landed on the broken asphalt in a crouch, bone claws slid out, spines and horns working their way through the rents in the skin along his back and head. Eldredge stumbled back a step, thrusting the knife out before him. Up close, Schweitzer felt the magic in it more strongly. It thrummed against his own, checking him, cooling his anger. He didn't want to go near that blade. He straightened instead, leaned in. "You want me to give you my son?"

"Even a small cut from this will destroy you," Eldredge said. "Don't come near me."

Schweitzer wasn't sure he believed him, but it didn't

matter. It would be easy enough to move around the blade, rip the old man's arm off at the shoulder. The key would be to get close enough to the wrist to control the weapon's movement.

"Listen to me," Eldredge said. "The Cell is everywhere. There is no place in this country where they can't reach you, probably no place in the world. Whoever you entrust with Patrick is going to be discovered, and that means they're going to be killed. Like it or not, Patrick is a death sentence."

Schweitzer thought of Perretto. He'd known this, of course, that to entrust Patrick to him was to condemn his own children to lives without a father, if they lived at all, but he had been desperate for a direction, for some kind of *hope* that Patrick could have something approaching a normal life. His rage surged as Eldredge spoke the words. Because once said, they couldn't be unsaid; because now he couldn't give Patrick to Perretto.

"You need someone who already has a death sentence." Eldredge spoke in a rush. "Someone with nothing to lose. Someone who will believe stories about a secret magical military unit that marshals an army of superpowered corpses. As far as I know, I'm the only person in existence with that resume, Jim. We need one another."

Schweitzer heard a rapping from behind him, turned to see Patrick banging on the locked glass door to the store. Schweitzer could hear the boy faintly through the barrier. "Daddy!" The same word he had cried when Schweitzer's enemies had broken into his home and ended his life.

Schweitzer moved just as quickly as he had against Eldredge. Before he knew it, he had raced to the door and ripped it open, the shattered lock flying. He reached down for his son.

Patrick paused, hand on Schweitzer's leg, stared shyly at Eldredge. Schweitzer ruffled his hair, only touching a few strands before his son detached from his leg, closed the distance to Eldredge, and froze, staring up into the old man's eyes. Eldredge lowered the knife, mouth crinkling into a smile. "There you are," he said to Patrick, then looked up at Schweitzer. "You're not a very good liar, Jim. You never were."

"Fuck you," Schweitzer said, heading toward his son. But Patrick had already closed the rest of the distance, grasped Eldredge's fingers. Schweitzer came closer, but didn't intervene as Eldredge bent down to the boy. *How long have you kept Patrick on the run?* Schweitzer asked himself. *How long has it been since he touched another warm, living hand? Looked into eyes that aren't made of fire?*

Schweitzer remembered when he had visited the Cell's command center before he'd escaped. He'd shaken hands with one of the analysts, thrilled to the warm pulse in her palm. He knew the power of that contact, knew what it meant to Patrick, young as he was.

You can never give him that. No matter what you do. Not ever.

"How the hell did you find us?"

Eldredge looked up, the ghost of the smile he'd had for Patrick still playing on his lips. "I got lucky. I caught a news segment on TV saying that you chucked a guy off a train."

"I didn't chuck anyone. I told him to jump. Is he okay?"

"Banged up but fine. It gave me a positive location for you and told me how you were travelling. There's only one cargo line through here, Jim, and it goes in a straight line. From there, it was a question of calculating time and distance. Luckily, we're in the middle of nowhere, Kentucky. There aren't a lot of towns, and I figured you'd have to resupply. The rest"—he hefted the knife—"came down to this."

Patrick stared up at Eldredge, and the old man ruffled his hair. "Ah, Jim. All those years shut underground. You get bent on a task and you start to forget why you do it. The thing itself becomes its own reason. There is no end state."

"Patrick is my end state, Eldredge. There's nothing else."

"And this is the only way Patrick will ever be safe," Eldredge said. "Take out the Cell, or sooner or later, they'll take out your son."

He was right, of course. Nothing would make Schweitzer happier than to see the program that had birthed him into this new life, that had kept him prisoner and lied to him about his family's survival, pay. He could see himself tearing through the hallways, the blood of his enemies, the soldiers, the analysts, painting the walls.

No. They are serving their country the best way they know how. They don't deserve this. Only the people at the top. You have the remember that. That is the difference between you and Ninip.

"Why did you run?" Schweitzer asked.

"The Director, he . . ."

"I thought you were the Director."

"No, Jim. I'm the 'Lead Scientist' in a program that involves no real science. I run things, but I took my orders from him."

"And he is?"

"He's an Operator, Jim. All the years I worked there, and I never knew. But I know now. He's as dead as you are."

Schweitzer looked at his face, smelled the chemicals in his bloodstream. He was telling the truth. "How did you find out?"

"We always communicated over video chat without the video. I finally went to see him."

"Why?"

"Because it's out of control, Jim. He's killing indiscriminately; by the time we caught up with you and Sarah, the Golds had wiped out an entire town."

"I know; I saw."

"No, you didn't. Not the aftermath, the gutted buildings and corpses. It was . . . It's too much. They got a Boy Scout troop later. Boy Scouts, Jim!"

Schweitzer said nothing, his eyes fixed on his son, who clung to Eldredge's leg now, cheek pressed against his thigh.

"And there's more," Eldredge said. "They brought in another Sorcerer to work with Jawid. She's . . . better than he is. They're Binding jinn into living subjects. We tried it before, years before you . . . before we got you. The subjects never lived through it, and eventually, we called it off. But this time, they've kept on trying, and they're having some success. They'll get it eventually."

"Why would they want to do that?"

"I don't know, but it's not hard to guess. A Gold Operator can't walk in the daylight, can't attend board meetings or make speeches. They are monsters, Jim. A jinn in a living person? They could go hidden. They could do something other than kill."

"No, they couldn't. You didn't live with a jinn, didn't share your body with one. Killing is all they know how to do."

"Maybe it's different with a living soul. Maybe it's different in a living body. Maybe it isn't different, but they've figured out some other way."

"I can't believe you expect me to believe any of this. I may be the corpse, Eldredge, but you're the monster. You've murdered and you've lied and you've worked in the shadows for years, and you expect me to believe that you've suddenly found a conscience. You expect me to leave my son with you and race off to my own destruction. How convenient that would be for you, for the Cell."

Eldredge's face twisted in grief and anger, but his smell didn't change. Schweitzer's words were hurting him, but he still wasn't lying. "You're right, Jim. I have done terrible things. I am the monster. Even dead, you're a better man than I am. But in this case, in this one case, we need one another. Everything I've done, I've done with the idea that it was better for the country, for humanity. I broke eggs to make an omelet. You mean to tell me that you never killed innocents on all your scores of operations?"

He was right. Schweitzer had killed people to keep ops from being compromised. In a small Eastern European hamlet owned by the self-styled "Amir of the Caucasus," he'd put a bullet in a girl in her early twenties for turning a corner too fast. She had just been a blur in his vision, and then she had been dead. His training had put her down; it helped him with the shock and grief, too, kept him focused on the op. It was within rules of engagement, but it still ate at him. He'd never discussed it with Sarah. Why bother? It wouldn't bring the girl back to life.

He didn't discuss it with Eldredge now, but he saw the man's point.

"It all went so fast," Eldredge said. "By the time I realized it was too much, Basye was already gone. I always assumed that I was working toward a goal I could understand, could share in. I was taking on a burden so that others wouldn't have to."

So others might live. Schweitzer knew the oath well, had almost sacrificed his own marriage on that altar.

"The Director is . . . maybe not a Gold. He's patient; he's smart. He has control of his appetites. I wonder if he's like you. He's definitely dead, Jim. Whatever he's got planned, it isn't part of the national agenda; it isn't event part of the *human* agenda. This Binding into the living, I shudder to think of what he plans to do with that."

"Put himself in a living body." The thought lanced through Schweitzer. A living body. A beating heart again. Warm arms to hold his son. *There's no end state,* Eldredge had just said, but if magic could put Schweitzer back in a living body, then maybe he was wrong. "Someone important," Schweitzer went on, grateful that his unlife enabled him to keep emotion out of his voice.

Eldredge nodded. "I don't want that to happen, Jim. I want to enjoy some of this freedom I've supposedly been fighting for. I want to live."

"Death's not so bad. You get used to it."

"Please, Jim. I'm not a SEAL. Nobody's going to bring me back."

Schweitzer looked at Patrick, reached out a hand toward him. Patrick took it tentatively, but he didn't let go of Eldredge's leg. "You are not taking my son."

"That's right," Eldredge said, detaching Patrick and gently pushing him back toward his father. "I'm not. I'm sitting tight with him, wherever you tell me, giving you whatever reassurances you want, until you've killed the

Director and whomever else you have to in order to make sure the program stays dead."

"That might be a lot of people."

Eldredge shrugged. "However many it takes, Jim. It isn't much of a chance, but it's a better idea than running until Patrick really does expire."

"I can't protect you, Eldredge." The thought of Sarah materialized too fast for him to squash it or the spike of remorse that followed. "I can't protect anyone."

"I don't want you to protect me. I want you to help me bring it all down. It's the only way I'll ever be safe. It's the only way your son will ever be safe."

CHAPTER XXII
NEW MANAGEMENT

Dadou knelt over Jawid's corpse for a long, long time.

His head had come open at the top, the skull cracking along the forehead, spilling its contents onto the rug. His nose was broken, both eyes swollen shut. If she looked at him from the right angle, he looked like he'd passed out after being in a barroom brawl. She followed the procedures, checked his pulse, both carotid and radial. Nothing. He was gone.

Her mind sorted through and discarded any number of excuses. He had turned traitor. He was going to run. He'd put his hands on her. But the truth made a cold and slow crawl up her spine until it seated, immovable, in her mind.

The fact was that she barely remembered the moments between Jawid telling her to come away with him and now. The rest was stuttering, red-tinted flashes, like glimpses of the countryside seen through the slats of a boxcar hurtling along the tracks, or when booze and *ariwana* had begun to shut off her mind.

She had been so *angry*. But the anger that had propelled her through the killing vanished as soon as the deed was done, leaving her only the memories of Jawid that she liked. His sweet shyness. His earnest honesty. His bone-deep understanding of what she lived with every day. She blinked at the corpse before her, the one she had made.

He was a man, and the worst kind of man, a *religious* man. All religions were built to subjugate women, to make them bend their knees and spread their legs for entitled children. She had seen what had become of that for her sister. Jawid wanted the same thing, no matter how sweet his sighs and protestations of love. She had tolerated them because they made him pliant in the short term at least, but combined with his desire to betray the program, they were past enduring.

So, why was she sorry he was gone?

Because the truth was this: the anger, the simmering rage, had made her another person. She had meant to hurt him, frighten him.

Not to kill him.

She looked up at the shrine she'd built, the picture of her mother and sister. She wondered what her sister was doing now. Married, she assumed, or dead in a ditch. It didn't matter; there was no way Dadou could talk to her now, no way to explain what had become of her life.

Maybe that was why she was sorry Jawid was gone. Because he was one of the few people who had known who she was now. Because that pool seemed to be forever shrinking.

The isolation gripped her, and she went mad for the second time that day. She sobbed, the tears turning into laughter. She grabbed the small, thin pillow off the bed, put it over his purple face, covered some of the blood and brain that pooled on the floor. He looked better that way, more peaceful. Dadou lay down, placed her head on his back, pulled the tight curls of his thick black hair. It was clotted with blood and tiny chips of bone, but it still had that delightful spring to it. "Boink," she said, with each pop of the curl. "Boink."

He was still warm. She nestled against him, felt some of

the blood reach her shoulder. It was still warm too. She was two Dadous, one who knew that lying beside Jawid's corpse was sick and crazy, and another who reveled in his warmth, in the close contact, in the knowing that another person was nearby.

"Ah, *chouchou*," she breathed. "I didn't mean to; I am sorry." It changed nothing, but it felt good to say it.

Dadou didn't realize she had fallen asleep until she was awakened by a low beeping. She had closed her laptop while she had touched herself before Jawid had come to her door, and she hadn't wanted the Director to be able to see. She was sure there were other cameras in the room, but she controlled what she could. Now the light on the side of the webcam flashed as the call came in.

Dadou shook sleep from her head. She was foggy, but her mind had returned to her. The blinding rage and crippling loneliness were gone, and she was Dadou again. Jawid's body had gone stiff and cool beneath her, his blood gelling to a thick paste that stuck to her neck and shoulders. She propped herself up on her elbows, blinked at the pallor in his skin, the dull copper smell rising from him. Too weak to be brought back as a Gold Operator, even though it was probably still soon enough to return his soul. She glanced at the laptop. It was likely the Director or his secretary. She would have to report what had happened here; it couldn't be hidden. Fear roiled in her belly. Her lack of control had cost the Cell one of its most valuable assets. The Director would be furious.

She calmed the fear with an effort, reminding herself that without Jawid, she was the Cell's *most* valuable asset. *No, they may have others.* Dadou doubted it, but there was no way to know.

The laptop's chime sounded again. The Director knew her whereabouts at all times; hell, he had probably seen what she did to Jawid already.

She flipped up the laptop to see the Director's secretary, disingenuous smile already melting away as her eyes roved over Dadou's shoulder to take in Jawid's corpse. "Miss Dadou . . . I. Are you all right? Is that Mister Rahimi?"

"*That*," Dadou said, "is none of your business. I will discuss it with the Director directly. Please put me through."

"No need." The secretary found her composure, smile springing back to her face, stretching her improbably bright lips. Dadou thought she looked like a circus clown. "The Director wanted to see you personally. He should be . . ."

The chime outside Dadou's door sounded and the transmission cut off. Dadou felt fear sinking in her belly, turned to face the door. Its stainless steel surface reflected a funhouse mirror image of herself, down to the knees where a spray of drying blood interrupted it.

She didn't have time to approach it before it clicked open, lock manipulated by the master electronic key. A man in a black suit entered, gun drawn, eyes roving the room, never alighting in one place. He ignored Jawid's corpse, gestured with the barrel at one corner. "Ma'am, I need you to step over there and face the wall. Do not turn around, no matter what happens."

"Do—"

The barrel hovered over her heart. "Ma'am, do not speak. Move to the corner and face it. Do it right now. I won't ask you again."

Dadou knew she should be angry, knew that if they already had decided to punish her for Jawid, that she was better served by going down fighting. *No. If he wanted you dead, he'd have shot you by now.* She stepped into the corner, so close that her nose almost touched the wall. She heard the man bustling around behind her, going through drawers, kneeling in front of the bed.

Her back and shoulders itched, anticipating the bullet that could come at any moment. *If it's my time, then it's my time. It is no great loss if the world goes on without me.* She thought of the long years ahead of her, angry and alone, and wondered if she might not like it better that way herself.

The thought gave her some peace, and she focused on

the ache in her heart and stomach that contemplating her own death brought.

She didn't know how long she'd been lost in thought when she finally noticed that all sound of movement had stopped. The room was silent. The air vents did not hiss. She shivered, cool air on her shoulders. She waited another moment before mustering the courage to speak. "Sir? I'm sorry; can I turn . . ."

No sound of movement, no breathing, no answer. Dadou risked a glance over her shoulder.

The door was closed; the man with the gun was gone. In his place was another man, tall and muscular. He also wore a suit, rumpled and threadbare, draped carelessly over his body. The chipped buttons were misaligned, the cuffs bagging around his black shoes. His hands were enclosed in black gloves, fake leather flaking off in patches. His head and neck were covered in stretched white fabric, giving only the vaguest outline of the depression of his eye sockets, stub of a nose, cut of a mouth. The cold air came from him. As if he had just been wheeled out of a refrigerator.

He was completely still. No rise and fall of his chest, no twitching of his fingers. For a moment, Dadou wondered if she was the victim of some prank, if the man had placed an eerily dressed mannequin behind her before he departed.

But then the thing in the suit spoke. "Do you know who I am?"

Its lips slid against the constraining fabric, adding a whisper to the crooning, monster-movie voice. She'd never heard it before, not without the aid of a computer modulator, but she knew precisely who he was, had always known, really.

"You are the Director."

"It's nice to meet you in person, Miss Alva."

Dadou said nothing. It was not nice to meet this thing in front of her, this freezing thing that didn't breathe, didn't move, save for its lips behind their mask.

One finger on the gloved hand twitched toward Jawid's corpse. Otherwise, the thing was stone. "I appreciate your work, Miss Alva, first for Scorpio Cell and now for our joint effort here. You've made stunning progress in a very short period of time, and I'm pleased to see the psychology reports indicating that Jawid had become more compliant thanks to your efforts to . . . convince him.

"So, you will forgive me," the Director went on, "if I find the evidence before us"—the finger twitched again toward Jawid—"somewhat to the contrary."

"I'm sorry," Dadou echoed what had become Jawid's favorite words since they'd first made love. It was the truth. She was deeply and truly sorry. She hadn't meant to kill him. But the deeper truth was that her remorse was far outmatched by the possibility of incurring the wrath of the thing standing before her.

"I am too," the Director said. "Mister Rahimi was an enormous asset to this program, and the most effective we ever employed. He'd have given you a run for your money in his early days, I'd wager. Would you mind telling me what happened?"

"He told me he loved me," Dadou said. "He wanted us to marry."

"Those were your orders, Miss Alva. To woo him. To win him. It sounds like you succeeded. Why, then, is he dead?"

"He wanted to take me home with him. He was planning to escape. You ordered me to deal with him if he turned traitor."

"And you are certain he would have been successful in this enterprise? You could not have subdued him, bound him, waited for assistance?"

Dadou swallowed. She didn't like being questioned. It made the anger burn behind her eyes, her throat tightening and her hands flexing. But she looked at the tall, thin figure, and the tension in her muscles went slack. She didn't think she could fight him. She didn't think she could win. "I got angry," she said, her hands making useless circles at her side.

"You got angry," he repeated.

"You don't understand," she said. "It was . . . like going crazy. There were some things that happened . . . to my sister, when we were little."

"You mean to tell me"—the Director cut her off—"that you murdered your coworker because you have unresolved issues from your childhood? You think that is an excuse?"

Now is where the rubber meets the road, Dadou thought. If she was going to pay, it would be now.

There was a long pause.

"This is most unfortunate," the Director said. "We cannot have team members inflicting violence on one another in the workplace, Miss Dadou. I'm afraid there will be consequences."

Dadou felt her fear reach a height where it finally lapped itself, leaving centered calm in its wake. She had seen the dead slaughter the living. Even in a world transformed by magic, dying was still dying. She was ready. When she answered, her voice was steady. "What will you do to me? Arrest me? Feed me to the Golds?"

The Director was silent.

Dadou laughed long and low. It was forced, but the action still felt good in the face of this thin, rumpled dead thing in her cell.

"I fail to see the humor," the Director said. "You have cost me one of my most important assets."

"No, *Direktè*," Dadou answered. "I took out your garbage. I did you a favor."

"The work he was doing for the program . . ."

"He was done working for the program. He was done working for you. It was time for him to go."

His horror-film voice sounded confused, frustrated. "That is not your decision to make, Miss Dadou. Give me one good reason why I shouldn't kill you right now."

She laughed again. "There isn't one, unless you've got another *Sèvitè* running around? Maybe there is another cell you can call for a replacement Sorcerer?"

"There are others."

"Others who can do what I do?"

The Director was silent. Dadou smiled wider. She had guessed right. "I am going to take that as a no."

"But you should not take that to mean you can write your own ticket. I can and will find other Sorcerers if I must, and you should not labor under the delusion that I will hesitate to kill you if I feel you are too far off the reservation. Is that clear?"

Dadou nodded. It was clear, but now that she knew she was the only resource the program had, the boundaries of the reservation had just become a whole lot wider. Dead or alive, all men were the same. Give them the illusion of control, and they were docile as sheep.

"Anyway"—the Director flicked a finger at Jawid's corpse again—"we now have a small problem."

"We have two problems," Dadou said, "and neither of them are small."

"I assume neither of these problems have anything to do with the act of unspeakable violence you have visited on my dear friend and colleague, Mister Rahimi."

Dadou shook her head.

"Then"—the Director's voice took on a hint of exasperation that made him a sliver less frightening behind his masked immobility—"kindly enlighten me as to your insights into the problems faced by this program."

"Your problems are people. One is a powerful man who wants to shut this program down. The other is James Schweitzer."

"Schweitzer is dead. I would hardly call him a person," the Director said.

"Yet the solution is the same for both of them."

"And that is?"

Dadou smiled. *"Se de bon ki fé bonbon."*

The Director was silent for a long time. "I know the French, but your dialect is hard for me to follow."

"How do you like to say it here? Kill two birds with one stone."

CHAPTER XXIII
RETURN

Eldredge shivered at the base of the tree. He'd seemed a big man when Schweitzer had been his prisoner, the perennial white lab coat giving him a heft that Schweitzer missed now that it was gone. He was all knees and elbows, white hair sprouting from his ears and nose, skin so pale and thin that Schweitzer could see the tracery of veins beneath. He looked like some crazy, homeless grandpa, and of course Patrick loved him.

It had been the same way with Steve, with the old man who took Sarah in just before Schweitzer came for her. It was always this way with men. Schweitzer tried to write it off as coincidence, a quirk of character baked into Patrick's DNA, but he was too smart to see it as anything other than the accusation it was, as bold and clear as a pointed finger. Without a real father figure at home, his son sought them out wherever he could. He sat on Eldredge's knee, tugging gently on the old man's ear. Eldredge smiled at him, the corners of his eyes crinkling with genuine joy. When he spoke, his voice was thick. "Such a cutie. I can see why you love him so much."

Schweitzer stifled the urge to snatch him away from Eldredge. He had done enough snatching of Patrick as of late. Let the boy experience something other than fear for five minutes. He could sense Eldredge's intentions in the speed of his heartbeat and the smell of his sweat. If he summoned the will to hurt Patrick, Schweitzer would be ready.

"I am sorry we kept you from him," Eldredge said, looking up. The remorse in his eyes was genuine. "We didn't see how reuniting you would do any good."

"Bullshit," Schweitzer rasped. "You thought separating us would help keep me under control."

Eldredge looked shamefacedly at the ground. "That's true. Guess it didn't work."

"Might as well come clean now, Eldredge. Since we're on the same side." Schweitzer intended the words to be sarcastic but found that even with his increased control over his voice, he lacked the nuance to carry the tone. Eldredge looked up hopefully.

"Was it deliberate?" Schweitzer asked. "Did the Cell have me killed deliberately so they could use my body? Did you leak my identity to the Body Farm on purpose?"

Eldredge was quiet for a long time. His increased heart rate and blood sugar told Schweitzer that the question rattled him but not why.

"If you'd asked on the day you escaped us, I'd have said absolutely not," Eldredge said. "But now, I don't know. The Director isn't human, Jim. Who the hell knows why he does anything?"

"Who is he working for? There has to be a human hand behind this."

"Does there? You don't work for anyone."

"I'm different. I'm . . ."

"Good? That's what I thought too, that your essential sense of ethics was the thing that made you different. It certainly seemed that your 'good' acts were the thing that pushed Ninip out and kept you in. But the truth is that nobody has any idea of how this works except for Jawid and the Scorpio Sorcerer they brought in, and even they don't fully understand it.

"This Senator I was telling you about. He pulls the purse strings. He'd been threatening to shut us down over the . . . excesses of the Gold Elements we put in the field to find you."

Schweitzer felt the lie in Eldredge's chemical cocktail. "Don't fuck with me, Eldredge."

"He was going to shut us down for failing to find you."

"So? You want the Cell shut down. I don't want to be found. Everybody wins."

"He's going to replace it with something worse. Some new corps under SOCOM. It wouldn't be the end of the Cell, Jim. New boss, same as the old boss. I didn't entertain any illusions that they'd keep any of the old staff, though. We'd all get tossed in the trash or put under some asshole Army three-star who thinks magic is a satanic conspiracy."

"How was he going to do it?"

"The same way government suits have done these things since they invented the red power tie. He was going to cut off our money."

"That got your Director's attention, I'll bet."

"It didn't. He didn't really care. Jim, you've been in government long enough to know that nobody ignores funding line items. *Nobody*, no matter how self-interested, no matter how altruistic, no matter how cynical or idealistic, ignores threats to their funding. I know it seems crazy, but that was the scariest thing of all."

It was Schweitzer's turn to be quiet for a while. "No, that makes sense."

"I don't know for sure, but I think that's the end game here. To put a jinn in him, to have the one man we answer to be our puppet."

"Our?" Schweitzer asked. "I thought you said you were done."

Patrick grew impatient at the adult talk, tangled his hands in Eldredge's hair, pulling his head down toward him. "Oh, hey, there! What have you found? Is there something on my head?" Eldredge asked.

"Don't get too comfortable." Schweitzer couldn't keep the bitterness from his words. This bastard who had kept him from his son could give him something he never could, warm arms to fold him against a chest that housed a beating heart. "You're not going to be with him long."

"I'll take what I can get," Eldredge said seriously. "You weren't the only prisoner down there, Jim. I was locked underground for years. I came topside for ops, but that was it. I can't remember the last time I just sat and smelled the wind in the trees, or had a kid play on my lap."

"Do you expect me to feel bad for you?"

"No, but I do expect you to understand that this isn't some sneak attack on your family. I am not lying to you, Jim. We are wasting time here. Every minute we delay is another minute for them to find us and make us fight them on ground of their choosing, pitted against the pawns instead of the king. We need to move east, Jim. They won't expect it."

Schweitzer ignored him, dialing his hearing out into the wind-tossed tops of the trees behind the building. It was a trap. It had to be—the Cell was desperate; both its regular and Gold teams had failed to bring Schweitzer to heel, so they'd set up this elaborate ruse to lure him in.

Come on. Ockham's Razor. What makes more sense? That Eldredge is on the run from his own leadership, or that you're being tricked?

Schweitzer laughed internally. This was the problem with the brave new world he now occupied. When the dead could walk and magic was real, all possibilities were equally unlikely. Logic wasn't going to work here.

Fine. What does your gut tell you?

He studied Eldredge as the man returned his attention to Patrick, patiently enduring the boy's fingers up his nose.

And then . . . something.

The stirring of something in his chest, like a wound reopening, a vein he'd thought severed and scabbed over pumping blood again. His dead heart clenched, his spiritual stomach turned over.

With Sarah's death, his sense of her, of the link that connected them, had gone dead. He'd been able to focus on it enough to confirm what he knew, that she twisted in the soul storm with the rest of the screaming dead, that she endured the torture that had turned Ninip into a monster over the course of millennia. He knew he would never find her in that morass, that trying would only pull him further from his son. He couldn't abandon the living for the sake of the dead. That was what the monsters did.

Schweitzer didn't know much about magic or how it worked, but as far as he understood, dead was dead. The dead could be returned to the world of the living, but that wasn't the same thing as being returned to life.

And with a thunderclap of sudden feeling, the instant resurgence of the link he shared with his wife, Schweitzer knew that was what had happened to Sarah. She wasn't alive. That was impossible. Much as he had tried to turn away from the sight, he couldn't. He had witnessed her horrible death. No, not alive.

But she was here. In the world of the living.

The link reported as it had when she lived: emotion and resonance, direction and distance. She was a long, long way away, battered and frightened.

And not alone.

"Jim?" Eldredge had been speaking, and Schweitzer stopped him now, raising a palm toward him. He concentrated again, wrestling with the strength of his certainty, matched only by the vagueness of the details he needed. She was northwest. Many, many miles. She needed him. He could feel her crushed in the grip of something, battered by it. His wife, pushed into a corner, fighting madly for . . . for herself.

Schweitzer knew that feeling, could remember the sweet sense of corruption, Ninip constantly trying to slide his demonic filter over Schweitzer's perception of the world. Sarah was facing something like that now, save that, where Ninip had tried to slyly persuade, she was being battered.

"I have to go," Schweitzer heard himself say absently. He was already moving.

"Where? What's wrong?" Eldredge stood, Patrick reached for Schweitzer, caught hold of his hand.

"It's Sarah; she's back."

"That's not . . ." Eldredge paused. "You're sure?"

Schweitzer nodded. He squeezed Patrick's hand, but the link yanked him in Sarah's direction as surely as if he were a fish on a line. The need to go to her was as overwhelming as it was instant. "I have to find her, Eldredge. I have to do it now."

"It's a trap, Jim. It has to be. They wouldn't have brought her back without a very specific reason. They're probably hoping you'll come. They're going to be ready."

"Maybe she's alive . . . You said they were binding jinn into living bodies."

Eldredge shook his head. "Not *her* body, Jim. I saw what happened to Sarah's body. There's no way to put anything back in it."

"Maybe—"

"Jim," Eldredge cut him off. "This is the *Cell*. They don't do things to be nice. If Sarah's spirit is back in this world, it's because it suits them to have it here."

The need burned in Schweitzer. Already it was blotting out his senses, the strength of the link so intense that he set his shoulders back to stop it from physically dragging him forward. He knew he had an obligation to Patrick, but it felt fuzzy. It was hard to focus on anything other than the blazing, white-hot sensation of Sarah's presence. She was in the same world. She was so *near*. "I still have to go. I don't expect you to understand."

"I don't need to understand," Eldredge said. "I ran that program for years without understanding a goddamn thing. Makes things simpler. Jim, this is not a good idea."

"She's *hurting*, damn it!" Schweitzer snarled. "There's something . . . with her."

"They've paired her up with another soul, then."

"That doesn't make sense." The jinn had always been summoned into the body of the dead. "This would mean . . . *she's* the jinn. She's not a monster, Eldredge."

"This new Sorcerer is good," Eldredge said. "Really good. Who the hell knows what she can do?"

"You know." Jim was surprised at how angry he was. The link ran on emotion, and it fed his jinn side, crushing the cool professionalism of his training, making him itch to get underway and moving toward her, to *do* something. "You're the one who's supposed to know!"

Patrick shrank into Eldredge's side. Schweitzer knew he was scaring the boy, but he could feel Sarah again, backed into a corner, savaged. He could picture her in his mind, arms up, sheltering under a rain of blows. Eldredge leaned forward. "I don't know what you're going to find when you reach her, Jim, but it won't be friendly."

"I have to help her." The link to her pulsed like an ache in his chest.

"I know you do," Eldredge said, "and I also know that the only way to do that is to put her back in the void."

Schweitzer nodded. "If I have to," he said, not at all sure that he meant it. The maddening feeling of Sarah *alive* and so close . . . *No. She's not alive. It's not the same.* But he couldn't think, couldn't focus. He had to get to Sarah. He would deal with the rest then.

"Jim, I—"

"I'm going, Eldredge." In the face of the emotional onslaught, all resistance to the thought of leaving Patrick with Eldredge crumbled. "I can't . . . I just can't . . ."

Eldredge sighed. "Okay. You have to go to her. I've got it. Let me help you." He drew out the KA-BAR, teal light spilling over them both.

"Jim, look at me. I know this is hard for you, but you have to focus."

The light from the knife blazed in Schweitzer's vision. It was a weapon; it could hurt him. The thought distracted him from the tug of Sarah's presence, let the SEAL in him assert himself just enough. A few more moments wouldn't make a difference. If he went after Sarah, he had to do it right.

Schweitzer forced his feet to stay where they were. "You said that knife would destroy me. What's in it?"

"A jinn. One that can't abide others. I've killed a Gold with it already. The Director had three . . . I don't know what they were. Gold Operators, but wearing ancient jewelry. They had crowns. They looked like mummified kings. One of them came for me. I killed it with this knife."

"You want me to take it."

Eldredge nodded. "There are only two ways I know to send a jinn back to the void: complete destruction of the body, or what I have in my hand here. The first option would be . . . hard on you. You want to help Sarah, you're going to need this."

Schweitzer stared at the knife. It was insane, but the thought of sending Sarah back into the void felt like killing her all over again. Which was, of course, what the Cell was counting on him to feel. *You'll do what needs to be done. You owe her that.*

Schweitzer felt the tug in his chest again, stumbled a step forward.

"We both know it's going to be one hell of a fight, Jim," Eldredge said, "and we both know we can't just stash Patrick in an alley and go mix it up. Someone's got to look after him. You have a better chance with this knife than I do. Go find Sarah. Wherever she is, the Gemini Cell will be there too."

Schweitzer put out his hand. Eldredge slapped the knife handle-first into it. It glowed so brightly that Schweitzer had to dial his vision back to take it in. "Careful of that blade," Eldredge said. "So far as I know, it works at a scratch. Keep it sheathed. You don't want to send this whole thing south because you accidentally cut yourself."

Schweitzer slid the knife into its leather sheath, held it in his hand, adjusting his vision as the light winked out. "Will it even work on me? Maybe it only affects Golds."

"I'd rather not risk finding out. It's sure as hell glowing brightly enough for you."

"If I cut Sarah with this . . ."

"It'll send her back to the storm, Jim. I'm sorry."

Schweitzer stared at the knife.

"Maybe she's not a jinn, Jim," Eldredge said, "maybe they've found some other way to bring her back. You're certain she's in this world?"

Schweitzer reached inward, felt the unerring compass needle of his link to her. "Absolutely."

"Magic is new," Eldredge sighed. "There's more we don't know about it than we do. But I only know of one way a soul exits this world, and only one way it can reenter. Sarah definitely exited. If she's back, it's because the Cell brought her here for some reason and by some means you're not going to like."

"I don't know if I can kill her."

"She's dead, Jim. You can't kill her."

"You know what I mean."

Eldredge shrugged. "Think of it as a mercy killing. Maybe you can find a way to . . . make her like you. Either way, you must destroy the Cell."

Schweitzer looked up at him, held his eyes for a long time. Eldredge shrugged again. "I'm not all bad, Jim. Wanting to live without fear isn't a crime. It doesn't mean I'm not trustworthy. The likes of you and Sarah are beyond me." He gave Patrick a squeeze. "Now, this lad here, this lad I can look out for. We're going to have a fine time together, won't we?"

Schweitzer was silent for a long time, fighting against the pulling of the link. At long last, he felt himself regain some kind of balance. The insistent tug continued, but it wasn't yanking him off his feet now. He looked down at his son. Patrick looked back, and Schweitzer could see the trust in the boy's eyes. But Eldredge's leg was visible over his son's shoulder, the heat of his blood visible to Schweitzer's augmented vision. The warm pulse in Eldredge's femoral was in and of itself more fatherhood than Schweitzer could ever muster on his own. The boy would be better off with anyone other than him. Eldredge was right. If he was an agent of the Gemini Cell, Schweitzer would be destroyed and Patrick dead by now. And even life with the Gemini Cell was still more life than Schweitzer could give him. Living was beyond him.

"How will I find you?" Schweitzer asked. And even though living was beyond him, Schweitzer felt a little piece of himself die with the question.

"Craigslist," Eldredge answered so quickly that Schweitzer knew he'd already thought it through. "I'll put an ad in the personals once a week. I'll say I'm more Mark Twain than Bettie Page. You can find it in a Google search; whatever city it's posted under is where I'll be. Respond to the ad and we'll go from there."

Schweitzer held up his mangled fingers. "The fuck am I supposed to Google anything?"

Eldredge rolled his eyes. "You have to be the first zombie prima donna in history. You're a goddamn SEAL, Jim. You can figure out how to use a computer with no skin on your fingers."

They were quiet for a long time, Eldredge locking eyes with the flames in Schweitzer's sockets. He could smell the fear stink on the old man, but Schweitzer had to admit, he did a damn good job of not showing it. He was right, of course. Schweitzer was going after Sarah, and he was leaving Patrick with the good doctor, and he would break into a library and do a Google search if there was anything left of him bigger than a breadbox after it was all over.

Schweitzer shook his head. "I'll figure something out."

Eldredge nodded. "This is likely certain death for both of us . . . well, death for me. Whatever passes for death for you. Can you give me anything?"

Schweitzer handed him the child's backpack that was all their supplies. "I won't need it."

Eldredge took the pack, stared at it dangling from his hand. Schweitzer felt the pull of his link to Sarah. *Be patient. A few more minutes. For Patrick.*

"I know it's not exactly Gucci," Schweitzer said, "but it's what I've got."

Eldredge rolled his eyes, but he didn't return the pack. "This is great, but that's not what I meant. I mean, is there anywhere for me to go? Do you have family who would take us in? Friends?"

"I've only got one, and it's a long shot, but it's away from here. West."

"How far west?"

"San Diego. Guy named Dan Perretto, Coast Guard Maritime Enforcement Specialist First Class. Assigned to PACTACLET. I don't know where he lives, but if you found me, you can sure as hell find him."

"And he'll help?"

"Not sure, but I think so. Dan's a good man. Got kids of his own. We went through a lot together."

Eldredge paused. "You know this could bring . . . scrutiny on your friend, Jim?"

"Yeah," Schweitzer said. "But I also don't have a lot of options here. And I'm not just dumping Patrick off with him. You're going to keep him with you, and you're going to find a way to keep this out of Perretto's living room."

"If he'll even talk to me."

"If. Anyway, whether you find Perretto or not, west is still a direction to move in."

"That's pretty thin, Jim."

"Whole fucking thing is pretty thin," Schweitzer answered. "Entire world's turned on its head lately, or didn't you notice? If you've got a better idea, I'm all ears."

"How are you going to get there?"

"I'll have to fly. Wherever she is, it's much too far to walk."

"You can tell that?"

Schweitzer nodded. "We're joined; it's a kind of magic. Similar to what bound Ninip to me. I can tell direction, and distance more or less. She's a long way away, to the northwest. You got any idea what's there?"

"Canada?"

"That doesn't make sense. Why bring her back outside the country?"

"Idaho? I don't fucking know. North of here is . . . Ohio, I think."

"What's in Ohio? Does the Cell have a facility there?"

"Not that I know of. We had one in California, Scorpio Cell, but we shut that down and pulled the Sorcerer over to Virginia when you flew the coop."

"What's north? Think, Eldredge. This . . . makes it hard to concentrate." He gestured at his chest, as if Eldredge could see the magic link to Sarah.

"Jesus, Jim. I'm a doctor, not a cartographer." Schweitzer stared at him, stone-faced. "Okay, fine. I-states. Indiana. Illinois. Iowa . . . Fuck, Jim. Iowa."

"What about Iowa?"

"That's where Hodges is from."

"Hodges . . . Don Hodges?"

Eldredge nodded. "The Senator. He's the one I was telling you about. The one who knows about our budget and authorizes funding." He met Schweitzer's eyes. "Someone important."

"Doesn't mean anything. Maybe they're taking Sarah to him for a demo."

"Maybe we're completely off base and she's in Nebraska. Or the Dakotas. Jesus, Jim. It's all a wing and a fucking prayer."

"You got any other details on Hodges? Where does he live?"

Eldredge rolled his eyes again. "How the hell should I know? He's a Senator. Start with the state house. Look him up on Goo— Oh, Jesus Christ."

Schweitzer waved a hand. "It doesn't matter. I can find Sarah. I can always find Sarah."

He knelt down before his son, wrestling with his impatience to be away. It would be so easy to just stand and go, leave Eldredge to make his excuses. Patrick was too young to understand. *No. That's bullshit and you know it. He's busted up enough by all of this. Do it right this time.*

"Hey, little man." Patrick tucked himself against Eldredge's leg. Schweitzer winced. "Daddy's got to go away for a little while, but I'll be back soon. Uncle . . ." He realized with a start that he didn't know Eldredge's first name. He looked up at the older man.

"Julius," Eldredge said.

"Are you serious?"

"I fail to see how that's any less of a decent name than James. And my last name isn't Eldredge. It's Whiting."

Schweitzer stared, smelled the truth in him. "You're serious."

Eldredge shrugged. "They're just names. It's not like it matters now anyway."

"It matters to me."

Eldredge looked embarrassed. "It's funny; I haven't used either name in so long. No, I think I'll stick with Eldredge. Julius Whiting died a long time ago."

"Eldredge it is," Schweitzer said.

"My middle name is Eustis. Glad to be shot of that."

Schweitzer turned back to Patrick. "Uncle Julius is going to take care of you until I come back. He's going to keep you safe until I can catch up to you"—he looked back up at Eldredge—"because Uncle Julius understands that if he doesn't, no matter what Hallmark moment we may just have shared, I will find him. Uncle Julius knows that if any harm should come to even a single hair on your head, then I will find him and I will make him pay."

"Uncle Julius is a coward," Eldredge said to Schweitzer, "and you can always count on cowards acting in the interest of self-preservation."

Schweitzer ignored him, reached out, touched his son's cheek. "I'll come back for you."

Patrick nodded, looked at the ground. His eyes were already somewhere else, taking him to the faraway place where none of this was happening, a world where dead men lay down and stayed dead. It was the best Schweitzer was going to get, and he took it.

Schweitzer felt his spiritual stomach clench with grief.

This may be the last time you see him. His son. *Oh, Patrick. We never had a chance.* He opened his mouth to say something more, but he didn't bother. What good would it do? In the end, all that came out was "Take care of him, Eldredge. And don't forget to keep in touch."

Eldredge's hand tightened on Patrick's shoulder. "Westward bound, Jim. We'll leave a light on for you."

Schweitzer knew he should feel fear. He knew he should feel regret, disgust that he was leaving his son in the hands of a stranger.

But the truth was that as he turned to the northwest and began to move, as he gave himself over to the impulse to follow the link wherever it led, he felt his dead heart lift. His limbs felt light, his step longer. Every cell in his body vibrated with the pulse of the magic, every foot a foot closer to her. It was right. Going after her was right.

Schweitzer broke into a run and the trees around him lengthened into brown and green blurs. He didn't know where he was going, but for now, it felt good just to run, away from Eldredge and his son, toward Sarah. He didn't have the details he needed: where she was, who she was with, what he could expect.

He'd played for higher stakes on less. No plan survived contact with the enemy, anyway. He put on speed and let the woods fall away behind him.

CHAPTER XXIV
THE FLIGHT IN

Ashland Regional Airport was a postage stamp, a tiny smudge of runway surrounded by poplars growing so thick that they blocked the breeze. A few planes dotted the flight line, two-seater private jobs for the most part, though he made out one small postal service cargo plane and an Air National Guard training jet.

It was too small for a control tower, just a collection of aluminum Quonset huts huddling together off the tarmac, beneath a ragged-looking wind sock and a fluttering American flag. There was no fence, no guards, nothing that marked the terror-addled culture of big-city airports, where he wouldn't have been able to get within half a klick of the runway without alerting a dozen armed guards.

Schweitzer kept his ears tuned, heard the footsteps of someone down on the runway's far end, probably a night watchman, given the late hour. He heard the droning of the last flight to take off, the angry-insect sound he'd used to find the airport in the first place, homing in as the plane taxied and took off.

He sized up the tail numbers of the parked planes and

then made for the largest of the white huts, a two-story building with a long bank of tinted windows facing the runway. If the flight controller had a desk, that's where it would be.

The door to the tarmac wasn't even locked, and Schweitzer made his way through the rows of desks and chairs unmolested, moving silently through the litter of real lives. Trophies, motivational posters, framed pictures of families. There was something about the small-town setting that tugged at him. Partly because it reminded him of his life back in Little Creek. Partly because, once again, it dangled the existence of families just outside of his grasp. But the tug was nothing compared to the tug he felt toward Sarah. It kept him focused, kept him moving.

The controller's desk was where he expected it. An old microphone stood beside a bank of dark equipment. Schweitzer could still smell the ozone from their being powered on to see the last flight off. He must have arrived just behind the departing shift.

He dug in drawers until he found what he sought, yellowed hanging folders, FLIGHT PLANS written in black marker across the top. He thumbed through them, checking the time and date against the huge red LED readout of the twenty-four-hour clock hanging above the desk. He paged back and through again, cursing under his breath. There was a flight due to leave tomorrow morning, ten hours from now. He had no choice. Unless he suddenly learned to fly a plane, he would have to wait.

The aircraft was also unlocked. It was a tiny, blue-striped single-engine plane, so clean that if Schweitzer hadn't just seen three logged flights for it in the past week, he'd have sworn it was brand-new. There was barely room for him behind the narrow seats, just enough to wedge himself into the tight space, lying on his back, knees drawn up to his chest. A blanket had been laid out there, loosely draped over a pile of towels, flip-flops, and bottles of sun block. Schweitzer huddled under it now, the odd plastic shapes digging into his back. As always, he was aware of the sensation of the discomfort, but it had no power to disturb him. Being dead had its advantages.

It grew hot in the back of the plane, long past the point where a living man would have been stifled, forced to throw the blanket aside to gasp for air, where the stink of his sweat would have filled the cockpit. It would have made him move, do any number of things that would have alerted others to Schweitzer's presence. But in death, he was completely still, the last hours of night finally shrugging off, the sun peeking above the treetops just as the rumble of engines announced the first members of the flight crew reporting for duty.

The pilot was late. Schweitzer didn't have a watch, but his augmented senses did give him a heightened sense of time passing, of the air heating by degrees as the sun rose. Before long, he heard a man making his way to the plane's side, whistling to himself tunelessly. He was overweight, the labored beating of his heart speaking of clogged arteries and old age. The door opened with a click, and Schweitzer felt the plane sag as the man lowered his weight into the pilot's chair.

Schweitzer listened to the preflight checks, the man's deep southern twang as he went down the list, the dull scratching on the pen against the clipboard. Schweitzer would wait until they were airborne and away from the airport. He hadn't paid attention to the destination. It wouldn't matter. He just hoped the old man's ticker would hold out, given what was about to happen.

At last, the engine coughed into life, and the pilot spoke into his radio headset. "Ashland Regional Unicom, five niner one niner for a radio check, over."

The response was muffled by the cups of his headphones, drowned out by the roar of the engines. Schweitzer dialed in his hearing, shutting out the engine noise and focusing on the buzzing crackle of the radio. "Ashland Regional Unicom has you, Lima Charlie. Good morning, Frank."

Frank smiled. "Good morning, Paul. Five niner one niner is departing two-six."

"Roger that. Have fun and be safe."

Schweitzer felt the plane begin to move slowly. It picked up speed, and Schweitzer watched the shadows play along the inside of the cockpit, racing faster and faster, until at last, Schweitzer felt the plane's nose come up, taking his weight as it pushed its way up into the sky.

The plane banked as Frank circled out from the pattern, and Schweitzer felt the airframe sag, shuddering. "What the fuc . . ." Frank muttered, looking over his instruments. He turned around and looked behind him, straight at Schweitzer's hiding place, then forward again as the plane banked once more.

"Ashland Regional, five niner one niner."

"Everything okay, Frank?"

"Plane doesn't feel right. I'm dragging ass up here."

"Okay, how worried should I be right now?"

Frank looked at his instruments, shrugged. "Not worried. Everything's responding; it just doesn't feel right. I'm going to set her back down. Is there anyone else on approach I didn't see?"

"No, you're . . ."

No time. Schweitzer slid out from under the blanket. Pushed his upper body into the passenger seat, never rising high enough to be seen over the canopy's edge. He lifted one skeletal hand, duct tape peeling away from the rents, and for the first time was grateful for his horrific appearance. He placed it on the pilot's chest. "Don't say a goddamn thing into that radio. You speak and you're fucking dead."

The man, strictly speaking, obeyed him. He screamed, a high whining sound that made Schweitzer think of cats fucking, but Schweitzer didn't hear the rasping click that would have meant he'd toggled the radio. His meaty face went white, shook.

"You pass out, and I'll fucking kill you," Schweitzer rasped.

The man did not pass out; his chins quivered, tears leaked out the corners of his eyes, but he kept his grip on consciousness.

"You want to get through this alive, you do exactly as I say. I'm already dead, so you better fucking believe that crashing this aircraft is no big deal to me. I will walk away from it. You won't. You read me?"

The man nodded.

"Radio back and tell them you figured it out. Tell them you're good to go."

"But I just told them that I'm dragging." The man's voice was high, whining. "How do I explain—"

"You're the fucking pilot. You figure it out. And God as my witness, you'd better figure it out."

"I can't believe this. This isn't happening."

Schweitzer let one bone claw extend far enough to pierce the man's shirt, brought it gently across his collarbone. *You bastard. This guy's done nothing wrong. He doesn't deserve this.*

Fuck that. This guy is your chance to find Sarah. Mission first. Focus.

"You feel that?" Schweitzer asked.

The man nodded. Whimpered.

"That's real blood coming out of you, pal. *Your* blood. You better fucking believe this is happening, and you better start believing it right now."

"Okay."

"Good. Now use that radio and keep us in the air."

The buzzing click of the radio sounded as the pilot switched over. "Ashland Regional, five niner one niner." His voice was halting, on the verge of a stutter.

"Lock it up," Schweitzer whispered. "If they guess something's wrong, it's over."

The man's terrified eyes rolled over, his face asking the question: *A corpse just rolled out from behind me and is hijacking my plane. I'm fucking terrified. How do you expect me to sound like everything's normal?*

Schweitzer bared his teeth. "Find. A. Way."

The radio crackled as the tower replied. "Frank, what's going on?"

"It's me. I'm an idiot," the pilot said, still sounding

rattled but better than before. "I forgot my cooler from last time. Left it in the back. It's fine."

The voice on the other end of the radio sounded doubtful. "You sure?"

"Yeah, everything checks out. Everything responds. It must have been the cooler and a crosswind. I just got in a clear patch and the plane feels fine. Sorry about that."

A long pause. "Dude. Don't scare me like that."

"Yeah," Frank laughed nervously. "Sorry about that."

"Well done," Schweitzer said. "You just bought yourself another fifteen minutes. Now get us to cruising altitude."

"I have a wife," the man said. "Children, grandchildren, please."

"You think I give a fuck about any of that?" Schweitzer growled. But the truth was that he did care, that the words twisted in his spiritual gut. *Patrick was wrong. You are a bad monster. No better than the terrorists and human traffickers you operated against for years. It doesn't matter why you're doing this.* He remembered standing over the "Amir of the Caucasus." The man had set fire to a school for daring to teach girls to read. Schweitzer had taken great pleasure in kicking down his door and putting a bullet in his gut.

The man had stared up at him from the floor, trying to keep the tangled mess of his guts from spilling up. There was pain in his eyes, but righteous fury too, and that had angered Schweitzer. He didn't want him to die feeling like he was in the right. "How could you do that? You burned down a *school*, you fucker. You killed dozens of little girls. Don't you have daughters of your own?"

"I did," the Amir whispered, blood bubbling out with the words. "Your drones killed them. Why should my children die and yours live?"

Schweitzer hadn't had an answer for him. He probably twisted in the soul storm now, there to while away the millennia until someone like Jawid brought him back. He'd make an excellent jinn.

"You're not going to kill me, are you?" The pilot asked.

"Not if you do exactly as I say," Schweitzer answered. "Get us up and where I want to go, and then I'll be out of your hair and you can fly on home to that family of yours. This isn't personal. I just need a ride."

"Are you dead?"

Schweitzer knew he should tell him to shut up, that revealing anything personal was a risk, but there was a limit to how much of a monster he could be. He waited until he saw the man gently pull on the yoke and the he felt the plane's nose lift.

"Yes, Frank," Schweitzer said, watching Frank's eyes widen as he discovered Schweitzer already knew his name. "I am."

"Jesus," the man said.

"Magic is real, Frank. Sorry you had to find out this way."

"Where am I taking you?"

"You have a smartphone?"

Frank nodded.

"Hand it to me."

Frank dug in his pocket and handed it to Schweitzer. "It's not locked." Schweitzer drew a finger across the virtual keyboard to open it up. No reaction. *You fucking idiot. These things work off the heat in your fingers.* He bit back on the spasm of grief that accompanied the reminder that he lacked even the body heat to work a phone.

"Looks like I'm going to need your help here, Frank." He handed the phone back. "I need you to look something up for me."

"Okay." Frank took the phone, hovered his thumb over it.

"I need the Iowa offices for Senator Don Hodges."

"You mean the address? Why?"

"Because you're going to fly me there."

"Why?"

The cooling air told Schweitzer that they were well airborne now. He wouldn't be seen from the ground. He crawled up into the seat and turned to look at Frank. "You have got to be out of your fucking mind, asking me questions like that, Frank. Did you miss the whole part of me walking away from a plane crash?"

"You'll be too messed up in a plane crash to walk, even if you are dead. You'd be burned to a crisp or in pieces."

"You want to test that theory?" Schweitzer reached out and nudged the control stick forward. The nose of the plane dipped sharply and Frank let out a terrified squeal.

"Okay! Okay! I'll look it up!"

"Good boy."

Frank tapped on his phone for a moment. "I have the address. Des Moines."

"Outstanding. Take me there." Hodges likely wouldn't be at his Iowa office, but it didn't matter. He would feel it as they drew nearer to Sarah, and the closer they came, the better he would know where she was.

"Flight plan says Little Rock, man," Frank said. "We don't have the fuel to make it there. We'll crash, and then neither of us gets what we want."

"Look at me, Frank." Schweitzer leaned toward him. His elbow brushed a bobblehead hula dancer Frank had suctioned to the dash. "Look at me."

Frank looked at him sidelong, head still facing forward. The effect was comical, and Schweitzer felt a phantom smile rise to his face, a ghost of the man he'd once been, a living man who could laugh and appreciate irony. But his face was a skull now, and skulls grinned all the time, whether the joke was funny or not. "Do you think that, in life, I was a stupid man, Frank?"

No answer. Frank looked back out the windshield.

"I said, fucking look at me!"

The eyes jerked back over. "I'm looking at you!"

"Do you think I was stupid?"

"How should I know? I didn't know you."

"I'm very smart, Frank. Dying hasn't changed that. Smart guys like me know that Little Rock isn't much farther than even the far side of Iowa. I used to drop from light aircraft like this. I knew a thing or two about reckoning fuel. You can make it, Frank. You can make it and to spare. And if you try to trick me again, I will kick your ass out of the cockpit and see if all that hot air can float you down slowly enough to land on your feet."

Frank said nothing, the tears still leaking out of the corners of his eyes.

"You may look away now, Frank. Always want to keep your eyes on the road."

Frank looked back out the windshield and Schweitzer quelled his rebel conscience yet again. The ground was a swath of green pasteboard beneath them, the clouds a flat line of white over their heads. Schweitzer had the weird sensation of buzzing through a layer of a landscape painting, the reality above and below him too perfectly rendered to be real.

Schweitzer heard the light click of Frank engaging the radio, whipped a claw out to hover below his chin. "Don't."

"I have to radio the course change, man. I can't just fly wherever the hell I want. It's not like driving a car," he said, and Schweitzer's augmented senses assured him that Frank believed it to be true. "Please, I'm not lying. I'm not trying to trick you; don't hurt me."

Schweitzer considered. The midair course change would require a reason, would set the authorities on alert. An unreported and unscheduled flight change would also raise alarms, but it would take more time for ground crews to figure out what the problem was and to coordinate a response. "Just keep flying," he said.

"Even if you don't kill me, man, you're going to get me arrested as soon as I land."

"You can tell them there was a stowaway."

"A zombie stowaway." Frank rolled his eyes. "Nobody is going to believe that. I don't even believe that."

"Believe it. And tell them that I had a gun on you if it helps."

"It won't."

Schweitzer shrugged. "I'm fucking dead, dude. You'll forgive me if I lack sympathy for your predicament. Just keep flying and you'll live through this. Keep it as low as you can without drawing attention."

Schweitzer felt the plane slowly shed altitude as Frank obeyed. The man started to speak again and stopped at a shushing from Schweitzer. The next two hours were an odd silence, Frank with his eyes straight ahead, the plane engines droning, and the airframe shaking under the pressure of the currents of wind and Schweitzer's dead weight on the cockpit floor. Schweitzer could feel Sarah's signal getting stronger, the emotions passed along the link more intense. They were moving in the right direction. Schweitzer imagined the distance dropping away, stifled the urge to drum his fingers on his knees as the agitation at her growing nearness almost overwhelmed him.

Schweitzer kept his bone claw extended and near Frank's throat, a reminder of what was at stake. Schweitzer could feel Frank's chemical scent change as he calmed, slowly realizing that he wasn't going to die, at least not yet. Schweitzer could hear his heart slowing, feel the pressure in him change as his veins dilated back to their regular diameter. Schweitzer thought of amping his fear up again with some menacing gesture but decided he didn't want to. It was exhausting being a monster. He had done it enough to Patrick. He wanted a break.

Schweitzer knew Frank was going to speak before he opened his mouth. "So . . . who were when you were alive?"

"The fuck do you care about me?"

A spike in the fear, but not as high as before. "Hey, man. It's a long flight. We might as well make conversation."

"I was a man."

Frank actually smiled. "Well, I figured."

Schweitzer knew this wasn't good. There was no reason to connect with this man, no reason to communicate with him at all. He was the ride to Sarah, nothing more. Schweitzer's training tried to kick in, to dehumanize, to reduce Frank to his functional role, to keep Schweitzer's situational awareness. But the truth was that Schweitzer was exhausted. Since his death, Schweitzer's every conversation had been fraught.

Cutting deals with Eldredge, getting briefed by Jawid, explaining the new lie of the world to Sarah. He had forgotten the gentle rhythms of easy, adult conversation, the micro-connections that small talk forged. And once he remembered, he realized that he wanted it, desperately.

"I had a family." Schweitzer said.

"They died too?" Frank asked.

"Yes," Schweitzer answered. Best not to let the man know there were any levers on him.

"I'm really sorry to hear that. I don't know what I'd do if my kids died."

"You'd find a way to go on, same as everyone else."

"Not everybody finds a way. I know I couldn't.".

"You'd be surprised at what you can do. You ever serve?"

Frank arched an eyebrow at that. The question itself gave him information Schweitzer knew the man probably shouldn't have, but he cared less and less. He'd lost his life. He'd lost Sarah. He could have this one thing. "You were . . . in the military? When you were alive? I kinda guessed when you talked about dropping out of planes."

Schweitzer nodded.

"What branch?"

"None of your fucking business."

"Hey, man. That's fine. I was in the Army. I only did four years, though. You could do four and get out back then. I drove trucks."

"Then you remember what it was like. They take you in, they break you down, they build you back up. By the time they're done with you, you're capable of amazing things. Things you never thought you'd be able to do." He'd had this conversation with Sarah when they'd first dated. *I could never paint like that,* he'd said. She'd fixed him with a serious look, and her voice had been stern, even scolding. *Yes, you could. If you were willing to put in the time, willing to give up your leisure and your freedom and your money, you could be the greatest painter that ever lived. The only difference between you and I is focus, commitment, and desire.*

He wasn't sure of the exact moment when he figured out that he would love her and no other for the rest of his life, but that was certainly a candidate.

Oh God. Sarah. I miss you so much.

Frank shrugged. "All I learned to do was drive a truck, man. And stand in line a lot."

"You'd adapt to it," Schweitzer said, "but I hope you never have to." Showing sympathy was a terrible idea, and it felt fantastic.

"Everybody's got to go sometime," Frank said. Schweitzer waited for him to say more, but he was content to fly on in silence, and eventually, Schweitzer settled into the lull of the throbbing engines and the whoosh of the air over the wings. He watched the clouds scud by above them. Frank was keeping the plane low per his orders, and Schweitzer watched the sun peek out between billowing white banks. The brightness was dazzling, but he had no eyes left to damage. For the first time in his existence, he stared directly into the center of the fiery ball, letting his vision play over the rippling plasma, seeing the sparking tendrils of heat even from this distance. It was amazing. Every moment he existed as a dead man, he found new ways to experience the world. In some ways, he was like a newborn baby.

I can look straight into the sun. For as long as I want.

He heard a dull click, felt the faint vibrations of the radio trembling through the headphones around Frank's ears. Schweitzer dialed his hearing up to pick up the frequency.

A normal human ear wouldn't have been able to hear over the ambient noise of the moving plane, but Schweitzer wasn't a normal human.

"Cessna one seven two, tail number November five niner one niner, November five niner one niner, this is Air National Guard India Alpha three one two. You have entered restricted airspace. I say again you have entered restricted military airspace. Assume heading two seven zero and depart the area immediately."

Frank stayed quiet, a bead of sweat slowly working its way from his forehead behind one of the earphones. His eyes flicked to Schweitzer, only for an instant, back to the windscreen. Schweitzer smelled the burned-sugar stink of his blood sugar spiking, the chemically sour odor of adrenaline, heard the hammering of his speeding heart.

Schweitzer waited for Frank to turn the plane.

He didn't. It wasn't an accident.

The radio crackled again. "November five niner one niner, this is India Alpha three one two. If you do not leave the airspace on heading two seven zero, we will engage you. If you are in distress and cannot respond, please toggle your radio three times in one-second intervals, over."

Schweitzer sat bolt upright. "What the fu . . ."

Frank kept his eyes straight ahead, his hand on the controls. With the other, he reached down and toggled his radio. *Click-click. Click-click . . .*

Frank didn't get a chance to sound a third click before Schweitzer snatched his wrist, but the radio was already sounding again. "November five niner one niner, this is India Alpha three one two. We are in receipt of your distress indicator and are inbound to intercept. Assume heading two seven zero and maintain speed and altitude. Toggle your radio twice in one-second intervals to indicate that you will comply, over."

Frank clicked two more times as Schweitzer reached over to snatch his wrist. "Roger that," the radio crackled. "We're on our way. India Alpha three one two out."

"Are you a fucking idiot?" Schweitzer asked.

"I don't know what you're talking about, man," Frank practically squeaked.

"I'm talking about you deliberately flying over a fucking Air National Guard base," Schweitzer hissed. "What part of 'Do what I say and you'll live through this' didn't you understand?"

"I didn't do anything!" Frank screamed.

Schweitzer sat up, his head and shoulders flattening against the canopy as he seized Frank's neck, the man's fat jowls spilling over his grip, eyes bugging out of his head. Schweitzer pointed at his throat with the other finger, letting the bone claw extend until it touched Frank's Adam's apple. "You stupid motherfucker."

"You know, man," Frank gasped, "I don't think you're going to hurt me. I don't think that's what you're going to do at all."

You idiot, Schweitzer screamed at himself. *Why did you fucking talk to him?* Too much sympathy, too much humanity. Enough to give Frank the glimmer of hope that Schweitzer was too soft to do the deed. Schweitzer wasn't too soft to do the deed, but he would have to do it now. There was no intimidating Frank into anything, and the Air National Guard jets that were scrambling would be there soon.

Schweitzer cursed, retracted the bone claw, and punched down on the controls. The plane's nose dipped sickeningly and Frank shrieked as it dove, engines roaring. Schweitzer saw the green paste of the Iowa plain below him, a flashing blue ribbon that he knew meant one of the rivers that crisscrossed the state. He'd always planned to travel there with Sarah, see the fields where the Indian Wars had been fought, the edges of the frontier where the nation had been born.

The ground rushed toward them; Frank grabbed the controls and pulled futilely against Schweitzer's strength. "Please! Please!"

Above them, a long way off but coming fast, Schweitzer could hear the high-pitched whine of a jet engine burning hard.

The Air National Guard jet, inbound at speed. An F-16, most likely. It wouldn't take them long to arrive, and he had to be gone by then.

"Please!" Spit trailed out of the corners of Frank's mouth. "Let me level her off! I have a family!"

The green stretch of ground sped toward them; a thick

swath of trees came and went. The bright, shining line of
the river rushed closer. "Keep us over the river," Schweitzer
said, and Frank nodded enthusiastically, hauling back on
the yoke as soon as Schweitzer released it.

It was a near thing. Frank pulled and the plane groaned,
straining as if, now that it was committed to the dive, it
didn't want to pull out of it, had its heart set on crashing
straight into the river glinting silver-white now that the sun
was behind them. Schweitzer heard the airframe groan as
the metal strained against the wind, the high-wire twanging
of the wings cutting through the rushing air. Frank couldn't
hear those sounds, had no idea how close his tiny little
airplane was coming to ripping itself apart. Better for him
that way.

The radio crackled again. "Five niner one niner, India
Alpha three one two. I say again, maintain your current
speed and altitude on bearing two seven zero or we will
open fire."

"They might kill you," Schweitzer said. "I definitely
will. Get as low and slow as you can get us without stalling.
Keep diving."

Frank banked the plane until the electronic compass
pointed to two seven zero but otherwise kept the aircraft
steady. Schweitzer pressed the claw into his throat. "Last
chance, Frank. I'm done being nice."

Frank swallowed and slowed the plane, pushing the nose
gently down. Schweitzer watched the river grow beneath
them until it filled the entire horizon. The whine of the jet
engine came louder.

"Fuck," Frank whispered. "They'll just fire a missile.
We won't even see it coming."

Schweitzer retracted the claw and squeezed Frank's
shoulder. "Then I'll get off. Thanks for the ride, man."

Schweitzer forced the side door open, struggling briefly
against the rush of wind that tried to hold it shut. He heard
Frank curse as he leapt.

The plane must have slowed to little more than fifty

knots, but the tail still swept over him so close that he could feel the rags of his clothing stirred by its passing. Then he was falling, letting his body stretch to keep himself stable, creating as much wind resistance as possible. The Iowa countryside was beautiful out here, the air sharp and clear, the river winking at him, breaking the sunlight into a shivering screen of diamonds. The whining of the jet engines became a roar as the river rushed upward and he arced into a graceful dive, tucking his chin, pointing his arms, and breaking the surface with little more than a splash.

The river wasn't deep down here. No sooner had the cold water admitted him than Schweitzer saw the sandy bottom racing upward, dotted with slimy rocks. He arched his back again, widening the angle of his descent and giving himself more time to shed speed. The resistance of the water continued to break his momentum, but not enough to keep him from colliding sharply with the bottom. He felt his ribs take the impact, flex enough to crush the lungs and heart of a living man but hold without more than a couple of minor breaks. He spun onto his back as he rebounded upward, swatting away a cloud of minnows and focusing his eyes up toward the surface.

The reflection of the sun and the wavering surface made it harder, but not impossible, for his magically augmented eyes to see out and into the open air, but it was still an oily and wave-washed image of Frank's little Cessna slowly gaining altitude below two gray streaks that were the F-16s finally arriving, overshooting at their higher airspeed, banking around for another pass. Schweitzer was certain that Frank was even now shouting into the radio, desperately telling them to wave off, that he'd been hijacked, that he was complying.

There was no fireball, no whoosh and roar of explosive ordnance being deployed. Schweitzer had gambled with Frank's life, to be sure, and there was a part of him that curdled at the thought, but it was a gamble that paid off as the Cessna motored on and out of sight.

Schweitzer nodded in satisfaction. Sarah was close, the tug of her through the link dragging him along like a fish on a lure. He gave into it, turning on his belly and swimming down into the dark, sweeping up against the current to where he knew his wife awaited him.

CHAPTER XXV
COMBINED

Schweitzer swam the river's oily length, pulling himself along the river bottom, ragged fingers digging into the silt and rock. He could feel the dark water pressing in on him from all sides, and the current worked furiously against him, desperately trying to sweep him down and out into the Mississippi, as if the water itself were trying to keep him from reaching his wife.

It could do as it liked. It couldn't stop him. Schweitzer pulled himself relentlessly along, so deep he knew he wasn't as much as a shadow to someone on the surface, even though the river was clear as glass and the day bright and sunny. He didn't need to rest, and his legs were strong enough to kick his way along upriver faster than a man could walk. With each yard, the maddening closeness of Sarah's presence grew, until he had to force himself to keep from scrabbling at the riverbed and take long, deliberate strokes. *Slow is smooth, smooth is fast. Focus.* Hand over hand, Schweitzer climbed the river bottom north and west.

The sun was setting, the rippling surface of the river blazing orange and red above him as he became aware of the shadows of buildings falling over the water's surface. He could hear the churning of motors, taste the rancid tang of garbage that told him he'd entered the dirtier water that carved its way through a major city. Sarah blazed like a coal forced down his throat and into his chest.

The sun sank farther as he pulled his way farther into the city, until the river bottom was shrouded in gloom, and Schweitzer had to adjust his vision to take advantage of the scarcer light. A few garbage bags had been sunk around him, old boots and crushed tin cans. Soggy fur and scattered bones. The detritus of a people living cheek by jowl. The river bent back on itself, and as he turned to follow it, he felt Sarah's presence growing farther. If he was going to find her, he'd have to go the rest of the way on land.

Schweitzer rolled onto his back, let himself surface by inches, fighting against the impulse to race up and out of the water, to go after her. *Go ahead; come up in the middle of a bunch of couples out for a stroll, or in front of a cop car.* He knew what he looked like. He could pass for a man if he had a man's clothes and at least something to cover his face, but his leering, dripping skull wouldn't leave room for doubt, especially with his burning silver eyes.

Des Moines was not New York, and while the water muted the sounds of those on the surface, Schweitzer could still hear the thrum of car wheels against the ground, the distant tread of footsteps. Nothing close. At night, it was a city of the dead.

Schweitzer let the top of his head break the surface, felt the soft touch of the air on his scalp. A high wall of gray stone rose sheer to one side, a wide stretch of grass between it and the road that wound its way along the river. As he watched, a car sped past, headlights painting two white cones on the asphalt. They wouldn't be able to see him from there. Not at night. Not even if they were looking.

He swam to the wall, tested the stone. It was uneven, the tiny ledges between the bricks slick with river slime, but he swarmed his way up with ease, his magically augmented muscles making short work of the climb, his shredded fingers and toes as strong as a living man's arm or leg. He threw a hand over the top, holding himself flat against the side of the wall as another car rushed past.

When he finally pulled himself up, he was greeted by a white stone building in classical style, flanked by bronze lamps and covered with sweeping arched windows. A wide stone staircase led up to the huge bronze double doors, closed and locked for the night. Some government building, full of the pompous grandeur that men used to deceive themselves into thinking the things they did had meaning, that they could protect anyone. That was fine. The architectural overstatement cast many shadows, offered an endless series of alcoves. It was perfect for a creature that wanted to shroud itself in darkness, to hide.

Schweitzer squatted beneath a stone eave and scanned the city skyline, feeling Sarah pulse in his throat, a steady rhythm that he could nearly hear. If his heart still beat, he knew it would be surging. A modern-sculpture park sprawled on the river's far side. Schweitzer could hear someone snoring fitfully beneath one of the pieces, a gang of kids whispering around a can of something just a few feet away from him. Easy to avoid, easier to scare off if they got wind of him. Beyond the park, tall glass-sided buildings reared into the night, limned in neon that only set them more starkly against the plain black-gray of the Iowa night sky.

There. Sarah was there.

Schweitzer bolted from cover, raced to the river's edge, leapt into the air. The river was at least fifty feet across. Schweitzer cleared it easily. A part of him knew that he should be amazed, filled with wonder at the fact that with a better running start, he could have jumped twice as far, but Schweitzer felt that part of him slipping away. This new creature, the one who could bend cold iron with its bare hands, the one that didn't need to eat, didn't need to sleep, didn't need to breathe, was more and more of who he was. That creature couldn't take care of a little boy, couldn't love a wife.

Lock it up. Patrick is with Eldredge now, for better or for worse. You can't do anything for him until you finish this.

For now, this creature was who he needed to be. All warriors needed to remember what they were fighting for, but it didn't change what the warrior had to do to win the fight. War was monstrous. To win, you had to be a monster.

And he was.

Schweitzer landed in a crouch on the far bank of the river, dropping into the shadows of the sculpture park. The kids stopped talking, swiveled their heads in his direction. There were whispers of "Did you see that?" But Schweitzer knew he had jumped too far and too fast. There would be too much for their minds to take in, and by the time they made sense of it, he'd be gone.

He took off at a sprint, sticking to the shadows of the office park, until he had to risk the streetlights along a broad avenue that wended its way toward the straight metal teeth of the skyline.

As the shadows of the buildings fell over him again, Sarah's signal grew focused, and Schweitzer fought against the edges of a tunnel vision threatening to settle on him. He had felt the same thing when he'd put down the kickstand on the stolen Harley-Davidson, stepping onto the front lawn of the farmhouse where Sarah had taken refuge while she'd still been alive.

The tallest of the buildings loomed closer, a modern, star-shaped tower with a beaten-copper roof that had failed to deliver the promised verdigris and instead turned a sick-looking dark brown. Schweitzer's powerful eyes could see the directory posted in the lobby, the prominent brass plaques posted below it, the guard behind the marble-topped desk. An office building, then. If Senator Hodges lived there, his was one of the very few residences.

But it didn't matter, because Sarah was in there. Schweitzer was sure of it. Schweitzer had thought that once he'd pushed Ninip out, he'd mastered his new self, was in complete control. He'd had no idea. The compulsion of his link to Sarah took hold of him now, batted all resistance aside. His years of training to be a SEAL, his gift for self-denial, his pridelessness, his endurance, all were swept away in an instant, replaced by an animal need to *get to her* no matter what the cost.

Schweitzer the SEAL wanted to case the target, to surveil the entrances, figure out the path of any guard patrols, to wait, to plan, to do things right. But Schweitzer the jinn just galloped across the road, vaulting over a parked BMW sports coupe and hammering through the front doors so quickly, he nearly took them off their hinges.

The one guard was already rising, eyes fixed on a monitor that no doubt showed Schweitzer's approach, so fast that he didn't have time to register what he was seeing. He winced as the doors banged open, turned to face Schweitzer, eyes widening, before one hand disappeared beneath the desk.

Schweitzer smoothly vaulted the countertop, closing the distance between them and seizing the man's wrist. He ripped it away from the white button the guard had been reaching for, bent it painfully back. The guard drew breath to cry out and Schweitzer seized his throat. "You can scream, or you can go on breathing, but you can't do both."

The guard was bald, in his thirties, his thick torso covered by a black cable-knit sweater. He stared at Schweitzer, slowly closing his mouth, raising his free hand. "It's cool, man. Be cool."

"Cool is my middle fucking name," Schweitzer whispered, running his hands over the man's waist. There was a thick utility belt there. Ring of keys, flashlight, handcuffs, radio. No gun.

Schweitzer did a quick once-over of the guard's armpits and ankles. No hidden holsters. He was unarmed. "What's your name?"

The guard was staring into Schweitzer's silver eyes. "Are you for fucking real, man?"

Schweitzer shook him hard enough to make his head rock side to side. "I ask the questions. What's your goddamn name?"

The man coughed, sputtered. "Raoul, man. Fucking Raoul."

"All right, Raoul. You're going to come with me, and you're going to be very quiet while you do, or I'm going to kill you."

"I'm going crazy. You're dead, man. You're dead."

"Yes, I am dead. But you're not, and you have a chance to keep it that way, but only if you do exactly as I say. Now, are you going to be good? Or are you going to be meat?" With the last word, Schweitzer let a single bone claw slide from his fingertip.

Raoul didn't answer, raised his hand instead. The terror in his face was evident, but he forced a weak smile.

Schweitzer relaxed a hair. "Good." He snatched the radio from Raoul's holster. "How often do you check in?"

"Every hour; due in another twenty minutes."

Schweitzer disconnected the battery and put the two pieces beside one another under Raoul's metal chair. "Stairs?"

Raoul pointed to a black door set in the reflective stainless steel of the lobby wall. A broad white sign glowed red above it, blaring the words EXIT to anyone looking. Schweitzer would have rolled his eyes had he had them to roll. His mouth reflexively stretched into a smile, failed as the taut skin met resistance from the metal armature beneath. But he was able to sound sheepish, at least. "Should have seen that. There an alarm on that door?"

Raoul shook his head, and Schweitzer pulled them both through the door and into the white-painted stairwell beyond. Metal stairs wound their way up out of Schweitzer's sight, obscured by a series of concrete landings above. Schweitzer glanced to his right, found what he was looking for, a water pipe rising out of the concrete floor, disappearing into the landing above. Schweitzer snatched Raoul's handcuffs out of his belt, slapped the guard's wrist to the pipe. The man resisted, but Schweitzer overpowered him as easily if he were a child. He wisely didn't raise his other hand.

"You're not going to kill me, are you?" Raoul asked.

"No," Schweitzer said, cuffing him to the pipe. "So long as you don't make a lot of noise. All you have to do is sit here quietly, and I'll be done and out of here in about fifteen minutes. You can be quiet for fifteen minutes, can't you?"

Raoul nodded vigorously. "Not a peep, man. I'm cool."

"You are cool," Schweitzer said, "which is why I'm not going to kill you. But, unfortunately, I am going to have to hurt you, but I promise not any more than I absolutely have to."

"Wait . . ." Raoul began, but Schweitzer had already lifted his shoulder, keeping his elbow hooked and raising his right hand in an uppercut that would have been the envy of a prizefighter. He planted it precisely on the point of Raoul's chin, snapping the guard's head back hard enough that his brain sloshed in the hard housing of his skull, the stem stretching and snapping back as the muscles and tendons engaged to keep his head from spinning all the way around. Raoul gave a brief groan, the light went out of his eyes, and he collapsed, hanging by his cuffed wrist.

He wouldn't be down long. He would scream when he came to. Schweitzer had to make sure that by then, it wouldn't matter.

He felt Sarah's signal, rising in his chest, pull him on and up. He surrendered to it, letting his legs and arms pump, taking the stairs two, then five, then entire flights at a time, pausing only to hook the railing with his arm to propel him around and up again at each landing. He lost count of how many floors he'd gone up, seeing only the flashing white of the cinder-block walls blurring along beside him. He could see the faint heat signatures of people on the floors, could hear hushed conversations, muted breathing, the sounds he'd expect to hear in a late-night office building. He ignored them all, listening only to the siren's call of Sarah growing more intense with each step.

Schweitzer realized that he was suddenly in silence. The SEAL side of him began to curse his lack of caution, even as the jinn continued to plunge upward, listening only for the sound of his lost love. He slowly mastered himself, ripping his eyes from the dwindling pinnacle of the stairwell, turned to the thickness of the wall and its black steel door leading out to the floor beyond. The floor number, 38, was painted in white stencil beside it. Schweitzer squinted, just barely able to make out the outlines of five heat signatures. They were incredibly faint, far more than they should have been, but Schweitzer could make out men lined up beside the door, each with his hand on the shoulder of the man before him.

Schweitzer knew the formation well, the snake formed behind the point man, stacked on the door. Trained professionals. Trouble.

Barreling ahead was not the answer here. They were ready. But he could feel Sarah's soul screaming down the link between them. Whatever she was paired with was hurting her. There was no way he could slow-roll this. Not when she was so close.

Schweitzer drove forward as the door slammed open, the first two operators buttonhooking into the stairwell, one mounting the stairs and the other moving to the corner of the landing. Cold came off them in waves, a light dusting of frost on their body armor and helmets. They had been hosed down with Freon, or stood in a refrigerator before being sent against him. He could smell the Composition B explosive in the oversized drums hanging beneath the barrels of their carbines. They'd been loaded out and prepared to fight against an enemy who could see into the infrared spectrum. The Comp B meant they knew that regular bullets weren't going to do the job. They were waiting for him. They were ready.

Schweitzer growled and leapt as the first one fired. The round ripped through the air, narrowly missing his head.

But instead of thudding into the wall, Schweitzer saw a light on the operator's weapon flash red and heard a dull *whump* behind him as the round exploded. A hot hand slapped his back, turning his leap into a spin. He crashed into the men, lowering his shoulder to catch one of them under the chin and slamming him into the wall. The operator's throat collapsed under the pressure, and he fell to the floor, clawing at his neck and rolling down the stairs into the boiling black smoke left by the round's detonation. Schweitzer didn't have time to fully assess the damage, but he could feel the backs of his ribs exposed where the shrapnel had torn the flesh away, the chips of concrete flaying the backs of his arms and thighs.

The other operator raised his weapon, cursed as he realized he was too close to fire the explosive round, and whipped the carbine off the sling. A long axe blade swung out of the stock with a loud click. He lifted the gun up by the barrel, stepping into the swing as another of the operators came through the doorway.

Schweitzer rolled to his knees, got a hand up in time to intercept the axe blade, catching the operator's wrist and crushing it with a quick squeeze. The bones snapped, grinding together, the operator screaming. But the weapon already had the momentum, and the axe blade was heavy. It flew down, sinking deep into Schweitzer's shoulder. The scar left by the fight with Jackrabbit had left a divot in that shoulder, a relic of where the bone cleaver had cut in, nearly severing the arm. The Gemini Cell had spent hours repairing the damage, shoring it up with metal cables that held the arm in place, giving Schweitzer the freedom of movement he needed, strength he could rely on. In the days since the repair, it had been so reliable that he'd forgotten about the damage.

But the divot guided the blade in, the axe biting into the old wound, sharp metal cutting effortlessly through the soft flesh until it caught on the fibers of the metal cable at the joint. Schweitzer could feel a few of the precious threads part, springing back on their own tension with a metallic twanging sound muted by the dead meat around them.

These men were trained to fight him. They weren't wasting time with bullets. They would blow him apart or cut him to pieces.

Schweitzer reached across his chest, grasping the back

of the axe blade. The operator was well trained, and he released the weapon, dropping his hand to a hatchet hanging at his waist. He jerked it out by the head, letting its own momentum carry it upward before catching it by the handle.

Schweitzer jerked the carbine-axe head up and out of his shoulder, spun it around so the blade faced his enemy. The operator's eyes widened briefly as he realized his mistake, and then Schweitzer plunged the axe head forward, punching it through the black Kevlar of his helmet, feeling it cut through his skull and into the soft brain behind. The enemy collapsed, sliding down the stairs, carbine bouncing against the metal as it trailed from the blade, still stuck in his head.

The other operator dropped his carbine to hang by its sling and already had his hatchet out. He swung it just as Schweitzer turned back to him, planting the head in the wound opened by the carbine-axe. The metal head cut deeper into the cable, more threads snapping, the arm going slack to hang by a slim line of gristle and metal wire. Glycerol squirted against the wall, dribbled down Schweitzer's side.

Schweitzer reached out and grabbed the man's throat, expecting him to try to back away, but he should have reckoned that an operator would follow Schweitzer's own oath: *so others might live*. Schweitzer was an enemy, a monster. Of course the operator would be willing to sacrifice himself. He had been training to die his entire professional life.

The operator leaned in, letting Schweitzer's hand cut off his windpipe. Schweitzer was lightning-fast, but the operator still had precious seconds to react before Schweitzer's magical strength collapsed the flesh of his neck onto his vertebrae, began crushing the bone. He used those seconds well, grasping Schweitzer's wrist and yanking it with surprising strength, the strands finally parting, the arm ripping away even as Schweitzer snapped his neck and he collapsed.

Schweitzer followed his corpse down, catching up the carbine with his remaining hand, leveling the weapon and firing even as the other operators tried to clear the doorway. The round sped so quickly that the contrail sucked the door in behind it, slamming it shut. The subsequent blast bent it, knocking it askew on its hinges, but it had been designed to hold back fire, the thick metal sagging but holding steady. The men beyond were not so lucky; Schweitzer could tell by the screams. His heat vision was suddenly alight as their warm remains were spattered by the explosive round, dripping off the walls and ceiling.

Through it all, Sarah's proximity, her agony, still vibrated through the link they shared. She was just a floor or two above, so close he couldn't concentrate. He stared down at his arm, looking tiny now that it was parted from him. The gray muscles were ragged, covered more by duct tape than skin, the metal cables trailing from the shoulder turned blue where the scraping of the hatchet and axe blades had heated them.

He left it where it lay. He was past sentiment, had no place for keepsakes. Only the Gemini Cell's technicians could fix it anyway, and they weren't exactly inclined to help him. He felt lighter as he bounded up the remaining stairs, compensating for the sudden change in his balance by leaning against the heavier pull of his remaining arm. At last, he could bear it no more and jumped straight up, cresting the metal railing and vaulting over to land at a crouch outside the landing doorway.

There were no heat signatures beyond it, but he could feel Sarah just a few feet away, separated from him only by the thick piece of metal on its well-oiled hinges. He reached for it instinctively with his missing arm, corrected himself, pulled it open with his real one. His senses screamed out in warning, the SEAL within him long since bludgeoned into silence by the jinn. This direct approach was idiocy, had already cost him an arm. That those operators had been cooled to dampen their heat signatures showed that the enemy was ready for him.

But the pull of the magic was far too strong. A wild, mad part of him truly believed that if he could only get close enough to Sarah, there wasn't a force in the world that could stop him. That love, contrary to everything he'd learned in a lifetime of running ops, really conquered all. The SEAL in him knew this was wrong, that he was running headlong into ambush, that he was down an arm. It didn't matter; the signal was all. Ninip had spoken of his addiction to the blood of the living, likened it to heroin. Schweitzer understood that now, as helpless as a rowboat on a storm-tossed sea. *Sarahsarahsarahsarahsarah.*

Schweitzer gave his jinn aspect free rein. The horns broke his scalp, the line of spikes punching through the open remains of his back, more vertebrae exposed than covered. His claws came out on his remaining hand, and he was surprised to feel a bone spike jut out from the stump of his shoulder, projecting out into the space where his arm used to be.

He reached out for the door handle, hesitated at a sudden strong sensation from just beyond the metal. Liquid power washed over and through him, as if he stood in the midst of a current, a tide that drowned and carried him up in the same moment. Magic. Sarah's terror and urgency, her love and anger, her need came roaring down the link that bound them, signal boosted by the presence of whatever magic was beyond the door.

Schweitzer could see a heat signature now, faint but growing as the human behind it drew closer. If it was another operator, he was alone.

And then the tide of magic and Sarah's nearness overwhelmed Schweitzer and he lost control, yanked the door handle so hard that it ripped free of the metal, sending slivers of metal sparkling through the air. Schweitzer stumbled back, victim to his own momentum, as the door shivered in its hinges and held fast.

Then it exploded.

The door flew out of the jamb, corner striking Schweitzer on his sternum, crushing him into the railing so hard that the metal bent. The door spun away, clattering down the stairwell. Schweitzer reached out to stop himself, realized the arm he'd used was missing, and flipped over sideways, tumbling. His face struck the stairs and he rolled, flopping down the steps until he skidded to a stop on the landing below, beside the broken remains of the door, his arm, and the operators he'd killed just moments before. The feeling of the magic at his back grew stronger, followed by the sound of heavy tread crunching on the metal fragments left by the shattered door.

"Jim Schweitzer." A woman's voice, rich and low, with the slightest trace of an accent. "You've lost an arm. *Pa bon.* That's government property, you know."

Schweitzer got himself up on the right hand this time, flipped himself over.

Raees Gruenen stood a few steps up, gray skin waxy under the fluorescent light.

The bullet hole Schweitzer had put in his forehead had been plugged and melted over, leaving a wet-looking round scar. The process of rebuilding his skull had stretched his face, as it had with Schweitzer, but with Raees, the Cell had been careless, favoring one side. The result was a leer, long and rising, his mouth lopsided as if mirth had dragged it too high and too hard, a dead man laughing out one side of his mouth. Long bone spines curved upward from his back, the frames of featherless wings. Others projected from his knees.

Over his shoulder, Schweitzer could see a woman, lean and muscular, her dreadlocked hair gathered into a long braid tossed over one shoulder. She was kitted out as an operator and carried a pistol, which she didn't bother to point at him. The tide of her magic was so strong that Schweitzer felt his dead skin prickle in response.

"'Lo, Jim," Gruenen said from the corner of his canted mouth. Schweitzer could tell from the wheezing flexion of his chest that he was doing the same bellows-dance Schweitzer had done before he pushed Ninip out and took control of his own corpse.

Schweitzer felt his link to Sarah vibrate, his wife's presence so close that she was almost on top of him. The edges of Schweitzer's vision narrowed again, the same sign he'd had when he'd first escaped the Cell and found Sarah, the surefire sign that the link they shared had reached its terminus.

He looked at the twisted smile with dawning horror. Gruenen took a step down, the link pulsed, and Schweitzer knew his wife was inside that mercenary's broken corpse.

CHAPTER XXVI
SO OTHERS MIGHT LIVE

Jim, the link throbbed. Gruenen took another step, his fists began to crackle, blue arcs of electricity spanning the knuckles. He could feel Gruenen battering Sarah aside, slamming her against the walls of the body they shared. *Jim.* Sarah's voice. *Jim, run.*

What did you expect, Schweitzer asked himself, *that she'd be walking and talking? Body whole and heart beating? That they'd truly brought her back to life?* The truth was that he hadn't had any expectations, that he had only been drunk on the bond between them. *Enough. She's trapped in there and she's hurting. Use the knife; set her free.*

"Jim." The Sorcerer's voice was soft, reasonable, but she was careful to keep Gruenen's corpse between her and Schweitzer. "Can you feel your wife, Jim? She's in there, you know. The love of your life."

They had brought her soul back. They had paired it with the still-cooling corpse of that mercenary. Their souls were linked, her memories and experiences laid bare as his had been to Ninip. The thought filled him with rage and grief, propelling him to his feet, sending him flying forward, an insensate growl escaping his mouth, a howl not unlike the one Ninip had uttered when he'd been in thrall to his bloodlust, scenting beating hearts and the stench of fear.

But Gruenen was not afraid. His eyes narrowed, the gold threaded with thick lines of silver that showed he was in control. He raised his buzzing hand and lightning exploded, blue arcs sizzling across Schweitzer's chest. Schweitzer's dead muscles seized, and he felt as if a hammer struck his chest, launching him back down to the landing. Smoke rose from his shoulders, flame licking the earlobe of his remaining ear.

Death had not robbed Gruenen of the magic he had commanded in life. Schweitzer could feel Gruenen's magical current looping and coiling around him. It felt the same as the magic he'd felt around the Golds. All a single element. Was it linked to the dead mercenary's body? His soul? "Stoo . . . pid," Gruenen managed, descended another step.

Jim. Another burst of emotion along the link they shared, carrying the hints of Sarah's voice.

"Don't be stupid," the Sorcerer said. "You're missing an arm, and what's left of you is held together by duct tape, literally. You want to be with your wife again, don't you? I can arrange that."

"That's not how it works," Schweitzer growled, struggling to get up.

"You don't know how it works," the Sorcerer answered. "Nobody does. You have only ever worked with Jawid. You don't know what I can do. I brought your wife back, and I can put you two together. How would you like to share a body with her, Jim? How would you like to be linked to her, soul to soul, for the rest of eternity? I can make that happen."

Schweitzer felt his dead heart jump at the thought. Eldredge had said that the Cell was learning how to put souls in living bodies. If there was a way . . . *No. If there is a way, it isn't this one.* "I'm not working for you again."

"Nothing in life is free, Jim. You know that." She nodded to Gruenen's corpse.

Schweitzer jumped onto his haunches, sprang aside as Gruenen extended his hand again, and Schweitzer felt the electrostatic charge building in the air around him. A thick cable of lightning arced into the landing, sizzling just behind Schweitzer's heel as he dove through the singed remains of the doorway, tumbling through the scattered bodies of the operators he'd fought before. There was precious little left to them, most of it spread across the blackened walls by the explosion of the airburst round. Schweitzer rolled in the ash and dust, putting out the fire Gruenen's lightning bolt had kindled on his back. The landing behind him burned brightly.

"Jim!" the Sorcerer called. "Stop playing games! What do you think is going to happen here? If by some miracle you beat this one, I'll bring your wife back in another body. And another. I am not Jawid. I can find anyone in the void. I can find your son after he is dead. I can even find you. Would you like a new body? A whole one? A strong one? I can make it happen for you.

"What do you plan to do, Jim? Kill Gruenen and Sarah goes back into the void. You lose her again."

She was right, of course. The link to his wife had dragged him all this way, and now all he could do was cut her free. "You only want one thing, Jim, and I have it. Let me give it to you."

The Sorcerer made her way around Gruenen's corpse. The dead thing put out an arm to hold her back, but the Sorcerer pushed the hand aside as confidently and easily as it had been a living man. "Jim, please." Her dark eyes were honest, sympathetic. Schweitzer tried to sniff out the scent of the chemicals in her bloodstream, listen to the beat of her heart, but the tide of her magic blotted out his senses. He couldn't focus, not with Sarah so near. "We didn't bring you back here to destroy you. Eldredge was right about you. You're unique. Your country still needs you. I can reunite you with your wife. Is that so much worse than life on the run? You can't care for your son. You must know that."

Gruenen stood on the stairs, the tension in his muscles making him shiver, but holding his position for now.

"Eldredge told me about the Director," Schweitzer said. "You work for a Gold."

Dadou smiled. "I work for a soul. Dead or living, we all have them. The body means nothing, Jim. You, of all people, should know that."

Schweitzer could feel her magic focusing, reaching out to him, probing and touching, tugging experimentally. "Let me get you out of this pile of rag and bone. Let me set you free."

Schweitzer thought of the feral madness of Ninip, of what he'd seen the Golds do to the old man and his wife when he'd fought to save Sarah at that Virginia farmhouse. He thought of the hours trapped in the clear white expanse of his underground cell.

He thought of the chance to be in a living body, to feel his heartbeat, to feel it in time with his son's, with his wife's.

But he felt the nearness of Sarah again, her agony pulsing along the link to him. Summoned back after death, it was stronger, clearer. He could hear her voice now. *No,* she sent. *Don't.*

Schweitzer let his hand drop, scooping up one of the operator's fallen carbines, angling the barrel up toward the ceiling.

The Sorcerer bared her teeth, not bothering to cry out. She raised her pistol, and Schweitzer felt the forty-five-caliber round tear through his chest, exit his shoulder. He went tumbling backward, but not before he felt the carbine fire, the airburst round tearing into the concrete slab overhead. It detonated with a sharp kick, the shock wave driving him into the floor and knocking Gruenen from his feet. Schweitzer felt the concrete fracture, the huge chunks of masonry tumbling down around them. He'd hoped to catch both the Sorcerer and her creation in the sudden fall, but the round in his chest had thrown off his aim. Most of the debris fell harmlessly down the stairwell.

At last, the momentum of the explosion spent itself, and Schweitzer got to his feet.

The Sorcerer lay on the floor of the hallway, her leg twisted at an unnatural angle, blood pooling beneath her knee. The joint was flattened beneath a piece of fallen concrete, the rebar support disappearing into the flesh below. Her face was twisted in pain, her breathing coming in great gulps.

Gruenen sprang to his feet behind her, pointed a finger at Schweitzer, who dove aside as the lightning tore a hole in the landing, leaving a ring of flames around a black scar in the floor.

"Gah!" the Sorcerer shouted to Gruenen. "Just rip that fucker to pieces! I'm done talking to it."

Schweitzer scrambled to his feet. He couldn't take Gruenen head to head, not if he hoped to win. But he could feel Eldredge's knife tucked into the waistband of his trousers, a cold firmness nestled into the small of his back. He reached for it now, drew it out, let the angry teal light wash over Gruenen's leering dead face.

"Come!" Gruenen bellowed, leaping down to the landing and standing in the pool of flame. "Come! Wife! Have!" *Jim*, Sarah sent along the link. *Run*. Then Gruenen bulled her aside and Schweitzer could feel the rage and pain along the link as she struggled against him.

No, Schweitzer sent back, not sure if she could hear him. *I'm going to set you free.*

SEALs trained for knife-fighting, and Schweitzer instinctively fell into his old stance, bringing the knife hand back, waving the free one forward as a visual distraction. It wasn't until Gruenen charged him that he realized that he'd once again forgotten his missing arm. He swung the blade crosswise, hoping Gruenen would be as careless as a Gold, let Schweitzer stab him in an effort to close.

But Gruenen wasn't a Gold. His burning eyes were threaded with silver, and they flicked to the glowing weapon, sensing the magic or guessing at it from the glow. He danced back, the knife tip missing him by inches, and then stepped in, grabbing Schweitzer's wrist and elbow carefully, pulling his arm across his chest.

With only one arm, Schweitzer had no leverage to grapple with him. He twisted his body violently away, and Gruenen slid his fingers up Schweitzer's wrist, pinching the KA-BAR by its metal hilt, yanking it from Schweitzer's grasp and tossing it down the stairwell.

The only real weapon he had. Gone. Schweitzer listened to the hollow-sounding clatter of the blade as it tumbled and finally came to a stop a floor below.

Gruenen laughed and punched Schweitzer in the face. The blow would have broken a bone jaw, but Schweitzer's was made of metal, and the shot only made his head spin as Gruenen threw him down the hallway.

Stupid move. He had me. He should have ripped me up. But while Gruenen was a trained Operator, he was no SEAL. The dead mercenary howled again, thumping his fists against his chest. *He's enjoying this.* That was good. It would make him careless.

Panic began to well in Schweitzer's spiritual gut at the thought of his disadvantage, but he pushed it aside. *Focus. He's got one up on you. You need to find another way to win.*

Going after the knife would take him straight into Gruenen's arms, so Schweitzer ran the other way, pelting down the industrial carpeting, faux-wooden office doors a blur to either side. Plexiglas plaques proclaimed business names beside windows reinforced with wire. Sarah's signal came behind him, maddeningly close, calling him back to her.

But there was no Sarah. Her soul was bound into the corpse that shambled after him. She was there and not there. She was with him and lost to him. Grief blurred his senses, even as he felt the electrostatic charge rise as Gruenen readied himself for another burst of lightning. Schweitzer shot to his right, yanking a door open as the blast tore after him, the electricity exploding the cheap pressboard into splinters, the glass melting and running down the wall. The cloud of dust filled the hallway, and Schweitzer knew he couldn't keep on like this. The narrow space was a shooting gallery, giving Gruenen the range and tight quarters he needed to hem his target in. Schweitzer had to get out of there until he could close the distance.

And then what? To kill Gruenen was to kill Sarah. *No, Sarah's already dead.* He remembered Jawid's words. *The great death. The last one.* If he destroyed Gruenen, would that condemn Sarah to something beyond the void? It didn't matter. He couldn't leave her tangled with Gruenen's rotten soul.

Position first. You need out of this hallway. It stretched out ahead of him for at least another thirty feet. He wouldn't make it before the dust cleared. Schweitzer veered left, throwing his shoulder into the next office door, smashing it open and sending himself hurtling into the darkness within.

The wall behind the reflective metal desk was made of the same cheap wood as the door, and Schweitzer caught his own reflection as he cleared the dust cloud and caught his hips against the desk, sending him flipping over and into the chair on the other side. A huge embossed seal dominated the wall, brass silhouette of a rifleman standing on farmland before an American flag. THE GREAT SEAL OF THE STATE OF IOWA.

Schweitzer rolled off the chair, picking it up and flinging it through the door. It wouldn't take Gruenen long to clear it, but it would buy him a second to survey his surroundings. There was nothing; a door led to adjacent offices from their side of the desk, and a small hatch in the wall likely led to a trash chute below. Schweitzer dared to hope that there was an incinerator at the bottom of it, but he already knew there wasn't. He would have been able to see the heated air wafting up the shaft.

A crash as Gruenen tore through the dust cloud and stumbled over the wreckage of the chair. He smashed through it, the bones rising from his shoulders tossing the twisted metal back down the hall, then pushed into the doorway, knuckle-walking like a gorilla. "Jim!"

Sarah. Schweitzer tried to reach back down the link, fumbling to connect to his wife. He tried to push his love to her, to give her some comfort as she struggled against Gruenen's relentless battering of her soul. He moved upstream against a strong current, as he had when he'd reached out to Jawid, Gruenen forcing the tide against him. For a moment, he felt Sarah's presence, so near it was like a physical touch. With that touch, he again lost the bubble, his training knocked aside by a need so powerful that he could no more stand against it than he could against gravity.

A professional never let grief or anger drive. A professional didn't believe in fair fights, let alone fights where they were at a disadvantage, down an arm, body slowly coming apart, skeletal integrity compromised by hundreds of breaks, flesh held together by duct tape. A professional chose their ground and their moment, made damn sure that they didn't take on fights they couldn't win.

But with Sarah so close, Schweitzer was a professional no longer. He stood, hurling the desk up and into Gruenen's face, following close behind. *No,* Sarah passed along the link as Gruenen rose, driving his head forward into the desk, breaking it in half. He strode through to meet Schweitzer, hands blazing lightning. Schweitzer kicked at his knee, succeeded only in nearly impaling one foot on the bone spike before Gruenen extended a hand. Schweitzer leaned aside as a lightning bolt sizzled over his shoulder, striking the hatch to the trash chute and sending it spinning away, leaving a dark, smoking hole in the wall.

Schweitzer swung back, head-butting Gruenen in the ribs and driving a bone horn into his side. He could feel it grate against the dead mercenary's ribs, locking in place between the two of them, taking Gruenen's weight. This close, Schweitzer could feel the tide of Gruenen's magic so strongly, it was nearly suffocating. He shouted, straightened, jerking his head back and feeling Gruenen's feet come off the ground.

Gruenen shouted, bringing his fists down against Schweitzer's lower back hard enough to make his whole skeleton vibrate. The impact set Schweitzer off-balance, and he fell backward a few steps. Gruenen's weight sagged forward, and he brought his knees down, driving the spikes into Schweitzer's chest, then ripped them free. Schweitzer could feel his dead flesh tearing as the bone projections pulled out, Gruenen's thighs tensing to drive them in again. He would not be able to hold against more of those blows. He had to get Gruenen off of him quickly.

Schweitzer let Gruenen's weight carry them the rest of the way, toppling over, waiting for the body to slide off the horn, freeing him to turn and fight. There was a shuddering impact and Schweitzer's forward momentum was halted. Gruenen flailed, legs kicking before he remembered the knee spines and tried to drive them forward again. Schweitzer got his good arm up in time to intercept Gruenen's right leg, but his left cleared the empty space where Schweitzer's other arm should have been, driving into his chest again. Schweitzer howled and wrenched his neck, desperate to get free. Gruenen worked to the same purpose, trying to rip himself off Schweitzer's horn. There was a moment of strain, a loud crack, and at last, Schweitzer felt the horn rip away from his skull, cracking in half along with Gruenen's ribs. The weight dropped away from his neck, and he whirled.

Gruenen was getting his feet under him, hands planted against the wall. Schweitzer's fall had slammed his head and shoulders into the trash chute, and the spider-webbing of cracks through the white cinder-block wall testified to the force of the impact. It wouldn't hold him for long.

Schweitzer didn't need long. He kicked Gruenen in his ass. The dead mercenary shuddered, shoulders breaking as he hammered forward into a chute designed to accommodate boxes of paper half his size. His hands ripped off the wall as his arms were pressed to his sides. His legs twitched.

Schweitzer could feel the rise in his magical current as he gathered it to him.

Schweitzer stepped back, ran forward, leaping into a final kick that drove Gruenen the rest of the way through the wall and down into the chute below, his body jerking as he flailed himself to a stop a few feet down, knee spikes digging into the thin metal of the chute sides, claws dragging rents through the bright surface. As he stopped, the metal's shriek was replaced by Gruenen's animal cry. "Jiiiiiiimmmmm!"

Schweitzer thrust his head and shoulders into the chute top, looked down at Gruenen's tangled corpse. The chute was twice the width of the entryway, and the dead mercenary jerked his broken shoulders, ripping his arms free, pulling himself forward and up.

Gruenen's shoulders were broken but still broad enough to wedge him into the tight space. Schweitzer was one arm slimmer and had the high ground. If he was going to fight Gruenen head on, circumstances would never favor him more.

Schweitzer came down the chute boot-first, planting his sole against Gruenen's forehead, snapping the dead mercenary's head back. Schweitzer heard a dull cracking of Gruenen's cervical vertebrae as they took on Schweitzer's full weight. Schweitzer jammed his fist against the chute side and pushed, wedging himself in and keeping himself from falling farther. He planted one foot on Gruenen's shoulder and lifted the other to stomp him again.

But Gruenen, for all the beating he had taken, was still more whole than Schweitzer, stability and skeletal integrity lending him speed. He swept a hand up, catching Schweitzer's ankle and yanking it down.

Schweitzer came off-balance, shoulder slamming into the rent left by Gruenen's claws. Gruenen pulled harder, pinning Schweitzer's arm against his side. Schweitzer struggled to free it, but even his magical strength was useless against the feet of concrete wall behind the thin metal sheeting. Gruenen hauled on the leg, pulling it taut and hauling himself up. He flailed out with another hand and grasped Schweitzer's other foot. Schweitzer tried to kick his feet free, but Gruenen held him fast, slowly hauling himself up Schweitzer's body, hand over hand.

Schweitzer swept a knee up as soon as Gruenen's hands left his ankles, but it was impossible to get enough leverage in the tight space, and he succeeded only in keeping Gruenen below him, pinned to the back of the chute. All the while, Sarah's nearness tore at him, a moth fluttering against the side of a glass jar.

"Got you," Gruenen whispered. "Got you."

The dead mercenary reached up, claws sliding out from his finger tips, and plunged them into Schweitzer's stomach. Schweitzer flailed, pushed, kicked, all for naught. Gruenen's feet were braced against the chute sides now, his broad bulk solidly wedged into the tight space, stable as if he stood on firm ground. Schweitzer felt the claws digging in, tunneling up as Schweitzer had done so long ago, when he and Sarah had fought the Golds in a Virginia field. But where Schweitzer had grasped his enemy's spine, Gruenen's hands curled around Schweitzer's floating ribs.

"Got you," Gruenen repeated, and began to pull.

Schweitzer felt the pressure torquing him in two directions, his spine quivering, sternum sliding off center. The tendons in his torso began to tear, ligaments straining, muscles starting to fray. Gruenen's leverage was unbreakable. He was going to tear Schweitzer in half.

Jim. Sarah's voice. She was so close. Schweitzer looked back up the shaft to the hatchless opening. He couldn't reach it with his arm trapped against his side. He flailed, pushed, stayed firmly locked in place.

He felt the first tiny cracks shudder through his ribcage.

He wondered if his soul would stay attached to his body once Gruenen broke him. How destroyed would he have to be before he was freed to return to the churning of the soul storm? Maybe he would be able to find Sarah there. With no way to resist Gruenen physically, he instead channeled his energy into the link with Sarah, trying to get a last touch of her. Maybe if he could scent her, truly feel her one last time, he would be able to follow her in the void. Maybe they could find one another in that churning chaos. He didn't think it was possible, but just a short while before, he had thought that life after death was impossible too.

Sarah, I'm sorry. He'd failed her; he'd failed the mission. Love didn't conquer all. Righteousness was not stronger than death, not when you were down an arm, not when you had more duct tape than skin holding you together. The SEAL never ascribed to idiot notions of failure not being an option. Failure was always an option, and understanding that was the first step to avoiding it. And understanding failure meant accepting it when it came.

Gruenen's focus was on breaking Schweitzer in two, and for the moment, Sarah swam back down the link to him, her love so intense and immediate that it made his senses buzz. He drowned in the sensation, the nearness of her, so close it felt as if the stuff that made them up was mingling.

Since Schweitzer's death and reanimation, their bodies had separated them, a gulf riven by her warm blood and beating heart. Now, here in the link forged by the magic that connected them, they were truly together, for the first time since a gun barrel had been shoved under Schweitzer's chin. He felt Sarah's soul anchored in the dead mercenary's body, as if only a branch of her flowed out to him. Schweitzer wrapped himself around it, wove into it.

And for a moment, it was as it had been in their apartment on the night he'd been killed, with the moonlight making hammered silver of their skin as they made love. As it had then, the line between the two of them blurred, until Schweitzer forgot where he left off and she began, and they were one thing, drowning in love.

Oh, baby. I'm so sorry, he whispered.

Patrick is . . .

He's safe. I'm sorry; I had to try . . .

It's okay. It's okay.

I can't leave you in here with him; I've got to get you out of here. I'll find a way. I'll come back.

And now Schweitzer could feel Gruenen's presence turning, reaching back from its focus on making the dead hands pry Schweitzer apart, focusing instead on the rosewater tide that linked Jim and Sarah Schweitzer blazing like a flower in the midst of the dark inner space within the dead mercenary.

Sarah turned from Schweitzer, facing her enemy, ready for the next round.

Schweitzer focused on the link, visualized Gruenen's presence, hulking and black, dwarfing the tiny silver light that was his wife. He could feel the mercenary's malevolence, his anger. Schweitzer had snuck into his spiritual backfield, and Sarah had helped. There would be plenty of time to tear Schweitzer's body apart. For now, Sarah would be made to pay for speaking to the enemy.

No! You fucker! I'll kill you! Schweitzer was vaguely aware of his physical mouth emitting a howl of rage that rebounded off the chute's reflective metal walls. He funneled his anger through the link, as if by the very heat of it, he could blast Gruenen back.

But the only person to hear his words, the only person to feel the heat of his anger, was Sarah. She squared herself against Gruenen, buzzing hate so strong that Schweitzer could feel it in the back of his throat. Schweitzer could see her spiritual form, the silver outline of her body glowing orange with the heat of Schweitzer's anger, growing.

It was impossible to tell in the darkness of Gruenen's inner space, in the confusion of emotions that buffeted him, but Schweitzer imagined that he saw Sarah look back down the link toward him, saw the silver-washed contours of her face. She smiled at him, turned away.

She launched herself against Gruenen, the rage making the dark space within him reverberate. Gruenen was driven back, his huge darkness staggering under the assault of Sarah's onslaught. He reeled, fell against the edges of himself. Sarah pressed forward, buffeting him, pushing him back.

But Gruenen was strong. It only took him a moment to

find his spiritual footing, to begin pressing back. Schweitzer continued to scream, helpless to move, to aid her. Unable to do anything but feel what she felt through the link.

And so it was that he saw the plan forming in her mind, knew what she was about to do.

And even now, when he knew it would free her from pain, he didn't want her to do it. Because he had fought so hard and come so far. Because at last, he had found her, and even agony was agony *together.*

Once Bound, two souls shared one corpse. The stronger could control the body. A spoken word, a bent finger, a footstep.

Sarah was not stronger than Gruenen, but the dead mercenary was knocked back for the moment.

Don't, Schweitzer found himself sending to Sarah, even as she swept up, seizing control of Gruenen's magic.

So others might live. Sarah's voice was faint, wracked with the agony of her constant struggle with Gruenen. Schweitzer felt her tap into the flow that Gruenen commanded, drawing it about them. Schweitzer's physical senses heard the crackle of electricity as it wreathed Gruenen's lower body, well clear of Schweitzer. He smelled the burned stink of ozone and metal.

So others might live, Sarah repeated.

His oath.

I lost you, Schweitzer said. No matter how badly he wanted her, there was no way to have her back, not now. Sarah was dead; there was no changing that. Patrick was still alive in the hands of a stranger. He had solved the mystery of Sarah's return. He had found as much as there was to find. Now he had to destroy the Cell so Patrick could go on living. The void wasn't going anywhere. It would be waiting for him when the tattered remnants of his body finally gave out. *But the longer she twists in the soul storm, the more insane she'll become.* He knew that Ninip had not always been the ravening monster who shared Schweitzer's corpse. He had been a man once, before the maelstrom had its way with him. Schweitzer couldn't bear the thought of

Sarah being slowly warped into a creature like that. *No,* Schweitzer thought. *Ninip had millennia. You'll end this one way or another in less than a month.*

The emotion travelled down the link, resonating with Sarah's spirit on the other end. The bolt of love and loss that she sent back up staggered him. *I'll find a way back to you, Jim. I always do.*

Gruenen growled, tore after her. Sarah gave him a final spiritual shove, sending Schweitzer one last message. *So others might live. I died, Jim. Help him.*

Patrick. Help Patrick.

Gruenen's presence slammed into Sarah, dragging her back from her control over his magic. His malice flowed down the link between them, so strong it threw Schweitzer back, knocking him into his own physical form, wedged into the chute, trapped between Gruenen and the concrete behind the thin reflective metal.

But not before he saw Sarah smile, release the magic she'd Drawn around them.

Bright blue lightning flashed down from Gruenen's waist. Arcs of electricity danced up the metal chute, the smell of smoke and ozone nearly overwhelming to Schweitzer's augmented senses. A sudden burst of heat engulfed his head and shoulders. He kicked off, pushing Gruenen away, launching himself up toward the chute entrance, throwing himself through.

Tongues of lightning chased him, the cool air of the office rising up to embrace him. The lightning storm inside the chute collapsed the wall, and Schweitzer could see it crackling, rebounding off the chute's reflective metal surface. Gruenen's corpse hung in the center, flesh smoking, tongues of flame rising as he was consumed by electricity of his own making. *Not his making. Sarah pulled that trigger.*

Gruenen tried to roar, the cry reduced to an insect buzzing as his throat melted. The flames of his eyes vanished as his face sheeted down, a gray liquid mixing with the sizzling ruin of his chest. Schweitzer tried to reach out for Sarah, but the link was static noise now. He had a vague sense of struggle, of agony, but nothing close to the detail he had known before Sarah had triggered Gruenen's magic against himself.

"Sarah!" Schweitzer shouted as the lightning reached a fever pitch, the blue arcs self-sustaining now, independent of the magic, the entire chute turned into a glittering column of fire. The heat forced Schweitzer to back away, throwing his arm across his face, but not before he saw Gruenen shiver and finally explode.

The dead mercenary's flesh pattered off Schweitzer's face and shoulders. The broken link with Sarah throbbed, her absence a punch in his gut. Smoke was rising from his head and shoulders, one of his eyes closing as the skin melted over it, fusing the socket shut until the silver flame burned back through a moment later. He stumbled back into the wreckage of the desk, his enhanced hearing picking up the splattering sound of the pieces of Gruenen pattering down into the Dumpster below.

The link with Sarah was silent, the emotional funnel gone dead. Gruenen's magical tide no longer eddied. Schweitzer tried to roll his shoulders, felt the melted ruin of his skin catching, inhibiting the movement. But in the confines of the chute, the damage had been magnified a hundredfold. Schweitzer didn't need to look back in the hole to know that Gruenen was gone, and with him, Sarah.

He went back out into the hallway. The Sorcerer had managed to drag herself most of the way toward a bigger office farther down, where Schweitzer could see the heat signatures of five men crouching by the cold, dark square of a window. One of them was bent, arms working to uncoil a rope ladder.

The Sorcerer looked hopefully over her shoulder, her expression turning sour as she realized that it was Schweitzer and not Gruenen who has returning for her. "You fucking . . . With one arm. You beat him with one arm!"

"Don't need it," Schweitzer managed, snatching her up

by her collar. Her shattered legs dragged on the carpet and she cried out.

"Shut up," he said. He dragged her the rest of the way to the door, the loss of Sarah making him savage. Her eyes rolled back in her head, and he felt her magical tide reaching out into the distance, and he knew she was seeking the void as Jawid had. Her magic washed over him and he bulled it aside. It got easier with practice. Each time he felt another's magic, he got a little better at controlling his own.

"You think because you are winning that you are a hero," the Sorcerer snarled. "*Salle bette*, you're a walking dead man. My kind created you. I'm the hero!"

"Uh-huh," Schweitzer said. "How're your legs?"

The Sorcerer twitched in his grasp. She flailed her fists, drumming them against the melted scar slurry of his hips. "You don't fucking own me! You don't control me!" she screamed.

"Not at all," Schweitzer said. "You're your own woman. You chose to lock my wife in with a monster. You chose to stand by while he hurt her. You chose to work for the enemy. All your choices. All your responsibility."

"Listen to me! I can still help you. I can bring you together with your wife. I can protect your son."

Schweitzer smiled his rictus grin. "I've run against people like you all my life. You always bargain at the end."

"Please! I know how you won out against Ninip, Jim! You have to be good. You can't murder me."

The final door was thick; a cipher lock blinked red beside a shaded glass window. The state seal hung below the great seal of the United States, the eagle pronouncing that from the many, they had built one. Schweitzer planted his foot in the center of the seal.

His grief had tripped the scales, gone so far into the red that it lapped itself. It gave him a hideous focus, a strength beyond even what he'd known when he'd first pushed Ninip out and taken control of his corpse. The door folded in on itself, bending double, the doorknob popping off, the cipher panel sparking. The figures beyond froze, hands dropping to pistols. Two of them pushed down another, forcing him to shelter behind the desk. The last redoubled his efforts to get the rope ladder out.

A second kick and the door flew inward. Schweitzer followed, the Sorcerer dragged in the wreckage, screaming as Schweitzer kicked the receptionist's desk out of the way and hauled her upright. The office was configured just as the last one, with doors at both sides of the room. Schweitzer went to the doorway where the red outlines of the figures ghosted the thickness of the walls. He heard the tension on trigger springs, the men around the Senator drawing down on the entrance. They would fire at the first thing to come through that door.

"I'm not going to murder you," he said.

"What the hell are you doing?" the Sorcerer asked him as he swung her around to the doorway.

"You're the hero," Schweitzer said, "prove it."

He shoved her forward, letting her go and sending her tumbling through the door.

The bullets tore into her even as she crumpled on her broken legs. She twitched in the air, spinning as she collapsed, her blood misting the far wall. Sarah had danced that way the last time Schweitzer had been alive, Patrick too. He supposed everyone looked like that when the gunfire came calling.

He felt her current wink out, saw her body sprawl, limp as a rag in a darkening pool. White dust settled slowly over her, broken away when the bullets had pierced her and torn divots in the wall.

Schweitzer knew that the shooters would stay covered down on the entrance, scanning after their target had dropped. He had done the same thing a dozen times himself, and so he knew that a few moments later, they would relax just a fraction, their guard dropping as they slowly came to believe that nothing was coming in after them. They would begin to move toward the door, confusion sapping their focus.

He waited, heard their footsteps, heard the miniscule creak of the triggers as they let them out just a fraction, just enough to give him the time he needed.

Schweitzer flowed around the door.

He immediately heard the trigger springs take on tension, could smell the adrenaline dumping into the gunmen's veins, wafting into the air from the sudden sheen of sweat that sprang out on their foreheads at the sight of him. They had just gunned down one of their own, flopping like a rag doll on broken legs; now they faced a one-armed monster, a shambling thing of ragged bone trailing scraps of meat.

Yet they still moved as if in slow motion. The operators in the stairwell had been prepped with cutting weapons, staged and ready to face him. These men had no such advantage. Schweitzer had been fighting the Golds for so long now that mere humans were no contest. The enemy closest to him swiveled his wrist to follow Schweitzer, loading the trigger, slapping it to the rear. Years on the range had taught Schweitzer that the rush would yank the pistol's muzzle low and to the left, and he leaned in the opposite direction, chopping out with his arm, expertly striking the man at the base of his neck, snapping it sideways. As the man fell forward, Schweitzer brought his knee up, cracking his ribs and sending him hurtling into the man with the rope ladder. He had just enough time to scream before the corpse of his comrade slammed into him, sending them both crashing through the window, his scream fading as they fell.

The next man got a shot off, and Schweitzer knew right away that his aim was true, could tell from the shooter's steady stance, his calm breathing. He also knew that the man was a professional, and professionals didn't shoot center mass. The bullet would be headed for the three-inch triangle that ran from the top of his mouth to the center of his forehead. Schweitzer tilted his head, bending his neck low enough to touch his ear to his shoulder, a move that would have given a living man whiplash.

The bullet skidded through the flesh, digging a furrow

as it whined along the surface of his skull. Schweitzer felt the intense heat of its touch, and then it was gone again, flying on and through the wall behind him. The man had been so sure of his shot that he'd released the trigger, giving himself a split second to see that his target was down. It would have been a fatal mistake for a lesser shot, but this man was good and he knew it. His eyes widened in shock as the round missed and Schweitzer closed the rest of the distance, kicking straight up, catching the enemy on his chin and snapping his neck. He turned a twitching somersault, landing in a limp pile.

The final enemy reached down behind the desk, dragging an older man into view. His hair was immaculate despite sheltering in the midst of the fight, his kind features crunched with worry. He stayed low, crab-walking with his escort, clearly a man trained for protective security details.

"Senator Hodges," Schweitzer said as the last enemy leveled his gun at him.

"Stop right there!" The man's voice was panicked; he knew he couldn't beat Schweitzer. He'd just watched him take out his three squadmates in as many seconds.

Hodges had more sangfroid. He shook off the man's hand, straightening. "Hello, Jim."

Schweitzer turned to the remaining man. "Time for you to go," he said. "I've had enough killing. You can tell your bosses that you blew it."

The man looked at the Senator, and Hodges put a hand on his shoulder. "I'm glad you're being reasonable, Jim." Hodges's voice was a cartoon of New England gentry, and Schweitzer remembered it now from televised committee hearings.

"I'm not being reasonable," Schweitzer said. "I'm being exhausted. Last chance." He nodded to the man.

"Now, Jim." Hodges patted the air with his palms. "I understand that you're angry . . ."

Schweitzer heard the tension coming out of the trigger spring in the man's hand. He couldn't leave his charge. He was a professional. Schweitzer could respect that. He would have done the same thing, had taken the same oath. So others might live.

He punched the man's wrist, the gun going off, bullet discharging harmlessly into the ceiling. The pistol's hammer struck the man in the eye at the same time his wristbone snapped, and Schweitzer heard him groan as he dropped to the floor, hand clapped to the bleeding socket, desperately trying to hold the popped remains of his eye in his skull.

Hodges winced. "Christ, Jim. It's hard to believe you used to be a good man."

"I'm not a man anymore," Schweitzer said, "but good or bad, I just saved your life."

"You just took the lives of four service members, Jim. Men just doing their jobs. Men protecting me."

"They weren't protecting you," Schweitzer said. "They were holding you hostage."

The man on the ground groaned, driving the heel of his hand into the ruined remains of his eye. His free hand held the broken wrist. He was definitely out of the fight. Schweitzer jerked his thumb at the Sorcerer. If she was like Jawid, there would probably be more. Who knew if they would all be able to do what Eldredge said she could have done? Hodges wouldn't be safe, not now.

"Why the hell would my own people hold me hostage?" Hodges asked, but Schweitzer could hear the vibration in his throat, the tiny upward lilt at the end of his words. The seeds of doubt were already planted.

"That"—Schweitzer gestured to the Sorcerer again—"was going to do something terrible to you. I take it you know about the Gemini Cell?"

"I'm not going to tell—"

"So, yes, you do. Eldredge had mentioned that there was only one person in the government who knew about it."

"Doctor Eldredge is a traitor. He is in the employ of a foreign—"

Schweitzer waved the statement away. "Maybe, but the truth is that I don't care. You know about the jinn. What you don't know is that that woman was going to put one in you. Because they wanted to keep the program going. Because they knew you would shut it down."

"You're lying," Hodges said, but Schweitzer could tell that the Senator believed him.

Schweitzer shrugged, feeling the tension in his melted skin. "Maybe, but you're out of choices, Senator. You can't fight me and I'm not letting you go."

"Where are you taking me?"

"Away. There'll be more coming. There are always more. First, we're going get someplace safe, then you're going to call off the dogs and save my son. After that, we can work on taking this program apart."

"Just who do you think you are?" Hodges's voice was full of wonder.

"I'm the monster who saved your life," Schweitzer answered. He took hold of Hodges's elbow, began to steer him toward the rope ladder. "They had the right idea, at least. Makes more sense than going out through the lobby."

Hodges shook off Schweitzer's hand. He had courage. Schweitzer would credit him with that, but he knew it was always the way with people used to being in charge. "What do you want?" the Senator asked.

Schweitzer thought about that for a moment before answering. "I want my wife back."

Schweitzer wasn't sure if Hodges was genuinely sympathetic or merely seeking leverage, but his voice sounded genuine enough, sorrowful. "She's dead."

Schweitzer gave Hodges a shove, steadying the Senator as he got his feet onto the rope ladder. The man refused to climb down, staring up into Schweitzer's face. "I'm truly sorry, Jim, but she's dead."

Schweitzer didn't bother trying to smile. He was too tired. The fatigue gave him strength, put an edge on his doggedness. This life after death had painted the whole world with a patina of despair, but it had turned everything he'd ever known about what it meant to be alive on its ear.

That wasn't quite hope, but it was close. "That never stopped her before," Schweitzer said. "Come on, Senator. It's a long climb down."

Hodges went, and Schweitzer followed. The Iowa night was cool and still. A thick sheet of cloud had rolled out over the sky, blotting out the stars behind a wall of spun cotton. It pooled shadows around the base of the building, wrapping itself around an island of sodium street lights marching in orderly rows all the way to the river.

Hodges looked up at Schweitzer, and Schweitzer saw no fear in him, knew that if he listened for his heartbeat, he would find it steady and calm. "You're not going to hurt me, are you?"

Schweitzer shook his head. "Hurt enough in the world already."

Hodges nodded and started moving again, until his feet touched down on top of an access ledge that marked the rope ladder's end. From there, Schweitzer scooped him up over his shoulder and vaulted the rest of the way down. Hodges suffered the indignity until they reached the lake of shadows around the tower's base, and the darkness swallowed them whole.

EPILOGUE
COASTLINE

"You're late," Eldredge said, tapping his watch. "If we're going to be in business together, we can't have that. I need to be able to trust you."

"This isn't exactly what I call a big purchase," the kid answered. "You want to be treated like a high roller, you have to pay for it." A breeze blew in from San Diego Bay, ruffling the kid's hair. He couldn't have been older than sixteen. The thought of one so young making a living at crime twisted Eldredge's gut, but he quelled the sympathy before it had a chance to make him lose focus. He had one kid to take care of already.

"I only get a fifteen-minute break." Eldredge nodded at the night watchman's booth behind him. "I'm gone too long, I can get in trouble." Knuckling under to his twenty-something manager for minimum wage stuck in his craw, but it was the only job Eldredge could find where they wouldn't ask questions.

"No way you can afford this from this bitch-ass job." The kid gestured at the booth. "Where you get this kind of money?"

"Let's just say I have some other skills. I moonlight."

"The fuck you do. You're like ninety, dude."

"I don't have time for this. Do you have it or not?"

"Relax, man. I have it." The kid produced a manila envelope. Eldredge took it, but the kid held on. "Dude. Money."

Eldredge passed him a wad of cash and the kid let go. Eldredge tore the envelope open, trying not to let his eagerness show. The birth certificate looked real enough, right down to the raised seal. "Carlos?" he asked.

The kid shrugged. "I wrote a script that generates the names randomly. Trust me, a lot less likely to get caught that way."

"This backstopped?"

"Yeah. I told you. I've got remote access to the citizens registry database. You want out of this job? I can get you a fucking doctor's license if you want. It'll check out."

"Thanks; if this works out, I will definitely be back for some more items."

"I always appreciate repeat customers, man."

Eldredge knew he should end it there, but he couldn't help himself. "Look, kid. You need to get an interlocutor. You don't want to be meeting with your clients in person."

The kid looked up at him, eyes hard. "The fuck you know about it?"

"I was in a . . . similar business for a long time."

"Yeah? Well, then, you know that the more people involved, the more chance you're going to have a fuck-ing rat."

"That's why you need someone you trust."

"You trying to get in on my business?"

Eldredge laughed. "No, no. I've got enough on my plate. I'm just saying that you're getting lucky here. Sooner or later, you're going to get burned. If you don't have someone you trust, you need to use a dead drop to drop off the goods and pick up the money."

"What the fuck is a dead drop?"

Eldredge looked back down at his watch. "Google it."

He turned to go. "Hey," the kid said.

"Yeah?" Eldredge turned.

"What do you need that for? You're not . . . like you're not . . ." There was a glimmer there of the kid he'd been before whatever had happened to him had flipped the switch that made the difference between legitimate computer programmers and hackers.

"I'm not a kid-toucher," Eldredge said. "He's my grandson. His dad's a violent drunk who also happens to be a cop. Court wouldn't give me custody, and his dad was about one bender away from killing him. I had to get him out of there."

The kid raised a skeptical eyebrow, but Eldredge knew the tells on his face. He'd wanted a story he could repeat to himself when his conscience came calling, and Eldredge had given him one. He wasn't dumb enough to go chasing the truth. Besides, what he wanted to know *was* true. Eldredge wasn't exploiting Patrick.

"Okay," the kid finally said, turning to go.

"Oh, hey, one more thing," Eldredge said. "You know Sector San Diego? That Coast Guard building near the . . ."

"The museum, on Guadalcanal Avenue. Yeah, I know it."

"Do you know if they take Transport Workers Identity Cards to get on the pier near there?"

"I don't know, but I can get you a TWIC. Email me at the same address."

"All right, I will. You remember what I told you about dead drops. Google brush passes while you're at it."

"Whatever. What do you want with the Coast Guard?"

"Old friend," Eldredge said. "Fan of my grandson. I figured he'd like to see me again."

The kid nodded and vanished into the gloom. Eldredge turned and headed back to the booth. He'd probably said more to the kid than he should have, but that was the trick with these sorts of things. Sooner or later, you had to stick your neck out if you wanted to get anything done. When he tried to think about the complexity of the way forward, how he was going to contact Schweitzer's old shipmate, how to approach him, how to keep himself and Patrick hidden until he was ready, what to do if Perretto wasn't sympathetic, it seemed overwhelming. Best to take baby steps, then. Eat the elephant one bite at a time.

First, he would go back to the booth and call Patrick's babysitter, make sure everything was okay. Second, he would finish his shift doing research on schools where he could get Patrick enrolled with the forged birth certificate. That was enough for tonight.

Eldredge looked up at the pink streaks on the horizon. Tomorrow was coming on fast.

GLOSSARY OF MILITARY
ACRONYMS AND SLANG

ABC'S—Airway, breathing, circulation. First responders check these to ensure a patient's vitality. Direct-action teams check them to ensure a target has been neutralized.

BIRD—Aviation asset such as a helicopter or fixed-wing aircraft.

BLEED OUT—Die via blood loss.

BMF—Boat Maintenance Facility.

BUD/S—Basic Underwater Demolition/SEAL training. The six-month training course that all sailors must graduate to become US Navy SEALs. BUD/S alone does not make one a SEAL, and additional training is required. BUD/S is intensely grueling, with an 80 percent attrition rate.

CARBINE—A long gun with a shorter barrel than a rifle. Carbines are better suited to combat in close quarters than their longer cousins.

CAS—Close air support. Action taken by fixed or rotary-wing platforms to assist ground troops.

CHEMLIGHT—Also known as "glow sticks." A short plastic tube filled with chemical compounds in separate compartments. When the stick is bent, the barrier between the compartments breaks, allowing the compounds to mix. The resultant chemical reaction causes the tube to emit a strong colored glow.

CLEARED HOT—Authorized to open fire.

CO—Commanding Officer.

CONDITION BLACK—A state of paralysis brought on by sudden, unanticipated violence.

CONDITION YELLOW—A state of hypervigilance where a person is constantly anticipating sudden violence.

CONEX—A type of intermodal shipping container.

COP—Combat Outpost.

CORPSMAN—Job title for United States Navy personnel assigned to field medical duties.

CQB—Close quarters battle. Refers to the tactics of breaching and clearing confined spaces, such as a building or ship.

DANGER CLOSE—Indicates a friendly force in close proximity to a target of fire, usually from artillery or close air support.

DFAC—Dining facility.

DUST OFF—Evacuate via helicopter.

DYNAMIC—An operational state wherein the enemy is aware of the assault team's presence, rendering stealth unnecessary.

EMBED—Embedded or one who is embedded.

EMT—Emergency Medical Technician.

"EYES ON"—Indicates the speaker is observing the subject of the sentence. "I have eyes on the door."

FIRE TEAM—The smallest operational military unit, usually composed of 4–5 members.

FNG—Fucking New Guy/Girl. A person who is newly assigned to a military unit. This friendly pejorative is meant to indicate the likelihood that the described will make mistakes.

GROM—Grupa Reagowania Operacyjno-Manewrowego. Poland's elite counterterrorism unit.

HAWK—Armed aviation asset such as a helicopter or fixed-wing aircraft.

"HONEY TRAP"—A clandestine operation in which an agent sexually attractive to the target is used to entice the target into a compromised position. Honey traps are also used to elicit information from pliant targets.

HVAC—Heating, Ventilation, and Air-Conditioning.

K-9—Canine. A unit that employs working dogs for law enforcement or military operations. The term is also used to refer to the dogs themselves.

KC—Kill-Capture. A direct-action mission wherein the team's first goal is to capture a human target. If the team is unable to capture the target without risking harm to their own number, they will kill him/her. A successful KC must conclude with the target either captured or dead.

KLICK—Slang for a kilometer.

LNO—Liaison Officer.

MAM—Military-aged male.

MANPAD—Man-portable air-defense system. A shoulder-mounted missile launcher.

MCPO—Master Chief Petty Officer.

MEDEVAC—Medical evacuation. An emergency retrieval and removal of a casualty from a crisis zone. The patient is stabilized and transferred as quickly as possible to a medical facility where adequate care can be provided.

MGRS—Military Grid Reference System.

"MIKES"—Minutes.

MWR—Morale, Welfare, and Recreation center.

NODS—Night Optical Devices. Mechanical devices that permit the user to see in the dark.

"OFF TO SEE THE WIZARD"—Slang used to indicate a visit to a mental health professional.

OP—Operation. Refers to any military undertaking with a discrete beginning and end.

OPERATOR—Members of Special Forces elements who engage in special operations. Term connotes members of direct-action elements whose primary tasking is breaching hardened targets and neutralizing a dug-in enemy.

PAX—Passenger or passengers.

"PINNING ON" OR "PINNED ON"—The act of physically attaching the insignia of a new rank or qualification to a uniform.

PIPE HITTER—A fighter. A person whose principal occupation is the use of force.

PJ—Pararescue Jumpers, also known as Pararescuemen. A special operations element within the United States Air Force.

PLATOON—A military organizational unit consisting of twenty-eight to sixty-four members.

PTSD—Post-Traumatic Stress Disorder.

QRF—Quick Reaction Force. A standby troop of warfighters positioned to respond rapidly to an emergency.

R AND R—Rest and Relaxation.

ROE—Rules of Engagement.

SEABEES—CBs, the construction battalions of the United States Navy.

SEAL—"Sea, Air, and Land." A special operations force of the United States Navy.

SITREP—Situation Report.

SO2—Special Warfare Operator 2nd Class.

SOAR—Special Operations Aviation Regiment. A special operations force of the United States Army that provides both general and specialized aviation support.

SOC—Supernatural Operations Corps.

SOCOM—Special Operations Command.

SOF—Special Operations Forces. Also referred to as "SF," as an acronym for "Special Forces."

SPECTER—A flying gunship.

SQT—SEAL Qualification Training.

SQUIRTERS—A colloquial term for those enemy who flee a targeted location.

SSG—Special Services Group. Pakistan's special operations forces.

SSRI—Selective Serotonin Reuptake Inhibitor. Medication typically used to treat anxiety and depression.

SST—Special Security Team. An elite counterterrorism unit in the Japanese Coast Guard.

TCCC—Tactical Combat Casualty Care. First-responder medical training given to operators. It is designed to allow nonmedical personnel to engage in triage under fire, and to stabilize casualties for medevac.

TIC—Troops in Contact. Indicates that the speaker is engaged and fighting with the enemy.

VTC—Video Teleconference.

WIA—Wounded in Action.

YN1—Yeoman First Class. A senior enlisted member of the US Navy or Coast Guard specializing in administration.